THE
COWARDS

* * * * * * * * *

OSEF ŠKVORECKÝ

anslated by Jeanne Němcová

Neglected Books of
the 20th Century

Sybille Bedford, *A Legacy*

Elizabeth Bishop, *The Diary of "Helena Morley"*

Elizabeth Bowen, *Bowen's Court*

Jane Bowles, *My Sister's Hand in Mine*
(an expanded edition of *The Collected Works*)

Paul Bowles, *The Sheltering Sky*

Mary Butts, *Scenes from the Life of Cleopatra*

Italo Calvino, *The Path to the Nest of Spiders*

Caresse Crosby, *The Passionate Years*

Ford Madox Ford, *Provence*

Cecily Mackworth, *The Destiny of Isabelle Eberhardt*

Josef Škvorecký, *The Cowards*

The Cowards

The Cowards

Josef Škvorecký

Translated by Jeanne Němcová

The Ecco Press / New York

To Zdena, the girl I met in Prague

The American edition of this book is
dedicated to all my friends to whom
the old Latin saying, *Donec eris felix . . .*
does not apply.

Copyright © 1970 by Grove Press, Inc.
Originally published by Československý Spisovatel
in Prague, Czechoslovakia, under the title Zbabělci.
© 1958 by Josef Škvorecký
All rights reserved
Issued in 1980 by The Ecco Press,
1 West 30th Street, New York, N.Y. 10001
The Ecco Press logo by Ahmed Yacoubi
Printed in the United States of America
Library of Congress Cataloging in Publication Data
Škvorecký, Josef. / The cowards.
(Neglected books of the twentieth century)
Translation of Zbabělci.
I. Title. II. Series.
PZ4.S61973CO *1980* [PG5038.S527] 891.8'635
ISBN 0-912-94675-X *(pbk)* 80-13087

Author's Preface

A human being, like everything else in the world, develops and changes, and that is why I believe it is impossible to revise a novel written fifteen years ago. I wrote *The Cowards* when I was twenty-four years old, so it has all the imperfections and shortcomings of youth. But I am afraid that what the critics wrote after the first edition appeared had nothing to do with the actual shortcomings of the novel but stemmed rather from a number of misunderstandings. Specifically, they charged that the novel was an offense against concepts sacred to the Czech and Slovak people and that it caricatures and insults the Red Army. It is common knowledge, however, that certain concepts which are expressed by the words "homeland" and "revolution," for instance, have one meaning for the bourgeoisie and another for Marxists. The heroes of *The Cowards*, who come from bourgeois homes but who are at the same time in revolt against the world of their bourgeois fathers, use these words ironically and derisively, yet still with the same limited, bourgeois meaning, simply because they know no other. The rehabilitation of "sacred" concepts was a matter for the future and for other social classes and this is not what *The Cowards* is about. Danny and his friends do not insult the revolution, but mock the way the bourgeoisie play at making one.

As far as offending the Red Army is concerned, I think this is a misunderstanding, a classic example of the clash, so frequent in Czechoslovakia in the past, between two

7

esthetic-philosophical outlooks, two ways of thinking, two views of the function of literature. Symbolically speaking, it is an encounter between Babel and Babayevsky, between the painting and the poster. I have come to the conclusion that if we have real respect for something, we express it best in art by absolute realism, "harsh" realism, if you like. And I don't think that realism means polishing to parade-ground luster the boots of an army fighting tooth and nail or pouring eau de cologne over its sweaty, grubby soldiers. I refuse to argue with those critics who objected to the fact that the Soviet soldiers and POWs represented in the novel are, for the most part, people whom Danny refers to as "Mongolians." I'm not a racist.

I have made a few revisions in the text of this edition in order to avoid these and similar misunderstandings in this book, which makes no claim to being an objective history but is instead an analytic novel about the thoughts, feelings, and experiences of a member of the Czech provincial "golden youth" at a time of world-shaking historical events. These revisions do not, of course, imply any change in my own opinions or in Danny's outlook on the world or an act of obedience, etc. Most of these changes were made simply to point up the fundamental ideas which the passages in question originally expressed but which might not have been clear enough because of excessive brevity or provocative stylization.

The Cowards remains just as it was when it was written in 1948–49. I hope that, aside from its juvenile mistakes and shortcomings, the book also reflects the candid, impertinent, Hans Christian Andersen-truths of youth which many of us so persistently overlook on our pilgrimage to the grave.

December, 1963   Josef Škvorecký

[*-see Notes following text.]

The Cowards

"*Any work of art that lives was created out of the very substance of its times. The artist did not build it himself. The work describes the sufferings, loves and dreams of his friends.*" —ROMAIN ROLLAND

"*A writer's job is to tell the truth.*"
—ERNEST HEMINGWAY

"*There was a revolution simmering in Chicago, led by a gang of pink-cheeked high school kids. These rebels in plus-fours, huddled on a bandstand instead of a soap-box, passed out riffs instead of handbills, but the effect was the same. Their jazz was a collectively improvised nosethumbing at all pillars of all communities, one big syncopated Bronx cheer for the righteous squares everywhere. Jazz was the only language they could find to preach their fire-eating message. These upstart small-fries . . . started hatching their plots way out in . . . a well-to-do suburb where all the days were Sabbaths, a sleepy-time neighborhood big as a yawn and just about as lively, loaded with shade-trees and clipped lawns and a groggy-eyed population that never came out of its coma except to turn over . . . They wanted to blast every highminded citizen clear out of his easy chair with their yarddog growls and gully-low howls.*" —MILTON "MEZZ" MEZZROW

Friday, May 4, 1945

We were all sitting over at the Port Arthur and Benno said, "Well, it looks like the revolution's been postponed for a while."

"Yes," I said and stuck the reed in my mouth. "For technical reasons, right?" The bamboo reed tasted good, as it always did. One of the reasons I played tenor was because I liked to suck on the reed. But that's not the only reason. When you play it makes such a nice buzzing noise. It reverberates inside your skull, good and solid and rounded and high class. It's a great feeling, playing a tenor sax. Which is another reason why I played it.

Benno took off his hat and hung it on the rack above Helena. He put his trumpet case on the table and took out his horn. "That's it, for technical reasons," he said. "They don't have enough guns or enough guts and there're still too many Germans around."

"Anyway, it's crazy," said Fonda. "We should all be glad things are going as well as they have so far."

"Except they're not going all that well," said Benno.

"What do you mean?"

Benno raised his eyebrows, stuck the mouthpiece into his trumpet, and pressed it against those thick Hapsburg lips of his. Fonda watched him, his mouth half open, and waited. Benno blew into the trumpet and pressed the valves. He raised his eyebrows even higher and didn't say a word. He wanted to keep Fonda in suspense. Fonda was always getting worked up over something. It didn't take much to get a rise out of Fonda.

"What do you mean?" he kept on. "Has there been any trouble?"

Benno blew a long note and it sounded hard and very sure, so I stopped worrying about him losing his tone while he was in the concentration camp. He hadn't. He definitely hadn't lost it. Just from that one note you could tell he hadn't.

"There was a fight over in Chodov yesterday," he said, and unscrewed one of the valves.

"What happened?"

"Somebody got tight and hung out the Czech flag and then people tried to make the Germans give up their guns." Benno spat on the valve and stuck it back in.

"And what happened?" Fonda persisted.

"The Germans didn't cooperate."

"Anybody get hurt?" asked Haryk.

"Yes," said Benno laconically.

"How many?"

"About four."

"How do you know?"

"Pop was there this morning with Sabata."

"And what's going on over there now?"

"Everything's quiet. Everybody's cooled off."

"Are the Germans still there?"

"They are."

"Hell," said Haryk. "What did you mean anyway when you said what you did before?"

"About what?"

"About the revolution being postponed."

"Well, old man Weiss wanted to stage an uprising today. He had it all arranged with people in Chodov and Rohnice but when the trouble started up in Chodov ahead of schedule, they decided to forget it."

"How do you know, for Chrissake?" said Fonda.

"Also from Pop. Pop's on some kind of national committee or something."

"Don't believe him," said Helena. "He's just trying to get

you all worked up. Now sit down like a good boy and play, Benny!"

Benno picked up his trumpet and went over to sit down. Old Winter shuffled in from the taproom and set a glass of pink soda pop down in front of Helena.

"Hey," said Lucie, "don't you have any lime soda?"

"I'll be right with you," said Winter, and slowly shuffled back to the tap. He had three rolls of fat at the back of his neck and his seat sagged. He reminded me of an elephant —I don't know whether it was male or female—I saw in a circus once. It kept tramping around the ring, its behind hanging down, limp and deflated, just like old Winter's. Josef Winter said his old man had progressive paralysis, but then he was mad at him because his old man wouldn't give him any money and only grumbled about Josef's loafing around all the time and never doing anything. Even if he did have progressive paralysis, I don't know whether that would have any connection with his pants. Anyway, it was only an idea. Kind of a dumb idea, the kind a person has subconsciously. Because inside, people are dirty dogs. Everybody. The only difference is some people try to hide it and others don't bother. The door opened and Jindra Kotyk came into the Port.

"Hello," he said, and started off to pick up his bass fiddle which he kept in the Winters' bedroom.

"About time," said Fonda.

"I couldn't get here any sooner. Boy, did all hell ever break loose at our place today!"

"Where?"

"At the factory."

"Huh?" said Haryk.

"At Messerschmidt. At the factory."

"You mean you went to work today?" said Haryk.

"Well, what's wrong with . . ."

"Man, you're dumb," said Fonda.

"What'd you want me to do?"

"Well, certainly not make a fool of yourself," said Haryk. "What's the point in showing up for work at the factory any more?"

Mrs. Winter appeared in the kitchen door with the bass fiddle. This saved Jindra just when he'd worked himself into a pretty tight spot.

"Thanks," he said and ducked behind his fiddle. He pretended he was tuning up but that wasn't very shrewd of him since everybody knew he wasn't. He couldn't. He didn't know how. The fact was he was just a sort of stopgap since we hadn't been able to find another bass player. To be more exact, we hadn't even been able to round up a bass, so when Jindra bought one we were glad to at least have somebody propping up a bass behind us when we appeared in public. The only trouble was we had to let him play it, too. Otherwise he wouldn't let us use his fiddle at all. So we chalked some marks up under the wires so the sounds he did make wouldn't be too far off and in time he actually learned to plunk away pretty well. He even had a red hot solo in one number. All that saved it from being a complete fiasco was the terrific energy he brought to his playing. All you could hear were those wires, which he plucked like mad, snapping away against the neck; applause usually covered up the sour notes. Jindra was very proud of his solo and called his technique the "Jan Hammer style"—after the Czech swing-bassist—and we let him call it whatever he wanted to. It would have been stupid to cross him up, since his old man owned a dry goods store and had some pull with City Hall and the Germans, which came in handy when we were trying to get an engagement.

"Oh, God!" said Haryk. "Hitler's dead and he still goes off to work."

"Well, it just so happens things at the factory have been very interesting these past few days."

"Interesting? I beg your pardon?"

Jindra took advantage of the opening. Now he could talk away and cover up the bad impression he'd made. I looked at him and saw him tightening up the key on the bass, pretending to be listening for the pitch but meanwhile saying casually, "There was a riot at Messerschmidt. The workers stopped work and asked for a raise."

"Oh, God!" said Haryk again. "Hitler's dead, the Reich's

going up in smoke, and all the Messerschmidt workers think about is trying to get a raise."

"They were just trying to raise hell. But the biggest joke is that it was Bartosik who led the whole strike."

"Who's that?"

"You don't know him? Herr Bartosik from the pay office."

"Oh, him. You mean those idiots let themselves be led by a collaborator like him?"

"Yes," said Jindra, and that was all. He stopped tuning his bass and flipped open the sheet music in front of him. We were all watching him. From the way he'd said it you could tell there was more to it than that. He waited a little while till the room got quiet, and when it was he went on.

"They let him lead 'em. But only up to Fenik's office, and then they grabbed both of 'em and locked 'em up in the basement."

"Jesus!" said Haryk. "I'm beginning to develop a healthy respect for the working class."

"You should have seen it! Especially the look on Bartosik's face when they locked him up. You can't imagine. . . ."

"Oh, yes I can. Because I was around when he made a bad mistake like that once before," said Benno.

"When?"

"When he found out I was going to be shipped off to a concentration camp for racial reasons."

We laughed, and Jindra laughed loudest. He had good reason to. He could be glad to get let off as easy as he had been after acting like such an eager beaver. Imagine, working in a German aircraft plant in Kostelec on the Fourth of May, 1945. Benno started off on a Bob Cats solo, softly, just for himself, and we turned to our parts, too. Before they shipped him off to the camp, Benno had been Bartosik's secretary. I can just imagine how surprised Mr. Bartosik must have been when he found out he'd had a half-Jew working for him in such a responsible position. And when he remembered all those half days he'd let Benno goof off! I stuck my saxophone in my mouth and hummed into it the opening bars of the first chorus of "Annie Laurie." At the next desk Haryk opened up "Annie

Laurie" too, except on his score he'd written "Lucie."
"Annie Lucie." Old Winter pried himself loose from the tap
and brought over some green soda pop on a tray. He
shuffled over to the table by the window and set it down
in front of Lucie. Lucie took a straw, tore off the wrapper,
and dipped the straw into the soda pop. Then she bent over
the glass and started to sip. She sat there in her nice thin
dress, with her golden hair, sipping the emerald-colored
soda pop through which shone the setting sun. She was
awfully pretty. I thought about Irena and wondered what
she was doing. But I knew. I was pretty sure I knew what
she was doing. Zdenek hadn't been going to the factory for
a long time so it was pretty clear what he was up to also.
Benno sounded off behind me, playing his rough, big,
beautiful pre-concentration camp solo from "St. James Infirmary." I looked out the window and there hung the
dusky silhouette of the castle and the sky was all red and
orange with little clouds and clear patches and the first
tiny stars. Lights glimmered in the castle windows. The
big shots were probably putting their heads together.
About how to make themselves scarce, most likely. The
place was crawling with them. They'd come here from all
over the Reich and now things were closing in on them
from all sides and there they sat in their plush-upholstered
rooms like in a trap. There was something kind of poignant
about it. Kostelec was right in the middle of Europe, so
they'd all gathered here. I guess they thought they could
still save their skins somehow or other. One of that bunch
was a queen of Württemberg—Ema, the housekeeper's
daughter up at the castle, had pointed her out to me—and
she was very good looking. I wasn't interested in her
though. Falling in love with her would have been like falling in love with Deanna Durbin or something. The only
way I could ever get her would be to take her by force
when everything fell apart. But the thought of taking
somebody by force when everything fell apart didn't appeal
to me. As a matter of fact, I've never felt like taking anybody by force ever. The only thing was that this Queen of
Württemberg was pretty and I've always had a soft spot
for a pretty woman. I didn't have much faith in spiritual

beauty. It's all right for people to have a soft spot for pretty girls, because that's only natural and it would be crazy to deny it. That's just our nature. Anyway I was convinced that Fonda Cemelik had a crush on the Queen of Württemberg, too, even though he said he didn't and that he couldn't care less about her, because she really was awfully good looking. Prettier than Irena—I had to admit it objectively. Except that I was in love with Irena, and Fonda had all sorts of prejudices and moral scruples. Something anyway. And all I felt for the Württemberg queen was sympathy. Nothing else.

Fonda rapped on the piano lid. "Okay, let's tune up," he said. He gave us A and we tuned up. Meanwhile I went on thinking about the Queen of Württemberg. Fonda didn't waste any time on Jindra but he was very strict with the rest of us. He had absolute pitch and sometimes really made a show of it. Venca was sweating from the way Fonda kept nagging at him. He made Venca slide his trombone all the way out but still it didn't sound right. When I finally told him the horn couldn't possibly still be off pitch, Fonda insisted there must have been a slip-up somewhere when the thing was made, or that the heat must have done things to it, but that nobody could question the fact that he had a perfect sense of pitch. Anyway, we were all on pitch at last and then quieted down. Fonda rapped four times on the top of Winter's upright piano and we began to play. Lexa wailed shrilly in the highest register of his clarinet, Venca sank down to the explosive depths of his trombone to build up the bass, and I was playing around with some fancy little flourishes in the middle range, while Benno came out above us with his rough, dirty, sobbing tones that sounded like they came from heaven. I started thinking about the Queen of Württemberg again, and about how good it was that there were beautiful girls in this world. It seemed only right there should be. I thought that here was this queen with a fancy family tree and ancestors and all kinds of class prejudices, but no kingdom to rule over, and that she could never, for instance, think of marrying me even if I wanted to marry her, but then it struck me maybe she would, now, because

I was a Czech and she was a German and maybe my look-out was a lot better than hers even if I didn't have any ancestors or prejudices like hers, but then I realized yes I did have ancestors, in fact just as many as she had, and I remembered those monogenetic and polygenetic theories I'd been reading about a while before and I remembered Forester Bauman who'd somehow found out that our family is actually an offshoot of the Smirickys of Smirice and if he was right, I thought, then I could marry the Württemberg queen after all, except suddenly I thought maybe an English lady might be a whole lot better when the war was over and with me coming from such a distinguished family, and while I was thinking all these things over we went right on playing without a break. The idea that there might be a revolution or that we would see front line action didn't even occur to me. And when it was time for me to start off on my solo, I thought to myself, you fool, Irena's the only woman you've got and the only one you love and she's better than all the others and more important than anything else in the whole world, and I started thinking about dying a hero's death and how that would really impress Irena and how wonderful it must be to die a hero's death, except that she would have to get to know about all the details, and I was positive then that I was in love with Irena because it was so wonderful to feel so positive that I was.

When we'd finished the piece, Benno said, "I sure missed that in Schlausen, and that's a fact."

"I'll bet you did," said Fonda. "Only you came in half a bar too late on your solo."

"Like hell I did," said Benno.

"Well, you did. It's supposed to go like this: tadlladada-taaaa," Fonda sang out, waving a finger and tapping his foot and bobbing that curly little head of his on top of his long neck. Fonda was infallible. Every note was right on pitch and it had an authoritative sound.

"Yeah?" said Benno, humbled. Then he lifted his trumpet to his lips, played the opening bars, and looked at Fonda.

"No," said Fonda and sang it out once again. Benno re-

peated it. It was just right this time. I expected Fonda to
find something wrong with my playing, too, but he didn't.

All he said was, "We'll take it from the top," then
waited for us to quiet down, rapped, and we started in
again. In those days we didn't dare improvise very much
and just went by the score. We had a great band though.
Better than anything for miles around, that's for sure. We
played Bob Crosby-style Dixieland very well. The only
trouble was in the bass. Fortunately, though, the bass
played so softly that it didn't make much difference. I'd
memorized my part. I just closed my eyes and fingered the
keys on my sax, thinking how nice it would be to start
daydreaming again, as usual, since dreaming's been a
habit with me for as long as I can remember. Ever since
ninth grade, to be exact. That's when I fell in love with
Judy Garland and that's when it all began. I thought about
myself and about her, but mainly about myself, and I
thought how things would be *if*. And usually the thoughts
themselves were so wonderful that they were enough for
me. Sometimes I even thought it was probably better just
to think about something than to actually live through it
in real life, at least in some ways. So I started daydreaming
again. It was really a wonderful feeling to sit there playing
a piece of music that had practically become a part of your
own body and at the same time to be daydreaming with
your eyes closed. The syncopated rhythms echoed through
my skull and I thought about Irena, or rather about myself,
how much I loved her and how wonderful it would be to
be with her, and how it was really better to be with her
this way than for real and not know what to say or what
to do. This way I didn't have to say anything at all, or just
say something and then listen to how it sounded in my
imagination and not to think about anything particular,
just about Irena in general. There was supposed to be a
revolution coming up and it was nice to think about that,
too. And have your last will and testament all written up,
like I did. Saying that I'd never loved anybody in my life
except Irena and that all I wanted in the world was for her
to know, as she read these lines, that everything I'd done
and gone through was important only because it had all

been in some way connected with her, that I'd lived and died only for her and that I'd loved her. The best part of the whole thing was the past tense. But the rest was pretty good, too. That part about "these lines" and how I'd "never loved anyone else in my life" and that "I don't want anything in the world." Words like that—"world" and "life"— sounded great. They were impressive. And when I thought about it honestly, it was a good thing, too, that I was in love with Irena and that she was going with Zdenek and maybe I was better off just daydreaming and writing testimonials to my love. Of course it would have been nice, too, if I'd been going with her myself. Everything was nice. Absolutely everything. Actually, there wasn't anything bad in the whole wide world.

"Benno," said Lexa when we'd finished, "come on, tell the truth. You practiced while you were in the concentration camp, didn't you? Your blues sound like Armstrong."

"It was the bedbugs. They really bothered me," said Benno.

"Honest? There were bedbugs?"

"What did you think, man? The place was crawling with them."

"Why, Benny's still scared of them," said Helena.

"Scared stiff," said Benno.

"Where at?" said Lexa.

Helena raised her eyebrows and pretended she hadn't heard. "He practically takes the bed apart every night before he goes to sleep. Why, he even leaves the light on all night long."

"Why?" I said.

"Bedbugs are scared of light," said Benno.

"Really?"

"Sure. A simple trick like that's enough for them. As long as the light's on they don't come out. They're awfully dumb."

"They sure are," said Lexa.

"Except in camp we weren't allowed to keep the lights on and that was rough. Bedbugs leave some people alone, but I was all chewed up by morning."

"Well, they had plenty to work on with you," said Lexa.

Benno didn't say anything.

"You put on a little weight while you were away, Benny," said Haryk.

"Maybe he had pull with the camp boss," said Lexa.

"Yeah," said Benno. "I had to shine his boots every morning and pull 'em off for him every night."

"No kidding."

"Sure. Man, it was like something out of *Good Soldier Schweik.*"

"What do you mean?"

"Well, I'd always stick out my ass . . ."

"Benny!" said Helena.

"What's wrong?"

"You know I don't like you to talk dirty."

"But, honey . . ."

"No, I won't stand for it. One more dirty word out of you and I'm going home."

"But ass isn't such a dirty word."

"I'm going," said Helena, and got up. Benno jumped up and rushed after her. He waddled, he was so fat and lazy, and his white shirt stuck to his back.

"But, baby," he said.

"No, I told you not to use dirty words and you said it again."

"Aw, come on, baby!"

"No. Goodby."

We all watched the scene with interest and I stopped daydreaming. Benno was completely under Helena's thumb. Henpecked. A classic example. I couldn't understand it. She could make him do absolutely anything. He trotted behind her and the folds of his sticky shirt quivered.

"Aw, baby!" he implored in a frightened whine. He ran up and grabbed her hand.

"Leave me alone," she said.

"But, honey, where you going?"

"Home."

"Why?"

"Because you said a dirty word."

"But I didn't say anything!"

"Yes, you did. Don't deny it."

"But it wasn't *that* bad."

"No. I said you weren't supposed to use words like that. You know I don't like it."

"Aw, come on, baby!"

"Leave me alone! Let go of me!"

"Don't be mad at me."

"Let *go!*"

"Helena, please, don't be mad at me!"

"I said let go of me!"

"Come on, baby! Please! Stay here."

Helena stopped pulling away. You could see how she led him around by the nose. He had a soft heart, like they say all fat people have. I don't know whether it's true in all cases but Benno anyway sure had one helluva soft heart. Helena looked sulky.

"Apologize!" she said.

"Helena, please excuse me," he muttered in a fast whisper. We were all listening, fascinated.

"Promise you won't ever say any more dirty words."

"I'll never say any more dirty words again."

"Not one!"

"Not one dirty word."

"No, the whole thing!"

"Huh?"

"Say the whole thing."

"Again?"

"Uh huh."

"But, baby . . ."

"Benny!"

"But, baby . . ."

"Well, are you going to say it or aren't you?"

"But, baby, I just said it!"

"Are you going to say it or aren't you?"

I couldn't understand how he could be so dumb. Not dumb in general, just dumb with her.

"I'll never say a single dirty word again."

"And apologize."

"Helena, please excuse me and I'll never say a single

dirty word again," he said quickly and softly to get it over with. He was annihilated.

"All right, now go and play," said Helena and sat down. He turned and obediently trudged back to his place. We acted as though nothing had happened. I picked up my sax from the stand and slung the cord around my neck.

"Let's go. What'll it be now?" I said.

"Wait a minute," said Fonda. "What's the story about taking off those boots?"

"Yeah. What happened, Benno?" said Lexa.

Benno picked up his trumpet. "Well, I always had to stick out my rear and grab his leg between my knees and he pushed against my rear with his other foot until I pulled off his boot."

"I see," said Lexa. "Yeah, I know what you mean."

"Let's play, gang. Let's get going," I said again.

"Okay," said Fonda. "Get out the 'Bob Cats.'"

There was a shuffling of paper as the boys hunted for "Bob Cats." I found it right away, and as I shifted around in my chair to get comfortable I noticed the way Lucie was making eyes at Haryk. She had pretty eyes. The green soda pop in front of her still sparkled like emeralds, and behind her the sky outside was blood red and the windows in the castle glittered. A whole row was lit up on the first floor, where the ballroom named after Piccolomini was, and then two or three windows on the second floor. The big shots were probably starting to panic. A little star twinkled right over the turret of the castle. Fonda rapped four times, Brynych started off on a drum solo. We waited till it was over and then we all came in, Venca with a wonderful, gutty glissando sliding up and down the scale and Lexa's heartbreaking moan. It was good. We hit it just right. I saw a smile spread over Fonda's face. Then I started thinking about Benno. It was funny, I knew, but this was something I couldn't and probably never would understand. Allowing yourself to be roped up and led around and humiliated like that, losing control over yourself that way. I've never lost control of myself. I could never get so mad at anybody that I'd really blow my top, and love never made me lose my head either. When I had my arms around some girl and was jabbering away, I had to act as though I was talking like that out of sheer ecstasy and excitement and all that kind of thing. I really could have talked pretty sensibly, only that probably would have made her mad, and so I'd always talk a lot of nonsense. I had to act like I was completely gone on her and that she took my breath away and so on, and at the same time I always had an embarrassing feeling that girls could see right through my act and that they were laughing at me. But none of them ever really saw through it. They asked for it. Probably everybody talks that way in such situations, so it doesn't seem funny to girls. Only it was hard to imagine a guy really meaning what he said. God knows. Certainly none of the girls ever found out. Probably boys really are smarter than girls. All of a sudden it occurred to me that I ought to be thinking about Irena if I was supposed to be in love with her. So I started thinking about her. At first I couldn't. I tried to picture her and I couldn't. So then I remembered how I'd looked down her bosom at the swimming pool recently and then it worked. I thought about how nice it would be to sleep with her and that Zdenek was sleeping with her and I started to be pleasantly jealous and that was fine. Then it was my turn for the tenor solo and I started to gulp away in the middle registers where the tenor sax sounds best and I forgot all about Irena, but she was still there in the back of my mind while I played my big solo from "Bob Cats." My nice big solo and I felt fine. I didn't even mind that there was probably going to be a revolution and that it wouldn't be so nice to really get hurt or killed. Instead, it was nice to think about my Last Will and Testament and heroism and things like that. When I finished my solo, I looked up and noticed old Winter sitting behind the tap staring into nowhere with those bloodshot eyes of his. He had dull eyes that wobbled in a watery kind of way and he was daydreaming just like me, except not about Irena but probably about the station restaurant he'd wanted to lease ever since he'd been a kid like us, or about some big hotel with four waiters, or maybe just getting hold of some real good Scotch and selling it to us. He didn't drink himself, maybe just to be different or something, or maybe he really did have progressive paralysis. His bald head glistened behind the taps and the brass pipes gleamed. Outside the windows the blood-red glow darkened and the stars began to shine. We finished "Bob Cats" by heart, playing it in the dark.

"Helena, turn on the lights over there, will you?" said Fonda when we'd finished. Helena reached up above her head, felt along the wall for a minute, then found the switch. The bulb in the ceiling came on and the way things looked surprised us all. All of a sudden you could see everything clearly. I noticed Lucie's mouth, how red it was in the electric light, and how dark it had gotten outside the windows. Haryk started strumming some kind of bouncy, romantic improvisation on the guitar and he grinned over at Lucie. I leafed through the sheet music.

"I saw Uippelt from Messerschmidt today," said Haryk, "heading out of town on his bike as fast as he could go."

"What about his old lady?"

"I don't know. He was all by himself."

"Anyway, it's funny he stuck around here so long since everybody knows him and the kind of bastard he is," said Lexa.

"You should have pushed him off his bike and grabbed it," said Fonda.

"Very clever. And then he pulls out a gun and kills me, right?"

"Don't forget, there's a revolution going on," said Lexa.

Benno called out from the back, "That's been postponed until further notice."

"You really think anything's going to happen?" asked Fonda.

"Why, sure." Lexa spoke with an authoritative tone because the Germans had executed his father. Since then, he always knew more than we did. But as far as this was concerned, I knew more than he did.

"No," said Benno. "You don't think our city fathers can do anything, do you?"

"Well, wait and see."

"I'll have to wait a long time then. They're all scared

shitless. The revolution's simply going to be put off indefinitely, that's all."

I looked over at Helena, but she didn't say anything. She was reading the paper.

I said, "No, not the city fathers. You'll see, though. Something's going to happen."

"And Chief of Police Rimbalnik's going to run the whole show I suppose?"

"Not him. You just wait."

"You talk as if you were mixed up in something," said Haryk.

I laughed. I was glad the boys didn't know what was going on. They didn't believe me because they weren't in on anything themselves but they weren't sure whether maybe I wasn't. I wasn't in very deep but at least I knew a little bit. I knew about something, but wasn't too sure myself what it really added up to. I'd found out about it from Prema and wasn't supposed to tell anybody.

"Oh, come on, kid, don't act so mysterious," said Benno.

I didn't feel like acting mysterious because that was silly. Even though the others didn't know anything, they still knew enough to realize that anything I was mixed up with couldn't be anything very earthshaking. So for a while I just kind of played like I was somebody who's in on a secret, and then I told what I knew. Prema had told me, and he was in contact with Perlik who'd been arrested by the Gestapo a month ago. He must have known something. It couldn't have been much, though, because probably nobody knew much. Anyway, the whole thing was just being improvised. But I didn't care and I was glad to get it off my chest and it made me seem important and if nothing finally came of the whole affair, the boys would forget about it.

"All I know," I said, "is that something's supposed to start when Radio Prague stops broadcasting."

"Where'd you hear that?"

I shrugged.

"I know it."

"Come on. Who told you?"

"Look, I had to promise I wouldn't tell, but you just wait and see."

"Don't tell me you guys really think something's going to happen?" said Fonda.

"Well, what d'you think?"

"Nothing's going to happen. Anyway, the Germans are done for—finished."

I laughed. I agreed with him but I had to laugh because it wouldn't have looked right for me to agree with him now. I was supposed to be mixed up in something and I had to want something to happen. Besides, I didn't have any objections to it. It opened up all those different possibilities as far as Irena was concerned. Heroism. And Zdenek getting killed maybe. Yes, I realized, he could get killed. That would be better than if I got killed, though there was something to be said for that, too. But I didn't mean it seriously. Not now, because now I wasn't daydreaming. It opened up a whole new perspective that, this way, I could get rid of Zdenek very effectively. If he was killed, I'd be glad to go to visit his grave with Irena. Irena would feel that was very noble of me and I'd be very gentle and understanding so as not to awaken any painful memories in her. I'd go visit his grave with her absolutely unselfishly. With Zdenek out of the picture, I'd be extremely unselfish. So I didn't have anything against an uprising. But that was the only good reason I could see for one. Otherwise I agreed with Fonda. I didn't feel like fighting for any patriotic or strategic reasons. The Germans had already lost the war anyway, so it didn't make any sense. It was only because of Irena that I wanted to get into it. To show off. That's all. So when Fonda said the Germans were already finished, I laughed as if I thought they were anything but.

"No, listen. I mean, what's the point?" Fonda persisted.

"I'm not saying what the point of it all is. I'm just telling you what I know," I said.

"Well, anyhow, there'll be a lot of laughs," said Haryk and he winked at Lucie again. She sat there with her elbows propped on the table and the straw between her lips, sipping her soda pop. When Haryk grinned at her, she squinted up her eyes. Boy, were they in tune. It got under my skin.

"It'll be a laugh, all right, the day Pop closes the store and starts out after the Germans with his squirrel gun," said Benno.

"And when old Cemelik leads the attack on the high school," said Haryk.

"Has your old man had his uniform cleaned already?" asked Lexa.

"You bet," said Fonda. "And the moths had really done a job on it."

"Where?"

"On the ass," said Lexa.

"Lexa!" bleated Haryk so he sounded exactly like Helena. "What?"

"You know you're not supposed to talk dirty."

"But, honey . . ."

"All right, boys. That's enough of that!" screamed Helena.

"Apologize!" continued Haryk.

"Helena, ple . . . ple . . . please forgive me," Lexa stuttered and Helena kept yelling, "Now you quit that right now or I'm going home!"

"Aw, honey," said Lexa. Helena rose, turned, and opened the door. Then she left without a word. There was a clatter behind me as if somebody had knocked over a music stand and then Benno's voice.

"Helena! Wait! Where you going?" Benno bumped into me from behind as he hurried toward the door with that waddling gait of his. His white shirt glimmered in the dark hallway and then he disappeared after Helena.

"Well, he's really in for it now," said Lexa and laughed.

"Jesus, Benno's dumb," said Haryk.

"I'll say. And she sure does make the most of it."

"If only she was worth it."

"She hasn't got a brain in her head," said Lexa.

"Oh," said Fonda, "she's not all that bad."

"Jeee-sus," said Haryk.

"Well, she's got a nice face anyway."

"Her ass is better," said Haryk.

"Haryk! Remember, Lucie's here," said Lexa.

I looked over at Lucie.

"I'm used to it," she said.

"Used to a foulmouth like Haryk? That's saying a lot, if you ask me," said Lexa.

"Look who's talking," said Haryk.

That was the way they usually talked. They never meant it seriously—just thought that kind of talk was very witty, and maybe it was. In reality, I mean. Books and novels always bubble with wit and sparkling repartee but in real life there's nothing very witty. Usually all it amounts to is a kind of teasing, the way boys and girls tease each other when they're together, though boys do it even among themselves. I don't know whether girls talk that way among themselves, too, but boys do. Because if you can't at least get each other all worked up by talking, then there really wouldn't be anything to talk about if nothing special happens to be going on right then—like at a dance, for instance—or you don't have anything really urgent to say. There wouldn't be any point in talking all that junk you talk about at dances if it weren't for the fun of teasing. Between boys and girls it's as natural as the day is long. Talking is probably about the same for them as sniffing is for dogs—and that's the honest truth, nothing dirty or exaggerated about it. I know it and I think everybody else does too, except not everybody admits it. I do. Boys say all sorts of things and crack all sorts of corny jokes just so finally they can kiss their girls out in the hall. That's true, at least as far as boys talking with girls is concerned. And it's certainly true when boys talk among themselves in front of a girl. Maybe it isn't always like that when they're by themselves but then boys usually talk about girls when they're by themselves, so even then it's true, too. So that's probably how it is with witty talk in general.

Then Benno appeared in the doorway with Helena. He was looking as deflated as before and Helena sat down, looking peeved.

"Let's finish up early today. I've got to get back home," he said.

"How come?" said Lexa.

"I've got to take a bath."

"First time since you got back from concentration camp, huh?"

"Aw, no. You ought to know Benny better than that," said Fonda.

"Shut up. Let's go through 'Riverside' again, then I'm taking off."

"Aw, don't be silly."

"I've got to."

"Well, you don't have to get so mad about it."

"What the hell? I'm not mad. I've just got to go home, that's all."

"Take it easy on him. I'm going home early too," I said.

"How come? Helena got you wrapped around her little finger, too?" quipped Lexa.

"Not Helena, Irena," said Haryk.

"Okay," I said calmly. "Let's play, shall we?" I didn't mind Haryk saying what he did because in general I didn't mind if the boys knew about it. I'd gotten so I didn't mind anything that had to do with Irena, I was so crazy about her. Fonda rapped on the piano.

"All right, 'Riverside' then. And Venca, watch out so you don't louse up the beginning again."

"Don't worry," said Venca and emptied out his trombone. I looked into my sax and saw a little puddle shining at the bottom. The bigger the puddle, the more fun it was to empty it out.

"Ready?" demanded Fonda.

"Ready," said Benno.

Fonda rapped slowly and the brush on the cymbals led into "Riverside Blues." Old Winter was dozing behind the counter and white drops trickled down from the tap into a mug underneath. Helena was browsing through another newspaper, bored. Music bored her, but she liked being married to the best trumpet player in the county so she stuck it out. Some old geezer stood planted in the doorway with a half pint of beer in his hand, staring at us. I could read his mind. His eyes looked like two bugles and he had a mouth like a tuba. He certainly didn't think the stuff we were producing was music. We didn't either, really. Not *just* music. For us it was something more like the world. Like before Christ and after Christ. I couldn't even remember what it had been like before jazz. I was probably interested in soccer or something—like our fathers who used to go to the stadium every Sunday and shout themselves hoarse. I wasn't much more than a kind of miniature dad myself then. A dad shrunk down to about four foot five. And then along came Benno with his records and jazz and the first experiments in Benno's house with a trumpet, piano, an old xylophone I'd dug up in the attic and two violins that Lexa and Haryk were learning to play because their parents wanted them to. And then Jimmy Lunceford. And Chick Webb. And Louis Armstrong. And Bob Crosby. And then everything else was After Jazz. So that it really wasn't just music at all. But that old geezer over there couldn't understand that. He'd been ruined a long time ago by soccer and beer and brass band music. Hopelessly ruined and for all time. But Lucie wasn't ruined, sitting there over what was left of her soda pop, her tanned legs gleaming underneath her skirt, one knee crossed over the other, and I remembered the greatest joke I'd ever thought up in my life, when I asked her to kiss me in the Petrin hall of mirrors so it would be like a thousand kisses all at once, and I began to regret I'd ever thrown her over, but then I realized it hadn't been me at all but her who'd thrown me over, though I still had hopes there, plenty of hopes, and then my conscience bothered me that I wasn't thinking about Irena so I started thinking about her and I joined in on the lament with everybody else and we wound up "Riverside" like we never had before. Like we never had about twenty times before.

When we'd finished, Helena got up and said, "Let's go, Benny."

"Sure, right away, Helena," said Benno and put away his music.

Fonda got up. "All right, that's all. Boys, we're going to play for a dance down at the spa any day now."

"You already lined it up?" asked Haryk.

"Yes. Medilek's cleaned up the outdoor dance floor so we can go any day now."

"Great. That means money, men," said Venca.

"That's right. Millions," said Haryk, and put his guitar in the case.

I got up and unscrewed the top of the saxophone. Then I tipped it over on one side where there aren't any valves on the bottom and poured the puddle out on the floor. I put in the brush and twirled the tenor elegantly in my hand. The weight dropped out through the narrow end and I had a good feeling as I slowly pulled the brush up through the saxophone. Then I put it into the case, took the head, pulled out the mouthpiece and cleaned it with a wire. I unscrewed the reed, dried it and wiped off the bakelite mouthpiece. Then I put everything into the case, locked it and put on my coat. Everybody else was ready. There was always more work with a saxophone. I went over to old man Winter and paid my bill. All I'd had was one beer. With his drowsy eyes, old Winter got up behind the counter and gave me back fifty German pfennigs change. That reminded me of the revolution. "Good night," I called after the others into the May night.

It was warm and starry, and as I came out into the darkness I was sort of blinded. At first all I could see against the grayish black of the night mist hanging over the town was a bunch of dark silhouettes. The windows of the castle still glittered on the other side of the valley. They weren't paying any attention to the blackout. The dark figures in front of the Port Arthur were saying goodby. "So long," I said and tagged along with Benno's short fat figure and Helena's female form. The others headed left toward the hospital. We were the only ones who went down toward the woods and around the brewery and over the bridge to the other side of the river where Benno's house was. It was quiet. Our footsteps beat a three-part rhythm on the pavement and we didn't talk. The silence was like before a storm. But maybe that was because I knew what was probably going to happen. Otherwise it was an ordinary kind of silence. We went past Dr. Stras' villa where

German officers were quartered. The main gate was open; the Germans had probably already left. It's always like that. The big brass clears out leaving the poor soldiers holding the bag. They'd made a field hospital out of the hotel on the square and there the wounded lay or hobbled around, sick and full of lice and puss. But Herr Regierungs- kommissar Kühl wasn't around any more. He'd had a five- room apartment in the hotel until not long ago. And now God knows where he was. He left the whole job up in the air. The town was without a ruling military commander. Wounded Wehrmacht soldiers were hanging around de- jectedly in Kühl's apartment, which he'd generously turned over to the wounded. Everywhere it was quiet. People were holed up at home, waiting. An ordinary kind of silence. It was only the fact that I knew what was going to happen before very long that made this silence seem like the silence before a storm. We reached the brewery and turned left, down toward the bridge. It arched gently over the river and the bulging paving stones glimmered whitely. Beyond it the road ran straight to the railroad station. A red light shone at the crossing. The huge smokestack of the power station stood out against the phosphorescent sky.

"Wait a minute, boys," said Helena, and she stopped. We stood there in the middle of the bridge. Helena leaned against the railing and we leaned over, too, on either side of her. I looked down. Beneath us the tranquil river flowed and you could feel how its dark surface was moving silently. The woods on the right were low and dark and the trees on the shore dipped their lower branches in the water. It was quiet. I strained my ears, but couldn't hear a thing. If you listened carefully, you could sometimes hear shooting from the front. On Black Mountain you could even hear the heavy machine guns sometimes. Now, though, I couldn't hear a thing. Just quiet. And that abso- lutely inaudible and subconscious rushing of the river underneath the bridge. Benno sighed.

"Oh, Jesus," he said and spat over the side of the bridge. The big white blob fell downward like a woman in a white veil committing suicide and splattered on the surface of the water.

"What's wrong, Benny?" said Helena.

"I don't feel good. I've got a fever."

"Let me feel," she said, touching his forehead. "No, you don't."

"I do, too."

"No, you don't. You're just imagining things again."

"No, I'm not. I got it from the camp."

"Well, come on, then. You'd better lie down."

"Wait," said Benno, and he was silent for a moment. "I just feel sort of stupid and sad."

"But why, Benny? Everything's going to be all right soon."

"Yeah, I know. But I still feel lousy."

Helena didn't say anything. She just reached over and took Benno's hand. I stood beside her and all of a sudden it was as if there were only two people standing there next to each other. Oh, I knew why Benno felt sad. I did, too. I hadn't ten minutes before, but now I did. It wasn't a terrible kind of sadness, like Benno's maybe, because he'd been in a concentration camp and half his relatives had died there, but just sad because of the river and those poor German clods with their skulls all bandaged up in the hotel, and because of the front which was getting closer and which was already senseless, and because of the woods and the little stars and everything. And because of Irena. Mainly because of Irena. And because now all of a sudden something was ending, something big and long, six years long, something which wouldn't ever happen again. I looked across at Irena's house on the other side of the river. I could see her window through the leaves on the tree that grew in front of her house and the light was on. She was probably reading or necking with Zdenek. I felt a terrific yearning to kiss somebody, too. And I was sad. Beside me, Benno and Helena were cooing to each other and I was standing there next to them, alone and melancholy and all too aware of how lonely I was. So what? What the hell. Maybe nobody understands me and that's why I'm alone. Maybe I really can't love anybody. Not in the dumb way Benno loved Helena. I remembered them all, Vera and Eva and Jarka and Irena, and it was as though I'd never loved any of them. I'd forgotten what being in love with them felt like. All I could remember were all kinds of problems and difficulties and embarrassing feelings. That was all. Maybe I wasn't made for it. It would have been nice to know that there was at least one girl in the world who wouldn't leave me feeling like that. Just one. I had a saxophone and I'd been on the honor roll in my senior year and my father had influence and everybody figured I had it good and that I was satisfied. I wasn't, though I had lots of success with old ladies. I talked politics with them over the tea cups. Boy, did I ever talk. And I was awfully mature and sensible for my age. And at home I wrote sentimental Last Will and Testaments for Irena and I wanted to love her and I'd held onto this feeling that I loved her for a long time. But I couldn't always and forever. And then I felt sad. Maybe it really would be better if I got knocked off in this revolution. I worked up a big ball of spit in my mouth and leaned over the railing. I let it go slowly and watched it fall. It fell straight because there wasn't any wind. It grew rapidly smaller and disappeared in the dark. All you could hear was a faint splat. The river down below rushed on quietly and evenly. I looked at the couple beside me. They stood there with their arms around each other's waists and their heads together, watching the river. Suddenly I was above them. Superior to them. Well, all right. What did they have anyway with their hugging and cooing and bothering the life out of each other? I was alone and free. Wonderfully free. And the revolution was approaching and I could hardly wait for it. And then later I'd go away. To Prague and to foreign countries and who knows where. But then it all collapsed inside me. Go away to what? And what would I do there? Live. Yes, just live. Look around at things and eat and fall in love with lots of girls. Yes. Well, yes, then. Well, all right, why not? It's interesting enough, living. Better than getting knocked off in some revolution. The river rippled and hummed and it was warm and dark. I stood up straighter. "Well," I said, "let's go."

"Sure," said Benno and we started off. Our steps echoed in the darkness. We went past the County Office Building and the sound of our footsteps boomed through the arcade.

"Are you coming over tomorrow?" Benno asked me.

"I don't know. It all depends."

"You really think something's going to happen tomorrow?"

"I don't know. Maybe."

"Listen, what do you really know?"

"Oh, nothing."

"Don't play dumb with me. Come on, tell me."

"But if . . . it's kind of hard."

"Tell us, Danny," said Helena.

"But really, I don't know anything."

"What was that you said about the radio then?"

"What radio?"

"About Radio Prague stopping broadcasting."

"Oh, well, yeah. I heard something like that."

"What?"

"Well, just that Prague's supposed to stop broadcasting and that that's supposed to be the sign it's going to begin."

"Where? Here, too?"

"I don't know. Maybe just in Prague. I don't know."

"Who told you?"

"Some kid, that's all."

"Listen, I'm scared those kids are up to some kind of trouble."

"How do you mean?"

"It's always the same gang, isn't it? Skocdopole and Vahar and Perlik and Benda—that whole crowd, right?"

"I don't know. Well, maybe."

"Don't kid me. You know what they're up to all right."

"No, I don't. Honest."

"But you're always hanging around with Skocdopole."

"Yeah, but he never tells me anything."

"Still, you know more than you're letting on you do."

"I do not. They're up to something but Prema won't tell me what, and I'm not going to pump him if he doesn't want to tell me himself, am I?"

"But they are planning to do something."

"Could be. But I don't know what."

"They're nuts. A bunch of idiots like that'll mess around

and all they'll do is get the Germans mad and then we'll all be in the shit."

"Benny!" whispered Helena.

"Well, it's the truth. Dad's the same way. They're nuts. He and Dr. Sabata and old Cemelik are planning an uprising."

"With Sabata?"

"Yeah."

"Who else is in on it?"

"I don't know for sure. Major Weiss and Krocan—the one that owns the factory—and Jirka Krocan and Dr. Bohadlo and people like that."

"Boy, I wonder what they're going to do."

"All I hope is that they'll wait till the Germans have all cleared out."

"And what if the communists won't wait that long?" I said.

Benno looked up with a jerk. "Hey, you do know something."

"What do you mean?"

"Well, what's this about the communists?"

"Nothing. All I know is that they're getting something ready, too."

"And Skocdopole and the others are in with them?"

"With the communists?"

"Yeah."

"No."

"So what are they up to?"

"They've got something else. They're probably hooked up with London or something."

"And how . . . what are their connections with the communists?"

"I don't know. All I know is that they're each doing it on their own."

"And the communists have their orders?"

"Sure, I guess so anyway."

"Then we're in for it."

"In for what?"

"You'll see. The communists want a revolution and so we all get dragged into the shit heap."

"You're not afraid, are you?"

"Afraid? No. I'm just fed up."

"Don't argue like that, Benny," said Helena.

"We're not arguing," I said.

"Maybe not. But Benny's using dirty words again."

"Don't blame him for that, Helena. We're all talking dirty these days. It's nerves."

"Yes, nerves!"

"What a future to look forward to!" said Benno. "If our old men don't louse it up, then Skocdopole and his gang will, and if they don't, then the communists certainly will. Either way, we've got something to look forward to."

"Benno, go to bed and sleep it off," I said. I knew how he felt and I should have pitied him, only I couldn't. I knew he'd been in a concentration camp and so he had good reason for being scared of shooting and dying and things like that. He'd seen death and I hadn't. So I acted like I would have acted if I'd felt sorry for him—out of respect for his nerves.

"Yes, Benny," said Helena. "Come on and get some sleep. You're worn out."

"I won't be able to sleep anyway."

"Sure you will. I'll give you a sleeping pill."

"I'm so goddamn fed up!"

"Benny! Don't swear!"

"I mean it, Helena. You hardly get to sit down for a minute and these fools start ruining everything."

"Oh, Benno," I said, "nothing's going to happen. They can't do a thing."

"I hope to God they can't."

"Not a chance. There's nothing to worry about. I know them."

"Idiots."

"Sure."

"Let's go," snapped Benno suddenly. "So long."

"Good night. Sleep tight," I said.

"Good night, Danny," said Helena.

"Good night."

They turned and hurried past the County Office Building toward Benno's family's house. They were arm in arm and they were hurrying. I watched them go. The Manes place was in the middle of a garden and the tall-windowed drawing room shone luxuriously into the night. They weren't paying any attention to the blackout either. I knew that Eva and Mr. and Mrs. Manes were sitting there, digesting their supper. There were wonderful paintings on the wall, a Persian rug on the floor, and everybody had his own room. Benno and Eva and all the others. It was a huge two-story mansion with a drawing room and veranda and a salon and a music room with potted palms. So Mr. Manes, export-import, was going to stage a revolution, too. Besides his business, all he cared about was Freud. And he knew how to live. He called himself a liberal. He was an Aryan but he looked like a Jew. His wife was kind and generous. She was Jewish and, besides Benno, there was also a very pretty daughter.

I watched the two of them until they disappeared through the garden gate. Then I turned around and headed toward the station.

I was all alone on the sidewalk now, not a soul in sight. On the left the park lay quiet and I would have bet anything that tonight there wasn't a single person in it, though it was a fine night for a stroll. Everybody, every family with all its little daughters, was getting ready to creep down in the cellar and stay there until it was all over. They were all imagining the craziest kinds of things. About the Russians and raping and so on. Goebbels had seen to that. If they catch you, you're done for. People joked about it at the grocery store and in all the shops, but deep down inside they were scared. So, in their different ways, people were getting ready and, just to be on the safe side, stitching together red flags out of old feather-bed ticking. Fathers were plotting in their offices and boys were hatching conspiracies in the taverns and back rooms. And dreaming of being heroes. Just like me.

I walked past a block of apartment houses that stretched all the way down to the railroad station. Dagmar Dreslerova lived in the last house. My refuge in distress. I'd been crazy about her when I was a sophomore and then I wasn't any more. But she was pretty and I didn't like thinking that maybe she wasn't crazy about me any more either. So every once in a while when I was feeling low on account of Irena, I'd visit Dagmar and tell her I loved her just so I could hear her tell me how much she loved me. Then, too, I felt kind of sorry for her because I wasn't in love with her any more. She'd taken it very hard when I broke off with her. Then she started going with Franta Kocandrle but he must have given her a rough time. And she was giving a rough time to Rosta Pitterman, who was in love with her in spite of the fact that she couldn't care less about him. She was ready to throw Franta over anytime I wanted her to, but I didn't take much advantage of the situation. My conscience bothered me. Not because it would hurt Franta but because I was mixing Dagmar up, getting her mentally and morally all snarled up and doing all sorts of things with her which I didn't really enjoy at all any more. I just didn't have the heart to disappoint her if it meant so much to her. I felt sorry for her, so I tried to give her pleasure. Sometimes I took refuge in Dagmar when I'd convinced myself I'd had enough of Irena, but that hardly ever happened. It was rare that I felt I couldn't take it any more. But when I did, I went to see Dagmar to make that feeling stand out even sharper, as if I needed consolation, and I consoled myself with Dagmar as well as I could so the feeling wouldn't go away too soon. There wasn't any light on in Dagmar's room. She'd probably gone to bed early with her unfortunate crush on me and was probably feeling damn good about it, too. An unhappy love affair ought to make her glad. I would have been glad if I'd had one. But, to tell the truth, I was feeling pretty satisfied. I was a bit tired, the saxophone case was heavy, and I was looking forward to going to bed. Even being tired felt good. Or being hungry. Or being shut up inside the Messerschmidt plant shortly before the end-of-the-shift whistle blew. I crossed the tracks and looked around the station. The trains weren't running any more. A row of freight cars fixed up so people could live in them stood on a siding. It was a munitions train and it was guarded by a couple of Vlasov men with submachine guns. It had got stuck here because the partisans had torn up the tracks to Germany. I could see somebody with his collar turned up, shuffling slowly along the line of cars—a sub-machine gun slung across his shoulder, a cigarette gleaming like a glow-worm under his nose. I shifted my sax case to my other hand and turned left along Jirasek Boulevard. The Messerschmidt plant lay on one side, dark and quiet. Only stars were reflected in the glass roof over the assembly department. Not even the little night light was on. The blue-painted glass shone under the starry sky. I'd spent a lot of time in there, too. A year and a half of drudgery and boredom. Mainly boredom because I didn't do much drudgery. Now that I looked back at it, it hadn't been so bad. The boys and the pneumatic drill and the cool aluminum frames and the factory guards and the toilets and the welding and the Germans and all the other things, and reading surrealist poetry in the john. Reading "Women in the Plural" and "The Bridge" and "The Absolute Grave-digger." Poems like that. My father teased me about it. I didn't mind because he made fun of jazz, too. And even though I probably didn't understand them very well, I liked those poems. I went over the footbridge that crossed the creek and came out on Jirasek Boulevard. It was narrow, high, and deserted. I walked fast. My footsteps echoed rhythmically on the pavement. The lights were on at the Krocans's. Across the street at the Kaldouns's, too. All the factory owners were getting ready for the liberation. So was Chief of Police Rimbalnik, who wore white gloves and lived at the Kaldouns's. The town was in good hands. We could all rest easy.

I got to our house and took my key out of my pocket. Out of habit, I looked up at the sky again and then at the outline of the castle. It was already dark up there and only the stars were shining. I stood in the doorway and felt around for the keyhole. I stuck the key in and unlocked the door. I didn't turn on the light. I always went upstairs in the dark. It was nicer that way. You could daydream and practically fall asleep on the stairs. I felt pleasantly tired. I slid one hand along the banister and dragged my saxophone case along in the other. It was dark on the first floor. There was a light under the door on the second floor.

B*

I went up as far as our balcony and felt like taking a look around outside again. I set the case down on the floor and opened the balcony door. I went out and leaned over the iron railing. It was just a thin railing and I always got a pleasantly threatening sense of insecurity when I leaned against it, hanging in thin air above the town. As I leaned there against the railing, the balcony disappeared and there I was, dangling in space. Down below me was the courtyard. I looked down and saw Bonza, the dog, looking up at me. I mewed. Bonza barked. He watched me and couldn't figure out what was going on. He barked suspiciously and inquisitively; I reached in my pocket and felt a piece of roll left over from lunch. I threw it down to Bonza. It made a dull *bonk* when it hit the concrete. Bonza quieted down right away. I looked out over the town. It lay in a valley, dark and quiet, the steeple of the Czech Brethren Church rising up over the little houses around it and only here and there a lone window gleaming. The lights were still on at the Port Arthur. I could imagine old Winter sitting there behind the counter with his drowsy eyes while beside him the beer tap dripped, slowly and steadily. And it was already quarter past eleven. I couldn't imagine a life like that. Sitting beside the tap every day and most of the night. Maybe he didn't even sleep in bed. It was unimaginable. Bonza barked again from down below. I reached in my pocket and felt a little box of the peppermint drops I sometimes suck on account of my breath. I took one out and pitched it down to Bonza. He stopped barking and snuffled around trying to find it. I looked out over the town again. Beyond it, the woods started up the side of the hill and out of the woods rose the bare peak of Black Mountain with the hotel on top. Now it was dark. I remembered those long Sunday afternoons we used to kill up there during the war, playing cards and billiards and drinking tea. That was all over now. All that was over now. Something new was beginning now. I tipped my head back and looked up at the wide sky that was swollen with stars. The Milky Way stretched across it and didn't move. A foamy spring-time silence hung over the town. It didn't look like there was going to be a revolution. But there was supposed to be a revolution. And there had to be one. A lot of people wanted a revolution. A lot of important people, too. And a lot of these had bad records that needed cleaning up fast. A revolution would be very handy for them. I could already see how Mr. Machacek would write it up: *The History of the Kostelec Revolution,* "Dedicated to the Honorable Dr. Sabata, Mayor of Kostelec," and it'd be published by B. Minarik who owned one of the bookstores in Kostelec. He'll write it and peddle it around, and Mr. Kaldoun and Mr. Krocan and Mr. Moutelik will tuck it away in their bookcases alongside the collected works of Master Alois Jirasek* and next to the memorial volume put out in honor of the ninetieth birthday of Mr. Josef Serpon-Domanin, the Czech industrialist. And they'll read it, but mostly just the parts that mention them. And they'll be in there. Everybody will be. Mr. Machacek won't forget anybody. Mr. Kaldoun was gracious enough to donate the use of his warehouse for a first-aid station, he'll write. And Mrs. Krocanova and Mrs. Moutelikova made soup for the partisans. Mr. Machacek will write about everything. Everything accurate and in great detail so the truth will be preserved for all posterity. About how Mrs. Krocanova made soup for the partisans. Well, anyway, it'll be good to have it preserved for all posterity. At least posterity'll have something to laugh about.

Bonza barked again from down below. He was starting to get on my nerves. You dumb mutt, I thought, all you care about is something to eat. I turned around and went off the balcony. I closed the door, picked up my saxophone case, and went up the last flight of stairs to our apartment. It was dark under the door. I unlocked it and went in. I didn't turn on the light in the hall so I wouldn't wake up my father and mother. But Mother probably wasn't asleep anyway. She always waited up until I came in and then fell asleep. Often she didn't even fall asleep then. She suffered from high blood pressure and insomnia. I felt sorry for her. Once, when I committed sabotage by mistake and was scared the Gestapo would come for me, I suddenly realized that I loved her. She was the only person I really loved. Otherwise I more or less always acted like I loved people, but I really did love Mother. Except she was always around and so I often forgot about her. I could hear Father softly snoring in the bedroom. I hung my hat on the rack and looked at myself in the dark mirror. I could see my silhouette. I always looked in the mirror when I came home at night. Sometimes, when I turned on the light, I looked handsome and aristocratic in the mirror. That was because of the way the light shone on me from above. I had a long face and hollow—but not too hollow—cheeks and a straight nose and eyes with shadows underneath and a nice mouth. I used to imagine myself on the movie screen. With Judy Garland. But that was a long time ago. Now I couldn't imagine myself like that any more. Only the habit still stuck with me, looking at myself in the mirror at night. I tiptoed across the carpet to my room, shut the door behind me, and set the case on the floor. Then I groped along in front of me until I felt the upright piano. Irena's picture stood on top. Before, Vera's picture used to stand there, and before that Lucie's. And before that Dagmar Dreslerova's. I always had to have some-body's picture on the piano. I touched the cool metal of the lamp and turned the switch. A sickly light seeped over the room. That was because I had a 220-volt bulb in the lamp which was too strong for the current in our house. I had the impression the light couldn't spread around the room as far as it should. The wardrobe and the table by the radio were almost in the dark. I turned to the bed. It was made up and a pair of carefully folded pajamas lay on the sheet. Just like my mother. I shoved the case under the bed and sat down. I felt tired. I pulled off my shoes, first one and then the other, untied my necktie and took off my shirt. Then I took off my pants, then my shorts and socks. I sat down on the bed naked. It felt good. I lay down on my back and put my feet up on the eiderdown quilt folded up at the foot of the bed. I lay there naked and the pillow and the sheet felt cool and good against my back. I gazed down at myself. I didn't look so bad with nothing on. I had a well-proportioned body and chest and slim hips. Without any athlete around to compare myself with,

I looked almost Grecian. The way the lamp was shining on me from behind, a shadow fell on my hips and suddenly I had those sharp angles around the pelvis like the statue by Praxiteles, whatever it is called. Those angles always looked unnatural and out of proportion to me but now I saw them there on my own body. I lifted one leg and stretched it out. It was nice to be tired. I lay there for a while, then sat up and put on my pajamas. I turned off the light and pulled the quilt up over me. Everything was quiet. In the name of the Father, Son, and Holy Ghost, I said to myself, and started to say my prayers. Dear God, make Irena care for me so she'll marry me and I can live with her happily ever after. That's what I'm praying for, Lord—that more than anything else in the world. I recited Our Father Who Art and thought about Benno and Helena and Kaldoun and Machacek and old man Winter and Bonza and the revolution and about everything, and then I realized that I wasn't saying my prayers in a very reverent way and so I said the Lord's Prayer over again and tried to think about God, but I couldn't unless I pictured him sitting on his throne in whiskers and a nightshirt. And then I said Hail Mary and that went better because I've always thought of the Virgin Mary as being very beautiful and sweet until you get to the part about Jesus, and then I bowed my head and imagined her together with Irena, Irena standing in front of the Virgin, wearing a white veil and carrying a bunch of lilies in her hand and smiling at me. When I finished that I repeated Dear Lord, please help me to make Irena care for me, and I crossed myself. I felt better. That duty was over with. Now I could think about whatever I wanted to. I wanted to think about Irena. And how it would be with her. I thought about me sleeping in bed and Irena sleeping next to me. We just went right on sleeping and I kept wanting to open my eyes and tell her, Irena, and she'd say, Yes, what is it? And I'd say, Irena, you know. . . And then I couldn't think what to say next and so we just went on sleeping and I kept on waiting for me to say something but I didn't say anything at all.

Saturday, May 5, 1945

I woke up at about half past eight. Outside the sun was shining and it was hot in the room. I lay in bed. I had a slight headache and a bad taste in my mouth. I lay there and looked up at Rosta's portrait of me that hung on the wall by my bed. I looked very distinguished. He'd given me a huge head and narrow shoulders so I looked scholarly. And what was interesting about the picture was the contrast between that intellectual-looking head and the grimy collar of my shirt which I wore without a tie. I remember when he did it. It was once right after I'd gotten home from work at Messerschmidt. I was wearing a cotton shirt that was spattered all over with ferroflux oil. I looked at the painting and thought to myself, that's a nice portrait, and if I die, at least I'll leave one good thing behind. Otherwise it was a lousy morning. I closed my eyes but I wasn't tired enough to sleep any more, or even doze.

It was time to get up. So finally I sprang out of bed. If you've got to do it sometimes it's best to do it fast. I went to the window and looked out. Nothing. The town looked just the same as yesterday. No sign of a revolution. Who could tell if anything was going to happen? I wasn't so sure anything would. Things like that do happen but that it would actually take place right here in our own town seemed awfully unlikely to me. Revolution. I couldn't imagine anybody shooting. The druggist, or Mr. Krocan who owned the factory? Crazy. Prema possibly. Prema had a killer's face and he had some weapons in his warehouse, that much I knew. And maybe Perlik, too. Otherwise the whole thing sounded pretty absurd. Completely absurd. I turned away from the window and switched on the radio. I waited a while and it irritated me. Waiting for the radio to warm up always irritated me. Some kind of Prussian march came booming out. So nothing had happened yet. Naturally. Nothing would. The Russians would come from the east and the Americans from the west and they'd liberate us in a moment of glory, and then the glorious moment would be over. Or maybe it would more likely just get off to a start with all the city fathers puffing around pinning medals on each other's chest. What a farce. I went to the bathroom and turned on the water. I washed and rubbed myself briskly with a Turkish towel until my skin was nearly red. A terrific feeling. I went back to the room, opened the window, and turned back the covers. Cool air rushed in through the open window. The sun, already up, shone bright and new. I went to the kitchen and put on the tea kettle, got some rolls from the pantry and started buttering them. First one, then another—like on an assembly line. Then I looked out the window and almost fell over. Across the street, a Czech flag was flying from architect Bauman's house.

It gave me a weird sensation. Like when I was fourteen years old and we were celebrating our Independence Day, the 28th of October. That flag hadn't flown for six years and now all of a sudden, there it was—flying again. And it didn't seem new or strange at all. It was a beautiful flag, at least nine feet wide, freshly laundered, and the red and white colors were strong and clear. I thought of the radio, ran back to my room, turned it on and waited. Meantime I noticed that flags were flying in front of the hospital and official buildings, too. Somebody was just hanging one out at Vasata's house. Yes. It was starting to happen now. As though everything was already won. But the Germans were still here. The radio came on. Music. I listened, but it wasn't German music. Some march by Kmoch. I should have known they wouldn't have come up with anything better than some dumb oompah Kmoch. What a revolution. I listened disgustedly to the tinny music. It spoiled my good mood. Then I went back into the kitchen, ate breakfast and decided that, whatever happened, I was going into this in style. I took my dark brown jacket out of the closet, put on a white shirt and light pants. Then I put on my boldly patterned bluish-yellow silk necktie, tied a neat little knot and buttoned the jacket. I took my perforated brown shoes, brushed them, and went to take a look at myself in the mirror. I was looking pretty sharp. That made me feel good. I put on a light colored hat, took one more look in the mirror, and left the apartment. When I got to the second floor and was passing the door of the Strnads' apartment, Mrs. Strnadova suddenly appeared in the doorway.

"Danny! Danny!" she cried hysterically. Tears were streaming down her cheeks.

"Good morning, Mrs. Strnadova," I said, took off my hat and gave her a big smile.

"The day has come, Danny! At long last we're free again!"

"Well, not quite yet!" I said in the same tone, as if I was saying, That's right! Free at last! Meanwhile I kept a polite smile fixed on my face.

"Isn't it just wonderful? I'm so happy! So happy!" she yelled without even bothering to listen to what I was saying.

"Wonderful. Yes. Wonderful."

"Oh, my word, I'm so happy I hardly know what I'm doing—aren't you?"

"Oh, absolutely."

"It'll be a joy to live again. And as for those butchers—they ought to shoot them all!"

"They certainly should."

"Yes. And not only them but everybody who collaborated with them, too. Mercy would be wasted on them."

"Absolutely," I said. I knew why the old girl was talking so wildly. Her neighbor's husband was a collaborator, and she couldn't stand her neighbor. So naturally she was all in favor of shooting.

"They all ought to be locked up. And anybody with a life

on his conscience—no mercy for them. The firing squad's all they deserve!"

"Oh there'll be shooting all right," I said.

"Oh yes," she said avidly. "You know, personally, I wouldn't hurt a fly, but when it comes to those monsters I don't have an ounce of pity."

"Who does?" I said.

"You'd be surprised. There are some people around here who'd just like to forgive and forget. But I'll never forget. Not me!"

"How could you?" I said.

"Because if we forget now, then we'll have the Germans back again in twenty years. We've suffered long enough under them. It mustn't happen again."

"That's for sure," I said.

"What would our children say? They'd never let us forget how foolish we'd been, how completely irresponsible and how we hadn't learned our lesson."

"Right," I said. "Excuse me, Mrs. Strnadova, but I've got an important appointment and I'll have to be going."

The old lady beamed at me.

"Aha, I understand," she said. "Well, I won't keep you, Danny, run along. And remember me to Miss Irena. She'll be so happy, too."

"Yes, thank you. Goodby," I said sweetly, and trotted down the stairs. The old girl was omniscient. She snooped out everything. I would have liked to have known where she found out that I was crazy about Irena. Actually, though, it was simple. Irena was Berty Moutelik's cousin, and Berty Moutelik couldn't keep anything to himself. And Miss Cihak, the schoolteacher, was Berty Moutelik's aunt. And Miss Cihak was a friend of Miss Strnad. And the little Strnad girl didn't go around with anybody except her mother. That was how she'd found out. It was simple. I didn't care. I rushed out to the street.

There were lots of people milling around. Flags were flying from most of the houses by now, shining in the sunshine. Crowds of laughing people swarmed through the streets. Everybody was grinning. I put on a scornful expression. All that gay laughter made me sick. A stupid happiness. One should sneer. Sneer about the Germans and the German Reich. I stuck one hand in my pocket and ambled along with the mob. Old men and young thronged alongside me and everybody wore something in his buttonhole. Mr. Petrbok, all dressed up in his band leader's uniform, rushed out of his house and hurried off toward the square. He was wearing white gloves and carrying a baton with a gold ball on the end. The idiot. This poor sap was the one who always made trouble about our permit to play and said that since jazz wasn't our national music it should be prohibited. And now he thought he would welcome the Russians with his idiotic tin-can band. Well, we'd welcome them too. And we wouldn't make any concessions, either—Petrbok could bet his last cent on that. We'll welcome them with some real fine Dixieland, with Venca's throaty, hoarse trombone and Benno's sobbing trumpet. We'll welcome them. And not Mr. Petrbok. And we'll play for dances down at the spa. And we'll jitterbug and have a party and hang up paper lanterns around the pool. I sauntered along and looked around. The sun was shining and the air was fresh and soft as May. Mr. Vladyka, the collaborator who worked at Dad's bank, was hunched up in front of the bank, all jittery. He was pale as a ghost and in his buttonhole he wore a big rosette made out of linden leaves and all sorts of junk as if he'd gotten himself all dressed for inspection. He was shaking all over, so that even his rosette trembled. He looked around him in terror but nobody paid any attention to him. I made a face and went past him. I saw Pedro Gershwin at the corner by Novotny's. I headed toward him.

"Hi," I said.

"Hi," he said, and touched two fingers to the rim of his hat. He was leaning up against the antitank barrier that stood there and his legs were crossed with elaborate casualness.

"How're things?" I said.

"I'm just watching the crowds," he said.

"Aren't you going on downtown?"

"No. I'm waiting for Haryk."

"Where is he?"

"He went for some paint."

"What for?"

"We're going to do some painting."

"Huh?"

"Painting."

"What are you going to paint?"

"We're going over the German signs."

"Oh, I see. Then I'll stick around, too. Anybody else coming?"

"Benno and Lexa went for a ladder."

"They're coming here?"

"Yeah."

We were silent.

Pedro was cool as a cucumber and terse. He always was. He didn't have much between the ears, but what little he did have he doled out so carefully that he made out better than lots of kids who knew ten times as much.

"What do you think? You think there's going to be any shooting here?" I said.

"I'm afraid so."

"You don't think maybe they ought to hold off for a while?"

"Sure."

"I think so, too. Guys are rushing into this like mad without even waiting till they've got enough guns and . . ."

"Let 'em, if they want to push up daisies for the communists."

"You think that's what's going to happen?"

"Why, sure."

"That the communists are going to take over?"

"No doubt about it."

"Well, I don't know. That'd be bad, all right. Yeah, but Benes . . ."

"There's nothing he can do about it."

I didn't say anything for a while. Then I said, "Well, what're you going to do?"

"Me?"

"Yeah. If the commies take over."

"Listen, pal—but this is strictly between you and me . . ."

"Sure."

Pedro looked at me quizzically.

"As soon as the highways are clear," he said, "I'm going to hop on my motorcycle and get the hell out of here."

"Where to?"

"To the Americans, where else?"

"Yeah, sure," I said. "You're right. That'd be the best thing to do."

"Greetings, gents," somebody said behind us. It was Haryk. He was wearing a white druggist's smock and in one hand he held a can of paint, in the other a paint brush, and he was grinning.

"Hi," I said. "Well, congratulations and welcome to freedom."

"Same to you, same to you," said Haryk.

"Man, did you see old Petrbok?"

"Yeah. With gloves and a big baton."

"He's nuts. But just wait till this afternoon when he marches his brass band out to the customs house."

"I hope he does. At least he could get mixed up in something out there and that would be the end of him," I said.

"Right," said Haryk. "Only then we'd have to play for all the funerals in town instead of him."

Pedro laughed.

"Yeah. Here everybody's celebrating victory and freedom and they forget the front hasn't gotten here yet."

"You think it'll come this way?" said Haryk.

"Well, what do *you* think? The Germans are just going to evaporate?"

"Maybe the Russians'll catch up with 'em before they get here."

"I wouldn't bet on it."

"Why?"

"Because the Germans are running their asses off trying to get back to the Americans."

"Maybe you're right," said Haryk. Silently, we watched the crowds. Lexa and Benno emerged from the Cinema Lido arcade. They were carrying a ladder. Lexa was dressed in his ordinary clothes but Benno was wearing a white smock and a hat made out of a newspaper. They came over to us.

"It's about time," said Haryk.

"Old man Matejka didn't want to lend us the ladder. He was scared we'd break it."

"Let's go. Let's do something," said Benno. I looked at him. He didn't look scared. I went over to him.

"How're you doing?"

"Huh?"

"How'd you sleep?"

"Swell," he said. "You?"

"Me, too. Everything's running real smooth, huh?"

"Just wait. Dad's down at City Hall now."

"Yeah," said Lexa. "So's old man Cemelik. From what I heard, they're going to proclaim an independent state of Kostelec at noon and elect Sabata president and declare war against Germany."

"Or declare neutrality, maybe?" said Haryk.

"That's possible, too."

"What the hell, let's get going," said Benno.

"Let's go," said Haryk.

"Where'll we go first?" I asked.

"First let's go over to our store," said Benno. We started off. People looked after us and some of them were laughing.

"That's the spirit, boys," some old timer said. "Smear it all up."

"You bet. We're going to wipe it all out," said Haryk.

"The whole past," said Pedro.

"And all that suffering," said Haryk.

The old guy looked at us and you could tell he didn't know what to think. But we kept right on going. The people kept streaming along, up one side of the street toward the square and back down on the other side. Flags were flying everywhere. Mr. Kodet was just sticking a bust of Benes in his shop window and his wife was fixing up the backdrop, draping the Czechoslovak flag into neat folds and then stepping back to see how it looked. Next door, the Shuberts had six flags in their store window. One for each of the Allies. They even had a Chinese flag. We kept on going. Mr. Moutelik was standing out in front of the City of London department store, passing out tricolors. A big crowd was elbowing around him, mostly boys, and begging him, "Me too, Mr. Moutelik, me too!" Mr. Moutelik was cutting out the tricolors and giving them away. Boy, was he bighearted! Man, was he a big patriot. He also owned the biggest store in Kostelec. He was absolutely bald and his head shone in the sunshine. When we reached him, he'd just finished cutting out the last piece. He threw up his hands and yelled, "That's all there is. Don't push! You can see for yourselves I don't have anymore."

Haryk stopped.

"Want us to paint you, Mr. Moutelik?"

"How's that, Haryk?"

"Do you want us to paint your sign for you?"

"Oh, that's it. Well, come on, boys," said Mr. Moutelik. "Come on. I'll be much obliged to you."

Lexa and Benno propped the ladder up in front of the door and Haryk slowly made his way up.

"Careful," said Mr. Moutelik. "Don't spill any paint on the Czech lettering now."

"Don't worry," said Haryk and he expertly began to paint over the German inscription.

"Careful," said Mr. Moutelik, looking up at him. Haryk calmly went on painting. But all of a sudden, a thin trickle of black paint dribbled off the brush and dripped down the signboard over the Czech letters.

"Watch out!" shrieked Mr. Moutelik. "Wipe it off, Haryk!"

"I don't have anything to wipe it off with," said Haryk.

"Wait a second," called Mr. Moutelik. "Rosie! Hurry! Bring a rag!"

"Yes, sir," said Rosie, looked up in amazement, then disappeared into the store. Haryk sat there on the ladder and didn't do a thing. We waited. Rosie didn't come. Haryk shifted the brush to his other hand and tried to rub off the paint with his hand. But he only made it worse.

"Careful! No! Don't do that!" cried Mr. Moutelik. "Here comes Rosie! Hurry up!"

Rosie rushed back with a rag and handed it up to Haryk. Haryk took the rag and rubbed. The Czech inscription and Mr. Moutelik's huge signature were veiled in a gray film. Mr. Moutelik looked grieved.

"Wait a minute, Harry, old boy," he said.

"It won't come off," said Haryk.

"Leave it be."

But Haryk kept on smearing the paint over the sign.

"Leave it!" Mr. Moutelik said heroically. "Anyway, I've got to have a new signboard painted. This is just temporary."

"That's right," I said. "This is just a kind of symbol, right?"

"Exactly, Danny," said Mr. Moutelik. "A symbol of the evil past."

Haryk slid down off the ladder and Benno and Lexa brought it down onto their shoulders.

"There we are," said Haryk. "Sorry, Mr. Moutelik . . ."

Mr. Moutelik waved his hand.

"Ah, don't give it a thought. What do I care? So what? At a time like this! Thanks, boys. Thank you."

"You're quite welcome," said Haryk. We all said goodby to him and then shoved off from the store. Haryk hurried on ahead. When we were out of earshot, Haryk turned to us.

"Man, I sure made a mess of that, didn't I?"

"You're telling me," said Lexa.

"Wait and see, he'll send you a bill for his new sign yet," said Benno.

"I wouldn't put it past him," said Haryk.

We strolled on toward the square. I walked with Pedro. Benno and Lexa were in front of us, carrying the ladder. The square looked like an anthill. People were walking back and forth in their Sunday best, pretending to be very jolly. Some were. But lots of them weren't. At least not all that jolly. It wasn't over yet. Nothing was certain yet and God only knew how it was going to turn out. The Russians were heading this way from the east. Still, everybody was acting as if they were jolly. An incredibly long flag was already hanging from one church steeple like a red and white noodle. Another was just being hung from another steeple. They were shoving it out through a window in the belfry like an anchor rope. It was a yellow and white flag. Some guy next to me started to cheer.

"Long live the Czechoslovak Republic! Long live President Benes!"

He looked drunk. When the yellow and white flag flapped out, he stopped and stared.

"What's that?" he said.

I leaned over and said, "It's the Pope's flag."

"That?" he said, turning toward me. "So that's the Pope's flag, is it?"

"Yes."

Then the guy began to cheer again. "Long live the Pope! Long live Jesus Christ! Long live the Czechoslovak Republic!"

We made our way across the square. All of a sudden a murmur ran through the crowd. Somebody was cheering, though it sounded pretty timid for a real cheer. I looked up and saw a huge flag majestically fluttering from the turret of the castle. The Czech flag. The sun was shining on it and the cupola of the castle was bright red; the hill on which the castle stood was bright with lilacs in bloom. It was like a picture on a candy box. An extremely patriotic picture. A picture to remember! It would certainly inspire Mr. Leitner to paint it, working in a bunch of people in Sokol dress and little girls in old-fashioned peasant costumes and, over in one corner, Alois Jirasek. No. Alois Jirasek in one corner and Bozena Nemcova* in the other. President Masaryk in the upper left hand corner, President Benes in the right and at the bottom Alois Jirasek and Bozena Nemcova. And then he'd display it in his shop window. And Mr. Machecek would use it for the frontispiece of his *History of the Kostelec Revolution.* Yes. That's how it would be. Everything'd be worked in, everything would be preserved. In word and picture. The revolution was in good hands. It sure was in our town anyway. All of a sudden the crowd behind us started laughing. I looked around. People were shoving and shouting, "Watch out!"

"What's going on?" asked Haryk.

Somebody up front turned around and called, "Watch out! They're going to throw Hitler out!"

I got the idea. We were standing in front of City Hall on the paved square where they used to have band concerts and speeches. I looked up. The building's main tower was very high and the top looked awfully small when you looked up at it from down below. Somebody was leaning out of the little cupola and holding something in his hands. He displayed it to the crowd below. It was the bronze bust of Hitler that used to stand in the main lobby of City Hall and the sun gleamed against it. "All right, let 'er go," somebody yelled, and everybody laughed again. Then somebody came racing out into the square. It was Petracek who worked out at the Messerschmidt plant. He was waving his arms and yelling to quiet the crowd.

"Now then, everybody," said Petracek. "Let's help him off on his long way down! Get ready!"

The crowd was with him. From the crowd came a long, drawn-out "Get setttt . . ." The man up there holding the bust caught on too, and after lifting up the bust with both hands as high over the railing as he could, he waited. Petracek sprang off to one side. Then somebody shouted and the whole crowd joined in with a thunderous "Go!" and that same second, the man in the tower let the bust drop. It fell through the crisp air and glittered in the sunshine. There was absolute silence. The bust sailed down and smashed on the pavement like a flower pot. It wasn't bronze at all, just some cheap ersatz material. The people broke into cheers. I could still recognize the tip of Hitler's nose with the little mustache underneath, and then even that was gone as the crowd rushed forward and trampled the pieces to dust.

"Let's go, gang. We've still got work to do," said Benno.

We started off. The flag on the castle was still flying and snapping in the sunshine. I suddenly thought of the Queen of Württemberg as I elbowed my way through the crowd. What do you suppose the Queen of Württemberg was doing? She was probably scared. We made our way over to the other side of the square. Things certainly looked as if the war had been already won. I didn't find it fun anymore. We stopped in front of Manes's shop. Benno set up the ladder and started to climb. He looked like a big blown-up white balloon. People were still streaming around.

"Hey, listen," I said to Pedro, "I'm going down to the post office to see if maybe they know what's going on in Prague."

I said it because it just occurred to me that maybe Irena was on duty now, and because I wanted to be alone.

"Okay," said Pedro and I turned and headed off the other way. Happy faces streamed against me and laughed in my face. I gave them a mean, squinting, scornful look. The flag was still flying from the castle. To hell with the Queen of Württemberg. To hell with everything. To hell with the Württemberg queen. She could go jump in the lake. She wasn't worth anything to anybody anyway.

I wanted to see Irena and so I walked toward the post office. Out in front, a crowd had gathered. I pushed through the crowd. There on the sidewalk in front of the post office was a platoon of German kids, armed to the teeth. It was a wild sight. They couldn't have been more than fourteen years old and their helmets were so big that only the tips of their noses stuck out underneath. And out of their helmets' shadows their little eyes gleamed scared and embarrassed and confused. You could see they were only little kids despite the potato-masher grenades and submachine guns they had draped around them— *Hitlerjugend.* They didn't say a word and they didn't know what to do. There was a wide space between them and the people who encircled them, swearing at them. I heard some really good swear words and saw clenched fists. I shoved my way up front. The Hitler kids wore mud-caked boots and they looked exhausted. Just then somebody jumped out of the crowd and tore a submachine gun out of the hands of one of the kids. Somebody else yelled, probably an order, and the cluster of soldiers bristled with guns. They peered around with their hollow black eyes and I felt an unpleasant tightening in my belly. Jesus. It was like I already had a bullet in me. It didn't feel good at all. I realized it must be pretty damned unpleasant to be wounded. I drew back impulsively, but suddenly stopped. Christ, what if Irena was watching from somewhere? I didn't want her to think I was scared. It was silly to be scared. I looked around, but I couldn't see Irena. Everybody was moving back now. I was standing all by myself between the retreating crowd and the bristling platoon of Germans. That was fine because now I could retreat too. I stuck my hands in my pockets and turned. I got that same feeling again, only this time it was in my back. My nerves grew taut. But I wanted to act casual. I moseyed along after the crowd. A sharp German command rang out behind me and I stiffened. Again my impulse was to drop to the ground, but I controlled myself. Nuts. They'd hit me anyway. The thing was not to get scared—and, especially, not to let it show. I made a face at the people in front of me as they moved backward. They stumbled and pushed frantically against the ones farther back who couldn't see and so didn't know what was going on. Nobody said a word. People gaped at me in amazement. I ambled after them nonchalantly, a prickly feeling running down my spine. Then, as if somebody had barked out an order, all those faces suddenly focused elsewhere and stopped retreating behind me. I heard the shuffle and scrape of many boots. I looked around. The German kids, their submachine guns trained on the crowd, were moving off without a word. The throng in front of them parted swiftly, like the Red Sea opening for the Jews.

"Take their guns away from 'em!" some brave soul yelled from the rear of the crowd, but nobody seemed to want to try. I watched the platoon go. Two little runts brought up the rear in oversized boots. A funny sight, that pair. Still, they had their submachine guns and the guns were loaded and that inspired respect. Again the curses began to fly. By then, though, the Germans had already disappeared around the corner. The crowd milled and followed. The post office square emptied out. I turned around and saw Irena, looking out the first floor window. She saw me and smiled.

"Hello, Danny," she called. She was wearing a white blouse with a tricolor pinned on it.

"Hello, Irena," I said and strolled over to the window.

"Did you see that?" she asked.

"Yeah."

"Spooky, wasn't it?"

"What?"

"Those kids. Why, they're no more than children."

"Oh, them. Yes, you're right. That's all they are."

"Who'd you think I meant?"

"I thought you were talking about the people."

"How do you mean?"

"Well, the people."

"I don't understand you."

I grinned, "All those big heroes."

"Oh, them. But what did you expect them to do without any guns?"

"I know, but . . ."

"But you think of yourself as a hero, I suppose?"

"Naturally," I said. Apparently she'd seen me after all. I'd have to make the most of it but the best way to play it would be to make myself look like a fool; otherwise I'd have to think up some logical explanation and I didn't feel like thinking logically. All I felt like doing was looking at Irena and kidding around with her.

"Well then," she said, "why didn't you do something?"

"I wasn't in the mood." I raised my eyebrows and gave her my Clark Gable look. It always seemed to me he didn't know how to do anything except twist his mouth around; still that was enough to impress women. At least in the movies. I discovered in real life, too, that that's usually about all you need. In most cases anyway. So now I twisted my mouth at Irena and went on.

"Why should I act like a hero, anyway? What's the point?"

"Well—to . . . to show you're not afraid."

"And why should I need to do that?"

"Why, to prove you're a man."

"There're other ways of proving that," I said inanely, and waited to see how Irena would react. She reacted just the way I expected her to. She was dumb. But I loved her.

"Now that's enough," she said, so I'd understand that she'd understood. It never even occurred to her that she hadn't really. Apparently her head wasn't really equipped to understand. Girls' mental equipment is generally pretty primitive. It would have been nice to know there was at least one girl in the world who could understand something. Not just what a person says, but what he means, too. And that maybe he means something entirely different from what he says. And that he says it for completely different reasons than he says. It would have been nice to know there was at least one girl like that in the world. Anyway, then I switched over to the track Irena's little brain was running on.

"Or maybe you think there isn't any other way to prove it?" I said.

"Oh well, sure there is, but that's about enough of that now, don't you think?"

"The other proofs are more fun, though."

"Danny, that's enough now. Just stop or I won't say another word to you."

"Okay," I said, and flashed her another one of my Gable grins. But it gave me a cramp in my cheek muscle and I had to hurry and hold my hand under my nose and massage it as though nothing had happened. Luckily, the cramp went away almost immediately. Irena hadn't even noticed it. It was all right.

"Well, so we've got our freedom back again, huh?" I said.

"No, now, be serious. You make a joke out of everything, Danny," said Irena.

"No, I don't."

"You do."

"I don't."

"Go on, I know you."

"Think so?"

"Absolutely."

"Well, I'm not so sure."

"Oh yes I do."

Irena was a grown-up young lady. She'd gone through

puberty but not very far beyond. Breasts and periods and a whole way of thinking. So she knows me, does she? That was good, too.

"Well, that's tough," I said.

"What?"

"That you know me so well."

"Why's it tough?"

"Well—since you know me so well I can't have any secrets from you, can I?"

Irena laughed.

"I don't know you all that well, Danny. You don't need to worry."

"But you know me pretty well, right?"

"Oh—pretty well, I think."

"And what do you know?"

"Hmmm?"

"What do you know that's so special about me anyway?"

"Special? Well, you're awfully conceited, for one thing."

"Aw, go on."

"You are, Danny."

I acted like this had really sobered me up, then I looked into her eyes.

"No, Irena. I'm not conceited. Not at all."

"No?"

"No."

"Well, I still think you're pretty conceited, Danny."

"I'm not, though."

"And I say you are, though."

"No. And I'll tell you why you're wrong, Irena. Because there just so happens to be something I don't think is true about you, and you know very well that it's true about me."

"Yes? What?" she said. Her eyes lit up when I switched to this other tone. We'd just been kidding around before, but now I'd struck a deeper chord. Now I'd touched on something that lay beneath all that kidding which was serious. At least that's what her biological feelers told her. Her fine little biological-psychological-acoustical feelers. I didn't contradict her.

"What is it?" I said slowly, and moved toward the wall.

I lifted my arms and leaned up against the wall under Irena's window.

"You know, Irena," I said.

She smiled wisely, the smile she kept handy for such occasions. It was a tender smile. Then she reached out and gently caressed the back of my hand.

"You know very well, Irena," I repeated. "I'm in love with you."

She stroked my hand again. Then she whispered, "I know."

I held onto her fingers.

"Irena, I'm terribly in love with you. Everything I do is just for you."

"I know, Danny."

"Look, this whole war and the liberation and everything won't really have any sense for me if you . . ."

I stopped right there and, instead of talking, squeezed her hand.

"I know, Danny."

"Irena, couldn't you . . ."

She pressed my hand. "No, Danny. Shh. Don't let's talk about it."

"Well, why not, Irena?"

"You know I—it's simply impossible."

"I know it is, Irena. But it's . . . awful."

"Danny."

"All right, I won't say any more about it."

"But don't be angry with me."

"I'm not angry with you. How could I be angry with you?"

"In matters like this, a person's simply helpless, you know that."

"I know, Irena."

"I think an awful lot of you, Danny, really. But—"

"You're in love with Zdenek."

She looked straight at me. Now it was getting very serious. Now she was going to make me face up to the facts, for about the sixth or seventh time.

"Yes," she said.

I squeezed her hand and gulped. I gulped so my Adam's apple would wobble and I made the corners of my eyelids twitch. I bowed my head slightly to one side and tears came to my eyes. I squeezed her hand.

"Okay, Irena, I know. Not much I can do about it, is there?"

"But you're not angry, are you?"

"No."

"You mustn't be angry."

"I'm not. I'm something else, though."

"What?"

"I'm in love with you," I said.

She drew back her hand and her smile changed. "You . . ." she said.

"Terribly in love with you."

"That's nice."

"I love you and I worship you and I want you."

Irena started to laugh. Then she spoke in a changed tone.

"Save some of your energy, Danny. Maybe you'll need it for something else."

I could see right through her. I could tell it made her feel good. Oh, I knew her. It flattered her, hearing all that over and over. It must be a nice feeling to know somebody's in love with you. But to be in love was also nice, which was why I was.

"Look," said Irena all of a sudden.

"What is it?" I said, and looked up at her. She was looking out over my head toward the square. I turned around. The sun stood blazing above the castle, flooding the square with its white light. The church cast a dark shadow on the cobblestones and as the crowd eddied around it, the women's dresses flashed as they moved out of the shadow into the sun. But that wasn't it. Something was going on. People were milling around on both sides of the church. They were running away from the square behind the church and jamming the streets on either side of the square. Something was going on behind the church but you couldn't see what. Clusters of people had stopped in front of the post office to stare. All I could see was the backs of people's heads, tilted hats, and disheveled hairdos. Soon it was almost deserted on both sides of the church. I watched Mrs. Salacova, the lame seamstress, swinging along fast on her crutches. My curiosity was aroused. From around the left side of the church a soldier emerged with fixed bayonet and the square grew silent. The soldier advanced slowly in his gray helmet and jackboots, an ominous figure. A second one came out close behind him. Then from behind the other side of the church more soldiers appeared. They moved forward, fanning out around the church. Some held submachine guns, others rifles with fixed bayonets. They came on quietly, slowly, steadily. Behind them, the square was empty. The crowd silently pressed back into side streets and doorways. Mrs. Salacova hurried along frantically on her crutches. I watched her go. Her body swung in frenzied arcs like a pendulum or as if she was doing calisthenics on the parallel bars. She was going as fast as she could, but not fast enough to escape the soldiers. The fan slowed down behind her. I could see that the soldier who was driving her on didn't know what to do. He was embarrassed. He didn't know whether to pass her and let her go on behind him or to wait until she'd hobbled into some doorway. He slowed down and soon the whole column came to a standstill. The soldiers on the other side of the square were nearly halfway across it now. Officers with drawn revolvers moved up behind the soldiers. I heard them yelling something at the people who still hadn't managed to find a place to duck into. I looked over at Mrs. Salacova again. She was nearly home. She had a little store in one of the houses on the left side of the square. The soldier with the submachine gun slowly trailed her. He looked like a Boy Scout doing a good deed, as if the gun was hers and he was just carrying it home for her. It was quiet, except for the officers yelling on the other side of the square and, in the distance, the squeak of Mrs. Salacova's crutches. They were a couple of steps away from her shop. She made three more lurches and vanished inside. The soldier turned and hurried along the row of houses to the end of the street. Behind him came an officer brandishing a revolver in his gloved hand. The two advancing columns had already circled the church and joined up in a single row. The end men stopped at the corners where the side streets entered the square while the center fanned out swiftly. The last remnants of the crowd dashed past me behind the post office toward the old ghetto and shoved through the doors into City Hall. It was quiet. Behind the soldiers the square was completely empty. Apparently they'd come from the emergency hospital behind the church where part of the Kostelec garrison was stationed. The rejoicing of the crowds had probably made them mad. The officers, anyway. My impression was that all the soldiers really cared about was clearing out before the Russians arrived. These last days anyway. They couldn't get out fast enough. But the officers wouldn't budge. Discipline to the bitter end. No matter how pointless—order and discipline right up to the end. And the soldiers obeyed. That much had been drilled into them. More soldiers appeared in the empty half of the square. They advanced in dead silence. They were sullen and ready for combat. Ammunition belts bounced against their chests and hand grenades jutted out of their boot tops.

"Danny!" said Irena nervously. I could tell right away she was scared.

"What?" I said without turning around.

"Danny, come inside!"

"Wait a while."

"Danny, please come inside. You can't kid around with them."

"Don't worry."

"Don't be crazy, Danny."

"Oh, don't worry, Irena. If I just stand here, they won't even notice me."

"Danny, please. Don't be silly."

I turned slowly and looked her in the eye. She was really scared. For me. I could tell she was scared, but on the other hand this was something I couldn't understand. I'd never been scared for anybody else. Just for myself. I didn't know what it was to feel that way. I couldn't understand how anybody could care that much about somebody else. Whether something was going to happen to somebody else, I mean. If somebody else was in a bad spot, I felt bad too, but I didn't know what it was to be scared for them. What's the sense in being scared, anyway? After all, nothing can happen except what happens to me. And you can stand everything else. I felt completely alone. I wouldn't have been scared for Irena. Why should I ever be scared for her? I wasn't really in love with her anyway. Or rather, I was in love with her because there wasn't anything better. When it came to things to be in love with, there was always a chronic shortage. And so I was in love with Irena. She wasn't in love with me and I loved her, but it didn't really matter that much to me. I looked straight at her.

"Are you scared?"

"Danny, please, don't put on an act."

"Are you?"

She looked over my head and there was fear in her eyes.

"Danny, come inside. This is no joke!"

"Are you scared?"

"Yes, sure I am."

"On account of me?"

"Oh, please, Danny, you know I am."

"But you don't love me?"

"Danny, please, come inside."

"But you don't love me, do you?" I said slowly.

Her eyes looked terrified. I was hamming it up. See, Irena, nothing matters to me. Let 'em shoot me for all I care, if you don't love me. Let 'em hang me, see? I gazed at her fixedly. All of a sudden her eyes started following something that was very close behind me. I could feel there was something behind me. And I knew what it was. I got the feeling again that I had a bullet in my back. And I also had the feeling that I'd put on a wonderful act for Irena, that I'd given a great performance. Irena's eyes followed whatever it was with terrified attention, her mouth half open. I turned, leaned back against the post office and stuck my hands in my pockets. I felt like the whole world was watching me. There in front of me, quite close now, stood a soldier aiming his submachine gun straight at me.

"*Also los,*" he said, but he didn't move. He had a broad, beefy face and a gray stubble on his chin. He had a gas mask slung over his shoulder and the gray head of a German bazooka stuck up above his ear. He was an old guy. A hand grenade was stuck in each boot and he looked as if he didn't know what to do. I gave him a friendly, cocky grin. He stepped up close. There was fear and bewilderment in his eyes. He was scared. He was scared of what was going to happen today or within the next few days. But he was also scared of the officers behind him. He stepped up to me and said in a confidential tone, "*Schauen Sie, es hat doch keinen Zweck. Gehen Sie weg bitte.*"

Suddenly I felt sorry for him. He kind of trusted me. I don't know what I would have done if he'd yelled at me, but he had so much trust in me I didn't want to disappoint him.

"All right," I said and took my hands out of my pocket. He stood there in front of me, waiting. I buttoned my jacket and figured I'd set off, slow but sure, around the corner.

"Well, so long, Irena, I'll be back," I said, and started off.

But as I turned toward the side street which led past the post office, I bumped into another soldier. He was wearing an Iron Cross ribbon in his button hole. An officer. I raised my head and looked him right in the eye. He had narrow, cold, Germanic eyes. He looked as if he'd never had a human feeling in his life.

"*Was ist hier los?*" he said menacingly. "*Haben Sie nicht gehört?*"

That made me mad. I knew these guys were done for. I didn't feel scared at all. Just that it was all over. The finale. I made a face.

"Shut up!" I said and squinted at him. I hadn't meant to say it in English. It just slipped out. Funny. I always reacted in English to all that German bellowing. Even when I was working at the factory, only then I said it under my breath. This time I 'd said it out loud.

"*Was?*" howled the officer.

"Shut up," I said quite logically. I stood opposite him with my hands in my pockets again.

"*Na warte, du Schwein, du!*" screamed the officer, and grabbed hold of my jacket with his left hand. He was holding a pistol in his right hand. I grabbed for it. He jerked me to one side. He was awfully damn strong. I tried to get my footing but couldn't. He shook me back and forth. A mess. A real mess. I must have looked pretty silly. And Irena was watching. I braced myself once again but had to spread my feet wide apart and let my knees sag. I looked ridiculous and what made it worse was that it all had to happen right in front of Irena. The officer gave me one more sharp jerk and let go. I lost my balance and fell over. I could feel I was blushing. Oh, God. Damn it. What a mess. I lay there on the ground. They'd caught me. Like a farmer catching a little kid stealing pears. It was anything but fun. Damn it, it wasn't fun at all. I blushed with shame. I thought about getting up and jumping that officer, but quickly dropped the idea. He was awfully strong. He'd just throw me again. Maybe he'd knock me around and that would be even more humiliating. Oh, I'd really messed things up. I looked up. The officer was standing over me and brandishing a pistol in front of my face.

"*Aufstehen!*" he ordered icily. I decided to preserve at least a remnant of decorum. I got up slowly and, as I rose, brushed off my jacket, taking my time about it. I felt I'd brushed off the bad impression I'd made, now that I looked decent again. In the movies, the hero always gets the first punch. Slowly I drew myself erect. The officer was watching me with cold scorn. He raised the muzzle of his revolver.

"*Hände hoch! Schnell!*"

I knew how to do that. Like they did it in Chicago. I could see myself like in a gangster movie. I was glad I was wearing such a sharp-looking jacket. I grimaced and slowly raised my hands over my head. Taking my time. And not too high. I bent my arms at the elbows and raised my palms so they came to about my ears. Nice and slow. I stood there with my feet planted wide, watching the officer. I felt like Al Capone and the square looked like Bloody Corner after a gun battle with the cops. Soon the G-men would come and take me away. I stared the officer right in the eye. I held his eye but it seemed to me as though all his anger had gone out of him. Naturally he'd had a steady diet of discipline, but after all, Hitler was dead and the Russians only a few miles away. It seemed to me he was looking at me with disgust. I gave him a sneering smile. The officer turned away. Behind him stood two guys with submachine guns.

"*Haftnehmen!*" said the officer. The two guys stepped up to me, one on each side. I turned around.

"*Los. Gehn Wir!*" one of them said. We started off. I turned around to see Irena. She was standing in the window, one hand clenched to her mouth. I made a face and winked at her.

"Danny!" she screamed hysterically.

"Don't worry," I called to her.

"*Los, los!*" said one of the guys beside me and grabbed my arm. I tried to turn around again to see Irena, but he yanked me back. The other one grabbed my other arm.

"Let me go. I'll walk by myself," I said in broken German.

"*Na gut,*" said the guy on my left and let go of my arm. I looked at him and saw he was the same beefy-faced soldier who'd talked to me before.

"*Machen Sie keine Dummheiten, es hat doch keinen Zweck,*" he advised me again in a confidential tone.

"Okay," I said and went quietly with them. They led me to the church. A couple of soldiers and one civilian were standing in front of the door to the choir loft. We came closer. I recognized him. It was Lenecek, the hairdresser. Another patriot. So they'd picked him up too. He was pale as death and looked solemn. I winked at him. He smiled gloomily and then looked as glum as before. My soldiers put me beside him.

"What'd you do?" I whispered.

"I slugged one of them. And you?"

"Oh, something like that."

We stopped talking. We stood by the church and the sun shone down on us. The church had a nice, massive, flaking, yellow-painted wall. Hell, I thought, they might stand us up against that wall! But when I looked at Lenecek, it didn't seem possible. I couldn't picture him slumping over, crumpling up. Too crazy. Or me either. Crazy too. They'd lock us up and let us out in a couple of days. But it would be a damn shame to be locked up now. I looked over at the officers. They were conferring about something. Lenecek stood there, white faced and motionless. The officers' conference broke up and they looked over at us. My heart was in my throat. They were going to line us up against the wall. Jesus! Suddenly I was scared. Not that, for Chrissake, don't do that! Anything but that! One of the officers gave an order of some kind and the soldiers lined up, a group on each side of us. Oh, God! Oh, damn! They're taking us off now. Lenecek turned even whiter.

We started off. Oh, God! Oh, God! Oh, Jesus! This was really bad. We marched out of the square at a brisk pace. You couldn't even take your own sweet time. I had to step along like in some kind of firemen's parade. Jesus! You ought at least to be able to go to your death elegantly. We turned off on the street that led past the Sokol* Hall. Yes. They were taking us to the high school. That was where the garrison was. And they'd shoot us in the courtyard. Oh, Jesus! The street was empty. Our steps echoed rhythmically. The doorways were jammed with people. You could tell they were scared. We went past them. I looked at them, huddled and trembling in the doorways, and I couldn't help making a face at them. The fools! Safe as houses and still scared shitless. And here we were, being led away to our execution. A chill ran down my spine. Just then I saw Lucie. She'd poked her head out of Manes's store. She saw me. I saw how surprised she was—astonished. Good. I stuck one hand in my pocket because I knew that made nice folds in my jacket and I gave Lucie a big smile. Then I noticed Haryk watching behind her. And Pedro Gershwin's face above Haryk's head. One on top of the other, those three heads, and they were looking at me and didn't know what to say. I grinned and nodded my head at them. They gaped back at me stupidly. Then we passed them. Lenecek marched alongside me, his head held high. Almost too high. It looked as though he had a crick in his neck. Otherwise he held up well. We hurried down a narrow street and past the savings bank and around the print shop. Everybody was watching us. And past Sokol Hall. All our friends were watching us. We were national heroes. We marched along and everybody knew us and we were surrounded by silent Germans in their grubby uniforms, draped with weapons. St. Matthew's Church rose beyond the viaduct and behind it the big yellow high-school building. My heart dropped, then rushed back up into my throat again. Boy, was I scared! Oh, Jesus God, this was all wrong! I certainly didn't feel like dying. Not even for my country. My country could get along without my life but I couldn't. Oh, this was bad. Now maybe Irena would reconsider. Now maybe she'd drop Zdenek and start going with me. It would really be dumb to have to die now. My God, would it ever!

We went past Welch's stationery store toward the viaduct. We were getting closer to the high school. I looked frantically around me. There was nobody there. Not a soul. And then all of a sudden my heart started jumping around inside my chest. Prema was heading toward us from under the viaduct. His pockets were stuffed with something and then he saw me and stopped. Behind him Jerry and Vasek Vostal appeared and a bunch of other guys. I could tell that Prema understood right away what was going on. He just looked at me and I looked at him. One glance was enough. Then he whirled around and said something to the boys. Prema! We turned off around the viaduct. Prema waited. By now it was clear we were going to the high school. I stared hard at Prema. Prema nodded and gave me the V-for-Victory sign. Prema was great. Then all the boys ducked around the corner and started to run. The path behind the viaduct was the shortest way to Skocdopole's warehouse. There were guns there. That I knew. My brain started working again. I quickly calculated how long it would take them to get to the warehouse. Then how long it would take before the Germans had led us into the big schoolyard and shot us. If they had some

kind of ceremony first, the boys might just make it in time.
Awfully risky. But terrific, too. So this was how the Kostelec
revolution was going to start. All on account of me, really.
Yes. Great. I tried to picture how it would be when the
boys would turn up. A shot. An explosion. Part of the
high school blown up and falling in. We're standing up
against the wall facing a row of armed Krauts, and all of
a sudden part of the high school blows up and boys jump
over the fence into the yard, carrying rifles and submachine guns. They had them too. Prema told me they'd
disarmed a whole platoon of Germans some place. I believed him because Prema didn't kid around. I could just
see them jumping over the principal's garden fence through
the smoke and dust and hollering. And the Germans
throwing away their guns. Or, no—they'd fight back. And
the two of us would dash away from the wall, I'd jump
that officer and now he'd be all mixed up and I'd sock him
in the eye and take away his revolver and we'd move in
on them from all sides. Lenecek would tell Irena all about
it afterward when she'd go to his shop for a permanent.
I could just see those Germans huddled together and then
moving back against the wall of the gym and we'd be
blasting away at them and they'd drop, one after the other.
And then I saw Prema, saw him taking an old egg-shaped
Czech Army grenade out of his pocket, pull the pin, count
three and pitch it, and the grenade exploding right in the
middle of the huddle. Germans fall in all directions, their
weapons drop from their hands and we move through
the high-school yard, our guns smoking, and so the Kostelec revolution begins.

We were getting closer to the high-school gate. I could
see the gatehouse that stood beside it. A soldier with his
bayonet fixed was marching up and down in front of the
gatehouse. A row of windows on the side of the high school
gleamed in the sunshine and here and there a German
face stared out. Inside you could hear the quiet buzz of
many voices, just as though school was still in session.
It always sounded like that in high school during recess.
Exactly the same. You couldn't even tell it was German
buzzing. We marched past the house where the Sisters of

c*

Mercy lived, straight toward the school gate. Their Franciscan swans' caps shone whitely behind the closed windows. The sisters were probably crossing themselves. This made me think of death and I started feeling pretty bad again. Christ. Christ! There were the four big windows of the chapel above the school entrance. Memories of how we used to go there every Sunday flashed through my head. My God, maybe there really is a God. And hell and heaven and stuff. Oh, God! And heaven's weeping now. It couldn't help but weep after all the sins I'd committed. Ever since sixth grade. We sixth-graders used to sit in the first row in chapel and we behaved ourselves pretty well because we were still scared of the religion teacher. But by the time we were in seventh grade we'd already started sinning. We'd moved back to the second row so they couldn't see us so well from the altar and we weren't so scared of the teacher any more, and instead of praying and singing hymns we fought and horsed around. During every mass we committed one sin on top of another. And then in eighth grade we were in the third row. Oh, boy! And in ninth grade and so on until we didn't sit downstairs anymore. We had chairs on the platform up alongside the organ. And we'd think up dirty words for the hymns. And we'd egg on Josef Stola who played the organ and he'd play a foxtrot from *Rose Marie,* for instance, during the elevation of the Host, or "San Francisco," and the religion teacher would even commend him for it. He liked those preludes so much that he recommended Joska to the choirmaster at the cathedral but when Joska played there for the first time and had nerve to play a prelude from *Rose Marie,* the choirmaster, who played the fiddle on week nights in a town night-club, recognized it immediately, kicked Joska out of the organ loft in the middle of the prelude, and told the teacher on him. So Joska got a D– in deportment and he had to do a lot of penance before he was allowed to play again, in chapel at least.

Oh, Christ! That's how we'd sinned. And it was wonderful to remember the past—all those memories of high school were wrapped in a sunny haze now. And now there the school stood in front of me, big and yellow, and the

Germans were taking me in for my own execution. My legs balked and I got the absolutely crazy idea that I simply wouldn't go any farther. But I went. I still couldn't believe what was happening and how it was happening. The high-school gate loomed closer. I looked over at Lenecek. He was white as alabaster now, but he was still holding his head up. Christ! Why act like a hero on top of everything else? But why not act like a hero, after all? What's the point of being scared to death if there's no help for us anymore anyway? Sure. It's better to stand up straight when you're facing a firing squad, and maybe even yell something. No, not that, though. Better not. That's the kind of thing Chief of Police Rimbalnik would do. No. Ask for a cigarette or something like that. Except I didn't smoke. And when the officer raises his sword over his head, then make a face at him. If he actually does have a sword, that is. We stopped right under the school motto inscribed over the gate: *"Cultivate feeling, enlighten reason and, oh school, plant the roots of resolute character!"* Oh, God! Or wouldn't it be better to just forget about being so resolute and get down on my knees and ask forgiveness for all my sins. Except maybe there really wasn't any God anyway, so why should I? I didn't want to make a fool of myself like that. Just like I'd never quite been able to make myself make a clear and obvious sign of the cross when I passed the church, like the priest always told us to do. I'd just kind of scratch myself on the forehead and then slide my thumb down over my face and scratch myself again on the chest. Because there might actually be a God after all. But it's not for sure. If it was, then I'd fall down on my knees right here and that would certainly soften him up. But the thing is, you can't be sure. So a person's got to be scared all the time—of God, if there is one, and of looking like a fool if there isn't.

The officers went on past us and into the high school. *"Los,"* said one of the soldiers and we followed them in. Light came through the row of windows and the corridor was clean and bright. We turned off toward the principal's office and there we stopped. Only the officers went inside. The doors swung shut behind them. Instead of the old name plate, there was a sign there now with the inscription KOMMANDANTUR. I looked at Lenecek. I felt like talking to convince myself that this was all just a joke.

"Well?" I said.

"We're in for it now," said Lenecek.

"You think they'll bump us off?"

"I think you can count on that, Mr. Smiricky."

"Jesus!" I said. All of a sudden the word sounded unpleasantly sinful. So I added, "That's bad."

Lenecek didn't say anything. He was so pale by now he looked almost transparent. The Germans guarding us stood there mute and listless. I wondered whether I shouldn't say something to them. But what? I looked out the window. The schoolyard looked like it always did. Even the volleyball net was up. The Germans had probably been playing volleyball. My God, so now it's all over. So now—and suddenly I remembered my Last Will and Testament. And then I realized that this was it. Instinctively. So now my will would serve its purpose. Irena could read it now. About how I'd never loved anybody else in my life, only her, how I didn't want anything in the world except now, as she reads these lines, for her to know that everything I've done and lived for was important only because it was all somehow for her, that I'd lived and died only for her and that I'd loved her. And how nothing mattered to me, even dying, because there was no sense in living since she didn't love me. Tears came to my eyes. I could see her, see her walking behind the coffin and it would really be some funeral, too, because I'd be a hero and it would be a great feeling—only there wouldn't be any feeling at all! Now was the time for feeling, I suddenly realized, and afterward, when it was all over for me, I wouldn't feel anything at all. Brrr! Not that. To hell with Irena. My Last Will and Testament was great when I wrote it. No Last Will and Testament was ever better. To hell with the will. I'd rather stay alive without Irena. She should try dying herself sometime. I didn't want to. Let Irena do it instead of me. It'd be better if I could go to her funeral instead of her going to mine. That certainly roused plenty of feelings. And what feelings! How sad I would be and crushed and noble and alone. Christ! I'd a thousand times rather be lonely than not be at all. Absolutely. But soldiers with guns were standing around me and that was a bad feeling. I thought about Prema again, wondering if he'd make it. God, let him make it! God, let him get here in time! God, please, please, God, let Prema get here in time!

Just then the door opened and there stood Dr. Sabata. My throat tightened from joy. I forgot all about Prema. Dr. Sabata was wearing a black suit and he had his pince-nez on his nose. Dr. Sabata. This was great. I felt safe immediately. I'd known it all along. Of course. They couldn't shoot us. That was all a lot of nonsense. I'd known it right from the start. They couldn't shoot us, now that Dr. Sabata was here. Dr. Sabata looked at me sadly and said, "Mr. Smiricky, what in the world have you been doing?"

"Why, nothing, Doctor. I was at the square and they picked me up," I said innocently. Now everything was all right again.

"You provoked them, didn't you? And you know what the situation is like. I'd thought we could at least depend on you students to be sensible."

"But I really wasn't doing anything, Doctor."

"Look here, Mr. Smiricky. We're negotiating now with the Commander about withdrawing the troops from the town so there won't be any needless destruction and you students are making things very difficult for us."

"I'm really awfully sorry, sir. I really didn't mean to . . ."

"Well, all right, I believe you. Mr. Kuelpe promised me he'd release you but I had to give him my word of honor that the townspeople will allow the troops to leave peacefully and take their arms with them."

I remembered Prema. Jesus! Dr. Sabata's word of honor wouldn't be worth a damn now. Jesus! All I wanted was to get out of there fast. So I said rapidly, "Thank you, Doctor."

"Don't mention it," said Dr. Sabata. "But please tell your friends not to do anything imprudent. Everything will be arranged. Just be patient."

"Yes," I said. Mayor Prudivy peeked out of the principal's office. The Kostelec city fathers were negotiating. I knew it.

I could see the revolution was in good hands. Dr. Sabata shook hands with me. "Thank you, Doctor," I said.

He smiled humbly. "You're quite welcome. I'm glad I could help you. Remember me to your father."

"Yes, thank you, I will."

"Goodby."

"Goodby."

I turned around. Lenecek came over to me. Dr. Sabata hadn't shaken hands with Lenecek. But Lenecek didn't mind. I noticed he wasn't so pale any more. We hurried down the stairs to the main floor. It was all over and now I could start living again. And it'd certainly make an impression on Irena. And maybe there'll be shooting anyway. Now all of a sudden I felt like shooting again. Now that nobody was going to stand me up against a wall and shoot at me. I had a terrific urge to start shooting. I ran down the steps in front of the high school and there I was, out in the bright sunshine. I waited for Lenecek.

"Are you going downtown?" I asked him.

"No, I've got to go home. My old lady'll have the shit scared out of her already by now. They've probably told her."

"Well, I'm going into town," I said.

"Take care of yourself, Mr. Smiricky," said Lenecek.

"Well, goodby," I said with a smile and held out my hand. He pressed it and his palm was still wet with fear.

I walked along Rampart Street in the direction of Skocdopole's warehouse. I saw them as soon as I turned the corner and they looked terrific. Vahar was carrying a flag and the others were clustered around him with Prema in the lead. Prema was holding a submachine gun, all polished and oiled, and he had a leather belt strapped around his waist over his coat with a couple rounds of ammunition in it. Hand-grenade pins stuck out of both pockets. I raised my hand and waved at them. The boys slowed down and stopped.

"What is it?" called Prema.

"They let us go," I said and hurried toward them. Vahar set the flag staff down on the ground. The boys stood there and set the butts of their guns down on the pavement. They were pretty well armed. Perlik had two bazookas and Jerry wore hand grenades draped around his neck like a rosary. I saw Prochazka and Vasek Vostal and Benda and Kocandrle. Benda and Vasek had submachine guns and Kocandrle and Prochazka had automatics.

"Thanks, guys," I said.

"So they let you go, huh?" said Prema and he sounded almost disappointed.

"Yeah. That is, Dr. Sabata got us out of it."

"Sabata was there?"

"Yeah. With old Prudivy. Maybe there were more of them."

"They came there after you?"

"No. They were there when we got there."

"What were they doing?"

"Probably negotiating with the Germans."

"What about, do you know?"

"Dr. Sabata said it was about letting the soldiers get out of town."

"Jesus!" said Prema. That made him mad. "What're those yellow-bellied bastards fouling things up for?"

"They're cautious all right. It doesn't surprise me," said Perlik.

"What're we going to do?" asked Benda.

"Shall we go after 'em?" said Vahar in a bloodthirsty tone.

"I don't think it would make much sense right now," I said. "Thanks a lot for wanting to help me, but it'd be a pretty risky business now."

"When do the Germans plan to pull out? Did Sabata say?" asked Prema.

"No. He didn't say."

"If we knew when they were going to pull out we could wait for 'em up on Sugarloaf."

"Yeah, but if we don't know?" said Benda.

"It's simple," Vahar said. "We'll keep our eye on 'em, right?"

"That's about all we can do," said Prema. "You don't know what else they were talking about?"

"I don't know. But I guess you know that Sabata and

Prudivy and the rest of them have some kind of an organization, don't you?"

Prema looked at me.

"We know about it."

Suddenly I felt hot all over. I'd thought I was going to tell them something new and instead I'd put my foot in it.

"Are you in contact with them?" I asked.

"Well—yes. I guess it's safe to talk about that now."

It was embarrassing. I knew Prema was mixed up in something. But he'd never really told me anything and I didn't want to pump it out of him if he didn't trust me enough to tell me himself. But now the opportunity had arisen.

"I want to join," I said. "Take me with you."

Prema acted very grave. "You want to join?"

"Yes," I said.

Prema's face took on an expression like one of the Founding Fathers'. He was really pretty naïve. I had different ideas about the revolution than he had. I was more of a gangster, whereas he was a real rebel. But I needed a gun and they certainly had them. This was the easiest way to get one. I knew the boys had been playing partisans for two months already and they must have a regular arsenal by now in Skocdopole's warehouse. Prema shook my hand. Very touching. But I needed that gun. Mutely, I pressed his hand.

"All right, then," said Prema. "We can use everybody except sissies and old maids."

I blushed. It was like something out of a grade-school primer. But I stopped blushing right away. After all, the main thing was that I'd have a gun. Once the shooting started, there wouldn't be time for a lot of speeches and sentimentality anymore. And then it'd probably be great. Even with these guys in their corduroy pants and stubble-beard faces. Even with all this rebel talk. Rebelling had its appeal for me, too. Again I could just imagine the smoke and the shooting and, in the midst of the smoke, Vahar with the flag. It was good.

"Well, let's pack up again, right?" said Benda.

"Yep," said Prema.

"Let's go," said Vahar. "We going to take it all back to the warehouse?"

"Yep," said Prema. Vahar picked up the flag and the boys slung their rifles over their shoulders. As they turned, I noticed that Vasek and Jerry had submachine guns slung across their backs, too. Apparently they had a surplus of them.

"Listen," I asked Prema. "How is it really? Is Sabata running the whole show or what?"

"Yeah. Sabata's running it," Prema said.

"And you have things all planned out already?"

"Well, Sabata's supposed to give the order over the loudspeaker."

"For the uprising?"

"No. Just for a mobilization."

"And when's the uprising supposed to start?"

"As soon as Cemelik gives the word."

"He's a colonel, isn't he?"

"Yeah."

I was silent. Then I asked, "And . . . and do you think Sabata'll start anything?"

Prema shrugged.

"And are you really going to wait till you get the word?" I said. I could tell Prema was fed up.

"I don't know," he said. "I'm beginning to have my doubts."

"Did anybody tell you to collect all these guns and stuff?"

"No. We did it on our own," he chuckled.

"Boy," I said. "I think Sabata's scared."

"I think so, too."

"I don't trust those guys anyway. All they care about is saving their own skins," I said.

Prema didn't say anything for awhile. Then he said, "We've known each other ever since we were kids, so I guess I can trust you, can't I?"

"Sure," I said.

"We're in this together with Sabata. But if he starts fooling around, we'll take off on our own, see?"

"Yeah."

"Because I know what a bunch of yellow bastards they are, too."

"Well, why did you get mixed up with them then?"

"Sabata has connections with Prague."

"I see."

"But if he starts something funny, we'll shit on the whole thing."

"Sure," I said. "And how's the mobilization going to go?"

"Aw, that might not be so bad. The loudspeakers are supposed to tell the people to report to the brewery, where they'll all get guns, and there'll be instructions, too, I guess."

"And you're going to be in on that, too?"

"I guess so. But if we don't like the looks of it, we pull out."

I didn't say anything for a while again. I had to get a gun out of Prema somehow.

"Listen—you think there'll be anything for me?"

"What do you mean?"

"Oh, maybe a submachine gun or something like that."

"Sure, don't worry. We've got lots more weapons back at the warehouse."

"You're not saving them for somebody else then?"

"No. We thought we'd distribute what we couldn't use once things get started."

"Well, thanks."

We came to the warehouse. The corrugated-iron overhead door was pulled halfway down and Mr. Skocdopole stood in front of it. When he saw me, he looked surprised.

"Well, so you did it, eh boys? How come you didn't have to shoot?"

"They let me go. Sabata put in a good word for us," I said.

"Oh, that's different," said Mr. Skocdopole. "Anyway, it'd still be a bit too early."

Vahar rolled up the flag and crawled inside. The boys went in after him, one after the other. Prema stayed outside with me. Mr. Skocdopole came up to us. He had a black patch on his left eye. He'd lost his eye in Siberia when he was in the Czech Legion.*

"Now, just be careful, boys," he said. "The essential thing is not to do anything rash and to think things through. But when things get rough, don't get scared."

"Wait a minute," said Prema. "I can use you."

"Yeah?" I said.

"I'm supposed to meet the Lof kid at Serpon's place. Know him?"

"That's the redhead from Messerschmidt, huh?"

"That's the one. He worked in the factory."

"Yeah, I know him."

"All right, listen. He's supposed to bring me a report from Black Mountain. Could you go there instead of me?"

"Sure."

"And tell him they're supposed to come here to the warehouse tomorrow morning. Got that?"

"Yeah. What time?"

"Oh, around eight."

"Okay."

"You'll go there then, right?"

"Sure. Have you got any password?"

"No. Just tell him I sent you. He knows you, doesn't he?"

"Sure."

"So I can depend on you?"

"Sure. And listen—I can count on that gun, can't I?"

"Naturally. When they announce mobilization, come straight to the warehouse."

"Thanks."

"That's all right. And you bring me Lof's report back to the warehouse too, huh?"

"You're going to be here this afternoon?"

"Yeah. We've still got to clean the guns."

"I'll be there. Is that all?"

"That's all."

I gave him my hand. He shook it.

"Well, cheers."

"Cheers, and thanks," I said.

"That's okay."

"Goodby," said Mr. Skocdopole.

"Goodby," I said, and turned.

So I had a gun. But that thing with Lof was a nuisance. Only there wasn't much I could do about it. One good turn deserves another. I went under the viaduct and headed back toward the square. It was only then that I noticed there were people standing on the opposite sidewalk looking toward the warehouse. And they were watching me, too. It gave me a good feeling. Too bad I hadn't had a gun when I walked up to the boys. But maybe it looked good that way. As if I was their superior or something. I hurried toward the square, feeling fine, and forgot all about Lof. The sun wasn't shining any longer because, in the meantime, the sky had grown overcast with rain clouds. They had blown in from the north and covered the sun and soon the whole sky was clouded over. I turned into Jew Street. It was narrow, cobbled, and deserted. Flags hung out from a few of the houses. I looked at my watch. It was already past twelve o'clock and people had probably gone home for lunch. Not even the revolution could interfere with that. I turned the corner and passed the post office on the square. People were already walking around normally again, but the crowds had dispersed. Flags flew from the church and the loan association office and it looked like noon on the 28th of October.* The flags gave me a kind of frustrated feeling of emptiness. It seemed to me you could almost smell nice, fat geese roasting in the ovens in all those houses. That was it. Roast goose. You could bet on it. That's how things go. Fear, cheers, brass bands, speeches, and roast goose with sauerkraut and dumplings. Everything would be the same again. Nothing would ever change. A couple of exciting days and then the same old bowl of oatmeal, stiff and gummy like it always used to be. And belching after lunch. I'd been feeling fine a little while ago, but now all of a sudden I was fed up. At least I had jazz. But even that didn't help just then. At least I'd be going to Prague, to the university. That didn't help either. Christ! Irena, at least. Nothing. I felt completely numb, stunned. I felt like I'd gone lame or blind and that I'd never see again, never feel again. Nothing, either pleasant or unpleasant, just this dull monotony of a life without any future. Quick! Look forward to something! Be glad about something! Love something! Or get furious at something! But nothing happened. I stood at the corner by the post office and I didn't feel a thing. It was awful. Suddenly my life had no goal whatsoever. All there was to do was to lie down and sleep. But I wouldn't be able to fall asleep. I was too jittery, too keyed up. Lord, one had to at least have something! At least Irena. I tried to imagine her and I did imagine her, but nothing happened. Nothing but numbness. I'd have to see her in the flesh. Maybe that would help me, at least. Yes. See her and kid around with her. At least that would help. I rushed into the post office. The frosted window was closed. The room was quiet. I went up to the telephone window and knocked. The window slid up and behind it sat the big-nosed girl with bleached hair who alternated with Irena. Irena wasn't there any more.

"Has Irena gone already?" I asked hurriedly.

The girl peered at me curiously and nodded.

"Thank you," I said and hurried out of the room. The heavy, brass-bound door gave me a hard time. My God! Where's Irena? Where's anything? The sky above the square was completely overcast by now. A chilly light lay over everything. The red in the flags had faded and a handful of people were loitering around the church. The church! I clutched at that bulbous steeple as if it was a lifebelt. Its windows in their deep niches and its blind sundial on the wall. To the church, fast! Feel something, say something to wake an echo in me, to break up this numbness, to find some sort of resonance inside. An empty, a desolate life. What did I care about Irena? About jazz? About anything? My whole life. I practically ran into the church. The doors were ajar. I burst inside. There was a little table in the vestibule with religious brochures and a cashbox. At the left there was a crucifix and, on the right, an old gravestone of some nobleman or other. I panicked, afraid that the glass doors into the main nave were locked. They usually were. I grabbed the latch. They weren't locked. I went inside and a churchly chill wafted over me. I dipped my thumb into the holy water and made a damp sign of the cross on my forehead and on my chin and on my chest.

A few old ladies were sitting in the pews—quite a few, more than usual. A white light poured in through the windows and dissolved into a little puddle of cold twilight. God, why doesn't it have stained-glass windows? But they'd taken them out on account of the danger of air raids. Three arched Gothic windows behind the main altar had just turned frigid in the unpleasant chill. God! The whole church was bright and clean. Too bright. You couldn't do anything here. You couldn't feel a thing in this church. How in hell could a person imagine God in such a light? And I needed to feel something, quick. My eyes skidded over the altar that had been ridiculously restored and was all polished up. The pewter baptismal font stood by the left altar. That's where I'd been baptized. Next to it rose the last pillar supporting the side wing of the choir loft. I looked over there. That was what I was looking for!

It was dim there. There was a little altar with a Virgin Mary in front of which a little red lamp burned. There at least it was dim. I went over. My heels made an awful noise on the floor and a couple of old ladies stared at me. I knelt in front of the altar and looked up at the Virgin Mary. She wasn't the prettiest I'd ever seen. I closed my eyes and imagined mine instead. She had red lips and green eyes. Like Irena. In fact, she looked just like Irena.

"Hail Queen, Mother of Mercy, our life and desire," I began. I felt the Virgin Mary was actually listening to me. And she was. "Our hope, we the outcast children of Eve, call out to Thee from this vale of tears." The Virgin Mary listened and watched me. "Speak. Speak to me," I implored. "My God, say something so I'll be able to feel something at least."

But she didn't say a thing. All she did was listen. But she never said a thing. All she'd ever done was listen dumbly like that.

"Turn upon us Thy gracious gaze," I pleaded, and I could see her turn her lovely eyes toward me and that was wonderful and it excited me and her pretty ruby-red lips were parted and it was night and her eyes were half closed.

Maybe she'd reconsider and marry me after all. It wouldn't be bad at all to get married to her. It would mean an end to everything, to all my plans and so on, but then plans never work out anyway and being married to her would be good. Good. Very good. My God! To sleep with her and make love to her, but then what? What the hell else can you do with Irena? You can't talk to her. All you can do is kid around and I'd soon get fed up with all that all the time. Nuts. I'd just as soon she wouldn't reconsider, that she'd just go on making Zdenek happy. Sure. I'd be better off without her. A lot better off. There're probably dozens of Irenas in Prague. Nuts to Irena. She's not bad, but that's only because there wasn't much choice. I looked up at the altar and remembered I'd wanted to pray.

"Our Father," I began, but what was it I'd wanted to pray about? Oh, yeah, to feel something again. But I was already feeling again. I didn't need to pray any more. I had lots of feelings now. About Irena and all those other Irenas in Prague. And how I'd fascinate them with my saxophone—the sexiest instrument there is. Sexophone. A real honey pot for girls. I wanted to hurry through my prayers and get out of there because everything was all right already but first I had to pray about something. At least an Our Father and a Hail Mary. Maybe God wants us to get bored saying our prayers so he can test us that way and find out whether we're willing to do something for him or not. I started in on the Our Father but couldn't get through it. I kept getting it all mixed up with Irena and saxophones and Prague and night clubs and all those girls and then the revolution and Prema and guns and where I was supposed to go this afternoon to meet Lof, and I couldn't finish the prayer. Finally I concentrated so hard my head ached, but I managed to get through to the end. I sighed with relief and crossed myself hurriedly. My conscience bothered me a bit, but not for long. It disappeared as soon as I was out in front of the church again. The cross I'd made on my forehead felt chilly and it was like I still had a drop of water there. I quickly wiped it off so nobody'd see and headed around the church toward home. There were only a few people out on the street and I didn't run into anybody I knew. Slowly I went up the apartment-house steps. I remembered how the German soldiers had taken me through the streets. I hoped Mother hadn't found out about it. She probably hadn't. It wouldn't be good for her if she had. She was nervous and had high blood pressure. I unlocked the door and went into the apartment. I expected something to happen. But Father and Mother were just sitting at the table in the dining room.

"Hello," I said.

"Greetings," said Father. "Well, what's going on outside?"

"Nothing. Dr. Sabata's negotiating with the Germans."

"Oh, gracious, let's just hope we all get through this safely," said Mother. She hadn't heard anything. That was good.

"We will. Don't worry," I said and sat down at the table.

Mother got up, took the soup tureen and filled my bowl with the aluminum ladle. It was beef broth.

"We spent the morning painting over the German signs," I said to break the silence.

"So I heard. And tell me, what happened at the square?" Father said.

"Nothing. The Germans just made everybody go away and then they left."

"You were there?"

"Yes," I said. Then I quickly changed the subject away from what had happened at the square. "Listen, what's with Vladyka?"

Father made a wry face. "Nothing, for the time being. This morning we told him to go home and wait for further decisions."

"I saw him in front of the bank. He was wearing a tri-color in his buttonhole as big as the side of a barn."

"Really? Oh, he'll be a big patriot now, you can be sure of that."

"Will you make things hot for him?"

"Well, I could, I suppose. But it all depends what the other men at the bank decide," Father said.

Father was a soft-hearted man, a good man. I knew him.

"You really ought to," I said. The soup was good. I didn't leave a drop.

"What's next?" Father asked.

"Roast sirloin," said Mother.

"Horse meat?"

"Why do you ask? You know very well there's nothing else these days."

"Oh, I'm not complaining. Horse sirloin is even better than the real thing."

Mother went into the kitchen. I picked up a book which lay on the radio. *Bread of the Sea* by Willibald Yöring. I opened it and was bored right away. This Yöring was interested in the life of Norwegian fishermen. I wasn't interested in the life of Norwegian fishermen. I put the book back. Books are awful, most of them anyway. Records are better. I was interested in food. In life, too, or my own life anyway. Mother appeared in the doorway, carrying a casserole on a wooden tray which she set down on the table. Father carefully lifted the lid.

"Aaaah," he said.

Then he served himself a nice big helping of meat and poured gravy over the whole plate. He dunked six dumplings in it. Father was a nice guy. I liked him. He was a good guy because he didn't pretend to be something he wasn't. That's why I liked him. I'd noticed a long time ago that whatever a man lives by, or for, becomes the most striking feature of his anatomy, his physiognomy. That's strictly according to Darwin, or whoever it was who wrote about the effect of habit on the adaption and development of characteristics. Maybe it was Spencer. There's nothing funnier than a big-mouthed, high-brow intellectual. You can tell right off which it is they work with more —their brains or their bellies. But Father didn't make any pretenses. He had a beautiful big mouth and jaws, his cheeks were like pouches and when he ate—and he always ate with his mouth closed—you could hear how everything was being ground up and mashed and kneaded and pulverized inside that great big mouth of his, even though he didn't smack his lips at all while he ate, because he always kept his mouth closed. Otherwise he was jolly and full of fun and he knew how to tell awful jokes and he kept on telling the same ones over and over, and the funny thing was that he always made a big hit with them. Those jokes seemed pretty lousy to me, but I guess other people didn't think so. I used to think that nothing could move him, but when Aunt Manya died he bawled all day and when he tried to talk he sobbed like a little kid. Yes, he was a good guy and I liked him. He didn't understand me but I didn't care. The main thing was, he gave me my allowance and let me do whatever I felt like doing. That he did.

I helped myself to the meat and dumplings and gravy and polished it off in a couple minutes. It was awfully good. I'm not surprised that there're people who live just to eat. If I could have food like this all the time without going to a lot of effort to get it, and if I didn't have any digestion problems, I could easily live for food too. The fact that I ate to live, instead of the other way around, was just because most of the time Mother cooked meals that weren't worth living for, because of the food shortage. That's why I had to think up other reasons for living.

After lunch Mother cleaned off the table and Father went to lie down on the couch in the kitchen. I got up from the table and sat down in the armchair by the radio. You could hear the clatter of dishes from the kitchen. I switched on the radio and looked out the window. It was nice to let all sorts of thoughts run through your head after lunch. Clouds were piling up over the town and it started to rain in the valley. All I could see from the window were hillsides and woods and houses, but no people. The people were out of sight, down in the streets. The set had warmed up and a desperate voice rang out from Prague Radio: "We are calling all Czech police, constabulary, and national troops in the region to report immediately to the Radio Building! The SS are trying to kill us! Report immediately!" My heart jumped into my throat. This was sensational! Nothing like this had ever happened before! An uprising set off and directed over the radio! I wanted to be in on it too. Well, so it'd already started in Prague. So they were already shooting inside the Radio Building.

That's on Foch Boulevard, the place guarded by a Kraut wearing a tin half moon on his chest. So they were shooting there. Maybe they were already dead. I closed my eyes and tried to imagine it. A guy in a sharp-looking suit with a rifle, crouched behind an overturned streetcar. A smooth-looking guy in a light tan hat, carrying a submachine gun, crouched behind a lamppost. That was my idea of a revolution. Uniforms didn't appeal to me. Uniforms were something for the Germans. This was more like it—the zootsuiters, as the German magazines scornfully called them, all dressed up and chewing gum. This was the way to stage an uprising against the Germans. To hell with uniforms. I went on listening. Just music now, no voice. Then it came on again. My spine felt chilly this time. Maybe things were really bad in Prague. Maybe they'd blow up the whole city. I felt like fighting. The Old Town Hall was on fire, they said. The best place to be would be on Kobylisy Hill where you get a nice view of Prague, kind of an unusual one, and from up there the town looks gray and flat, just chimneys and little turrets sticking up above the flat mass. And now I could imagine columns of smoke rising up toward the rainy skies and the wind blowing and shifting the smoke, and the fires springing up all over town as far as Vysehrad, and as dusk fell over the city, the fires burning brighter and brighter and huge flames licking at the Museum and the little towers and the Liben gas works, and in the distance the fires burning, smaller and smaller, while black columns of smoke wave and twist toward the stars. Prague was in ruins and there I sat in an armchair and I had a funny feeling in my stomach and in my brain, too. And it wasn't entirely unpleasant, either. So we weren't going to get by unscathed after all. So we weren't as spineless and weak as some of us thought. We were going to have it like they'd had it in Stalingrad, in London, in Warsaw. Prague, too, is burning. I turned up the radio and the announcer began reporting excitedly that German tanks were approaching Prague from Benesov and then he said in Czech-accented English: *"Attention! Attention! German tanks are approaching Prague from Benesov. We need air support! Attention, Allied Air Force!*

•

We need air support!" That sounded great. Then he repeated it in Russian, but I didn't understand that. And I could see those huge Typhoons and Thunderbolts with machine guns jutting out of their wings diving through the fine rain above the Benesov highway and blowing up the whole column of German tanks. I could just see those Tigers and Panthers burning and SS men in leather helmets tumbling out of the tank turrets, falling in the mud and racing off across the fields and the little green Spitfires going after them, diving low.

I felt fine. The room was warm and dim, the score for "Yellow Dog Blues" lay open on the piano, lunch was over, and outside the window the flags hung limply in the rain. I sat that way for quite a while daydreaming about it all, and then a bit about Irena again, and all of a sudden the clock struck in its nice deep tone and it was nearly three. I'd have to go meet Lof. I was glad. It felt good now to put on a raincoat and leave the warm room and go out into the misty rain on a conspiratorial mission to the castle drive, while everybody else'd still be digesting lunch and waiting till things blew over. Setting off alone to prepare for the uprising. It was great. I went into the hall and put on my raincoat. The glass door into the kitchen was closed. Then it suddenly occurred to me that I ought to change my clothes. I still had on my best clothes and it was raining out. It'd be too bad to get them wet. I took off my raincoat again and went into my room. I took off my brown jacket and pants and opened the closet. I got out my everyday suit—a dark blue double-breasted pin-striped suit—and put it on. I carefully hung my best suit on a hanger and put it back in the closet. Then I went out into the hall again and opened the storage closet. It was called the maid's room actually, though we hadn't had a maid for a long time. But it really was a maid's room. At least nothing else would fit into it except a maid. It was terribly tiny and it didn't have a window, just sort of an airhole that opened onto the corridor, so it was almost completely dark inside. The maids must have gone crazy in there. It was like a dungeon in a castle. It didn't surprise me at all that our last maid had thrown herself in front of a train. Boy, living in a hole like that would drive me crazy, too. Maybe not to suicide, but I'd have given notice. Only that had been during the Depression and she'd found out she was pregnant and so she was in a pretty tight spot, I guess. I opened the shoe cupboard and took out a pair of my most beat-up shoes. I took off my good pair, stuck in the shoe trees, and put them away in the cupboard. Then I put on my old shoes and came out of the closet. I put on my raincoat by the coatrack and fixed my hat in front of the mirror. Then I opened the kitchen door.

"Well, so long," I said.

"Where're you going?" Mother asked.

"Over to Benno's probably, to listen to some records," I said.

"Be careful, Danny. I wish you'd stay, though, just to be on the safe side today."

"Don't worry."

"Now listen to your mother, son. And be careful," said Father from the couch.

"Sure. Don't worry. Goodby," I said.

"Goodby, Danny," Mother said.

"So long," said Father.

I closed the door and went out in the corridor. I hurried down the stairs without getting stopped this time. Old lady Strnadova was probably washing her dishes. As soon as I was out on the street, I headed toward Serpon's mansion. There were still clusters of people milling around on the streets, all decked out in tricolors and cockades. Only it was raining, so a lot of them had stayed home and were just looking out their windows. Most of those who were still outside were young kids in raincoats, the same faces you saw out strolling around every Sunday. They must never eat lunch, since no matter when you go out they're almost always there. I hurried along and a thin rain drizzled on my head. It was chilly against my face and felt like at the seashore. I got into my part right away. I was hurrying through occupied Paris in the rain with important documents for the Intelligence Service. The rain drenched my face and I walked quickly down the street toward the square. It was practically empty. I crossed it and doffed my hat as I passed the church but made it look as if I was just adjusting my hat. I turned off the square, went past the drug store, and turned right at the loan association office toward Serpon's place. I soon saw it. It stood on a little elevation among a lot of rose beds which weren't in bloom yet. There was a high wall with spikes on top all around the whole property and behind it there was a rock garden and a bit of French-style garden. There was a huge iron gate which always reminded me of a cage in a zoo, and a little booth for the gatekeeper. I knew him. He had two boys who'd gone to grade school with me. He lived in the big house and I always envied him on account of the gate. He had a daughter, too, besides the two boys, and just recently his wife had had another child but it had died. A wide sandy driveway led from the gate up to the house and ended in front of an imposing-looking row of columns that supported the balcony. Above the columns the windows of the banquet hall were a gray gleam. It was a modern mansion, almost a palace. Built in the 1930s. Inside, there were potted palms, a winter garden, a fountain, a ballroom and a music room, and lots of bedrooms and bathrooms. Lada Serpon had his own three-room suite on the top floor of the tower. There was a wonderful view of the town from there and you could see far beyond the frontier. Lada had a piano in his room and a phonograph and a huge ten-tube radio set. We used to go up there sometimes during the war, generally in spring, because the tower was flat on top and you could dance there at night, right under the moon, and since there wasn't any railing around it, it had a special kind of charm, as if you were dancing on the edge of the world. Lada Serpon was crazy about Irena, too, but she didn't care about him either, because he was as ugly as a Hapsburg. I liked Lada. Now the windows in the mansion were dark in the rain. They stared boldly up at the next hill where the old castle was enthroned. Through the trees you could get only a small glimpse of the ramparts with their old gun emplacements, a couple of windows, and the turret. The hillside was steep so I saw the castle from a very sharp angle. Grayish-white clouds scudded low over the top of the turret, but the top itself stood there motionless.

The rain grew heavier and fell with a soft murmur on the trees in the drive. I turned up my collar and it made my neck feel cold. I quickly turned it down again. Why hadn't I had sense enough to turn it up when I first went out? Now I wouldn't be able to any more. I started off on the path that ran along the stone wall of Serpon's place. The path was filling up with puddles and I could already feel mud underfoot. It was raining harder and by now it was almost a downpour. Lousy weather. I got to the drive and tried to take shelter under the trees, but the rain was coming down too hard and there weren't many leaves on the trees yet. I looked at my watch. Quarter past three. I was late. I'd have to wait here. I dawdled along up the drive. I could feel I was rapidly getting soaked through my raincoat. Christ! A new downpour drenched my trousers. My shoes were full of water and the cold wet chilled my feet and legs halfway up to my knees. Damn! That dumb Lof. Why couldn't he come on time? Or maybe he'd already been and had left. I dragged myself slowly up the hill and the cold climbed up my legs. I was mad. I tried thinking about Paris again and the rain and the Intelligence Service, but it was raining too hard for that now. I was going to come down with the flu. I could already feel the flu coming on if I didn't get to bed in time. There on the road ahead I saw one of the castle gates. It was open. The Queen of Württemberg hadn't barricaded herself inside. A coat of arms of some sort was carved in sandstone over the gate—some kind of shield and a bunch of spears and old cannons and piles of funny-looking cannonballs. Underneath there was a plaque with a Latin inscription. Something about Octavio Piccolomini Anno Domini MDXXXVI or something like that. You couldn't make it out and, anyway, I can't read Roman numerals. I went through the gate and found myself in a courtyard. I could smell the manure from the stables. At the left was an archway with firewood stacked underneath. That was the steward's apartment and Ema lived there. In the tower. Ema was a sour grape. But I liked the archway. Lof must have come from Black Mountain along the drive from the other direction. He would have had to come through this courtyard and through the gate to get to Serpon's place. I stood under the archway and watched the rain come down. It was pouring in the courtyard, spattering off the tin sheeting on the old ramparts and on the stable roof and it made muddy puddles full of bubbles in the courtyard.

I was cold. That crazy Lof still didn't come. I looked at my watch again and it was half past three. I decided I'd wait till a quarter to four. Anyway, Prema and his Black Mountain headquarters were all just a joke. You couldn't expect any help from up there. The whole thing was nothing but a joke. The boys were just playing war. A bunch of fools, that's all they were.

I got awfully cold standing there in wet shoes in the wind and I could feel my cheeks getting hot. That was always a sign you were coming down with the flu. Damn fools! Why couldn't they fix a meeting in some better place? I could have kicked Prema in his teeth. And all the rest of them. What the hell do they need Lof for? Lof in particular and Black Mountain. There were dozens of villages all over the mountain, but no—he had to come here. Christ Almighty! Goddamn! I swore and whipped up my anger. The worst of it was that I had to stay put because I couldn't just walk off. I had to keep my idiotic promise. Prema set great store by that. Christ! I couldn't just drop the whole thing. And meantime Prema was sitting inside the warm warehouse with an electric light in the ceiling, oiling guns with the rest of the boys. And here I stood in the cold and wet, waiting for Lof who wasn't going to show up anyway. But I had to wait. A disgusting life. Nothing good ever lasted long. You climbed out of one mess only to stumble right into another. I was so mad I could have bawled.

I looked at my watch again. Twenty-five minutes to four. Ten more minutes. I decided to think about Irena. So I started thinking about her and it worked. Like now she was probably sitting at home in her bathrobe reading. She had a nice plaid bathrobe; I'd been at her place once when she'd been taking a bath. Her mother told me to sit down in an armchair in the livingroom and left me there. But I could hear the splashing from the bathroom and the rush of the shower and I could imagine Irena naked and soapy all over and how she was rinsing off the soapsuds with the big sponge, how her pretty naked body was glistening with the water and how she was completely naked except for a red shower cap on her head, and I got so excited, sitting there in the armchair, that I had to cross my legs so if anybody came in they couldn't tell. And there I sat inspecting the gilded backs of the *History of the Czech Nation,* and collected works of Alois Jirasek, and *Russian Adventures* by a local councilman, telling about his experiences in the Czech Legion, and then I looked at the artificial bananas and plums on the flowerstand by the window and the flourishing, thick-leaved rubber plant and some kind of green mess around it and at the various pictures and the bust of Jirasek on the bookcase and Kramar's* autographed photograph and a big yellow female torso by Lebeda that Irena had bought in Prague once when she suddenly got interested in art. And then Irena had come out with her hair tied up in a kerchief, German-style, wearing that thin plaid bathrobe, and as she walked, the bathrobe opened in front and you could see her suntanned thighs up as far as God knows where, and when she sat down, the bathrobe fell open and she left it like that for quite a while and I got a glimpse, but I couldn't get a good long look so I had to stare like I was nailed to my chair and there wasn't anything I could do about it, and then she closed her bathrobe and crossed her legs and it was all over. I thought about that and I felt good. I forgot about the rain and about Lof.

When I finished thinking about Irena I looked at my watch and it was already after a quarter to four. I could leave now, but I didn't feel like standing here until four o'clock either. It'd been fun with Irena and maybe she'd think it over after all. Even if you can't talk to her about anything. But she's pretty. Awfully pretty. Prettier than the Queen of Württemberg. She's dumb, but then all girls are dumb. Girls just weren't put on earth for their wisdom and you've got to pay a price for everything in life. Like, in exchange for the pleasure of being with Irena, you also have to pay sometimes by being bored stiff. I didn't feel like leaving yet. Then I had an idea. I felt like looking down at the town from up here. Toward where Irena lives. At her house. I forgot about Lof, jumped off the porch steps, and headed across the courtyard through the rain. The narrow embrasures flashed past, one after the other, as I passed and I went through the open gate into the second castle courtyard where there was a well. It was dim and I went up the stairs into a small stone courtyard surrounded by arcades on all sides with the base of the main tower rising from one corner. I went along a narrow passageway in the western gallery. There was no one around. It wasn't raining in here because the wind was coming from the north and so the roof, supported by a row of thin sandstone columns, shielded the gallery from the rain. From the western gallery you could see all the way down to Serpon's mansion with a regular little lake on the flat top of the square tower and, below it, Koletovic's villa built in Alpine style on an artificial hill. Behind it was the swimming pool where Lucie went swimming in the summertime and where I sometimes went to sunbathe. Sokol Hall stood a bit to the left, white in the middle of a sea of shabby-looking little houses at the edge of town—New World, they called it—and the railroad tracks ran glistening alongside leading out from under the viaduct, and above, there was St. Matthew's Church and the big yellow high school building.

Not a soul in sight. Not yet anyway. And Irena was sitting and reading in her little room with the desk and bookcase and armchair. I started back along the gallery and turned the corner. Somebody was sitting in the pergola in the middle of the gallery on the south side. I could see the edge of somebody's hat and the back of a green loden coat. I leaned against the stone balustrade and looked down over the town. I'd done that lots of times before. Black Mountain, the hillsides, the woods, the hospital, the Port Arthur, the commercial high school, the courthouse, the bridge, the county office building, and Irena's house behind it at the edge of the woods.

I could imagine the dim light inside and the armchair

and the table set for supper. And me down there in that house with a paunch and how I'm eating. And Irena sitting opposite me and she's pretty and has a nice red mouth. I looked around and saw the same person still sitting in the summer house. I wondered who it was. One of the nobility, no doubt. Maybe it was the Queen of Württemberg, bidding farewell to Kostelec in the rain. I moved slowly toward the summer house. The person in the loden coat didn't move. I came closer and closer. Then I saw who it was. He was sitting there with Irena and they were necking. It was Zdenek. It was Zdenek and Irena. They were absolutely glued together and he'd been sitting there kissing her the whole time I was looking out over the town.

I turned away and shivered. So that's the way things look in reality. Just like that. I left. That was the way things stood, then, and all those daydreams could go jump in the lake. To hell with daydreams. That was Irena. And that's the way it stood with Irena. She wouldn't reconsider. I was absolutely calm. I was unhappy. Spurned—or whatever you call it. I felt like curling up in the dark under the blankets and eating my heart out. I didn't want anything around to take my mind off it, didn't want to see or hear anything, all I wanted to do was just eat my heart out. Boy, the way they'd been kissing each other! I could just imagine her wet mouth and saliva and her darting tongue and it got me all excited. And now all that was his. I'd never had it like that with Irena and never would. I'd just stand under her window and pretend to be her friend, that's all. I hurried through the little courtyard, then past the well into the second courtyard, past the stables and through the gate out into the drive. I walked fast and I tried not to think about it too much. The tree branches swayed and I still felt a drizzle against my face. I loped past the wrought-iron gate of Serpon's mansion. Lof was nowhere to be seen. From the drive I headed straight for the loan association building. I wished I was already home. But I still had to go to the warehouse. Nuts. I decided I wouldn't go. I'd telephone Prema from Pilar's tavern. I went inside. The hallway was dark and full of kitchen smells. I used to go there every Wednesday for tripe soup when they still had tripe. Mrs. Pilarova always let me use the telephone. I went into the taproom. The phone was beside the tap. I picked up the receiver and dialed Skocdopole's number, 123. When Prema answered, I told him Lof hadn't come.

"That's bad," said Prema. "And you were at Serpon's place?"

"Sure I was. I waited there till half past three and then I walked up the drive toward the castle and back but he still hadn't shown."

"Well, I don't know. Probably something came up."

"Or else he decided he'd just skip the whole thing."

"That's possible, too."

Prema was silent.

"Listen," I said, "is there anything else I can do for you this afternoon?"

"No. Why?"

"Otherwise I think I'll go home to bed, all right? I'm soaked and I want to be in shape for tomorrow."

"Go on home, then. There's really nothing to do right now."

"And . . . listen," I said.

"Yeah?"

"I'm supposed to come over tomorrow morning, right?"

"That's right."

"And will you have that . . . thing, that . . . you know . . . for me?"

"Don't worry. It'll be here."

"Fine. I'll be there then."

"All right."

"Well, so long."

"So long."

So. That was that. I hung up. Now back home and to bed and to hell with everything. I stepped into the kitchen and laid a coin on a corner of the table.

"Thanks, Mrs. Pilarova," I said, and grinned at her.

"You're quite welcome. Come in again," she said.

I opened the door and went out into the hall. A cat mewed and I could see its green eyes shining in the darkness. I went on down the street toward the square. It wasn't raining at all any more. My face was hot and I felt chilled, but it wasn't so bad any more since I could look forward to an afternoon in bed and was thinking about Irena and felt pretty good. And awful, too. I'd make myself some hot tea and take an aspirin and pull down the blinds. I hurried across the square. It was full of people again. It was Saturday afternoon and mothers were out with their baby carriages. I saw pretty Mrs. Jurkova, Rosta Pitterman's sister, with her baby carriage and husband. She had nice wide eyes fringed with thick curly lashes. Her eyes looked surprised and pretty and dumb. There were lots of flags hanging along Jirasek Boulevard. At Kaldoun's there was a terribly long flag that hung from the attic window almost all the way to the ground. It was nearly sixty feet long. A real monster of a flag. Kaldoun's always had something unusual. Like that bronze statue of a naked Mercury that they had over their doorway, the only privately-owned statue like that in Kostelec. I hurried along and didn't pay any attention to people. Now all I wanted was to be alone, completely alone with myself and Irena.

But just as I got back to our building, I heard somebody yelling. I stopped and looked over to where the noise was coming from. Some people were racing past the Hotel Granada which stood on the corner. The Granada's manager was leaning out of one of the windows frantically trying wildly to yank the flagpole out of its holder. Finally he wrenched it out, then he snatched the flag inside. On the opposite side of the street, Mr. Pitterman was pulling his flag in through the window, hand over hand. He was in his shirtsleeves and wearing suspenders, and his hands flashed as he pulled at the cable. People were rushing along on both sides of the street, crowding into Pitterman's arcade and into the Granada. I stood in front of our house and watched. I could hear the roar of a motor and a big car turned into the street past Pitterman's house. A German soldier with a submachine gun was sitting on the roof of the car. Two other soldiers were perched on the front, their legs draped over the bumpers, wearing German jackboots with hand grenades stuck in the sides. They were both holding submachine guns in their laps, one on each side of the car. The car drove slowly along the street. An officer stood on the runningboard, holding on with his left hand through an open window, a pistol in his right hand. He was wearing gray gloves. He peered around at the houses. As the car drove slowly past, flags were snatched in from all the windows, one after another. The German officer looked at the windows and gestured with his pistol.

"*Los! Die Fahne weg!*" he screamed if somebody wasn't hauling in a flag fast enough. The street in front of the car had also emptied. Somebody was pulling Kaldoun's flag in through the attic window as fast as he could. It looked as though the dormer window up in the attic was swallowing a long piece of red and white macaroni. Away with that thing, fast. People had been in a little too much of a hurry. Get rid of it, fast. Wouldn't want to do anything to irritate the Germans. Have to keep this revolution safe. Everybody was playing it safe, all right. The officer with the pistol in his hand was staring, fascinated, at Kaldoun's flag. The car almost slowed to a halt. He watched the flag disappearing through the attic window and said nothing. Just then it got snagged on something at the front of the house. Whoever it was pulling it in began to jerk at it, but it wouldn't budge.

"*Los! Los!*" yelled the officer. The poor soul in the attic struggled to work the flag loose. I hoped it was Mr. Kaldoun himself. Fat, in his shirtsleeves and suspenders. It was probably the janitor though. Whoever it was, he wasn't getting anywhere.

"*Los!*" yelled the officer, but the flag was stuck fast. The officer raised his pistol and fired a shot into the attic window. The shot made an awful racket and the revolver flashed. The red and white macaroni started tumbling back out of the attic window. Now it looked like a waterfall of cloth and it seemed to have no end. Either the guy in the attic had been shot or else he got scared and dropped the thing. That was more likely. That was it for sure. I hoped it was Mr. Kaldoun. And that he got so scared he filled his pants. But if it wasn't Mr. Kaldoun, it was probably just the janitor. The officer on the running board laughed and the car drove on. All the houses were flagless now and the street looked as if it had been swept clean. I ducked inside the door and peeked out through the window. The car drove past me, the soldiers sitting on the bumpers, stiff and stupid. They were holding their guns at the ready and they wore shiny capes of ersatz rubber. Their gray helmets glistened from the rain and water dripped off the edges. As the car went past, I noticed the muzzles of a couple of submachine guns sticking out the back window. There were two more soldiers sitting inside and another behind, straddling the spare tire. It must have been pretty uncomfortable. Probably he could feel a bullet in his belly just like I had that morning. Except he was probably used to it by now. The car slowly moved on. I went inside. I got to our apartment and unlocked the door. As soon as I came into the hall, Mother ran out of the kitchen. She was frantic.

"Oh, Danny, thank heavens! I've been so frightened!"

"Why?"

"What was it? That shot?"

"That's all it was. Some German shot at Kaldoun's flag."

"Was anybody hurt?"

"Hurt? No."

"Thank goodness. Where were you, Danny? You shouldn't go out when things are like this."

"Oh, I was over at Serpon's. Could you make me some tea?"

"You got all wet, didn't you?"

"Yes. I'd like to sweat it out."

"You go right to bed. Otherwise you'll catch cold."

"And you'll make some tea for me?"

"Right away."

"Thanks," I said, and went into my room. I took off the red counterpane and turned back the eiderdown quilt. Then I took off my shoes and set them out in the hall to dry. I undressed and dropped my clothes on the floor. I put on my pajamas and laid my clothes over the chair. It felt good to have on a pair of dry pajamas. My pants were sopping wet. I slid my feet into my slippers and took my pants into the kitchen. Mother was standing at the table. The tea kettle was on the hot plate. She turned to me.

"You're absolutely soaking, aren't you?"

"Yeah."

"Hang your pants over the clothesline."

I tried to smooth a crease into the wet pants. They were all wrinkled up at the bottom. When I picked them up, they made me shiver.

"Leave them, Danny," Mother said. "I'll iron them for you as soon as they're dry."

"So I should just put 'em over the line?"

"Yes."

The tea kettle started to hiss. I tossed my pants over the clothesline. I shuddered again.

"Hurry up and get in bed, Danny. I'll bring you the tea," Mother said.

"Thanks. I'll take it myself."

Mother poured the water through a strainer into the cup.

"Do you want some rum in it?"

"Yes, please."

Mother took the bottle of rum and measured out two spoonfuls. She still thought I was a little kid as far as my needs were concerned. Then she set the cup on a tin tray.

"Wouldn't you like a piece of sponge cake, too?" she asked.

"No, thanks. I'll just take an aspirin."

"Yes, you do that, and cover up well. Do you want me to tuck you in?"

"No, I'm not going to sweat much. Just a bit."

"You really ought to work up a good sweat."

"No, I don't feel all that bad, Mother. I'll just pull down the blinds and sleep."

"That's the best thing you can do. You're sure you don't want me to tuck you in?"

"No, thanks," I said and smiled at her. Then I carried my tea out of the kitchen and into my room. I put the tea on a chair next to the bed, went over to the cupboard, opened it and took out a tube of aspirin, closed the cupboard and opened the inside window. It was pouring outside again.

A white curtain of rain veiled the river with a thin mist. I closed the window and pulled down the blinds. Now it was dark in the room and the window gleamed a yellowish brown. I went over to the door and closed it. I looked around. Tea, aspirin, blinds down, bed. I crawled into bed and propped two pillows behind my back so I could sit up. I took the tray with the tea and had a sip. The clock on the wall struck five. I took another sip of tea. It was awfully hot. I waited a while until it cooled off and then I began to drink it. I left a bit in the bottom of the cup and set the tray and the cup on the chair. And now for Irena. I fixed up the pillows so I could lie down and pulled the quilt up under my chin. Irena. But first I'd say my prayers. Dear Lord, please, and it went very fast. I rattled off the prayer and now it didn't matter that it wasn't very reverent. I didn't go back over it or repeat anything. And now for Irena. I thought about how I'd been at her place and she'd had on that plaid bathrobe and nothing underneath. I thought about that in every detail. And from there I went on to think about another time when I'd been at her place and Irena came into the hall in a blue Japanese kimono and held out her hand to me and I saw how her breasts pushed the kimono out in front and then it fell in a straight line down from her breasts and hung loose around the waist, and then Irena turned around and went into her room and she stumbled over the threshold and one of her slippers with a big blue pompon flew off, and she bent over to pick it up and as she did so her kimono opened in front a little bit so you could get a glimpse of her naked skin, and how one winter we were walking down Black Mountain and Irena fell and her skirt flew up and she had awfully pretty knees and white boots. I thought about all this and started thinking about how one morning in tenth grade when I'd waited for her under the viaduct by Skocdopole's warehouse she came, and she was wearing her blue coat with the white trimming around the hood and when I looked at her from the back it fell in a nice V on her back, and I thought about that and about the beach and her bathing suit with the white string across her back and so on, about her hips in that swimming suit

D*

and the narrow valley between her breasts that I could look down into when she was lying beside me on her stomach getting a suntan. That was my life. That had been my life. Irena. And I'd gotten a kick out of it. Kostelec and the revolution and the boys and Irena and all. I'd gotten a terrific kick out of it and I'd enjoyed it all. Every last little thing. I burrowed down under the quilt and closed my eyes. A good, warm, snug feeling came over me. I forgot about how they were fighting in Prague and that the Old Town Hall was on fire. Maybe my cousins were dying on the barricades. Or more likely they'd crept down in the cellar of their house. I felt great. They were fighting in Prague. Sensational. I lay in bed and felt nice and warm. Everything was great. The whole world in general. And I was happy. Then I just felt good and comfortable without thinking about anything at all and then I fell asleep. And I slept for a long time and I dreamed about something, but I forget what.

Sunday, May 6, 1945

I went around to Skocdopole's at about quarter to eight. It was drizzling and foggy outside. I'd hardly gotten out of the house before I could tell the revolution meant business. People in hiking clothes and berets were heading toward the brewery. They didn't have any weapons as far as I could see, but they had tricolors stitched on their berets and packs strapped to their backs.

I was wearing hiking clothes too, because it was raining and because I didn't want to ruin my best suit. I met Mr. Mozol under the viaduct near Skocdopole's warehouse. He was limping along, looking very pale, as he heroically made his way toward the brewery. He had strapped on an old Austrian saber and looked like something out of an American slapstick comedy. He had to act very heroic now because he hadn't been very heroic during the war. He'd worked his way up at the factory until finally he'd been made local construction supervisor of the German Air Transport Ministry. So now he had to act like a hero. I wondered whether the rest of that crowd would be down at the brewery. Probably. The poor saps would all have to be heroes now.

When I got to the warehouse, Prema was already sitting there on an empty crate, fully armed, wearing his corduroy hunting pants, and the rest of the boys were standing or sitting around. A dim light bulb, draped with cobwebs, shone down on them from the ceiling. They looked like Jesse James's gang. Prema had on high-laced hunting boots and an ammunition belt around his waist. A string of hand grenades were slung across his chest and a sub-machine gun over his shoulder. His face under the Masaryk cap was thin and with his gaunt cheeks he looked kind of Mongolian. Benda was wearing a shiny black fire-man's helmet. They were talking things over.

"Shit," said Prema. "I'm against going over there."

"Me, too. Once we get there, we're stuck," said Perlik.

"But. . ." said Benda.

"Anyway, all Sabata wants to do is lock us all up in the brewery."

"I still think it'd be better if we went over there," said Benda.

"Because you're scared, maybe?" said Perlik.

"Hell no. But what can we do all by ourselves?"

"We collected all these guns by ourselves, didn't we?"

"Okay, but when the SS-men come, then what? How many people do we have anyway?"

"Enough, but if you're scared, stay home."

"But. . ."

"Or else go over to the brewery."

"Aw, come on, for Chrissake."

"You're yellow."

"I am not."

"You are, too."

"No, I'm not."

"Shut up."

"Don't argue, guys," said Prema. "The point is whether we ought to go over there or not."

"I say we shouldn't," said Perlik.

"I think it'd be better if we did," said Vahar.

"You scared, too?" said Perlik.

"The fact is, we've got more guns than we know what to do with and it'd be a shame to let 'em go to waste," said Vahar.

"And on account of that you want to go report at the brewery, huh?"

"Well, and what do you want to do with the guns?"

"Pass 'em out to other guys."

"Yeah, but all the others are over at the brewery."

"So what do you say, fellas?" said Prema.

"What say we go to the brewery?" said Jerry.

I looked at them. They were standing around the up-turned packing crates like robbers in their den and, aside from Perlik, all of them wanted to go to the brewery. Only Prema was undecided. But he was their leader and he couldn't act hastily. I watched him through the glass doors and heard what he said. Then I opened the door and walked in.

"Hi," I said.

"Hiya. Come on in," said Prema.

"Well, are we going over to the brewery?" I said.

"We're just talking it over."

"And?"

"We can't make up our minds whether we ought to or not."

"Everybody's going."

"Sure," said Benda. "We're going, too. Come on."

"I'm not going," said Perlik.

"So stay here, then."

"I'd rather go over to the communists than sign up with Sabata."

"So go on, who's stopping you?" said Benda.

"Don't be nuts, Perlik," said Prema.

"So I'm the one who's nuts, am I? And how about the rest of you?"

"We'll wait and see how things look over there."

"You still don't know Dr. Sabata? You still don't know what a gutless bastard that guy is?"

"Aw, come off it."

"You think he'll let you take off with those guns? Why, you might annoy the Germans."

Perlik was angry and ironic. I knew him. The Germans sent him to a work camp once for being a chronic absentee. He was one of those people who are so brave they never show even a trace of fear. It was dangerous to be connected with a guy like that. But he was the only one. The rest were different.

"No, listen, fellas," said Prema. "The question is, can we get anywhere all by ourselves."

"That's right," said Jerry.

"The fact is that the German front's getting closer and closer and what can we do by ourselves against tanks?" said Benda.

"And what are you going to do against tanks together with Dr. Sabata?" said Perlik.

Benda ignored him.

"The fact is, we've got twice as many guns as we can use. Also, that there'll be guys over at the brewery who know how to use them."

"If Dr. Sabata'll let them use them, that is."

"What the hell, you want us to let the guns just lie around here?"

"And you're really dumb enough to think Sabata'll let anybody shoot 'em?"

"What've you got against Sabata, anyway? What makes you so sure he's so yellow?" said Vahar.

"What makes you think he isn't?"

"All I know is that he got my dad out of a concentration camp," said Vahar.

"That's right, he did," said Benda.

"But *how*?" said Perlik.

"The fact is, he did it," said Benda.

"Sure. By spending a lot of time drinking with the Gestapo down at headquarters."

"Well, he got him out, didn't he? And that wasn't the only case."

"All right now. Let's decide what we're going to do," said Prema.

"I'm for going over to the brewery," said Benda.

"Me, too," said Vahar.

"Me, too," said Jerry.

"All right," said Prema and looked at the others. Vasek Vostal and Prochazka were silent.

"How about it, you guys?"

"Oh, well, okay, let's go then," said Vostal.

"What about you?" Prema said to Prochazka.

"Sure, I guess so," Prochazka said.

"I'd rather not," said Kocandrle.

"What about you?" Prema said to me. I was kind of

surprised he was already counting me in. Also, I knew Perlik was right. But I wanted to go to the brewery anyway. I wanted to see the circus over there. The washing away of Protectorate sins. And besides, maybe Perlik was wrong after all. There'd be a lot of bloodthirsty guys over at the brewery, and once things got started not even Dr. Sabata could hold them back. I knew a lot of them personally. They didn't belong to any organization but they were crazy to have an uprising. Even at the brewery those pleasures would be provided for. And I wanted to see the others, too. I didn't want to miss Mr. Mozol. Or Mr. Moutelik either. I looked at Prema.

"I suppose we'd better go over to the brewery," I said. "If we don't like it, we can always clear out."

"That's right," said Benda.

"You guys are as dumb as they come," said Perlik.

"Shut up. The majority's for the brewery," said Benda.

"Because you're dumb."

"Quit arguing," said Prema. "Let's go."

"Right," said Benda, and they all got up.

"Morons," said Perlik.

Benda turned sharply on him. "Look, if you don't like it you don't have to come along!"

"Oh, shut up," said Perlik and got up too. I waited until they'd filed out of the warehouse and then went over to Prema.

"Oh, I almost forgot. Come on," said Prema. We went out.

In front of the warehouse stood a wagon whose load was covered up with a tarpaulin. The boys stood around it, silent, huddled in a circle in the rain, holding or shouldering their submachine guns and rifles. Vahar held the flag furled around its staff. Prema flipped back the tarpaulin and pulled a polished submachine gun out by its barrel.

"You know how to work this?" he said to me.

"No."

"Well, look. This is how you remove the safety. Here's where you load it and then this snaps down." Prema shoved the magazine into the barrel. The bullet heads shone through the holes. "Try it," said Prema.

I took out the magazine and then I put it in again. It worked fine.

"And when you shoot, press the butt up against your shoulder."

"Yeah."

Prema turned back to the wagon and pulled four clips of ammunition out from under the tarpaulin.

"Put these in your pocket."

"Thanks."

I stick the clips in my coat pocket. They just fit.

"Let's go," said Jerry.

"Let's go," said Prema.

Jerry grabbed the wagon shaft and Prochazka and Kocandrle pushed from behind. I stood on one side and helped them push. Vahar unfurled the flag and we started off. The wheels of the little wagon squeaked. We went slowly over the foot bridge, past the Czech Brethren Church and past the Social Democrat Workers Sports Club toward the brewery. I knew how we must look. Pretty fine. We all walked along without saying a word. We acted very casual. People in hiking knickers with tricolors on their berets stared at us. You could tell they admired us. It was great.

We got to the bridge. I looked up at Irena's window and hoped she was watching, but she wasn't. Naturally. She should see me now. But no such luck. I could already imagine fighting the Germans off in the woods and Irena hiding down in the cellar or somewhere. The whole thing lost all its charm if Irena couldn't see me. Why in hell was I letting myself in for this? A bunch of people were heading along the path from the bridge toward the brewery. Like going to the cemetery on All Saints' Day. A big Czechoslovak flag was flying from the brewery tower. I noticed that some of the guys in the crowd had Czechoslovak Army service rifles over their shoulders. And some were wearing old army uniforms and puttees. They looked quaint. I'd already forgotten there was such a thing as puttees anymore. Nobody wore them in this war. Silently we pushed our wagon slowly along with the crowd. People looked at us. You could tell some of them admired us, too.

Or else they were just scared. There were a lot of them who didn't enjoy looking at a real honest-to-goodness gun. Probably deep down they'd hoped everything would blow over nice and quiet. But nevertheless they were going to the brewery. They were all patriots. And heroes. Mr. Lobel was ahead of us. He used to be our landlord; he was Jewish but his wife was Aryan so he hadn't been sent to a concentration camp. He was carrying a shotgun over his shoulder. He'd always been a big hunter. I kind of expected to see his hunting dog, Bonza, trotting alongside. Bonza would have been glad to come along, I knew. We steered the wagon through the gate. Mr. Moutelik, wearing knickers and a ski cap, appeared with Berty beside him, his Leica on his chest. He beamed at me.

"Hi, Danny," Berty said.

"Hi. Going to take some pictures?" I said.

"You bet."

Better do it fast, I thought to myself. As we came through the gate, I noticed Mr. Mozol with a policeman's saber standing with a bunch of people from the Messerschmidt factory. They even stuck together here. They had it in their blood, the Messerschmidt people. Jerks! They stood in a bunch, chatting. Just three days ago, Mr. Mozol was crawling around, licking Uippelt's boots. Everybody knew that. And now he was scared again. He was always scared of something. And he always had good reason to be scared. He stood there, pale and silly looking and scared. We turned toward the main building. A long queue stood on the steps leading to the open doors. They were waiting to sign up. An army first has to be enlisted. I saw Mr. Stybl the barber, Dr. Bohadlo, Mr. Frinta the lawyer, the clerk from our bank, Mr. Jungwirth from the loan association, and others. They stood there waiting their turn. Mr. Jungwirth was eating a sandwich. We stopped the wagon. Prema turned.

"Wait here, fellows. I'm going to find Sabata."

"Okay," said Benda.

Prema went up the stairs and you could see how he was telling the guys at the door to let him through. I saw one guy at the door turn on him angrily, take one look at

Prema's gun and grenades, then slip aside fast. Sure. We didn't have to waste our time like all the rest of those people lined up there. Their eyes were full of envy because we were somebody, we had weapons. I held my gun by the muzzle and set it on the ground. The steel felt cool and good.

"Danny," I heard from behind me. There stood Berty with his Leica up to his eye.

"Stand over there and I'll take your picture."

"Thanks," I said. I didn't have any objection. I thought about Irena and how I'd show her my picture. I flashed my Gable smile and picked up my submachine gun so you couldn't miss it. Berty squinted at me through the finder and took two steps backward. I hoped Zdenek wasn't going to get a gun like mine. Or at least that nobody'd take Zdenek's picture with it. The camera clicked.

"Thanks. When can I get one, Berty?" I said.

"I'll develop it tonight."

"Can you make a few extras?"

"Sure. How many copies can I make up for you?" said Berty. He'd learned those expressions from his father. Berty was a businessman. His father was, too. They were both businessmen and they owned an apartment house. Berty's hobby was photography. He was always awfully obliging about taking pictures, but he never did anything for nothing. He was always taking pictures, at high school, at the A. C. Kostelec Athletic Club, at little-theater performances, and afterward he sold each snapshot at cost, plus a small fee. I still remembered how in high school he used to have a list of how much people owed him and he always kept after us about paying up. When it came to getting paid he didn't have any friends. Only customers.

"Oh, about six," I said, because I wanted to have plenty of copies. And I knew Mother would send one to Grandmother and another to Prague and another to my uncle in America, as soon as she could again.

"Can you save the negative, too?" I added as an afterthought.

"Certainly," said Berty.

"Well, thanks."

"You're quite welcome." Berty smiled broadly and moved on along the line with his camera all wound and ready for action again. He was pleased I'd let him take my picture. And after the revolution, he'd display the pictures in their show window with stupid captions. "*Valiantly into the Fray,*" he'd write under my picture. But that'd be fine with me. That kind of nonsense didn't bother Irena the way it did me. I was the only one sensitive about things like that. And the group in the band, too, of course. It'd be a big laugh. I could just see the people crowding around Moutelik's show window and bragging about the pictures. And I'd be there, too. I remembered Mr. Machacek. Of course. Berty would contribute the photographic illustrations. "*Photographs graciously donated by Mr. Albert Moutelik, Jr.*" it would say somewhere at the back of the book. And there would be one colored reproduction of an oil painting by Mr. Leitner, "*May 6th in Kostelec.*" I was already looking forward to that book. My picture would be in there, too. Mr. Machacek would put it in as a favor to Father. So I'd be immortalized. Immortalized for all eternity in Kostelec. I glanced around at the crowd. More people kept coming in through the gate and the line moved slowly. Jirka Vit came out of the icehouse, carrying two rifles over each shoulder. Behind him came Mr. Weiss in a major's uniform and behind him a bunch of fellows in Czech Army uniforms. One of them went up the steps of the main building and put up a sign next to the door. On it was written in black paint:

Order No. 1

ALL FIREARMS AND EXPLOSIVES ARE TO BE TURNED IN AT THE STOREROOM.

Col. Cemelik,

Commander

I immediately thought of Perlik. I turned to him. He was standing behind me, looking at the sign. Then he drew down his mouth and grimaced angrily.

"Well, isn't that nice," he said in an icy voice.

"That's really crazy," said Benda.

"So long, buddies," said Perlik and turned.

"Where're you going?" said Benda, but Perlik said nothing and hurried through the crowd toward the gate. I lost sight of him a couple of times as he pushed his way through the people with his submachine gun slung over his back, and then he disappeared.

"That's nonsense. We'll hang on to our guns," said Benda.

"Sure. Let everybody find his own," said Prochazka.

"We'll only turn in what's left over. That'll be enough for them anyway."

"You bet. Who else can give 'em so many?"

"So let's go to the storehouse and turn 'em in," said Vahar.

"Wait a minute, we'd better wait till they come for 'em," said Jerry.

"No, we'd better hand them in ourselves. They won't be able to hold it against us anyway."

"That's right. They won't scold us," said Benda. I could tell he was embarrassed now that he had seen in black and white that Perlik had probably been right all along.

"Aw, nuts, let's turn 'em in. That'll be better," said Vahar nervously.

"Think so?"

"Sure."

"Wait, let's wait for Prema," said Prochazka.

Vahar looked toward the main building. "All right," he said.

"Bringing weapons, boys?" somebody said in back of us. I turned around. There stood Major Weiss, looking very pleasant.

"Yes," said Benda.

"That's fine," said Major Weiss and turned back the tarpaulin revealing the pile of rifles, German bazookas and two submachine guns.

"Well, well, you've outdone yourselves, boys," said Major Weiss. "Come along with me now. We'll take them over to the storeroom."

"Yes, sir," said Benda and turned to us. The boys looked at him uncertainly.

"Let's go," said Benda, and didn't look at anybody. Major Weiss was already heading for the storeroom.

"I thought we were going to wait for Prema," said Prochazka.

"But he's ordered us," said Benda.

"But they're going to want us to turn in everything," said Kocandrle.

"Aw, no. You saw the way he just glanced at the wagon."

"I don't know."

"Oh, sure."

Major Weiss turned around. "Follow me, boys," he called to us.

"We're coming," said Benda and started to push the wagon.

"I don't know," repeated Kocandrle, but Vahar had already turned the shaft. The boys slowly began to push. It made me mad, too. I didn't want to part with my gun. Should I make a break for it? But it was probably too late now. Weiss had seen me. And what would I do with a gun all by myself, if the rest of the boys didn't have any weapons? But I could hide it someplace. Sure, it wouldn't be a bad idea to have it in the house somewhere. You could daydream a lot better that way. About gangsters and things like that. But Major Weiss was waiting for us and his assistants surrounded us. We were on the spot. We slowly trundled the wagon toward the storeroom. It was around the corner from the icehouse. Hruska from Messerschmidt stood in front of the doorway wearing a uniform and a helmet strapped under his chin. He was holding a rifle with a bayonet on it and staring straight ahead. One wing of the door was closed and there was a sign on it reading: ARSENAL. Slowly we approached the doorway. Hruska drew himself up straight and tall.

"Hey! Open up!" called Major Weiss.

Some guy with a pipe looked out. I knew him. It was the stockroom man at the brewery. He'd always been here. The stock had changed a bit, but otherwise there was no difference. He looked at us and shoved back the bolt. Then he leaned against the door and pushed it open.

"Bring it in, boys," said Major Weiss.

We pushed the wagon. The same kind of light fixture hung from the storeroom ceiling as in Skocdopole's warehouse. There was a table underneath and behind it sat the high-school janitor in his Czech Legion uniform with all his medals pinned on. He had a sheet of paper and a bottle of ink in front of him. There was somebody I knew by sight standing beside him, in a green cape and officer's cap. The man in the cape saluted. Major Weiss saluted, too.

"Another lot," said Major Weiss. "Boys, hand it over piece by piece to the lieutenant, and the sergeant will write it down."

I looked around. A row of rifles stood stacked up along the wall. At the end of the row I saw light Czechoslovak Army machine guns with tripods. There were a couple of sacks on the floor and on top, neat little pyramids of egg-shaped hand grenades. There were about twelve bazookas leaning against the other wall and a collection of all sorts of revolvers spread out on a table behind the janitor.

"Let's go," said the janitor. "First you'd better take off what you've got on so you can move around easier."

"Oh, that doesn't bother us," said Benda.

"You just take off those guns. You'll be more comfortable. You've got to do it sooner or later."

Benda stood silently in front of the janitor. I could see he was feeling uncomfortable. Then he spoke up slowly. "You want . . . the stuff we're carrying, too?"

The janitor looked at him in surprise. "Naturally."

"Well, now, look, we liberated this stuff ourselves."

"Yes, I know. Don't worry, we won't forget that."

"But . . ."

"I write down the name of the donor of every weapon, whenever there is one."

"But we'd like to keep them."

"Keep them?"

"Yes."

"I'm sorry, but that's impossible. Didn't you read the order?"

"The one on the door?"

"Yes."

"Well, yes . . ."

"You read the order?"

"Yes."

"Well, there you are."

"But, look. We . . ."

Major Weiss turned. "Yes?"

"Major, this gentleman refuses to hand over his weapons."

Major Weiss peered at Benda and assumed a military expression. "Do you know the order?"

"Yes, Major, but—"

"Quiet! You know the order, therefore you also know your duty."

"Yes—"

"Every soldier must obey without question orders given by a superior officer."

Benda flushed.

"I'm not a soldier!" he burst out.

"What's that?" said Major Weiss.

"I'm not a soldier," Benda repeated.

"When were you born?"

"The twenty-second of March, 1924."

"Then according to the proclamation of the chairman of the National Committee, you're mobilized."

"This is the first I ever heard of any proclamation."

"Well, I'm telling you now. Now turn in your weapons, please."

Benda didn't move.

"Are you going to hand them over? I'm giving you your last chance. Otherwise I'll have to regard this as a clear case of insubordination." Major Weiss waited in silence and watched Benda. Then he added, slowly and significantly, "And do you know what that means when a state is in extreme peril, as it is now?"

Benda stood in front of him, his face red, looking at the ground. The gun slung across his back looked silly now. He was whipped. He stood there in his black fireman's helmet and he'd been completely whipped. His round face burned. Major Weiss was watching him, icy and military. He was only doing his duty.

"Well?" he said. "This is it." I could hardly believe my own ears, but he really said it. "This is it." Probably it had popped up in his head from all those novels he'd consumed during the war when he'd worked in the municipal library. I looked at Benda. He was crushed. He stood there with his pants stretched tight over his big rump, in that funny-looking fireman's helmet with a silver seam down the middle. I felt sorry for him. I watched him and I would have helped him if I could. I thought about staging a mutiny. But it was just a thought. We had guns in our hands and they didn't have anything. We could easily have gotten out of there. But I put it out of my head right away. It'd be all over in a couple days and then they'd try us for sedition and we'd get sent to jail on account of it for God knows how long. There wasn't anything we could do. Slowly, Benda took off the string of hand grenades and laid them down on the table in front of the janitor. Then he took off the gun strapped over his shoulder and placed it on top of the grenades.

"Good. I see you've understood what your duty is," said Major Weiss. "And don't think we don't know what we're doing. These weapons will be distributed among experienced, trained soldiers."

Benda stepped back. I took his place in front of the janitor. Cautiously, Major Weiss picked up Benda's submachine gun.

"Write this down, sergeant," he said to the janitor. "One light machine gun, donated by Mr.—what's your name?"

"Submachine gun," I said quickly and casually.

"What?" said Major Weiss.

"That's a submachine gun."

I'd taken him by surprise. He was off balance now. He looked at me in embarrassment and his face flushed a little around his nose.

"It's a submachine gun, not a light machine gun," I repeated obligingly.

"Yes. I know, Mr. Smiricky. You don't need to instruct me," he said brusquely, to cover up.

"I thought maybe you didn't know," I said. I was capable of all kinds of insolence at that moment. Major Weiss turned pale with anger, but he was smart enough not to go on any further. He turned to the janitor and continued.

"Have you got that? One submachine gun, donated by Mr.—what's your name?"

"Benda," Benda said.

"Mr. Benda."

The janitor wrote it down. When he wrote submachine gun you could see how his pen hesitated. It was probably the first time he'd ever heard the word.

"Also six hand grenades," Major Weiss went on. The lieutenant took the grenades and Benda's submachine gun and put them aside. I laid my own submachine gun down on the table in front of the janitor and pulled the ammunition out of my pockets. I felt a bit like a thief, but then the whole thing was a farce anyway. And that's how we were disarmed. And we hadn't even fired a shot. It was a real farce. I felt a bit sad about giving up my gun, but at least I'd have a snapshot of it. That would be enough. And so I was out of it. Out of the army. And out of the uprising. And nobody could say I didn't have guts. And I'd be able to show Irena my picture. And I wasn't going to get mixed up in anything else. Let somebody else get mixed up. I'd done my part. Yesterday they'd practically put me in front of a firing squad and now today this business with our guns. I'd certainly done my part. Now Mr. Moutelik and Mr. Machacek could play at being heroes. I'd just sit by and watch. I stepped away from the table and stood next to Benda. Vahar moved in front of the janitor and put down his flag and staff.

"One Czechoslovak flag," Major Weiss dictated. "Donated by Mr.—?"

"Vahar," said Vahar, and stepped back to join us.

Then all the rest of the boys stepped up to the janitor's table, one after another. The lieutenant, his collar unbuttoned, checked the weapons and carried them over to the wall. You could tell from the way he picked up our submachine guns that it was the first time he'd ever laid his hands on one. Benda watched sadly. I watched with interest. When they were through with us, Major Weiss said, "Thank you. That's all. Now report to the office." He spoke briskly and officially because he was mad at us. Especially at me. Well, I'd shown him up. I turned around and went out. The first thing I saw was Berty Moutelik with his camera. He stood there with his camera up to his eye taking a picture of four gentlemen who were posing for him. I knew them all. They were from the Commercial Bank and they'd already been inducted because they had on red-and-white arm bands with some kind of gold inscription. When I got closer, I could read it. CS ARMY stood out like the letters on a ribbon on a funeral wreath. I noticed that there were already a lot of groups standing around in the yard with armbands on. We went on toward the main building. I saw the boys from the band standing over by the icehouse. I left the others and went over to them.

"Hi," I said. They turned to me.

"Hi," said Haryk. Benno was wearing his sheepskin cap. He wore it pulled down low over his eyes and he looked like a small-town hick. Benno was always good for a laugh. Day before yesterday he'd talked as if he was scared, but he hadn't lost his sense of humor. I remember him playing a hurdy-gurdy at a carnival once and the peasants, who didn't know who he was, threw money into his cap. We walked by him, too, and Haryk threw him a ten-crown note and Benno thanked him respectfully. He gave the guy who'd loaned him the hurdy-gurdy a thousand crowns for letting him use it half a day. But he could afford it. His dad's shop was doing good business.

"You're looking sharp, Benno," I said.

"Hail to our homeland," said Benno.

"All hail!" said Haryk.

"So you're in already?" I said, because I saw they were all wearing those mourning bands on their arms.

"You bet. Answering our country's call," said Lexa.

"I'm going to get in line."

"Go on, then come back here. We'll make up an exemplary body of fighting men."

I laughed and went up to the door and took my place in line. Hrob, a redheaded kid I'd known in grade school, was just ahead of me. He looked at me with those great big eyes of his.

"Hello," he said in a respectful voice.

"Hello," I answered, very friendly. Hrob had mild blue eyes. I remembered him—how he'd excelled in two things in school. He'd been absolutely incapable of learning the multiplication tables so he'd dropped out of school in fourth grade, but he was always so quiet and mild that the teacher had a hard time before finally deciding to flunk him. He really didn't excel so much in the second thing. It just brought him fame. That was one time in second grade, I guess, when we were still just little kids and we used to have peeing contests in the john at recess. Who could sprinkle the wall most. Ponykl won. He got all the way up to the strip of black tar paint and made a gorgeous palm tree on the wall. Hrob just watched us, but then all of a sudden he smiled, unbuttoned his fly, took out his little peter, bowed, and then a fine yellowish stream spurted out like a fountain and gradually went higher and higher up the wall. But still not as high as Ponykl's. Hrob leaned back a little bit more and he shouldn't have done that because the yellow stream dropped back from the wall and before the poor kid could duck, it fell back on his head, obeying the law of gravitation. The kids razzed him about it for the rest of his school career. Now there he stood in front of me, looking at me with those big, docile, respectful blue eyes. He had on a neat blue suit made of reject material by which you could always recognize the workers from Lewith's weaving mill on Sunday.

"You going to enlist too?" I said to him.

"Yes."

"Me, too," I said, and that was all.

Hrob said nothing. He never talked much. We stood there mutely and the line moved slowly into the building. We got into the hall and shuffled forward. The others who'd been through already came out, pulling on their armbands. Another guy in uniform stood by the office door with a fixed bayonet and whenever someone came out, he let in another one. The line was quiet. Nobody shoved. I was already nearly up to the door. They let Hrob go in and I stayed outside. The soldier with the bayonet was kidding around with some guy behind me. Then the door opened, Hrob emerged with a glowing face, reverently clutching his armband. I went in. Mr. Kuratko sat at the desk wearing a captain's uniform and with a big ledger opened up in front of him. Four paper flags—Czechoslovak, Soviet, American, and British—stood on his desk in a little vase. There was no water in it. On one side of Captain Kuratko sat old Cemelik with colonel's stars on his epaulets and on the other side was Mr. Manes with a blue armband with red trim and the inscription, NATIONAL COMMITTEE, in gold letters. Around a little table in the corner sat Dr. Sabata, Mr. Kaldoun, Mayor Prudivy, and Krocan the factory owner. So it wasn't Mr. Kaldoun who'd hauled in the flag, I realized. All of them were wearing those blue armbands with the red trim. The men behind the desk were watching me.

"Good morning," I said, but Mr. Manes and old Cemelik acted as if they didn't recognize me. They were acting very grim, like men at war. There they all sat, staging an uprising. People were pushing and shoving to get in and lay down their lives for their country while these men, in their own way, were doing their bit for their country, too. Mr. Kaldoun, Mr. Krocan, Dr. Sabata. They'd all gotten along pretty well with the Germans. Now they were running a revolution. Nobody could find any fault with them. Everybody was mobilized. Everybody had to obey. So everything was fine. And Colonel Cemelik was giving the orders.

"Name?" Captain Kuratko asked me.

"Daniel Smiricky."

Mr. Kuratko wrote my name down in the first column of his ledger and put a number in front of it. Then he went on.

"Occupation?"

"Student."

"Date of birth?"

"Twenty-seventh of September, 1924."

"Where?"

"In Kostelec."

"Kostelec County. Address?"

"Kostelec."

"Street?"

"123 Jirasek."

"Religion?"

"Roman Catholic."

"Inducted?"

"I beg your pardon?"

"Have you been inducted?"

"No."

"Has not done his military service."

Mr. Kuratko wrote a long sentence in his ledger, then took a mimeographed sheet of paper from a pile beside him, wrote something on it and handed it to me.

"Read this and sign it."

It read: "I, *Daniel Smiricky,*" which Mr. Kuratko had written in by hand, "*pledge on my honor and conscience that I will loyally obey all orders given by the local commander of the Czechoslovak Army in Kostelec and that I am ready if necessary to lay down my life for my country, the Czechoslovak Republic. Kostelec, — May, 1945.*" I took a pen, wrote in the date, May 6th, and signed my name. Mr. Kuratko gave the sheet of paper to Mr. Manes and he put it into a file in front of him. Then Mr. Kuratko shook hands with me.

"Thank you," he said.

"You're quite welcome," I said. Then old Cemelik shook hands with me, and Mr. Manes, too. He gave me a red-and-white armband from the basket beside the table. The basket was full of them.

"Thank you," I said and turned around. I opened the door and the soldier was already shoving somebody else inside. So now I was a private in the Czechoslovak Army. Now I belonged to the revolutionaries. I pulled on the armband and felt it looked silly. But nobody was looking at me any differently than usual. So this was an uprising. I went out of the building. The brewery yard was swarming with people. They were standing around in clusters, wearing all kinds of coats and jackets and raincoats, and they had knapsacks on their backs. They were smoking and talking. They looked more like a hiking club getting ready for an outing. But they were an army. These were revolutionaries. There wasn't much you could do about it. Colonel Cemelik was at the head of the army and the supreme commander was Dr. Sabata. It was an army. And I was in it.

I went down the stairs and looked for the boys. It had started raining again. Coat collars were turned up in the courtyard and people ducked into various doorways and sheds. But a lot of them still stood out in the yard. I buttoned my jacket up to my neck. Hell, why hadn't I worn a raincoat? I headed across the yard toward the icehouse. I didn't see the boys there but I heard the signal. We'd used that signal for as long as I can remember. It had caught on in town; even kids who didn't have anything to do with the band used it. I looked around. The rain started pouring down on the worn cobblestone pavement that led to the stable. People stood pressed up against the sides of buildings. I heard the signal again and looked around to see where it came from. I saw Benno's red face under his sheepskin cap and Haryk in his green raincoat. They were standing under a woodshed over by the fence. I hurried over to them.

"Greetings, brother," Haryk said to me.

"Greetings. Let me under," I said and crept in under the roof. It was dark and chilly and there were lots of other people in there, but you could hardly make them out in the dark. I stood between Benno and Haryk and looked out at the rain. It swept in sheets over the pavement and the fine chilly mist cooled my face. It felt good, standing there in the dark shed looking out at the rain.

"All actions canceled because of the weather," said Benno.

"In its first attempt to seize the offensive, the First Army Company got its feet wet," said Haryk.

"The offensive was repelled by Colonel Cemelik's unexpected attack of rheumatism," said Benno.

"Shut up," said Fonda from inside the shed. The boys stopped. I turned around and all I could make out in the darkness were a lot of pale faces and eyes. There was a little hole in the back wall of the shed that let in some light. We didn't say anything for a while. More people rushed over to the shed and pushed inside. But there was still plenty of room. By now all I could see was a patch of the courtyard over the dark heads of the people in front of me. Colonel Cemelik, wearing a green cape, walked across that little patch; the water trickled off his cap and down his face but he went on valiantly, taking his time. When he disappeared, the space was empty again. I leaned out and saw there was hardly anything left of the line now, just a handful of people up by the door. They must have been soaked to the skin by now. Then Cemelik appeared again and behind him came Hrob, his face glowing with enthusiasm, carrying a load of rifles on his back.

"Hey, look, reinforcements," said Haryk. Cemelik, with Hrob at his heels, disappeared into the main building. The rain kept on falling. The revolution was called off. Couldn't go on in a downpour like this. I could just imagine how glad this rain must have made Dr. Sabata feel. Sound the retreat and then there goes the army into a shed. Above the brewery the sky was white and gray with rain.

"Danny, is that you?" I heard behind me. It was Rosta. I recognized his voice immediately.

"Yeah, where are you?"

"Here. Come on and sit down."

I turned, but it was too dark to see. Somebody switched on a flashlight. The cone of light traveled over the ground. A pile of small logs was stacked up in the back of the shed. Some people were sitting on them, but there was still room. The flashlight gleamed from the top of the pile. Behind it I could see Rosta's face.

"Okay," I said and started to scramble up over the logs. It wasn't easy, but I made it. I sat down beside Rosta. The logs were rough so you could feel them on your behind, but it was better to sit down than stand up.

The rain was falling steadily on the roof of the shed, making an awful racket. We sat there high up in the dark on the pile of wood, and now I couldn't see into the yard at all. All I could see were the dark silhouettes of people standing at the edge of the shed and the milky gloomy light beyond. I was overcome by a feeling of security. The drumming of the rain on the roof awoke all sorts of recollections. About the Giant Mountains and Ledecsky Rocks, about a shed like this one, only that one was for hay, at

Ledec. And how I sat there that time with Irena and Zdenek and black clouds were scudding low and crooked across the sky, but there was still a narrow strip of blue sky at the horizon and the rays of the sun came through that strip of blue and shone on the tops of the rocks. And there in that strip of blue, birch trees swayed in the wind and a dead man was hanging from one of them and Irena screamed and clung to Zdenek. It was dark in that shed and I felt lonely and rejected and there were those black clouds and the light disappeared behind them and the rain streamed down over the cliffs. Irena's teeth were chattering and she clung to Zdenek and I crawled out of the shed and stood under the leaking eaves. Rain dripped on me as I stood out there looking down into the valley at the gilded tops of the cliffs and at the rainbow bulging above them and at the birch trees and at the dead man hanging there and at the dark pine woods in the rain, and behind me in the cabin was Irena with Zdenek and I was all alone and alone and alone.

It was dark inside the shed and suddenly warm and then suddenly cool again. It was very nice and we sat on the damp logs and for a while said nothing.

"Listen," said Rosta.

"What?"

"Aren't you fed up with this?"

"I'll say."

"Me, too."

"You look tired."

"I am."

"Why? What'd you do yesterday?"

"We had a binge up at the cabin."

"With Honza?"

"Yeah."

"And some girls?"

"Naturally."

I didn't say anything. I knew Rosta pretty well and I knew what was on his mind.

"How's it going with Dagmar?" I asked.

"Don't ask me."

"She still giving you a hard time?"

"I'll say."

"And you're still crazy about her?"

"I sure am. How's it going with you?"

"What?"

"With Irena?"

"Oh. Well, I'm still in love with her."

"So we're in the same boat, huh?"

"I guess we are."

Rosta fell silent. Then, "You know what we are?" he said. "We're a couple of . . ."

"Fools. I know."

"But still, you know something?"

"What?"

"I don't know quite how to say it, but I just wish those dumb girls had some idea how much a guy has to suffer on account of them."

"Yeah. You're right. But it's all for nothing—all that suffering."

"You think so?"

"I know so."

"Listen, though, I'm still going to marry Dagmar someday."

"Well, anything's possible."

"No, honest."

"Yeah, sure. You might do in a pinch."

"What do you mean by that?"

"Just what I say."

"Which is?"

"Well, I mean if she goes on horsing around."

"You mean—"

"Yeah, with Kocandrle. If he knocks her up—"

"You know something? That wouldn't even bother me," said Rosta.

"I know it wouldn't."

"Honest. I'm so crazy about her she could be a whore if she wanted to and it wouldn't make any difference to me."

"I know."

"Anyway, everything I do is just for her sake anyway."

I thought about my Last Will and Testament. That's what I'd written in it, too. Everything I've done has been for you only, Irena, or something to that effect.

"Rosta," I said.

"What?"

"Did you know that I've already written my Last Will and Testament?"

"Really?"

"Yes."

"And what'd you write in it?"

"Well, it's actually a letter to Irena, understand?"

"Yeah."

"A farewell message."

"Gee, I should have done that, too."

"Well, you still can."

"Who'd you give it to?"

"I've got it in my wallet. I addressed it to her."

"What'd you write in it?"

"Everything. How much I love her and so on."

"Hell, why didn't I write something like that, too?"

"It's not too late yet."

"Yeah, but where?"

"When it stops raining."

"I will, too," said Rosta, and then he fell silent again, thinking. After awhile he said, "Just imagine how it'll be when the girls get them."

"Boy, how about that?"

"Just imagine how they'll bawl."

"Or maybe not."

"Yeah, maybe not. But at least it'll make them feel pretty strange."

"Except it's never going to come to that."

"What do you mean?"

"You don't really think anybody's going to get killed in this thing, do you?"

"Maybe."

"Maybe. But I wouldn't count on it." I was silent. I could tell that Rosta didn't really believe anyone would get killed either. We sat there in silence looking at the light outside the shed.

"Oh, well," I said.

"Yeah, you said it," said Rosta. It felt good to sit there

and talk about girls and not to mean anything very seriously. And to go into this revolution as unhappy lovers. As I recalled, I was always most in love with Irena when I was in some kind of fix. That time with the sabotage at the factory. Or when they arrested Father and I was expecting them to arrest me, too. Still the trouble couldn't be too serious. When it was then I forgot all about Irena. Like yesterday when they were taking me off to be executed. Now, though, things weren't that bad. Now it was good, being in love with Irena and thinking about her.

"Listen," I said.

"What?"

"What are you here for anyway?"

"What do you mean?"

"Why are you risking your neck here?"

"Well . . ."

"I'm here on account of Irena," I said hurriedly so he couldn't get in ahead of me.

"Sure. Me, too. On account of Dagmar," said Rosta. Then he went on. "You think anything'll come of all this?"

"Could be."

"It sure doesn't look that way, though, does it?"

"Well, nothing'll happen down here at the brewery. But the communists'll pull something."

"You think so?"

"Absolutely."

"Well, fine. It's all the same to me."

"Me, too," I said, and it was. Not quite, though. I wanted them to pull something since it was pretty clear this army here wouldn't do much. And something had to happen. If the revolution had already started, then something had better happen, and I thought about Irena. The rain eased up a little. It was just drizzling now. We sat there in silence, thinking our separate thoughts. Time passed. All of a sudden some of the guys in front rushed out of the shed.

"What is it?" I called.

"They're going to read a proclamation," somebody yelled up in front.

"Should we go?" I said to Rosta.

"Okay," said Rosta and got up.

We climbed down the pile of logs and brushed off our pants. Outside, the yard was full again. The crowd had gathered in front of the main building. There on the steps by the front door stood Colonel Cemelik, Major Weiss, and Dr. Sabata. Colonel Cemelik wasn't wearing his cape any more and he was holding a sheaf of papers. The crowd, in their hiking outfits and raincoats, with their knapsacks strapped on their backs, pressed forward around the steps and stared up at the colonel. Cemelik started reading out something but we couldn't understand a word. The crowd buzzed and there were yells of "Quiet!" and "Listen!" Cemelik stopped reading and looked out over the crowd and gradually it quieted down. Then Cemelik started reading again, but he had such a weak voice you could just barely hear him. He said something about all squads being divided up into six-man patrol squads, each under the command of an older, more experienced soldier and that, in order to assure order and security, these teams would conduct three-hour patrols through the town. That really made me sore. I'd thought this army would at least put up antitank traps or something and lie in wait for the enemy. But patrol? Then Cemelik raised his voice.

"First Lieutenant Dr. Panozka!"

"Here!" somebody called out from the crowd.

"Lieutenant, you'll take charge of patrol team number one," said Cemelik. Then he told him to stand over by the icehouse and read out the names of his squad. He held the list in front of him and his voice sounded very crisp and military. Lexa and Pedro were in it. I could see them working their way through the crowd toward Dr. Panozka. He stood over by the icehouse in his hunting coat, his hands folded over his paunch, waiting for the members of his squad. I listened some more. They were all there. Mr. Moutelik, Commissioner Machacek, Attorney Frinta, Mr. Jungwirth. They were all older, more experienced soldiers and they each got their six picked privates. A magnificent army. And it was in good hands. Then all of a sudden Cemelik read out my name, too, and I belonged to Dr. Bohadlo's patrol. I knew him, too. He was a lawyer. I saw him standing by the icehouse in his tight-fitting knickers, a plump guy with a big bottom, chubby legs, a pudgy face, and a blue beret on top of his head. Benno in his cap and Haryk were already standing beside him and three other guys I only knew by sight. I joined them.

"How do you do?" I said to Dr. Bohadlo.

"Hello there. Welcome," he said benignly, and his mouth stretched a little as if he were smiling.

"Hi," said Haryk.

"Hi," I said.

Then we all stood there silently and waited until the army had been divided up. It was already noon and I was hungry. I'd had about all I could take of this rain and this hunger and these patrols and this army. I wanted some food. I wondered what was going to happen now. Whether they'd dismiss us to go home for lunch or whether they had a field kitchen somewhere and were going to serve soup. I would rather have gone home because it was Sunday. But a soup kitchen had its attractions, too.

"Jesus, I'm hungry," I said.

"Me, too," said Haryk. "Aren't you, Benno?"

"Shut up," said Benno. He was mad. With his dimensions, it was no surprise. I was convinced you could have heard his stomach growling with hunger if it hadn't been for all the noise. We looked at Cemelik. The crowd around him had thinned out and broken up into small groups scattered around the yard. Then Cemelik stopped reading and announced that all patrol commanders should report to his office for further instructions.

"Well, I'll be going, boys," said Dr. Bohadlo. "You'll wait here for me, right?"

"Yes," said Haryk.

"Sure," Benno and I said.

Dr. Bohadlo left. He trotted off on his chubby little legs, bouncing along because he suffered from shortened tendons or something. We stood there. It started raining again so we got up next to the wall of the icehouse and looked around. Steam rose from the woods beyond the brewery. It was noontime and quiet. I could imagine the fires crackling in kitchen stoves all over town and the pots on top of the stoves bubbling away and giving off good smells. But the menfolk wouldn't be coming home for lunch today because they'd patrol the town. It was like at a county Sokol festival or something. And then I thought about Irena again. Christ, I thought about her all the time. A two-seat Aero roadster drove into the yard and Jirka Krocan jumped out. He had on a leather coat. A Czechoslovak flag fluttered from the radiator cap. I thought about Irena. God, maybe that was all I could think about. And I was supposed to be one of the intelligentsia. I would have liked to know what the intelligentsia thinks about and if they really think about the things they say they do. Naturally, inventors and scientists and people like that think about their bacteria and electrodes and so on. But I meant the ordinary intelligentsia. Like me and Benno and Haryk. And Irena. Irena told me once that she went into the woods by herself with the dog to think. About literature and politics and I don't know what all. And I felt secretly embarrassed when she told me that, because when I'm alone usually all I ever think about is girls, and I felt inferior compared to her. But that had been a long time ago. An awfully long time ago. I wasn't like that any more. I didn't trouble my head with thoughts any more. I'd already caught on to what it was all about, to what really mattered. Nothing really mattered. Or, if anything did, then it was girls and having as much fun as you could with them. I wondered what Benno was thinking about and figured he was probably thinking about lunch now, and then once in a while about Helena and music, and Haryk was probably thinking about music, about "Swingin' the Blues" and "Sweet Sue" where he's got a big guitar solo, but you don't really think about music, you just get the whole band playing in your head and you play all the instruments simultaneously, getting dazzling effects from the trombone's lowest registers and letting the trumpet squeal away. That's how you think about music, and you don't need intellect for that either. In general, it seemed to me that intelligence was something awfully vague, even nonexistent, and that probably the only intelligent people were Socrates and Einstein and people like that. But besides them nobody. And so, so what if I was thinking about Irena? I liked thinking about her, about her mouth and her breasts and her hips and about how it'd feel to have it all there under your hands and about what's under her skirt and my thoughts were as common as dirt and I felt fine all the same.

"Shit," said Benno.

"What's wrong?" said Haryk.

"What're they shitting around for? They want us to sit around here all day without having lunch?"

"It looks that way."

"You'd think they could at least set up a goddamn field kitchen!"

Benno was so mad he couldn't see straight. Rain dripped off his cap and his ruddy face looked dangerous. The gentlemen with the blue-and-red armbands emerged from the main building. Each carried a sheet of paper. As they stepped out into the rain, they started turning up their collars and stuffing their papers into their pockets. Then each walked off to his own squad. Dr. Bohadlo, his face glowing and pompous, came over to us.

"Well, boys, let's form up and get going," he said.

"Where?" said Benno.

"We've been assigned the center of town as far as Pozner's factory, then down around the old Jewish Cemetery, through the ghetto, and then back here to the brewery."

"And what're we going to do?"

"We'll make the rounds every three hours and then have three hours free."

"And we're going right now?"

"Yes. It's half past twelve now, so this time we'll make an exception and patrol for only two and a half hours."

"You mean we're not going to have any lunch?"

"You'll survive. This once," smiled Dr. Bohadlo.

"That's a lousy trick to pull. Without food I'm not going anywhere," said Benno and he meant it.

Dr. Bohadlo took it as a joke though and he laughed. "Fine, then. A small sacrifice for the Fatherland," he said. "You're in the army now. Line up two by two behind me." Then he turned his back on us and lifted his hand like they do in Sokol when you're supposed to fall in.

"Shit," said Benno softly.

The three guys whose names I didn't know promptly fell in behind Dr. Bohadlo. The third one looked around at us and Benno shoved Haryk up to stand next to him. Haryk stuck his hands in his raincoat pockets. Meanwhile Dr. Bohadlo still stood there with his arm up in the air and his knickers stretching across his fat behind. The two boys in the first row stood at attention behind him. The guy next to Haryk did, too. Haryk stood hunched over, his collar turned up against the rain.

"In step now—hup!" said Dr. Bohadlo and flung out his left leg. The three boys leaned suddenly to the left and started off on their left feet, too. Haryk lagged behind, but soon got in step. Benno and I brought up the rear. Before long we were pretty far behind the others.

"Damn," I said.

"Jerks," said Benno and then we hurried up to join the column. With Dr. Bohadlo in the lead, we marched along over the cobblestone pavement toward the gate. It wasn't so bad, marching along in step. I looked around and saw nobody was looking at us. So it wasn't too bad. Anyway there were plenty of other centipedes just like us all following their red-and-blue armbanded leaders. As we neared the gate, I saw it was closed. A man in uniform stood in front of the gate, a sergeant's insignia on his epaulets. He held a rifle with a fixed bayonet. Dr. Bohadlo headed straight for the gate. The sergeant raised his rifle, opened the gate, and we swung right through like the London Horse Guard. Dr. Bohadlo executed a faultless left turn. We marched along the highway toward the bridge. I looked left, off toward the Port Arthur. Then we crossed the bridge and I looked up at Irena's window. Nobody there. Not a face in sight. We marched quietly toward the station. Mrs. Manesova was standing on the corner in front of the County Office Building. When she saw us, she hurried after us.

"When are you coming home, Benno?" she asked.

"I don't know."

"When will they let you go?"

"I don't know."

"Aren't you hungry? Don't you want something to eat?"

We kept marching along at an unslackened pace with Mrs. Manesova trotting alongside.

"Got anything with you?" asked Benno eagerly.

"No. I thought you were coming home."

"I don't know when I'll get back. No idea when they'll let us go."

"Where are you going?"

"To Pozner's and back."

"So then I . . . I'll pack you a lunch and wait here for you, all right?"

"Yes. Do that."

"All right," Mrs. Manesova stopped. Benno turned.

"Or else, maybe . . . how about bringing it to the brewery for me."

"Where?" said Mrs. Manesova, hurrying after us again.

"To the brewery, by the gate."

"All right. I'll wrap you up a piece of the rabbit. Would you like that?"

"Yeah. And some salami."

"Yes. By the brewery gate, is that right?"

"Yeah. So long now."

"Goodby."

Mrs. Manesova stood there looking after us. I glanced over at Benno. He was satisfied. Haryk turned around.

"Then you'll be ready to fight—right, Benno?" he said.

"Right."

"Quiet, boys. No talking on patrol," said Dr. Bohadlo.

We stopped talking. We crossed the tracks and turned up past the Messerschmidt plant on Jirasek Boulevard. There were only a few people out. Most of the men had gone to the brewery and the women were sitting at home. I saw my parents looking out the window. Father was an invalid from the First World War so he didn't have to take part in this. I pretended I hadn't seen them. I didn't know quite how I should have greeted them. We passed under our window and kept on going. Marching right out here on the street was the bad part. It was silly, marching around without any guns. Still, the few people we did come across

E*

looked at us respectfully. And it went right on raining. I was starting to feel cold. We marched across the square, around Sokol Hall, past the high school and down Kocanda Street to Pozner's factory. Pozner's house stood silent and the blinds were all down. I wondered what Blanka, Pozner's daughter, was doing. She always came to high school in a car driven by a chauffeur and I knew she must be scared now since she was hysterical anyway. Lucie had told me once that Blanka got temper tantrums and rolled all over the floor, and that she gave the servants there a very rough time. Lucie and Blanka had been sort of half friends but not close at all since Blanka wasn't really friendly with any of the local girls. And last year she'd gone off to take dancing lessons in Prague every week by car. I thought about her, because she was really very pretty, a special kind of beauty that was all mixed up with those millions that were waiting for her. Actually, they weren't waiting for her now since old Pozner would be locked up. Not that anybody really wanted to lock him up since none of the local bigwigs had anything special against him. They'd more or less all gone along with him, at least until up to just recently. But he'd compromised himself too much. It couldn't be overlooked any more. And then there was young Pozner. Rene, with his gold rings and sports clothes. And his post as chief engineer out at the factory. And going hunting with Miss Arnostova who came all the way from Moravia as Rene's fiancée and went out with the family to chamber concerts and to banquets thrown for the German officers. A stupid family, the Pozners. Lada Serpon was a millionaire, too, but he was a great guy compared to Rene. Rene was a dunce. I didn't have anything against millionaires or feel any envy at all, but Rene was a stuck-up jackass. I really wanted those Pozners to be sitting in their living-room or somewhere trembling all over with fright. We turned back around the factory and into the ghetto, past the old Jewish Cemetery with its toppled gravestones. There weren't any Jews in the ghetto any more. We passed the old Jewish school and I thought about Mr. Katz, the cantor I used to go to for my German lessons, and it made me feel sad. On Jew Street, the rain came down in an even more melancholy way than before and the battered old school stood there. I remembered the evenings long ago in the cantor's kitchen when we'd forget about grammar and literature for a while, forget about Goethe and Schiller and Chamisso, and just talk about the Germans and grumble and the old cantor would lament. What we Jews have gone through, he said, that is something nobody knows—nobody. And from the corner where the stove was and where the embers glowed, the cantor's fat old wife would murmur her agreement and the cantor would start telling me what the Germans were planning to do to the Jews and I'd reassure him that it wasn't going to be like that, but knew it would be, so then I'd change the subject and talk about the cantor's little granddaughter Hannerle, and then the cantor would forget all about everything else and take out the Hebrew primer he'd already bought for when she'd start to school, but she never did because less than a year later they were all shipped off to the gas ovens. They never came back. I thought about grubby ugly little Hannerle and about her black-haired mother and about the matzohs the cantor always gave me on holidays and about the times I'd cautiously slip out of school so nobody—not even any of my best friends—would notice that I still went to the cantor's house. And then as we marched through the ghetto, I remembered Bondy who used to live farther on down the street and at whose house we first began to put our band together, and the old xylophone on which I used to play "Donkey Serenade," and Bondy's rotting old grandfather dying in the next room of paralysis, and Mr. Bondy who hung on to his shop until the very last minute, and his pianist's fingers and his Mendelssohn, and as we passed the synagogue with its broken windows I remembered the cantor's daughter's wedding when the synagogue was full of hats and the rabbi's wedding sermon full of optimism and joy, and all the Kostelec Jews were there in all their finery, Mr. Pick, a director at our bank, Dr. Strass, all white and tiny, the Steins and the Goldsteins and the cantor's daughter and all the mystical talk about the prenuptial ceremonies for an Orthodox Jewish bride. I could imagine it all again, absolutely clear and distinct. I imagined her naked in the bath with all the Jewish women of Kostelec around, washing her and mumbling prayers. I didn't know whether that was the way they really did it or not but it was nice to think about and we kept on going, past the well with the Hebrew inscription at the end of the ghetto, and somehow it all made me feel terribly sad. Dr. Bohadlo, stuffed into his silly-looking knickers, the back of his fat little neck all red, marched along briskly. But all those others were gone—the cantor and the rabbi and Hannerle and all of them. Tears came to my eyes and my throat tightened up. Christ! I'm as sentimental as an old whore. But I felt sad. What did I care about the rabbi? What did I care about them? It was probably just all those memories. But they were nice memories. But then memories always were.

We were back on Jirasek Boulevard again and I didn't feel tears in my eyes any more. It disappointed me to feel there weren't tears in my eyes any more. We marched along the right side of the street. It was practically deserted and my feet were hurting me now and I was hungry and cold. The uprising wasn't fun at all any more. This whole damn uprising against the Germans and Dr. Bohadlo's military games. If other people wanted to play war with him I didn't mind, but I was fed up with the whole thing. A platoon of Germans, armed to the teeth, came toward us. For a minute I felt tense and wondered what was going to happen. But they didn't pay any attention to us. They just passed by and I noticed them peering out at us curiously from under their iron helmets. Of course. Dr. Sabata had arranged a truce. We marched down the street toward the station and past the County Office Building and over the bridge and back to the brewery. Mrs. Manesova was standing by the gate with a package. Dr. Bohadlo didn't even so much as glance at her, though normally he would have greeted her courteously. But now he was on patrol. He strode straight toward the gate. The sergeant opened it.

"Here you are, Benno," said Mrs. Manesova. "You think it'll be enough for you?"

"Yeah. Thanks," said Benno and took the package and

then we were in the courtyard again. I turned around and saw Mrs. Manesova standing at the gate looking at us through the bars. But Benno was already unwrapping the package.

"Company, halt!" said Dr. Bohadlo and wheeled around to face us.

"All right, boys, there'll be fifteen minutes' rest and then we go out again."

"What time is it, Doctor?" said Haryk.

"Quarter to two. Just time for one more round."

"Thank you."

"Wait here for me. I'll be right back," said Dr. Bohadlo and walked off. We leaned against the shed. My feet were hurting bad.

"You going to let us see what you got?" said Haryk.

Benno unwrapped the package and took out half a roast rabbit.

"I'll eat this myself," he said. Then he pulled out a long hunk of salami and a couple of bread-and-butter sandwiches. He gave me one and one to Haryk and told us to cut the salami in three. We divided it up and started eating. The salami tasted wonderful. We stood there and watched what was going on in the yard. Apparently everything was running smoothly. The patrols came and went, wet and hungry. Men in officer's capes crossed the yard now and then, carrying sheets of paper, and guys in red-and-white armbands crowded under the eaves around the buildings and sheds. A stream from the main building's rainspout trickled along the pavement toward the gate.

"See anybody?" said Haryk.

"No," I said. All the boys we knew were out on patrol apparently.

"I've got an ocean inside my shoes," said Haryk.

"Me, too."

We didn't say anything. After a while, Haryk said, "Boy, this really pisses me off."

"Me, too," said Benno.

"They can stuff this whole business. I sure didn't think it was going to be like this."

"Some fun," I said. "All we'll do is catch cold and then

we won't even be around for the liberation."

Dr. Bohadlo reappeared. "Well, boys, all rested up?" he said.

Benno growled.

"All right, let's go," said Dr. Bohadlo energetically, and he turned his rump toward us again. His fat hiker's calves got on my nerves. I was already aching all over from this marching around and I couldn't see any point in it. If we meet Irena, all wet and unarmed like this, I'd really look like a fool. Dr. Bohadlo flung up his arm; we fell into formation behind him and started off on another silent tramp. It was an awful bore. We went through town in a steady rain and finally tottered back to the brewery, half dead and soaked to the skin. Dr. Bohadlo still looked fresh though.

"Can we go home now?" I asked him.

He smiled. "Home? Why, no. You'll be staying in the barracks, boys."

"Barracks? Where?"

"Here, in the brewery. Now you've got three hours' rest and at six we start off on patrol again."

"Are we going to get something to eat?" said Benno.

"Go over to the warehouse. There's tea there. And everybody report back here by six. Right?"

"Right," said the three boys we didn't know.

"Dismissed," said Dr. Bohadlo.

The boys clicked their heels and snapped to attention.

"Adieu," said Benno.

Dr. Bohadlo walked away.

"What say we go get some tea?" I said.

"Why not? But where?" said Benno.

"I don't know. At the warehouse."

"Which warehouse?"

"Don't know. Let's ask."

Jirka Vit was just going by with some kind of papers. They'd apparently made him a messenger boy.

"Hey, Jirka, where're they giving out tea?" I yelled after him.

"Over there," he said and pointed to a big open door where a couple of guys were standing.

"Thanks," I said, and we went over.

It was dark with just one dim light bulb in the ceiling, and in that dim light you could make out a few shadowy figures going out through another door in the back of the building. Some sort of machines were stored off to one side in the dark. We opened the back door and in the light ahead of us saw a big arched room crowded with guys in rain-drenched clothes holding steaming cups and plates. In the back, white steam rose to the ceiling. We elbowed our way through the mob and I saw Mrs. Cemelikova in a white apron standing beside a big pot ladling out tea. There was another door in the back and two fat women were just bringing in a big tray piled with bread. Then in came Dagmar Dreslerova, also wearing a white apron and a dish towel. She went over to Mrs. Cemelikova and said something to her. Mrs. Cemelikova nodded and Dagmar turned. She looked pretty good in the middle of all that kitchen crew. I looked around to see if Irena was around somewhere. But she wasn't. We stood in line for the tea and slowly moved up toward the pot. I picked up a cup and Mrs. Cemelikova poured in a ladle of ersatz tea for me and I said hello and thank you and she gave me a nice smile and then I got a slice of dry bread from Mrs. Skocdopolova who was standing next to her. I stuck the bread in my pocket and we went around the corner. Somebody called to us. I turned. It was Lexa and he was sitting by the wall with Pedro on an upturned crate. We went over to them.

"Hi," said Haryk.

"Hi," said Lexa. "Well, have you already done your patriotic duty?"

"That's right. And now we're coming to fortify the inner man."

"Not much to fortify yourself with here."

"Well, here goes anyway," said Haryk and sat down next to Lexa. The next crate was empty and we pulled it over. Benno and I sat down opposite them. New guys kept crowding around us, wet and steaming, clutching their steaming cups. It reminded me of when they used to butcher at Count Humprecht's big farm where I'd gone once on a work brigade during vacation. They'd done that in a cellar, too, all murky and dark just like this one. Beside me, Benno noisily slurped his tea and Pedro and Lexa gnawed at the dry bread. The tea was hot and I thought about the past and the feeling I'd had when I was a little kid in bed and used to make a snowy igloo out of my eiderdown quilt, or how I'd lie there while Mother and Father were still reading and pretend I was camping, but in a meadow, and the feeble light of Father's bedside lamp was the dying light of the campfire. So there we sat in the steamy half-light and one shadow after another flitted across the faces of the boys in front of me and shadows danced and flickered and shifted on the wall beyond and I thought about the Countess Humprecht with her hawk-beak nose and the big dusty room in the castle and about me teaching her how to play the piano instead of working on the harvest and about her legs in her riding breeches, and my thoughts roamed out over the fields around Rounov with the girls in their bright-colored dresses and to the pheasants and the tree-lined drive and I saw the Gestapo taking the young Count Humprecht away that night before I was supposed to leave and then I remembered the Queen of Württemberg and Irena and it started all over again, like always. Those thoughts and memories wouldn't leave me alone and none of them had anything to do with anything I'd ever learned in school.

"Not bad, if you want to vomit," said Lexa and put his cup down on the floor.

"Boiled socks," said Benno.

"Think your old man drinks this stuff, too."

"Are you kidding?" said Pedro. "The command gets black coffee."

"What do they want with us anyway?" said Haryk.

"We're maintaining peace and order."

"And who's disturbing it?"

"Communists," said Pedro.

"I'd like to see 'em."

"Yeah, but they are. Seriously," said Lexa, "this afternoon they tried to loot the munitions train down at the station."

"Who said?"

"Dr. Sabata was there and got into a hassle with them."

"Well, did they finally loot it or not?"

"No. The guards wouldn't let them get in. They tried to talk the guards over and bribe them with booze but they wouldn't let them in."

"Sabata told you that?"

"No. Old man Cemelik told me. Now they're scared shitless that the commies are going to try and pull something tonight. They say they're going to step up the patrols."

"Are they going to give us guns?" I said.

"They don't give a shit about us," said Lexa.

"But we're supposed to go fight the commies, right?"

"Sure. For the sake of the nation."

"What a mess! What a goddamn stinking mess," said Benno.

"I'll second that motion," said Haryk.

"Nobody mentions the Germans any more, I guess."

"No. They've pulled out already."

"So what the hell are we still farting around for?"

Lexa grimaced. "Because there haven't been enough heroic deeds performed yet, that's why."

Suddenly people were shushing each other and the room quieted down and you could hear Mrs. Cemelikova saying in her shrill voice that all those who'd finished their tea should kindly make room for others. We picked ourselves up and took our cups over to the table. The hungry feeling I'd had was gone. We went out through the dark room with the light bulb in the ceiling and found ourselves back out in the yard again. In the meantime it had stopped raining but the sky was still overcast and mist from the woods hung low over the brewery. Men were strolling around the yard in clusters, their hands in their pockets, looking as if they had nothing to do. There wasn't a gun in sight.

"What the hell do they want to do with us anyway, keep us on ice?" said Haryk.

"Looks that way," said Lexa.

"Didn't old Cemelik say when he'd let us go home?" asked Benno.

"When the danger's over and everything's safe again."

"And all we're going to get is tea?"

"Bread, too," said Lexa.

"Look, I say we clear the hell out," said Haryk.

"Yeah, but how?"

"Over the fence."

"They got guards all over the place."

"Just like in a concentration camp," said Benno.

"Exactly."

"You mean we're just supposed to hang around here all day until . . ."

"You're in the army now," said Lexa.

"We got screwed," said Benno.

"Jesus bloody Christ," said Haryk.

"Shit. Just one big shit," said Lexa.

None of us said anything for a while. Then Haryk said, "Hell. Next time they send us out on patrol, I'm taking off."

"And the next thing you know you're up in front of a court-martial for desertion," said Lexa.

"Oh, don't feed me that."

"You don't think they can?"

"But the whole thing's a farce!"

"Except they take it seriously."

"Like hell."

"Sure. Just ask old Cemelik."

"What can they do to me?"

"They'll put you in jail so long you'll come out on crutches."

"Nuts."

"And you'll never be able to go to college either."

"Old Cemelik said that?"

"Yeah. I asked him because I wanted to clear out, too."

"To hell with the whole thing," I said. "Let's go over and sit in the shed."

"All right," said Lexa, and we started off. The shed where I'd sat that morning with Rosta was empty—except for Rosta, sitting on his old perch. We climbed up on a pile of logs and sat down. It was cold in there, but the darkness inside the shed and the bright view outside gave me the same good feeling I'd had before. I slid over next to Rosta.

"How's it going?" said Rosta.

"And with you?" I asked.

"Did you see Dagmar?"

"Yeah. She's looking fine."

"I was talking to her."

"Yeah? Well?"

"I told her again."

"And what did she say?"

"The same as always."

"What did you say?"

"That I hoped she'd remember me in case anything happened to me."

"What'd she say to that?"

"She said I got on her nerves."

"Huh?"

"That I got on her nerves."

"Why?"

"Because there were more important things to think about now and because she was getting pretty fed up with that kind of talk."

We didn't say anything for a while. Then I said, "You know something? She's just stupid."

"No, she isn't."

"She is, too."

"She is not."

"She is. Or else she really doesn't give a damn about you and is just giving you a rough time."

"That's more like it."

"Girls are bitches," I said.

"They sure are."

"I know the sort of more important things she's thinking about these days."

"Me, too. Kocandrle."

"She still going with him?"

"Yeah."

"You think he's already laid her?"

"Sure. He was bragging about it over at the Port Arthur."

"He talks big."

"Yeah, but I know it for a fact."

"How?"

"I ran into them at Habry on New Year's Eve. They were coming out of Kocandrle's cabin."

"Well, she's a tramp, that's all."

"That doesn't keep me from loving her though."

"I know."

"I can't help it. I don't care how much of a tramp she is, I'm still crazy about her."

"I know. It's the same with me," I said.

"You think Zdenek's laid Irena, too?" Rosta asked interestedly.

"Sure. They spent three days together at Ledecsky Rocks."

"And you're still crazy about her, right?"

"Sure. What would I do if I wasn't?"

"Anyway, it's nonsense the way so many guys get all worked up about whether a girl's a virgin or not."

"I'll say. It doesn't make any difference to me."

"Me neither."

"Then what are you worrying about anyway?"

"What? Well, that she won't let me lay her, too."

"And if she would, the fact that Kocandrle had had her before wouldn't bother you?"

"No."

"I'm not so sure, Rosta," I said.

Rosta shook his head. "Not a bit. I know it wouldn't."

"I'm not so sure."

"Absolutely. Wouldn't bother me at all."

"I think you're just talking."

"No, I'm not."

"Well, I'm not so sure. I wouldn't find it all that easy myself," I said.

"I would," said Rosta.

"You're easy to please then."

"I am." Rosta just sat there for a minute and then suddenly went on in an anguished voice, "Jesus, what I've had to take from that woman! If only she knew! If only she had any idea what I've gone through for her!"

"She'd still shit on you," I said.

"Maybe."

"Sure she would. Women get a real kick out of that kind of thing."

"I know. So I've been told."

"Told what?"

"That I shouldn't let her know how crazy I am about her."

"That's stupid too," I said.

"You think so?"

"Sure. If you stop showing how you feel about her, she'll warm up a little, but once she's got her hooks into you again she'll ditch you again and you'll be worse off than you are now."

"You're right."

"Besides, don't you find it sort of fun to tell her how much you love her?"

"No. Not when she tells me to forget it, it isn't."

"It does me," I said.

"And when she tells you it's hopeless."

"Even then."

"Well, it doesn't me."

"It doesn't bother me. Because I'll get her one of these days."

"Are you so sure?"

"Absolutely."

The guys in front stood up. Their silhouettes were etched against the white background outside. A thin buzz sounded in the distance and grew steadily louder.

"A plane," said Benno, and he sounded scared.

"Wait!" said Pedro and listened. The buzzing came closer. It was fast, but it sounded kind of funny. Pedro listened tensely. He was an expert when it came to airplane engines. Then he stood up quickly. "It's a Storch!"

"Yeah?" said Benno with relief.

"Sure. I recognized it right away. Let's go."

We all rushed out. Out in the yard some guys were staring up at the sky and others running for cover. People were hugging the walls all over the place. We looked off toward where the sound was coming from and it kept getting louder, and then all of a sudden a plane appeared over the woods, so low that it looked pretty big, wide-winged and fuzzy in the mist, but still you could pick out all the details —the sturdy-looking undercarriage, the little wheels, the glassed-in cockpit. At first I thought maybe it might start shooting, but then I thought, no it didn't look big enough to mount a machine gun on. The plane seemed to be flying sort of funny, as if it was bouncing around in a strong wind, and then all of a sudden a big bunch of little white pieces of paper dropped out and came fluttering down through the air. "Leaflets!" somebody yelled. They fell slowly and the wind carried them off over the yard toward the woods. We scrambled after them. Off they went, most of them settling down in the woods. They sidled down softly onto the earth. But the wind blew some back and the crowd lunged first one way and then the other as the wind played with the falling papers. Pedro jumped up and grabbed hold of one. The crowd was pressing in around the few guys who'd managed to catch a leaflet. Pedro looked at it.

"Read it!" said Benno.

We crowded around Pedro and more people crowded around behind us. Pedro smoothed the paper out and started to read:

> To all units of the Schörner forces. All units and soldiers of the Greater German Army are hereby ordered to assist all Czech organizations whose purpose is *Ordnung zu erhalten* . . . maintaining order . . . and resisting the *Bolschewistischen Ordnungs- störer* . . . order breakers. Signed: Generaloberst Kurt Scholze.

Pedro handed the leaflet to the guy standing beside him and told him to translate it. Then we worked our way out of the crowd.

"*Also,*" said Pedro when we got back to the woodshed.

"Lovely," said Haryk.

"It's in the bag," I said. "They're going to look after us. Nothing can happen to us now."

"So we can go home, right?" said Haryk.

"Home? And what about all those Bolsheviks who're disturbing the peace? Who's going to fight them?" said Lexa.

"That's right. I guess I'd forgotten about them," said Haryk.

Then I saw Benda. He saw me and came over to the shed. He looked pale and worried.

"What's up?" I asked him.

"Prema," he said.

"What about him?"

"They arrested him. He's locked up in the cellar."

"What? Why?"

"For refusing to obey orders."

Benda looked at me and didn't seem to want to say any more about it. I'd have to pump him. The boys gathered around.

"Well, what's the story? What happened anyway?" I said.

"When they told him he had to hand over his weapons, he refused."

"And they arrested him just for that?"

"They didn't much care for the way he talked to them either."

"What are they planning to do with him anyway?"

"I don't know. They'll probably try him for insurrection."

"Skocdopole?" said Lexa.

"Yeah."

"Because he wouldn't give up his gun?"

"Yeah."

"When's the trial going to be?"

"I don't know. Later on, I guess."

"If they don't decide to make it a court-martial," said Lexa.

"You think they will? They wouldn't do that," said Benno soberly.

"They're just dumb enough," said Lexa.

"What are we going to do?" I asked.

"I don't know. I'm going to round up the boys first."

"You got anything in mind?"

"Maybe. We'll see."

"Jesus, something ought to be done," said Haryk.

"Yeah, but it won't be easy. They've got him locked up in the cellar and guards posted at the door."

"How many?" I said.

"Two. And even if we could get them out of the way, we still don't have the key. Kuratko's got it."

"Jesus, couldn't old Cemelik do something?" I said.

"We could give it a try," said Lexa.

"Where's Fonda?"

"Probably inside with his old man."

"Then let's go, shall we?"

"Let's go."

Just then a guy appeared in one of the windows of the main building with a bugle. He put the bugle to his lips and, after a couple of false starts, managed to blow a few notes. Everybody looked toward the window. The guy with the bugle stepped back and Kuratko appeared in the window, holding a sheet of paper. Everybody stopped talking and Kuratko started to read.

"Order number two," he read. "The military commander hereby proclaims the city to be under a state of martial law. No person may appear on the streets after eight o'clock in the evening. Patrol units are ordered to apprehend any such individuals and instruct them to return home immediately. In case of resistance to this order, members of the patrol platoons are authorized to use force. Signed: Colonel Cemelik, Military Commander."

Kuratko folded the paper, announced that all patrols should prepare to report to their designated meeting places, and vanished. The crowd started chatting and laughing again.

"Let's go, huh?" I said.

"Yeah," said Lexa. We started off.

"Can I go with you?" said Benda.

"Sure," said Lexa. We went over to the main building. The guy posted in front of the entrance was wearing army pants and puttees but a civilian jacket. He had a rifle.

"We can't go in here?" asked Lexa.

"No," said the soldier.

"Would you please ask Cemelik to come out in case he's in?"

"What do you want him for?"

"We want to talk to him about something."

"In connection with what?"

"He doesn't mean the colonel. He means young Cemelik. Alphonse. Fonda. His son," I said.

"Oh, him," said the soldier. "Yeah, he's inside. I'll call him."

"If you would be so kind," said Lexa.

The soldier turned and stuck his head into the hall.

"Jirka," he yelled. "Tell 'em in there that young Cemelik's wanted outside."

"Okay," a voice replied from inside and then you could hear a door creak and a feeble voice saying that young Mr. Cemelik was wanted outside, and after awhile Fonda appeared.

"What's up?" he asked when he saw us.

"Come on out," said Lexa. Fonda came down the steps and joined us.

"What is it?" he said.

"Look," I said to him. "Your old man's locked up Prema Skocdopole for mutiny or insubordination or something because he didn't want to turn in his weapons to the arsenal. Tell him he should know better."

"Who? The old man?"

"That's right. Tell him to let him out because otherwise he's going to have the whole town against him."

"What did he do?"

"Hell, he didn't want to turn in his weapons. Your old man built it up into an insurrection."

"Yeah, but he's nuts if he does that when . . ."

"We know," said Lexa.

"What?" said Fonda.

"That your old man's nuts."

"But the Skocdopole kid's nuts, too, when he knows there's an order that all weapons have to be turned in."

"Fine," I said. "All we want is to get him out of this somehow, so smooth it over with your old man, will you?"

Fonda pulled a sour face and told us to wait. Then he turned and went back inside.

"You think they'll let him go?" asked Benda.

"Sure. Fonda'll fix it up with his old man. Old Cemelik gives him anything he wants," said Lexa.

"Yeah, an only child," said Haryk.

"The family's pride and joy," said Lexa.

"What time is it?" said Benno.

"Almost six," said Haryk.

"Jesus, we've got to go out on patrol again."

"That's right."

Fonda came back.

"Well?" I said.

"The old man says Skocdopole's a fool and won't let anyone tell him anything. It looks like there's not much he can do about it now anyway. He'll have to stay put."

"And will he let him go?"

"The old man says he'll fix it somehow later on, but he can't just now. It would enrage the people."

"Which people?" asked Lexa.

Fonda ignored him.

"But afterward he'll fix it up so they'll let him out, right?"

"Right."

"We can count on that?"

"If Pop says something, he'll do it."

"So Skocdopole's going to be locked up all through the revolution," said Benno.

"That's the way it looks. He is. But we're going to fight," said Haryk.

"Shit. We're going to be as locked up in this damn brewery as he is, except it's dry where he is and we'll be left out in the rain."

"Let's go. Thanks," I said to Fonda.

"Is it already six?" asked Benno.

"Yeah."

"Christ Almighty, another three hours of knocking ourselves out!" said Benno.

"Yeah, but it's for the Fatherland, remember?" said Lexa.

"Up yours," said Benno.

"Benno, what would Helena say?" said Haryk.

"Shit."

"Boy, you really let go when she's not around."

"Kiss my ass."

"Things look bad. Benno's manners are starting to crack," said Lexa.

"Why the hell shouldn't they?" said Benno.

"Easy, easy. Remember, only three hours to go until supper."

"They'll feed us shit."

"Come on, before we all catch whatever he's got," said Haryk.

"Let's go," said Lexa.

We tramped over to our assembly place. Dr. Bohadlo was already standing there looking at his watch and shuffling his feet.

"Punctuality, boys. We've got to learn to be more punctual!" he said. The other three boys were already standing there. We started off. I was so worn out I hardly knew what was going on. We circled the town three times and then Dr. Bohadlo, as sickeningly brisk and fresh as ever, led us back to the brewery.

"When can we go home, Doctor?" Benno asked him.

"When we're all demobilized, boys."

"You mean we have to stay here the whole time?"

"That's right."

"They'll give us something to eat?"

"Certainly. Only today everything's a bit makeshift. Now have yourselves some tea, then you can catch up on your rest."

"Where?"

"They've set up a lounge in the back of the main building. You go there and I'll come by for you at midnight."

"We're going out on patrol again?"

"Of course. Every three hours."

"Aha."

"Well, see you later, boys. Sleep well."

"See you," said Benno.

We had our tea and then went to the lounge. You had to go through the main entrance of the administration building to get there. It was a triangular room with mattresses in the corner and benches along the wall and tables out in the middle where some guys were playing cards and others were sleeping, their heads on their arms. The air was thick with cigarette smoke and damp and steamy from the wet clothes and the light was lousy. From the corner, somebody whistled our signal. It was Lexa. We went over to him. Benno saw an empty mattress next to the wall and flopped down on it. He lay on his back and stretched out his legs, bent at the knees. He looked like a bloated frog. We sat down next to Lexa; Haryk lit a cigarette.

"Well, did you take the Germans' guns away from them?" asked Lexa.

"No. You?"

"Yeah, we did. Really. There was this bunch of sad-assed bastards—five of them—followed us from the power station all the way to Sramova's whorehouse. They said they wanted to give up their guns. We didn't have the heart to turn them down."

"You kidding?"

"No, honest. Boy, when I saw those poor Krauts—worn out and fed up and practically ready to lick your shoes—suddenly it seemed pretty crazy to me. Really weird."

"What do you mean?"

"The whole thing," said Lexa in a tone of voice I'd never heard before. Then he said, "Hell, we make a big joke out of it, but actually the whole thing just makes you want to cry. I mean, I was really sorry for those guys."

"They shot your old man, you jerk," Benno said.

"Not those guys," said Lexa. "They really looked like they'd had it."

"What's wrong with you, you moron? Next thing you know you'll be bawling your eyes out for Hitler," said Benno.

I looked at Lexa. He'd always been pretty tough and ironic and a fast guy with women, but now he'd really been thrown off balance. He sat there, his eyes thoughtful, his coat collar turned up, the light bulb hanging from the ceiling shone into his face. With the light on him like that, you could see he had beautiful big dark eyes and all the lights around were reflected in his eyes.

"No, I won't do that," he said. "But I just remembered something that happened to me once in the war."

"What?" I asked.

"Oh, something with a girl."

"Naturally. No Lexa story without a woman in it," said Haryk.

"And what's the connection?" I said.

"None, really. Only this thing was pretty different from the usual kind of story. You want to hear it?"

"Is it dirty?" asked Benno.

"No. It's pathetic," said Lexa.

"Then skip it. My stomach's giving me trouble enough already," said Benno.

"Don't listen to him. Go on. Tell it," I said.

"Yeah? I'm warning you, though, it's not dirty, not even spicy."

"Get on with it, Lexa. Just cut the crap and tell your story," said Haryk.

"Okay," said Lexa, and took out a cigarette, got a light from Haryk's, and as he took a deep drag to get his cigarette going the glow lit up their faces. I thought about all the crazy things I'd lived through with them—the band and girls and so on—and I felt a wave of affection for those guys. Something pretty close to love. Then it suddenly struck me that this was love, too, a different kind of love than what I felt for Irena. But if there was any love in the world at all then this was real love. I loved them, these friends of mine. Irena had a nice body and I was crazy about her, but I really liked being with Benno, with Haryk, with Lexa. I felt good with them. Lexa sat up straight and shivered from the cold.

"Goddamn it," he said. "I haven't been dry all day. Or warm either." Then he started in on his story:

"Well, then. It was in May, 1943, in Kolin. One night—one of those nice, warm May nights when all the stars look wet—I was hanging around down by the railroad station when suddenly I see this woman standing there in the shadows. There was a great big suitcase and she must have just set it down because she was still catching her breath. In that light all I could see was that she had a nice figure and I was practically on my way over to gallantly offer to help her when the size of that suitcase sobered me up a little. Before lugging a thing like that I thought I'd better take a good look, so I walked past her first to see what she looked like from the front. She was standing under a blackout street light that was enough to see she was a real beauty. She was a blonde but not a peroxide blonde—I could see that—and there was something kind of exotic or strange about her, so I didn't care how big that suitcase was any more and I quickly sidled up toward her so nobody else'd try to beat me to it and politely asked if I could help her carry her suitcase. She looked at me suspiciously—I've never seen such obvious suspicion in a pair of eyes in my life—and then she said to me, '*Versteh nicht Tschechisch.*' So then I knew she must be one of those *Mädchen* from the *Luftwaffehilfefrauenfunkerschule* or whatever they called it, and I noticed she was wearing one of those dull brown coats of theirs. But instead of putting me off, it made me even more interested, because her powdered face, with those big mistrustful eyes blossoming out of that shabby uniform, was really something. Something very special. So anyway, I repeated my offer in German and Trudy—a dumb name, but then so what, she was a real beauty—Trudy smiled and said thank you and I picked up that suitcase and for a minute there I was sorry I'd ever offered to carry it, but that feeling was gone again in no time.

"'*Wohin?*' I asked her, and she said to the *Luftwaffehilfefrauenfunkerschule* and the way she said that awful word was very lovely—clear and smooth and distinct, without the usual kind of Kraut splutter, an intelligent kind of radio-announcer German. I liked the way she walked along next to me and I tried hard not to tilt way over to one side, but that suitcase was awfully damn heavy. I don't know what she had in it, maybe a transmitter or something; all I know is it weighed a ton. Then I asked her, '*Sie sind eine Luftwaffehilfefrauenfunkerschülerin?*' only I couldn't pronounce it right and she laughed and said, '*Jawohl . . .*' and that was when I decided I'd make a pass at her.

"I don't know, maybe you'll think it was pretty strange and wrong maybe—me trying to make time with a German girl while people were dying in concentration camps but, for one thing, how was I to know who was guilty and who wasn't, and, for another thing, I'd never had anything to do with the Germans before, but this girl was a real beauty and besides what I had in mind was just to have her once and then off I'd go and in a certain way I guess you could say that was hurting the enemy too. I can talk about the whole thing casually and easy enough now, but when it was all actually happening it wasn't like it sounds now. I didn't even know she was German when I started talking to her, and then how could I leave her there at night with that suitcase once I'd offered to help her? Anyway, what the hell! There's no sense in explaining it all to you anyway since it's obvious I'm just trying to justify my behavior and maybe show how dumb it is, too, to generalize and to get trapped by your own prejudices and irrational feelings.

"So anyway, we talked as we walked along side by side. Trudy asked me about Kolin and I answered her as I puffed along swearing away inside at that damn suitcase and I thought, I'm going to get what's coming to me, I'm not carrying this just for the fun of it. Of course that really wasn't the real reason. Actually, like I said, the fact that this pretty girl beside me spoke a foreign language gave her a special kind of charm. A scholar would probably say that, in this case, language assumed a secondary erotic function, but no matter how you put it the fact was, that's the way it was. And just when a beautiful silver moon came out from behind the clouds and most of those wet-looking little stars dimmed out, we got to the corner from where you could see the *Luftwaffehilfefrauenfunker-schule* and a Kraut was stomping back and forth in front of the gate in heavy boots with a bayonet and I stopped.

" 'So,' I said, '*dort ist die Luftwaffe . . . die Schule.*' Trudy laughed, then batted her eyes at me and said, 'Could you help me up to the door with my suitcase?' 'Sure,' I said. 'But first you've got to promise me something,' and I looked deep into her eyes. 'Me?' she asked, a little puzzled, and I told her she'd first have to promise to see me again. You ought to have seen what happened then! All at once her pretty face hardened up and everything she'd been indoctrinated to believe woke up in her and she said it was *unmöglich.* 'Why?' I asked her, and I tried to look into her eyes but couldn't. She looked away and didn't answer. *'Warum?'* I said again, and then she said, without even looking at me, *'Schauen Sie,* I'm grateful to you for helping me with the suitcase but it's impossible, *Sie verstehen doch.'* *'Ich versteh nicht,'* I said, but she just shrugged her shoulders.

"And then I said something to her I probably wouldn't have dared say if I'd been in my right mind, and she re-acted to it like a real Nazi. *'Is' es die Rasse?'* I said iron-ically, and smiled because I thought she'd look at the race business the same way I did, just so much bullshit, and I thought the whole situation was sort of intriguing. I was naïve enough to believe she'd think all those race theories of theirs were just as dumb as I did. Besides, Czechs were officially classed as Aryans, too. So I asked her, *'Is' es die Rasse?'* She turned to me and snapped, *'Ja wenn Sie's wissen wollen,'* and snatched up her suitcase and spun halfway around under the weight of it, but then turned again and started off across the square toward that Kraut with the bayonet, dragging the suitcase over the ground more than really carrying it. 'I'll help you,' I said and tried to help her again. *'Danke,'* she said sharply and walked faster, but then so did I and I just had time to say, *'Aber, Fräulein,'* when something flashed a couple yards ahead of us and I saw that it was that Kraut's bayonet and there he stood, legs widespread, watching us. Without saying a word and hardly even breaking my stride, I veered off to the left and disappeared into the darkness without even looking back. But when I'd got far enough away to feel safe, I started thinking about it.

"Dumb blonde, I thought to myself. So that kind of thing really exists. It really bothered her—me being so inferior— and I made up my mind I'd teach her a lesson. Maybe it sounds sort of strange, but I didn't have the slightest doubt that I'd get her sooner or later. For me the main thing was she was a pretty girl and I figured that for her, too, maybe the fact I was a boy was more important than anything else. That whole scene that night, right up to when I made my big pitch, seemed to point that way any-way. As soon as I got back to my room this whole race question seemed to add some kind of spice to the affair and I was already looking forward to making a pass at her. I was a sophomore then and had plenty of time to play around. Plenty of time and lots of interest in that kind of thing. Before going to sleep that night I cooked up all sorts of plans like you always do just before falling asleep. And when I finally fell asleep I dreamed about her—crazy dreams, all mixed up.

"The next afternoon I went and sat down in the park across from the airforcewomenassistantsradioschool—a mouthful in any language. I was hoping she'd show up but I still didn't have any clear plan of attack. I'd given up trying to plan things in detail a long time ago—back around my freshman year. I was so wet behind the ears even then that I always carried around a little black note-book in my back pocket, and whenever I fell in love with some girl I'd go out in the woods and write down a whole set of love dialogues and for each sentence I'd think up all sorts of answers. Then I'd memorize them instead of my Latin vocabulary or German history, which is probably why I flunked out that year. The trouble was, though, whenever a girl was really there, I could hardly get my mouth open. About all I could get out was to ask her very solemnly if maybe she'd like to go to a movie, and if she said no, that was that, I was finished and all I could say was, too bad, and then I'd just stand there. Like I say, there was this period when I was awfully dumb and inexperi-enced, but I picked up experience as time went on, so by the time I was a junior I was pretty much of a Don Juan with plenty of small talk to see me through and my condi-tioned reflexes in such good shape that nothing and no-body could shut me up. So there I sat that afternoon and I wasn't thinking about much in general—not of what I'd say to her in case she came by, anyway—just sort of day-dreaming about her and looking forward to seeing her again.

"And then around five o'clock she came. There she was in the dark doorway practically blinding me with that blonde hair of hers, and she was walking arm in arm with some ugly, dumpy, freckle-faced redheaded girl who made her look even greater by comparison. When she saw me, she put her nose in the air and pretended I wasn't even there. I got up from the bench, stuck my hands in my pockets and sauntered off after them.

"One thing, by the way—I really looked great. There wasn't another zootsuiter in Kolin back in those days who could even touch me—except for Tom Hojer, naturally. Except the fact that Tom had the edge on me wasn't so much his own doing as it was due to the fact that Mr. Buml had a real feud on with Tom's father. Mr. Buml was trying to get even with Tom Hojer's dad for something Tom Hojer's dad had done to him, I guess, and what he did was to get an article about Tom Hojer published in the *Aryan Struggle*. He wrote in demanding to know how, at a time when everyone was being called upon to make a supreme effort for the victory of the Reich, the nation could tolerate individuals who did nothing but loaf around in the Kolin square wearing a so-called Tatra hat and swinging a cane and whistling American hit tunes and adding that some of these young loafers had even been heard singing 'Lili Marlene' in English at the Beranek Café. Mr. Buml considered singing 'Lili Marlene' in English a particularly grave offense because it was such a purely German song and, to clear things up once and for all, he said he'd decided it was high time to publish the name of this shameful gang's ringleader in *Aryan Struggle*. This ringleader's name was Hojer, he was ostensibly a student, and to his cronies he was known as 'Tom' Hojer. Well, naturally, Tom couldn't have asked for any better publicity and there's no getting around it—he knew how to make the most of it. What he did was he sued Mr. Buml for libel and won. He got a statement signed by his doctor saying that he had a double fracture of his leg, so naturally he had to use a cane, and that the doctor had ordered him to take walks to exercise his leg. Then the head waiter at Beranek's and a couple other guys committed perjury for him and swore that Tom had sung 'Lili Marlene' in German, but in a Plattdeutsch dialect that Buml didn't understand, and then Mr. Buml really made a fool of himself when he tried to spout some German and it turned out that Plattdeutsch wasn't all he didn't know—he didn't even know plain Deutsch. So Tom Hojer came out a hero and Mr. Buml wound up as a first-class certified ass.

"Anyhow, so there I was sauntering along behind Trudy and the fat one and I was wearing a great pair of shoes with thick white rubber soles and my pants were so tight I could almost feel them stretching. On went the girls with me right behind them. They stopped in front of shop windows and I was biding my time, waiting for the fat one to finally go into some store so I could talk to Trudy. But they just kept going along arm in arm and didn't split up. Then all of a sudden, they turned and headed back toward me. Trudy frowned and looked stiff as a spinster when I said, '*Guten Tag*,' and sailed right past me without a word. That cooled me off a bit. I didn't want to make a big scene. So I decided I'd better just take it in my stride and so I walked on a little and then turned, too. I tailed them for about half an hour. Every once in a while Trudy would look back, spot me, scowl, and then face front again. I had a bad scare once when two officers suddenly came out of a store—big guys, with Iron Crosses, spiffy uniforms, super-Teutons. They stopped to chat with the girls and Trudy turned and gave me such a dirty look I thought, oh, oh, she's going to tell the officers, and I thought maybe I'd better take off fast. Nothing happened, though, and I was glad I hadn't run away because that must have impressed her. In fact, I think that was probably the main reason she finally talked to me after all.

"It was in front of the movie theater. The two officers said goodby to them, *heil*ed Hitler, and clicked their heels. There was this big picture poster of Hans Albers in front of the theater and I saw Trudy saying something to the fat one, who answered '*Gut*' and went into the lobby. As soon as she was gone, I headed straight over to Trudy, who spun around like she'd just been waiting for me to try. When I came up to her, before I could get a word out, she said, 'Why are you following me?' in a funny tone of voice —not so much unfriendly as sort of sad or reproving. '*Ich* *liebe Sie,*' I said promptly, but she didn't say a word. '*Ich liebe Sie,*' I went on, 'I'm madly in love with you and think of you all the time.' And still she didn't say anything. It was getting kind of embarrassing for me because my German wasn't so great that it couldn't get worse, especially when there was only this one thing to talk about. Then, just when I'd run out of words and had stopped talking too, she looked at me and spoke in that patient voice of hers, using the same clichés as the night before. '*Schauen Sie,*' she said, '*es hat wirklich keinen Zweck.* I believe you do really like me, but, really, there's just no point.' I gave her a passionate look and stepped in closer and said, '*Sagen Sie mir, ist es wirklich die Rasse?* Only *die Rasse? Nur die Nation?*' but this time she didn't react like a fanatic Nazi the way she had the night before and she answered calmly, '*Ja,*' and I said, 'It's that important?' Again she said, '*Ja,*' very short and sweet, looking at me patiently and sympathetically, as if she was sort of sorry for me. I took her hand and said—and it seemed to me it sounded better in German than in Czech, or maybe this time I really meant it—I said, or rather sighed, as they say in novels, '*Ich muss Sie sehen! Ich muss Sie sprechen!*' She jerked her hand away fast and looked around and in a quick whisper said, '*Das ist unmöglich,*' but I went right on. '*Ich muss, ich muss, bitte, bitte,* otherwise I'll go mad.' She made a face and all of a sudden her eyes didn't look so sure any more; she kept on glancing around nervously and again, but even quieter this time, she said, '*Nein, es geht nicht, wirklich nicht,*' which fired me up again and after I'd panted out a few more of those urgent *bitte, bitte's* all at once she said, '*Gut, ich komme,* but only once, we've got to get this cleared up.' Then she glanced around again. The fat one was coming back now so she said quickly, 'At the corner, tomorrow night at eight!' Then she turned around and called to her friend, '*Also, hast du's?*' and they linked arms. I knew which corner she meant.

"I just stood there and watched them and I felt wonderful, that kind of conquering feeling you always get when a girl says she'll go out with you, when a girl you've made up your mind you really want to make says yes. It's always the same feeling and what comes of it all depends on how things turn out. And I admit I didn't have any idea how that date was going to turn out, a bad jolt to a guy's self-confidence. But that wasn't the only jolt, since that wasn't so serious. It was all my ideas about people and about the world that got knocked around, too. I mean, so once more I'd seen that basically everybody's pretty much the same. All right. But on the other hand, what do they do? They fall for something so dumb they let themselves be pushed around, they let their lives get so screwed up that, well, that a guy with feelings and ideas like mine simply couldn't believe it if he hadn't seen it for himself.

"I waited at the corner for her. It was one of those starry nights again but pretty windy so the streets were nearly deserted. She appeared in the gate with typical German punctuality and the Kraut with the bayonet saluted, an unofficial flirt salute, I guess, because he grinned at her and she grinned back at him and then walked straight toward me, putting on her gloves as she came. I stayed put. I didn't go out to meet her because I was pretty well hidden in the shadows and figured, with that Kraut around, maybe she wouldn't like me racing out to pick her up, letting everybody know I had a date with her. So I stood there waiting in the shadows, and when she got there I took off my hat and said, 'Guten Abend,' and she nodded and said, 'Na kommen Sie,' and stuck her hands in her coat pockets without even stopping and kept right on going. This sort of threw me off balance, but I put my hat back on and caught up with her. So there we were, walking along side by side. 'Where're we going?' I asked, and when she said it was all the same to her I suggested the island. She said, 'Na gut,' and I was glad because there's no place like the island for the kind of thing I had in mind. And now—though I may have had my doubts before—I was absolutely convinced she'd have to not just surrender but completely capitulate. Then suddenly it struck me that I hadn't introduced myself yet and neither had she so I told her my name and naturally she absolutely couldn't get it straight so I had to repeat it three times. Then she told me hers was Trudy Krause. It probably sounds pretty awful to you, and there's no getting around it, it is one hell of a name. But that's only because German is such an awful language. If the Germans were all as dried up and full of belches as their names and language are they'd really be in sad shape. But this Trudy, she really made up for her horrible name and—objectively speaking and putting all prejudice aside—she was every bit as pretty as Deanna Durbin, for instance. As far as feminine beauty went, she had the very same quality. She was a woman, even though she was a Nazi. What's more, she was a German woman and I just couldn't believe, then anyway, that this could make her all that different from other girls, and from me. Instead, it seemed to me that her being a bit different only added to the fun, that being a foreigner she had an exotic charm, and even to this day I don't believe a German's really all that different or that this difference had to get in our way. I believe it didn't *have* to, but I also know it did.

"We crossed the iron bridge over to the island, a classic moon looking in through the trusses, the water below rushing over the weir, and the willows on the island rustling and whispering.

" 'Trudy,' I said when we were on the path with the black shadows changing to moonlight and then back to shadows again, '*Ich liebe Sie*,' and I took hold of her arm. At first she didn't say anything so I went on, telling her in my broken German that I didn't know quite how to explain it but that as soon as I'd seen her I felt suddenly . . . and all that junk you usually say in situations like that. Then we went over to a bench under a big weeping willow and the bench was almost hidden under the leaves and things were looking very promising. Trudy said we should sit down and so we sat down and I held Trudy's hand and then she started to talk.

" '*Es ist schön, was Sie mir sagen*,' she said, "and I believe you, but you must understand that it can't go on like this.'

" 'Why?' I said.

" 'Because—well, for the reasons you mentioned yourself.'

" 'But those aren't really reasons.'

" 'So you say,' she said mysteriously and fell silent.

" 'Trudy,' I said, 'do you really believe all that stuff?'

" '*Ja*,' she said.

" 'But it's all nonsense,' I said bravely. Only it wasn't bravery so much as the fact that I felt I could really trust this girl, even though she was obviously one of those hundred-percent Nazis. Even if she actually did believe all that nonsense, I was sure she wouldn't let it come between us. 'It's all crazy, can't you see that?' I said.

" 'So you say,' Trudy said. 'And that's what the Czechs think, and the Jews, too, because it's not very pleasant for them.'

" 'But we don't even take it seriously!'

" 'No,' she said, smiling slightly and shaking her head, 'and I can understand why. It can't be very nice to know you belong to an inferior race.'

"I must be dreaming, I thought. I couldn't believe my ears. And suddenly I had this weird feeling, she's actually sitting next to me and then, even weirder, I could feel how she must be feeling, sitting there next to somebody who belonged to an inferior race, and I thought, what does it feel like anyway—as if you're sitting next to a chimpanzee? And I couldn't believe it. And before I knew it, I asked her straight out.

" '*Sagen Sie mir*,' I said, 'how do I . . . what do you see me as anyway?'

" 'How do you mean?' she asked innocently, and again I simply couldn't believe she'd been serious before. It seemed to me she must have been just pulling my leg.

" 'Well, I mean from a racial point of view.'

" '*Ach so!* Well, you're Czech, aren't you?'

" 'Yes.'

" 'Well then, that's how I see you—as a Czech.'

" 'Fine, but then don't you have . . . I mean, don't I disgust you or something?'

" 'You aren't a Jew, are you?'

" 'No.'

" '*Na also*. Then you're an Aryan, and the only difference is that your racial mixture is an inferior kind.' She said this so innocently and in such a scholarly tone that it really floored me.

" 'Racial mixture?' I asked, stunned, and she started un-reeling a whole slew of lunatic theories—theories that really sounded crazy when you heard them the first time, about the German race being some kind of mixture of Nordic and I don't know what all races and how everybody in Europe originally came from this race and how they all had blond hair and blue eyes and she did too. Well, if that whole Nordic-German race looked as good as she did, it followed, I guess, that it really was a pretty noble race. The only trouble was that once she got started she couldn't stop talking all the nonsense about first-class Aryans and second-class Aryans and mixed races and hopelessly mixed-up races like the Jews, for instance, and I listened and I was shocked and I still couldn't believe she really meant it. Finally I stopped listening. I just couldn't figure out how she could go on sitting there next to me explain-ing all these theories if I was as awful as she made out I must be, or how she could find me anything *but* awful if she knew I was, racially, such an inferior blend. And then I figured this whole race theory must be something like that coffee they used to sell at Meinl's before the war, where the best and most expensive kind was blended out of about twenty different kinds of coffee and then there were cheaper blends made out of fewer kinds until you got all the way down to the ordinary Brazilian kind that didn't even say what it was blended out of, so it probably wasn't blended at all. But I didn't tell her that and when she stopped talking for a minute, I asked her what she would do if I was a Jew?

" 'I wouldn't be sitting here.'

" 'Why not?'

" 'I couldn't sit with a Jew.'

" 'But why? You mean it would upset you physically or what?'

" 'Yes. Of course it would.'

"Then I thought I'd give her a hard time and make her ditch that racial junk once and for all.

" 'Look,' I said in a fatherly tone. 'You're about eighteen, right?'

" 'Going on eighteen.'

" 'That means that ten years ago you weren't even eight.'

" 'That's right.'

" 'Then tell me—how many Jews have you seen anyway since you were eight years old?' I said as if that took care of that argument. She frowned again. I could tell I had her there.

" 'That has nothing to do with it,' she said.

" 'It certainly does. How can you judge about something you don't know from your own experience?'

" '*Schauen Sie*,' she said again, using one of her favorite expressions, 'you don't know from your own experience that the earth rotates around the sun and yet you believe that, don't you?'

"That little Jesuit trick caught me off guard. All I could come up with right then was, 'All right. But that has been scientifically proven.'

" 'Well,' she said, 'so has this.'

" 'I beg your pardon?'

" 'Have you read Rosenberg? Or Gobineau? Or Chamberlain? Or at least something by Streicher?'

" 'Well, no, but . . .'

" 'There, you see? And you talk about scientific proof. Well, these things have been proved just as scientifically as gravity and all those other things.'

"This wasn't the way I'd wanted things to go—getting all tangled up like this. But, believe me, arguing with her wasn't easy. You couldn't allow yourself to forget, even for a second, that you were arguing with a fanatical Nazi. And I still couldn't quite believe she was. 'You're right,' I said.

" '*Na, sehen Sie!*'

" 'Yes, you may be right. Still I don't think it would hurt you any to try some of your ideas out in practice and see how they hold up then.'

" 'There's no need for that.'

" 'But you could at least give it a try.'

" 'There's no need for that and I don't even think it's possible today.'

F*

" 'Why not?'

" 'Why, all the Jews have already been isolated.'

"That really made me mad. It was the casual way she said it that really made me mad. And all at once it struck me how awful and absurd it was—her sitting there talking about it so casually and at the same time looking so pretty and sweet, and yet what was coming out of her mouth was something a beast like Streicher would say. And she didn't even notice. It didn't even faze her. Just then the moon came out and drifted slowly over the branches of the willow we were sitting under. Trudy looked beautiful and her face was still flushed with the excitement of explaining her theories to me, but suddenly she seemed revolting—or not so much that as she horrified me somehow—seemed abnormal, a kind of monster with that pretty little face and all those horrible ideas inside. I got terribly angry, furious at her. Suddenly I got an idea and I didn't even stop to think what might happen but barged right ahead, wanting to hurt her, to mess up and knock apart that tidy little stiff neat world of hers with all its orderly varieties of racial mixtures like Meinl's blended coffees. Maybe it was stupid of me, maybe it wasn't, but I couldn't help it, I had to do it and I did. As that sentimental silvery moon drifted by and she said with godlike calm that all the Jews were isolated, as if they were lepers or something, and when I started thinking about what 'isolation' really meant, and when it dawned on me that while I was sitting there calmly kidding around with a pretty Brunhilde, boys I knew—Quido Hirsch and Alik Karpeles and Pavel Polak—maybe weren't even alive any more or were going through God knows what kind of hell right then—then I couldn't hold it in any more and I blurted it out, and it was a real pleasure to feel that venom flow.

" 'It might still be possible, though—even today,' I said.

" 'How do you mean?'

" 'Well, I mean there're still some *Mischlinge* left.'

" '*Na ja. Aber . . .*'

" 'I'm one,' I said satanically and squeezed her hand and tried to put my arm around her waist; deep down I still couldn't believe it would make any difference to her, but I had a kind of devilish wish it would. And it did, too. I could feel her whole body go stiff. She stared at me, her eyes nearly popping out of her head.

" '*Was?*' she gasped, and then for a second we both just sat there, motionless. I slid my right hand around her slim waist.

" 'I am a half-Jew—*ein Halbjude*,' I said in that same satanic voice and then she shuddered. She really shuddered, as if she'd touched a toad, and then jerked away from me so violently that I was really surprised. A crazy thought about conditioned and basically unnatural reflexes flashed through my head and she jumped up and I just sat there and her lovely hair looked bleached in the moonlight. She stood there in front of me, her empty hands still pushing out in front of her, and she was staring at me and saying, in a voice full of dread as if she couldn't believe her ears, '*Sie sind . . .*'

" '*Ein Halbjude*,' I repeated in a murderously calm tone of voice. She just groaned in a funny unnatural way, turned and ran away. All I saw was that Nordic head of hers shining from time to time as she ran out of the shadows into the moonlight. I sat there on the bench and didn't feel like ever getting up again. A real beauty, the picture of happiness and everything that makes life worth living—and that's what they'd done to her."

His story over, Lexa lit another cigarette. I looked at my watch. It was 11:30.

"And you never saw her again?" asked Haryk.

"No."

Haryk was silent for a minute and then he said, "Well, you never can tell. Maybe she was just a bitch to begin with."

"Maybe she wasn't," said Lexa.

Nobody said anything. Then Lexa sneezed.

"Christ, the way I feel now, I'll never live to see morning."

I looked over at Benno stretched out on the mattress and saw he was sound asleep with his mouth wide open. Then I looked around the room. The air was thick with smoke.

A few guys were still playing cards; others were flopped out on mattresses, sleeping; others who'd fallen asleep at their tables were still pillowing their heads on their arms, sleeping. I watched a kid across from me fighting to keep awake. His eyelids kept drooping lower and lower over his eyes and his face began to look stupid, and then all of a sudden his head would sag down on his chest and he'd jerk it up again and you could see what an effort it was. Then for a minute he'd sort of pull himself together and then his eyelids began to droop again and his face slowly grew stupid again, and he'd go through the whole thing again, exactly the same each time. Lexa sat there leaning his head back against the wall, blowing out smoke rings and thinking. Haryk sat there, his knees drawn up under his chin, and was silent, too. So there we sat and this was the revolution. You could hear the snap of cards from the corner and Benno snoring loudly from the mattress. I wanted to fall asleep, too. That's all I wanted to do—just sleep. I was tired and fed up with everything. I could feel my head starting to droop and each time it slumped over onto my chest I felt it and knew how stupid my own face probably looked but didn't care because everybody looks dumb when they're sleeping and it seemed to me that there wasn't anything either clever or decent in the whole wide world, that everything was a sham, a big bluff, and all I felt was this awful weariness and that chin of mine that kept dropping down and down and that kept getting harder and harder to lift up again.

It was Dr. Bohadlo who woke me up. He looked as sickeningly fresh and pink as ever and was wearing a plaid scarf around his neck. He tapped me on the shoulder and when I turned and looked up, he grinned.

"Time to get up!" he said. "We're on duty again." I was convinced I'd never make it, never be able to get up. It was the same feeling I'd had lots of times when we were on forced labor and when I felt so lousy at five in the morning I thought I'd never be able to get up, that I'd stay in bed and talk my way out of it somehow, that I'd play sick and stay home, while all the time I knew that I couldn't, that I already had two absences that month and that I'd have to go to the factory and rivet all day in the freezing cold. I just did not want to believe I'd really get up. I did though. Haryk was up and ready to go and Lexa had already gone. They'd probably come for him while I was asleep. Dr. Bohadlo took Benno by the shoulder and shook him. But Benno just grumbled something. Dr. Bohadlo shook him again. Benno opened his eyes, and when he saw Dr. Bohadlo he sat up.

"Time to get up! We're on duty again!" Dr. Bohadlo sang out like a Scoutmaster. He behaved like one of those hikers or mushroom collectors that get such a kick out of getting up early though they could sleep till noon if they wanted to. I never got any kick out of that kind of thing. Neither did Benno, from the way he looked.

"Come on now, boys. Hurry up!" said Dr. Bohadlo and moved toward the door.

Benno got up, rubbed his eyes, then shuffled after the doctor. Fat and sleepy, he stumbled between the sleeping figures to the door and said, "Shit."

We went out into the hall and buttoned our coats. A cold draft came in from outside. It was dark in the hall. I heard Dr. Bohadlo saying that our route had been changed for the night, that we'd be patrolling around the railroad station. Then I could hear him opening a door but still couldn't see any light. It was pitch dark outside. A cold wind swept into the hallway. Benno was swearing under his breath. We staggered out and the wind hit us hard.

Dr. Bohadlo switched on his flashlight. "Careful now, boys. Wouldn't want anyone to get lost," he said. We lined up. My whole body was trembling from the cold. I could practically feel myself catching the flu. We lurched across the yard. A lantern was shining at the corner of the administration building and in its light you could see little raindrops being blown around the corner of the building. The fine rain chilled my face. We headed toward the gate over which another lit lantern hung. Under it stood two soldiers with fixed bayonets and turned-up coat collars.

"All in step now," said Dr. Bohadlo when we got out to the paved part. Benno grunted something. We fell in step with the other boys and clattered across the cobblestones toward the gate. The drizzle shone as it slanted across the lantern in the gateway. We passed the two soldiers who paid no attention to us—just stamped their feet and clumped back and forth—and then marched off into the deep and windy darkness between us and the town. All I could see were a few little blue blacked-out street lights— points of light that dimly showed the way to the station. We went more by memory than sight and it wasn't much fun in that dark. I felt the bridge under my feet and, under the bridge, the river, but couldn't see a thing. The wind and rain didn't let up for a minute. We got to the tracks and went past a red signal. The station was dark. Suddenly there was a bright wedge of light, a door opened, a guy carrying a gun slipped out, and then the door closed. There stood the German munitions train. We crossed the tracks. Dr. Bohadlo halted.

"Hold it up, boys," he said.

We halted.

"Now then," said the doctor, "from this point on we're going to spread out, forming a column from one side of the street to the other. A human chain. That way, nobody can get by us."

"I thought we were only going to patrol around the station," said Benno.

"Well, and so we will, too. Down Jirasek Boulevard to Novotny's, then past the station and over to Schroll's and back again."

"Aha," said Benno.

Dr. Bohadlo switched his flashlight on again. The cone of light lit up a patch of the Messerschmidt factory wall.

"Let's go," said Dr. Bohadlo. We spread out across the width of the street and started off. We gradually all got into step again. Spread out like that we made a lot more noise than when we marched in a column. It was dark except for a thin band of feeble light where the rain clouds had torn, low on the horizon. From the distance you could hear the faint chatter of machine guns.

"Hear that?" said one of the other boys. We listened. The machine gun chattered in short bursts, and another machine gun chattered back.

"That's from the front," the boy said. "It's pretty close already. Somewhere around Ledecsky Rocks."

As we went on, I thought of Ledecsky Rocks and of the Eagle's Nest where we'd been sitting a week ago, all worn out from the climb up through the cone-shaped Chimney, me and Zdenek and Irena and Vasek, and listening to all that wonderful news blowing in from Germany. You could hear everything from up there. Machine guns and Tiger and Panther cannons and those Soviet T-34's, and the sky above us was blue and beautiful and under that sky, just beyond the horizon, there was a war going on. It was great, sitting up there with the war almost over and I'd almost regretted that it was all going to end, those afternoons when they drove us out of the factory into the spring fields and then, far off on the horizon, white ribbons of smoke appeared and then those shiny American planes—things like that, everything. And naturally I was sad, too, on account of Irena and Zdenek who were sitting there side by side, and Zdenek fastened his safety rope to Irena so they were tied together and, like a fool, I saw that as a symbol and thought maybe I could just accidentally help him tumble over the side of some cliff but naturally thinking about it was as far as I got. I didn't do a damn thing. As usual.

We marched east along the endless Messerschmidt wall.

"What's that?" said one of the boys. There was a light on in the nightwatchman's gatehouse. A weak watery splotch of light crept over puddles on the pavement. Dr. Bohadlo said nothing. As we went by, we saw a helmeted German, his coat collar turned up, standing guard under the gateway. When we'd gone a little farther the kid said, "I don't get it. What's a Kraut doing there anyway?"

"They're only quartering there for the night—a column retreating from the front," said Dr. Bohadlo.

"Shouldn't we disarm them?" the kid said.

"They want to surrender to the Americans with their weapons."

"But maybe they'll go on to Prague," the kid said. Dr. Bohadlo didn't answer. "We ought to disarm them," the kid said again.

"They're far too well armed and trained for that. It

would only lead to useless bloodshed," said Dr. Bohadlo.
The kid didn't say anything. We marched on in silence to
Shroll's factory, turned and headed back. It was raining
harder now. Benno was grumbling under his breath and I
was shivering all over again. Like a pack of robots back
we went—from the Messerschmidt plant to the station
again and all around it was pitch dark except for that light
in the watchman's office and the little red-and-green lights
at the station. We crossed the bridge and underneath the
water roared as if the river was crowded with water now,
and then we stepped into the canyon of tall buildings along
Jirasek Boulevard. Our footsteps echoed here. We marched
quickly down the deserted street. Benno and I were on the
left wing, on the sidewalk. It was quiet. The only sound
was the clump of our boots. The windows in the houses
were dark. Only two blackout lights were on in the entire
street. As we neared the one swinging above the antitank
barrier, by its dim light, we suddenly saw a man.

"Careful!" said Dr. Bohadlo and crossed quickly over to
the righthand side of the street. We walked slower now. I
could hear the man's fast footsteps. Dr. Bohadlo switched
on his flashlight and I saw the iron shutter that covered
Novotny's store window. The cone of light swiftly hunted
on down the sidewalk, groping for the stranger. Then it
caught him and he stopped. He was wearing a raincoat
and shielding his eyes with his hands.

"Halt!" shouted Dr. Bohadlo and rushed over, his flashlight aimed right into the man's eyes.

"What is all this?" said the man.

"Where are you going?"

"Home."

"And where have you been?"

"What business is that of yours?"

I saw the silhouette of Dr. Bohadlo in his knickers and
beret and the man caught in the bright light streaming out
of Dr. Bohadlo's fist.

"Don't you know this city is under martial law now?"

"Under what?"

"Martial law."

"So?"

"Don't you know no one is allowed out on the street after eight o'clock?"

"Why not?"

"Because this city is under martial law!"

The man dropped his hand from his face and blinked. Then he started to walk on. Dr. Bohadlo grabbed his arm and the man tried to jerk away. The cone of light leaped up along the front of the house, then into the sky, and back on the man again. I saw the three other guys on our squad grab him. Dr. Bohadlo turned the light on his face again.

"Damn it!" said the man. "Get your hands off me!"

"Hold onto him, boys," said Dr. Bohadlo. "Your identity card, please."

"What the hell do you want now?"

"Your identity card."

"What authority do you have to ask for that?"

"I'm not going to waste time discussing the issue. Just show me your papers, please."

"What proof do you have that you have any right to ask?"

Dr. Bohadlo turned the flashlight on his armband.

"Anybody could put one of those things on," the man said.

"All right now, either produce your identity card and take the shortest way home or I'll be forced to arrest you."

"You have no right to do that either," the man muttered as he slowly reached into his pocket. Dr. Bohadlo stuck out his hand, took the crumpled identity card, and shone his flashlight on it.

"Well, now, Mr. Mracek," he said, "where are you coming from and where are you going?"

"I told you, I'm going home," the man said angrily.

"And where've you been?"

"Why the hell do you have to know?"

"Just answer the question."

"I told you, I'm going home, all right? What the hell, I'm not at confession, am I?"

"If you don't tell me where you've been, I'm going to

have to arrest you. And I warn you, you'd better tell the truth. We'll check up."

"Jesus Christ, what you'd ever want to know for is beyond me."

"That's our business."

The man again tried to get away.

"Let me go."

"Answer the question."

"Christ, don't make such a fuss about it, will you?" the man said.

"Are you going to answer my question?"

"Shit."

"You're under arrest," said Dr. Bohadlo.

"Oh, take it easy. Don't get so goddamn worked up."

"Hold onto him, boys!"

"What the hell are you going to do with me?"

"You'll be brought before a court-martial."

"By what right?"

"As I said before, this city is under martial law now."

"Take your goddamn hands off me."

"Hold onto him, boys."

In the light of the flashlight you could see him struggling to work loose but the three boys had a good professional grip on him.

"Let's go!" said Dr. Bohadlo.

"All right, I'll tell you," the man said quickly.

"You're under arrest."

"Oh, forget all this junk about arrest. I'll tell you if you're so damn eager to know."

"You should have told me sooner."

"Well, sure, maybe I should have, but how was I supposed to know . . . ? And it's not all that simple either. But, all right, I'll tell you."

Dr. Bohadlo said nothing. The boys were pulling the man on down the street and the man was giving them a hard time and then suddenly he said, "All right. I was with a woman. There. Now you know. Now let go of me."

The boys still held onto him.

"I was with a woman and now I'm going home to get some sleep."

"Wait a minute," said Dr. Bohadlo. The boys stopped.

"And that's all there is to it," the man said. "I was with a woman and now I'm going home."

"Tell us the woman's name."

"But why?"

"How else can we check up on you?"

"Hell. I can't do that."

"Why not?"

"I can't, that's all."

"In that case, I won't be able to release you."

"Oh, Jesus," the fellow said. "Can't you understand that there're some things you don't just go around telling people?"

"If you're afraid of an indiscretion, it's unnecessary. In an interrogation like this all information is held in the strictest confidence."

"Like hell it is! With this bunch of squirts around the whole town'll know by morning."

"I advise you to keep your personal opinions of these men to yourself," said Dr. Bohadlo. "Do you refuse to give this woman's name in order not to compromise her?"

"Naturally. She's married."

"Nevertheless if you don't give me her name, I'll have to turn you in."

"Oh, for Chrissake!" said the man and then whispered something to Dr. Bohadlo but so loud we could all hear it. "Listen, her husband's over at the brewery, too. Do you see now why . . . ?"

"I'm sorry." Dr. Bohadlo shrugged his shoulders. "Furthermore I might point out that such activities are illegal, too."

"Well, sure. But it isn't *that* serious a crime, is it?" the man said.

"Let's go," said Dr. Bohadlo.

"All right, I'll tell you who," the man yelled. We all stopped.

"But only you," the man said to Dr. Bohadlo. Dr. Bohadlo stepped up close to him and the man whispered something into his ear and then Dr. Bohadlo drew back sharply and stared at him.

"Really?" he said.

"That's right," the man said.

"And the Mayor doesn't . . ." Dr. Bohadlo started to say.

"Shh!" the man said and Dr. Bohadlo bent over and whispered something into his ear to which the man nodded. Then he grabbed the doctor's hand imploringly and Dr. Bohadlo straightened up and said in a loud voice, "And you're on your way home now?"

"That's right."

Dr. Bohadlo thought it over for a while and then he said, "I'll make a note of your name and then you may go."

"But you'll keep it strictly confidential, right?"

"Of course," Dr. Bohadlo replied and jotted something down in his little notebook. Then he handed the man's identity card back to him and cleared his throat.

"Ahem, well, come to my office next week. And now go straight home, please, and remember—next time I'll be obliged to detain you."

"Yes. Thanks," said the man.

"Let him go, boys." I saw the boys suspiciously release the man and the man straightening his coat collar.

"Well, thanks," he said and then turned and strode off down the street toward the station. We just stood there in silence. It was raining and in the steady patter of the rain Mracek's footsteps grew fainter and fainter. We all just stood there until Dr. Bohadlo said, "All right, on we go, boys," and took his place in the lead and we stretched out in a line across the street again and as I passed Haryk, he said, "Hot stuff, huh?"

"You said it," I said and took my place on the left wing of the column. On we went, down Jirasek Boulevard, across the bridge, and then there we were back again between the station and Messerschmidt. You could hear a kind of humming roar coming from the direction of the frontier now. We went as far as Schroll's factory and the noise was getting louder now. Then a short string of lights appeared on the highway.

"We'll wait here," said Dr. Bohadlo. We lined up against the wall and waited. The lights came closer through the rain and the noise kept growing louder. It wasn't the usual kind of noise that cars or trucks make. As it came closer, I could feel the earth trembling but I still couldn't make out what it was. Until at last I heard a metallic clatter and then I knew it was a tank. Through the dark and the rain it was rapidly crawling toward us. We stood there, pressed up against the wall, waiting. The lights drew nearer and, above us, the blackout lamp danced in the wind. The rumbling got louder until it was almost deafening and then a huge dark tank lumbered out of the night into the dim circle of light, its armored turret shiny from the rain and giving off a stink of gas and exhaust fumes as it clanked by. The racket completely deafened me. Behind the tank came trucks—one, two, three, four, five of them. As they moved under the canopy of light I could see the soldiers sitting inside in two rows, facing each other silently in their wet helmets. Then the column had passed us by and the howling and racket was muffled among the tall apartment houses on Jirasek Boulevard until it gradually died away completely.

"They're on their way to Prague," one of the boys said glumly.

Dr. Bohadlo moved away from the wall. "To Prague? No," he said, "they're on their way to surrender to the Americans." Then he pulled up his armband which had slipped all the way down to his wrist and said, "All right now. Forward march, boys!"

We moved off, one after the other, and formed our line again. The rain was cold against our faces and you could hear Benno swearing away steadily under his breath. We marched back to town. From time to time we heard the receding rumble of a truck. We went along Jirasek Boulevard as far as Novotny's store, turned and headed back. It was getting kind of silly by now. The rain slanted across each street light as it poured down on the town and the little puddles glittered and splattered as the heavy drops fell into them. My shoes were sopping wet and I was shaking with a chill. We got to the Messerschmidt plant again, passed along it, then marched by the little park in front of the station. You could just barely make out the whitewashed fence of the railroad warehouse in front of us. It glimmered dimly through the dark. Suddenly a dark figure emerged from the darkness and started clambering up the white fence. All you could see was a kind of vague, four-legged shadow.

"Halt!" yelled Dr. Bohadlo and turned on his flashlight. It made a nice, clear circle on the flat face of the white fence and in the middle of it hung a drenched black silhouette trying to pull itself up and over.

"Halt!" Dr. Bohadlo yelled again and started running. We started running too. We raced up to the fence and Dr. Bohadlo yelled "Halt!" again but the guy paid no attention to him. You could see him pulling hard, then get one leg over and then the circle of light slid up over the fence and all I could see was the guy's back, a little bit lighter against the black sky, and then even that was gone as he jumped down on the other side and vanished. Dr. Bohadlo stood there. We crowded around him.

"Who was it?" asked one of the boys.

"No idea. Probably another of those people who're trying to break into the munitions train," said Dr. Bohadlo dejectedly.

"Who do you mean?"

"Communists," said Benno.

"No," said Dr. Bohadlo quickly. "I don't know who. Probably just a bunch of hoodlums, that's all."

"Communists," Benno said again.

"No, Mr. Manes. We have no cause to think so. But last night some gang or other tried to break into it, too."

"I know. Communists," said Benno.

For a minute nobody said anything. Then one kid said, "We ought to go to the station."

"No. Our orders are to patrol outside," said Dr. Bohadlo.

"Is anybody there now?"

"Well, there're some Germans, of course."

"Ukrainians," said Benno.

"Vlasov's men," said Dr. Bohadlo. "No, we most definitely will not go inside."

"But what if somebody's trying to get at the train?"

"That's none of our business. They do it at their own risk."

"Who knows what's going on? Anyway, it was only one guy," I said.

"No, we are not going inside," said Dr. Bohadlo, "but we will keep watch on the station."

"From here?" the kid asked.

"We'll conceal ourselves in the park."

That sounded more like it to me. We aboutfaced, went into the park, and took our stand behind the hedge. Standing right up against it I could feel its wet branches scratching my coat. Water dribbled down my face. For a second I felt I was in London. Or in Madrid during the Civil War. It was like in the movies and when I looked off to the side I could see the other guys crouched behind the hedge, in the dark, watching. I felt great, in spite of the wet and cold. Keeping our heads down, we stared across at the wood enclosure that walled off the station. Then all at once a bright light clicked on and then off again somewhere off to our right. Everything dark again. It must have come from somewhere close to the station.

"It came from a window—a skylight up on the roof," said one boy. I looked up at the roof of the stationhouse. The light went on, then off again. Then it went on again after a longer interval. Off, then on again.

"Morse code," said Dr. Bohadlo. "Any of you boys know Morse code?"

"I do," one of the boys said. "M-R-L-B. Mrlb," he said. "I don't get it."

We stared again, nobody saying a word.

"Who do you think it is?"

"Communists," said Benno.

"Shh! Look! Over there!" said Dr. Bohadlo.

"Where?" said Haryk.

I turned around. From the slope back of the Messerschmidt plant, from one of the workers' apartment buildings, you could see a light blinking on and off.

"The fools," said Dr. Bohadlo. "They ought to know better than to play games like that, with all those Germans quartered at Messerschmidt." None of us said anything. The light up on the hill stopped blinking. We turned again.

Somebody was signaling all right. Then the other light started blinking again.

"We ought to go and have a look," the boy said.

"Where?" said Benno.

"At the station."

"No, boys. As I said before, our orders are to stand watch in *front* of the station."

"And we're just going to stand here like this?"

"No. We'll send a report back to the brewery . . . that is, to headquarters," said Dr. Bohadlo. "Any volunteers?"

"I'll go." It was one of the kids we didn't know.

"Fine. I'll just write up my report and then . . ." Dr. Bohadlo took out his notebook. "Hold this flashlight for me, will you please?" The kid took the flashlight and turned it on. Dr. Bohadlo wrote something in his notebook. I tried to look over his shoulder but couldn't see anything.

"There," he said, ripped out the sheet of paper, and folded it.

"Deliver this to headquarters as quickly as possible and wait there for an answer."

"Yes, sir," said the kid.

"You may go."

"Yes, sir."

The kid turned and disappeared into the park. I turned to watch him but all I could see were the long branches of a weeping willow waving in the dark. It was raining. Then another figure appeared by the fence. He stood there for a moment, still as a statue.

"Careful now, boys!" whispered Dr. Bohadlo. "Follow me but keep quiet." Then with a tremendous crash, he pushed his way through the hedge. Our column moved after him. Dr. Bohadlo broke into a trot. You could hear him splashing through the mud puddles in front of the park.

"Quick!" said the figure by the fence in a low voice. He'd mistaken us, I suddenly realized, for somebody else. We ran up to him, surrounded him, and Dr. Bohadlo flashed the light on his face. The guy was wearing a cap, no overcoat, and a scarf around his neck. He squinted, blinded by the flashlight.

"What are you doing here?" said Dr. Bohadlo sharply.

"Turn that thing off!" said the fellow.

"What are you doing here?"

"What's it to you?"

"I asked you what you're doing here."

"And I say kiss my ass."

"It would be in your own interest if you'd show a little respect. Don't you know there's a curfew?"

"Why don't you just mind your own business. And turn that damn thing off."

"Tell me what you're doing here!"

"And like I told you—kiss my ass."

"You're under arrest. Take him, boys," said Dr. Bohadlo. The other two boys jumped him, but Benno and Haryk and I just stood there. He wasn't about to give himself up. First he punched one of the kids in the nose, then he jumped sideways, out of the light. The kid landed hard in the mud. There'd been a soft cracking noise when the guy hit him, then a little sigh. Dr. Bohadlo flashed the light around, trying to keep up with the guy now and the light slid sharply along the white fence, then picked him up slogging his way through the mud toward the station.

"After him!" yelled Dr. Bohadlo and started running. We all took off after him. Along the fence the mud was awful. The cone of light bounced around through the dark as Dr. Bohadlo ran and our feet sank and stuck in the mud, and then suddenly we heard a big splat in front of us and I saw the guy fall. The other kid jumped him and came down on his back. We ran up. Dr. Bohadlo trained his flashlight on him.

"Get up!" he said.

The guy lay there on his stomach, the boy straddling his back, and it didn't look as if he was in any hurry to get up. He kept his face down and with his right hand started groping for something inside his jacket. Then all at once he stuck something in his mouth and before Dr. Bohadlo could stop him a piercing whistle split the air. The kid on top of him grabbed his head and the whistling stopped but with a twist he threw the kid off and was up again. Dr. Bohadlo grabbed him clumsily around the waist. Then I got into it, too, moving in and getting an armlock around his neck.

He was struggling hard and he was very strong. Haryk had a hold on him now, too.

"You bastards!" the guy said savagely, breathing hard. "A great bunch of patriots you are—you sons of bitches."

"Quiet!" said Dr. Bohadlo.

"Why don't you go ask the Krauts for some help, huh?"

"Hold him, boys. I'll see if he's armed," said Dr. Bohadlo. I could feel the guy starting to squirm again, trying to break loose. Haryk let out a yell and sat down on the ground. Dr. Bohadlo grabbed the guy around the waist again.

"Jee-sus!" moaned Haryk.

"You hurt?" said Benno.

"He . . . he kicked me," said Haryk and moaned again. In the meantime the kid who'd landed in the mud before had taken over for Haryk and Benno was carefully holding onto one of his arms. The kid was clutching a bloody handkerchief.

"Are you bleeding?" said Dr. Bohadlo.

"Nothing serious," the boy said.

"Now hold him tight, boys," said Dr. Bohadlo. The guy tried to kick the first kid but he dodged to one side and then the kid told Haryk to help out so he could get the guy's legs.

Haryk got up, clutching his stomach.

"It hurts like hell," he said.

"Come on, come on," said the kid.

Haryk went over to the guy and got a hold on him.

"You sons of bitches! You're going to pay for this!" said the guy. The first boy knelt down and got a good grip on the guy's feet. Now we were all holding on somewhere. Dr. Bohadlo started searching his pockets.

"Ah, there we are," he said and pulled something out. He held it in the palm of his hand, then turned the light on it. It was a heavy German pistol.

"You sons of bitches! Traitors!"

Dr. Bohadlo was just putting the pistol into his own pocket when two short whistles came from somewhere off in the dark and the guy jerked his head back and yelled, "Over here! Here! Help!"

The kid with the bleeding nose quickly rammed his bloody handkerchief into the guy's mouth. The guy bit his hand. The kid howled. A light shone out of the darkness. It found us. I turned around. A couple of men were running toward us through the mud. I let go of the guy and got ready for a fight. I felt like pounding the hell out of somebody.

"Watch it, boys!" shouted Dr. Bohadlo and flashed his light on the men running at us.

"Son of a bitch!" I heard behind me. I spun around and saw that the guy had wrenched himself free. Which was fine with me. I didn't want to get into any fight with him. He jumped Dr. Bohadlo and knocked the flashlight out of his hand. It fell to the ground, rolled, and then lay there lighting up a long patch of mud. I saw the guy ram his knee into Dr. Bohadlo's belly, then roll over on the ground with him, and Dr. Bohadlo's knickered little legs churning around in the air, but that was all I saw because the guy's friends charged into us then. I went for one of them, but he got a leg behind me and over I went, but I didn't let go of him so we both went down. I could feel the soft, wet mud under me as I lay there on my back. I poked my fingers into the guy's eyes like we used to do when we were playing around with jujitsu. The guy let out a crazy howl and let go. I jumped up and kicked him in the belly. He doubled up in the mud and moaned. I looked around. In the patch of light from Dr. Bohadlo's flashlight I saw two bodies wrestling in the mud. A clumsy figure, splattering mud all over the place, tore by. It was Benno. A flashlight went on and I saw Haryk lying there on the ground, his face all bloody. The kid sitting next to him in the mud was holding a hanky to his nose. Then they both disappeared in the dark again because the guy with the flashlight was hunting around for something. The light slid over puddles and mud until it picked me out. The next thing I knew two figures leaped into the light and started barreling toward me. I didn't wait for them but turned and lit out after Benno. I heard them sloshing along noisily behind me. Then somebody yelled, "Let him go!" Though the footsteps stopped I kept right on going. I made a flying leap toward the hedge and burrowed through. The twigs slashed my face and I could hear my coat ripping. I went right on through.

"Danny?" said a voice out of the dark.

"Benno?" I said.

"Yeah. Where are you?"

"Here."

I groped my way over toward Benno's voice. Then I felt him next to me.

"Anybody else here?" I said.

"I don't know. I guess not."

"They still fighting?"

"Not any more. Look."

I looked over toward the battlefield. By now, Dr. Bohadlo's flashlight, half buried in mud, was only dimly shining on the back of the kid with the smashed-in nose. On the other hand, over by the wall, you could see a bunch of men helping each other over the fence one after the other.

"Well, that's that," said Benno.

"You said it!"

The last guy swung himself up, dropped, and vanished on the other side of the fence.

"Shall we go back?" said Benno.

"Sure," I said. We shoved our way back through the hedge. Somebody was picking the flashlight out of the mud and you could see a red hand cleaning it off. Then the cone of light circled. It picked up Haryk holding his hanky up to his cheek. A relief to see nothing worse had happened to him. We hurried over to the light. Dr. Bohadlo was standing there with his flashlight, staring off into the night. The two kids came up—one still clutching his nose, the other limping. We all crowded around Dr. Bohadlo.

"Are you all here?" he asked.

"Yeah," I said.

"I'll need one of you to run a report over to the brewery."

Nobody volunteered.

"Hold my flashlight," said Dr. Bohadlo. One of the kids held the flashlight and Dr. Bohadlo pulled out his notebook and I noticed that his sleeve was ripped all the way up to the elbow.

"What happened to you?" Benno asked Haryk.

"I got one right in the teeth."

"Let's see."

"Skip it. I checked. They're all still there."

"And all that blood?"

"I guess I got that when he knocked me down. How about yourself?"

"Me? I'm okay," said Benno.

"Were you in on the fight?"

"Are you kidding? I sure wasn't."

"How about you?" Haryk asked me.

"Yeah."

"You get hurt?"

"I won."

"Oh, come on!"

"Really. I did."

"You cleared out just like Benno."

"Honest to God, I was fighting like crazy."

"But you didn't win."

"I did, too."

"There," said Dr. Bohadlo and tore a page out of his notebook. "Now, who's going to . . ."

Just then a submachine gun started chattering in short bursts from the station. We stiffened. The machine-gun fire died down, then a few more shots cracked. Revolver shots this time.

"My God, that gang is going to get the whole city in trouble," said Dr. Bohadlo in a shocked tone of voice.

Behind the fence something flashed. Smoke rolled up. Somebody had thrown a hand grenade.

"Let's clear out of here," Benno muttered.

"Wait," stammered Dr. Bohadlo.

"Why? What's the point in waiting around here anyway?" Benno persisted. The submachine gun on the other side of the fence chattered again. Suddenly a floodlight blazed on over to the left. I turned. Germans armed with submachine guns and rifles came racing out around the corner of the warehouse. I heard a plop behind me. I turned and saw Benno stretched out flat in the mud. Dr.

Bohadlo didn't budge. The Germans rushed up to us and halted. An officer trained a flashlight on us.

"What are you doing here?" he demanded.

"We belong to the Czech Army," said Dr. Bohadlo quickly.

"*Aha! Herr Doktor Sabata, was?*"

"Exactly!"

"What's going on here?"

"We were attacked," said Dr. Bohadlo. "A group of men . . . armed men . . ."

"Where are they now?" the officer asked impatiently.

"There. At the station," said Dr. Bohadlo.

"*Gut,*" said the officer and turned to the soldiers. "*Los! Gehn wir!*" he barked and they all started running toward the station.

"Come on, let's get out of here!" said Benno.

"What the hell are we waiting for? Let's go, you guys," said Haryk. Behind the fence there was another explosion, then three more, one right after the other. In the light of one blast I saw three figures scrambling down over the fence and taking off in the direction of the workers' district up on the hill. The submachine gun started chattering again.

"Let's go, boys. There's nothing we can do here anyway," said Dr. Bohadlo.

"Exactly," said Benno.

We trotted past the park, heading for town. It was raining hard. Another explosion went off and the flash lit up one whole side of the buildings on Jirasek Boulevard.

"We'll go through the underpass," panted Dr. Bohadlo. We ran across the bridge, our footsteps booming, and switched left toward the underpass. Another long spatter of shots rang out from the station. We tramped through the underpass and came out onto a muddy path and then we all slowed down and I looked around and the railroad station was dark and silent again. Only the rain kept coming down.

"Boy, does that ever hurt!" said Haryk.

"What's wrong?" I asked.

"That guy really kicked me in the gut all right."

"Is anybody injured?" asked Dr. Bohadlo.

"Me," said Haryk.

"Where?"

"In the stomach. It really hurts."

"Can you walk?"

"Yes."

"As soon as we get back to the brewery, report to the first-aid station."

"I will."

"Anyone else have any injuries?"

Nobody spoke up. We cut through the park in front of the County Office Building.

"Know what I'd like to do?" Benno whispered to me. "Take off. Beat it."

"Don't. Don't do it, Benno."

"Do what?" said Haryk and slowed down for us. We let the others walk on ahead a little.

"I just said I'd like to take off," said Benno.

"Me, too," said Haryk.

"Don't. Stick around," I said, "for a while anyway."

"Stick around? Hell, once we're back inside we'll never get out again," Benno said.

"Sure we will."

"Well, how?"

"Don't worry. We'll manage."

"Yeah, but why crawl back in when we've got a perfect chance to take off now?"

I couldn't tell them that I wanted to be in on whatever was going on back at the brewery. That I wanted to see the army finally getting ready for action. And to see what Colonel Cemelik was up to. So all I said was, "Look, you know how dumb they are. They're just dumb enough to lock us all up."

"Shit," said Benno. "Anyway, we're already mixed up in this stupid business. And things can't get much worse for us than they are already."

"How do you mean?" I asked.

"Well, I mean what's already happened."

"What?"

"Jesus Christ! What happened with those communists."

"Yeah, so what?"

"Oh, come on, stop playing so dumb."

"I still don't get it."

"I mean that when the Russians come, they'll wipe us out because of that—that's what I mean."

"You kidding? Did you recognize any of those guys?"

"No. But they sure recognized us."

"In the dark?"

"Everybody recognizes me, even in the dark," said Benno.

"Yeah, but after all, all we did was obey orders. Anyway, the whole thing's crazy."

"Like hell it is."

"It is, too. The Russians'll have plenty of other worries."

"Hurry up, boys," a voice sang out from up front.

"Right," I said.

"I don't even want to think about what's going to happen," said Benno but he hurried up, too. We were nearing the gate now. It was closed and the lantern behind it turned the bars of the gate into long, fan-shaped shadows on the wet pavement. We got to the gate.

"Dr. Bohadlo's patrol," said Dr. Bohadlo. The gate opened and we marched inside. The soldier closed it behind us as soon as we all passed through. Crowds came up from all sides. Everybody wanted to know what was going on outside.

"Let us through," said Dr. Bohadlo.

"But what's going on?" somebody asked.

"Where was the shooting?"

"What's happening?"

Silently we made our way through the crowd, but they followed us, asking us questions all the way over to the administration building. None of us said a word. It was only when we passed under the lantern at the corner of the building that I realized how we looked. We were all covered with mud. Dr. Bohadlo's sleeve was torn and Haryk's face was bleeding. While we were standing there, Mr. Jungwirth came up to me.

"What's going on out there, Danny? They won't let us out of this place."

"The Germans are mixing it up with some communists at the railroad station," I said.

"With communists?" I could see this news really knocked him for a loop.

"Yes," I said.

"What's that? What'd he say?" voices called out behind Mr. Jungwirth. I left him to take care of the questions. We went up the steps toward the door and into the hallway. There was a light on.

"Wait here. I'll go and report," said Dr. Bohadlo. We sat down on a bench along the wall and Dr. Bohadlo went into the office.

"A nice mess," said Benno.

"You're not kidding," I said.

"Yeah, but this gut of mine has really had it!" said Haryk.

"It still hurts?" I asked.

"I'll say it does."

"Where abouts?"

"Right in the middle."

"You ought to go to the first-aid station."

"I'd rather go home."

"We should have beat it," said Benno.

"Wait a while. We will."

"Yeah. Now all we can do is wait."

"Oh, maybe they'll let us off."

"Like hell they will."

"Sure they will."

"Yeah? When?"

"Oh, by morning at the latest."

"I'll believe it when I see it," said Benno.

It was quiet in the hallway. The light in the hall shone murkily. We sat there on the bench, bloody, bleeding, filthy, drenched, and exhausted. So this was a revolution. It wasn't just a big lark after all. And that was all right, too. I liked that. I'd forgotten all about my flu. I remembered everything that had happened. It was pleasant to remember kicking that guy in the stomach. And how he'd groaned. It worried me a bit, though—maybe I'd really hurt him. I'd never have thought I was capable of kicking anybody like that, that hard. Apparently I was, though. Obviously I was capable of even worse things, too. Too bad I hadn't had a gun with me. I could have picked off those Germans as they came running up to us with their guns and bayonets. I could just see myself behind that hedge, firing away with my submachine gun, the short flame shooting out of the muzzle, the rain pouring down, the brief bursts of light, and the Germans turning to flee in their wet helmets and flapping trenchcoats. These brewery battalion leaders made me mad. Why didn't they let us do anything? If they'd only passed out all those guns they had lying around in the arsenal, they could have taken the station. Well, sure. But what's the good of taking the station away from the Germans if it costs lives? True. I could see that. And this way the Germans could escape easier and then they'd be out of our way. The communists **were** making things rough enough for us as it was. Take on the Germans, too? I shuddered.

"What the hell are they doing in there?" said Benno.

"What time is it?" asked Haryk.

"Nearly three. Those guys'll be gabbing away in there until morning."

I was trembling all over from the cold. I tried to think about shooting again but it didn't work. I was so cold my teeth were chattering.

"What's wrong with you?" said Benno.

"I'm cold."

"You see, you jerk. You could already be home in bed by now."

"Yeah, sure."

The longer we sat there the worse I felt. I tried to warm up by thinking about Irena, but that didn't help much. The lightbulb in the ceiling looked as cold as ice and Dr. Bohadlo didn't return. The minutes dragged by. At last Dr. Bohadlo appeared. He came out looking very grave, his full-moon face still spattered with mud, and he told us to go to the lounge.

"When are you going to let us go home?" said Benno.

"I've already told you—only when things have quieted down. You're in the army now. Go and get some rest," said Dr. Bohadlo testily. We got up. Dr. Bohadlo disappeared through another door.

"A great army," said Benno.

"A great screw-up, that's for sure," said Haryk.

"You coming?" said one of the other guys.

"Sure. You go on ahead. We'll be down in a while," said Benno. They headed off for the lounge. Benno turned to us. "Well, you want to stay here?"

"No," said Haryk.

"How about you?" Benno turned to me.

"I'm for clearing out."

"Okay. But how?"

"Come on, you guys. I know a place we can get over that fence in no time," said Haryk. I opened the door. A bunch of guys were still standing under the lantern, arguing.

"Careful. Follow me," said Haryk. We crept out, slipped quickly along the wall on the other side of the door and turned the corner. We found ourselves in complete darkness.

"Where are you?"

"Here," I said.

"Hold on."

I groped around until I felt Haryk's hand. Benno laid his hand on my shoulder. Slowly we picked our way through the darkness. It was still pouring and dark as the inside of your hat. Haryk stopped and let go of my hand.

"Well, here's the fence," he said.

"Where does it bring us out?" said Benno.

"On the Bucina road."

"I'll never make it over."

"We'll boost you. Danny, come here."

I stood next to Haryk.

"Come on, Benno."

Benno stepped up to the fence. It was an ordinary board fence.

"Grab hold at the top and stick out your ass. We'll help you," said Haryk.

"All right," said Benno. Haryk and I caught hold of his rear and boosted him up. He was awfully heavy. He started grunting and groaning.

"You got a hold up there?" asked Haryk.

"Yeah."

"Can we let go yet?"

"Wait, not yet." You could hear him wheezing and I could feel him frantically pulling himself up. Finally he started growing a bit lighter. It felt like most of him anyway was already over the fence.

"Okay," he said and we let go and I heard his shoes banging against the fence and then his body landing with a thud on the other side.

"You make it all right?" asked Haryk.

"Yeah. All banged up," said Benno from behind the fence.

"Can you get up?"

"Yeah. To hell with everything."

"Okay, Danny. Your turn," said Haryk. I swung myself up on the fence and Haryk helped push. I got one leg over, then the other and sat on top. You couldn't see a thing beyond the fence.

"Where are you, Benno?"

"Here." His voice came from right underneath me.

"Get out of the way so I don't land on top of you."

I could hear branches cracking as Benno moved off to one side. Then I jumped. I landed on my hands and feet on the sopping wet ground.

"Okay?" Haryk called out from the other side.

"Yeah. You can jump," I said and got up. Haryk jumped down behind me. We came out on the highway.

"Well, let's go," said Benno. We hurried past the brewery. When we got near the gate we made a detour to keep out of the lantern light. The soldier was still patrolling behind the gate. We crossed the bridge and went past the County Office Building. All the windows were dark. Benno stopped at the corner.

"Well, so long."

"See you," said Haryk.

"Good night," I said.

"You coming over to our place this afternoon, aren't you?"

"We'll be there," I said.

"Well, good night."

"Good night."

Haryk and I walked through the park and under the railroad underpass. It was wet and dark all around. We came out of the underpass and around the Hotel Granada on Jirasek Boulevard. We stopped in front of our building.

"See you at Benno's tomorrow?" I asked.

"Yeah."

"Well . . . good night."

"Good night," said Haryk, and vanished. I could hear his footsteps getting farther and farther away and then I unlocked the door. Then there I was in the hall and suddenly it was warm and dry. I shut the door and started shivering. I hurried up the stairs. It was dark at our place. I opened the door and closed it quietly behind me so as not to wake Mother. But I woke her up anyway or else she hadn't been asleep at all. A light went on in the bedroom and she rushed into the hall in her nightgown.

"Danny! Thank heavens! Are you all right?"

"Don't worry. I'm fine," I said.

"What was all that shooting then? I've been so worried and frightened that something had happened to you!"

"It was some kind of incident at the station. It's all over now."

"And they've let you go now?"

"No. But I caught cold so I came home."

"A good idea. Now you get right into bed. You'd like some tea?"

"Please."

Mother went into the kitchen and I slipped into the bathroom to wash up a bit and also so I wouldn't have to explain anything. She hadn't seen anything there in the dark hall, but when she saw my clothes she'd be in for quite a shock. But she wouldn't see them until morning. I stripped to the waist, washed, and rubbed myself dry with a Turkish towel. Then I went to my room, undressed, and crawled into bed. I was cold. Mother came in with a big mug of steaming hot tea and set it on the chair next to my bed.

"Well, the main thing is you're home again—thank God," she said.

"Right. And tomorrow I'll take a sweat cure and get rid of this cold."

"Of course. And we'll ask Dr. Labsky to write you a certificate so that you can't go back there any more."

"Well, we'll see," I said and picked up the mug of tea.

"Yes . . . Would you like anything else? A sandwich or . . ."

"No, thanks. Go back to bed, Mother."

"All right. Good night," she said, and leaned over me.

"Good night," I said and screwed up my mouth. She kissed me.

"And get a good long rest," she said, and went back to her bedroom. She closed the door behind her.

I was alone in my room with the tea. I drank it and then crawled down under the eiderdown quilt and curled up. That same old, familiar, eternally recurring and always wonderful feeling swept over me. I closed my eyes and started saying my prayers. Dear Lord, help me to win Irena. Our Father Which art in heaven, hallowed be Thy Name, Thy kingdom come, and I thought about Irena and could see her the way she'd looked up in the mountains, edging her way across a narrow traverse near the Chimney and moving slowly around the overhanging rock toward the big crevasse, her arms bare and tan up to her shoulders and the safety rope between her breasts and Holy Mary, Mother of God, pray for us now and at the moment of our death, Amen, and Irena still sitting there in the sunshine and I said, Dear God, help me to win Irena, and I crossed myself and started thinking about her up there on the mountain again and then about the brewery and how they were all locked up inside it like in a zoo behind bars, and about the bars, and about the explosions down at the station, and that hot, black, wet tank and us getting over that fence and then suddenly I was thinking of Prague where they were probably really fighting now and the barricades were blazing in the streets and the Germans were probably murdering people and raping pretty girls, girls like Irena, or maybe somewhere a girl, the girl I'd finally meet some day and marry, was going through hell right then, and then it astonished me, the thought that I probably hadn't even met the girl I would marry some day but that she must be living somewhere or that maybe she hadn't even been born yet, and that maybe I wouldn't get married until I was old and my bride would be young, except that I didn't believe I'd live to be very old, and suddenly I had a terrific desire to know her and I wondered what she was like and whether or not she really existed at all and I said to myself, that's all a lot of nonsense, I'll never meet one, and then I remembered I was supposed to be in love with Irena, but then there I was back again thinking about *her* again, that girl I was going to meet, and I tried to imagine how she looked but I couldn't, and all I knew was that she'd be pretty and I decided I could never love a girl who wasn't pretty and wondered how anybody ever could but then for a second that made me feel sort of ignoble, that all I thought about was physical beauty and not spiritual beauty, but I said to myself, skip the spirit, I don't believe in the spirit, I just believe in the body and only pretty ones at that and in all the pleasure you get out of looking and touching and I imagined myself embracing this girl I was going to meet and we were in bed together, both of us naked, and I was touching her breasts and kissing her and I went on dreaming it out in detail and then I felt worse than ever because it all wasn't real, and for a while I thought about Dr. Bohadlo and about Irena and about that guy I'd kicked in the stomach and about the communists and that, maybe, instead of just waiting around, the thing to do was get out and do something. But why? And then back came the girl and I whispered I love you, I love you, and saw her in a pretty dress in Prague at the university and beside the river on a fall evening; so I went on and hardly knew any more quite what it was I was thinking about and what was real and what wasn't until I fell asleep with all these pleasant thoughts, without even knowing how.

Monday, May 7, 1945

I woke up drenched with sweat from head to foot. It was already one o'clock. I lay there with the covers drawn up to my chin, my chest and neck cool from a draft seeping in under the blankets. Still, it was good I was sweating like that. I called Mother and asked her to bring me a towel. She brought two plus a fresh pair of pajamas.

"Should I call the doctor?" she asked.

"No," I said. "It's just an ordinary cold."

"Would you like some tea?"

"Yes. And some lunch, too, if it's ready."

Mother went out to the kitchen and I tossed off the covers and got out of my sweaty pajamas and rubbed myself down with a towel. I could feel the blood pulsing through my veins. I put on the clean pajamas, turned the quilt over and plumped it up, straightened the pillows, and climbed back into bed again. Then I rubbed my face and hair with the towel. I felt like I'd just had a bath. Mother brought lunch in on a tray and set it down in front of me. I finished it all off in no time and drank the tea. It warmed me up. Then I put the tray down next to the bed, crawled under the covers again, and closed my eyes. I felt fine. But then I started remembering again and the feeling started to fade. I remembered what had happened the night before, the explosion at the station, the whole thing, and wondered why they'd done it, what they got out of it, why they couldn't wait like everybody else until it all blew over, whether it was for glory or what, and for the life of me I couldn't see why and all it did was spoil that comfy feeling I had there in bed, so I switched over to thinking about Irena like I always did when I wanted to feel good, about all those evenings she'd left me feeling good, bad, or indifferent, though when I thought of her now it was only the good feelings that came to mind. I closed my eyes, listened to the clock tick, and thought about Irena, how once, the winter before, I'd gone with her from Stare Mesto by train and we'd sat there together in the dim compartment and I'd put my arm around her waist and told her I loved her and she'd pushed me away and started saying, as usual, that we were just good friends, I was back in my element then and went right on thinking about her. It seemed to me that my whole life was made up of only Irena and Vera and Eva and Jarinka, of what I'd had with them, and of nothing else really. And other people's lives were exactly the same. I thought about the other guys and was pretty sure that all they ever thought about was girls and that girls were all they talked about, too. Girls, and music. Yes. Music and girls. That was life. Music was great and, whether I was thinking about the past or about what the future would bring, it was always connected with either music or girls. Like, once we were rehearsing at the Lion Inn and the girls were sitting around a table, looking at us, and I sat there hunched over my saxophone and I could see Vera had her eye on me and I knew that with my sax to my lips and with that whole complicated array of valves working away under my fingertips I must look pretty terrific, and that made me feel good. And then there was that big graduation dance in 1940. It was in the big ballroom at the Lion. The chandeliers, high up, were all lit and the girls dressed up in their tulle evening gowns and then I got up in a white dinner jacket and played my fine, tender solo in "I've Got a Guy" or that wild solo in "Liza Likes Nobody" and I never felt so great in my whole life. Nobody feels better than when he's playing. I got up and Mr. Flux turned the spotlight on me and there I stood, all in white, with my sideburns and glistening saxophone and Irena was down there in the darkened ballroom watching. That's the way it was with music. Something wonderful,

G*

maybe even more wonderful than girls, except wherever there's music, there're girls, too. It was all part of the same piece of happiness, it was life, maybe the best thing about life there was, and when I thought of the future, I could see notes in front of me on a music stand and a band up on the stage and me with a golden saxophone and beautiful girls wearing low-cut gowns and a lost look in their eyes from the music and smiles on their lips when I looked their way and I could see myself out on my evening stroll through Prague and all those big, fancy, blasé houses and apartments and they were part of it, too, part of my jazz, and of life, and suddenly that kind of life scared me even though it looked as if that's just the way mine would turn out—full of jazz and girls, pretty, beautiful, sweet, gaudy girls I could look at as long as I lived, which probably wouldn't be very long, and then I thought about the others, about Fonda who wanted to be an architect and the only reason I could think of for him wanting to be an architect was that he could make a pile of money that way and live in a swanky house outside of Prague, because why else would a guy like Fonda want to be an architect? But that was life. Jazz and the girls and the memories. It couldn't be any other way, I thought. Because they were all that was worth living for. That business of working at the factory, of getting up at five in the morning and coming home at eight at night sure hadn't been living. No. This was life. Just this. And I couldn't help thinking how nice it would be if there was a God, and I thought to myself, too bad there isn't, at least not the kind you learn about in Sunday school and it's anybody's guess what He's really like and how it all began and maybe He's like they say in Sunday school after all, but I couldn't believe it and I couldn't believe He'd damn me to hell even if that was the kind of God He was, because I'd lived a pretty decent life and I had the feeling I'd never been very bad though I'd been pretty fresh a few times maybe and let a few girls down pretty hard when they thought I was serious and found out I wasn't, and I thought about, when I was little, that kid called Vocenil who sat right behind me in grade school, how he always smelled of bread and about those games we used to play in Bucina, the slingshots we had and the castles we built out of sticks and stones and it was all wrapped in a sort of autumnal haze and it was all so long ago, and after that came the winter evenings and high school and then the band and electric lights in the Manes' drawing room and the wine cellar at the Lion and the Port Arthur and the light on the sax and the trumpet and the way the moist reed tasted in my mouth and the swimming pool with girls in their bathing suits and it got all mixed up and swirled and danced all around me and I was in it, too, watching how I lived, and I couldn't tell whether it was good or bad or why I was living at all, but lying there in bed it didn't seem to matter, because I felt comfy and warm and that's all that mattered to me. Those memories were enough for me, and daydreaming about the future. It was all so peculiar, I could hardly believe it myself, because I knew I was living in 1945 and that the biggest war of all time was just coming to an end, a war in which millions of people had been killed and millions more had been horribly wounded and had lived through hell in the mud and the hospitals and millions more had been tortured and killed by the Germans in concentration camps— I thought of all those deaths and wondered what life was about, what the point was, and it seemed to me it didn't have any, unless maybe just thinking about girls and music, and I wondered if that was enough to live for, but nothing else came to mind so I left it at that and quickly started thinking about Irena again, about one walk we'd taken through the woods one night and how awfully inferior I'd felt when she started talking about Victor Hugo and Byron and I got Byron mixed up with Balzac and Balzac with Barbusse and I hadn't read anything by any of them, and it seemed to me I was as dumb as ever and that what was really important was inventing new things and new medicines—obviously very important—but that even without them you could still get along but that without girls and music life wouldn't be worth living, and so my thoughts cruised through my head until I fell asleep and when I woke up I saw it was already evening. Outside my window the sky was red and the windows of the other houses shone with the setting sun. It was spring and the end of the German Protectorate.

Father came into the room and said he was going to turn on the radio. I lay there sprawled out in bed, listening to the news from Prague which was interesting and exciting, and I could see it all going on in my head, and Father said things were quiet in town, that the Germans hadn't made a fuss about the raid last night and that this afternoon the whole garrison had moved out. I asked him if they'd let the people at the brewery go home and Father said yes, some, but that all the others were still there, and then I asked him if he knew anything about Prema but he didn't. Then they announced over the radio that Hradcany was on fire and Father clenched his fists and called the Germans beasts and vandals and I could see it, imagine it burning, and somehow it made me glad that it was and that now they'd have to build new buildings there and that now maybe everything would be new and better than it had been before and I looked forward to getting up the next morning and seeing Irena again and my friends and how we'd sit and play and I looked forward to playing my sax and to that unknown girl I'd meet in Prague. It was getting dark. Father switched off the radio and left. I was alone in my room. I turned off the light, looked out the window at the stars twinkling in the sky because the rain clouds had passed over and I thought about things and then my eyes wouldn't stay open and I fell asleep.

Tuesday, May 8, 1945

The next morning I'd just left the house and started walking down the street when I saw them—a bunch of men in green khaki uniforms and dusty shoes with knapsacks on their backs. The sun was shining and the men looked exhausted and they trudged on in silence. The minute I saw them I knew they were English. A tall, lean man with a gaunt face was in the lead and next to him an older, short, bowlegged guy who had sergeant's stripes on his sleeve. I caught up with the older one and asked, "Are you English?"

He stopped, looked at me in surprise and then said, "Yes."

"Welcome," I said. They gathered around me and the older guy said, "You speak English?"

"Sure," I said.

"Well," the sergeant said, "we are trying to get to the Americans. Think we might find a car around here anywhere?"

I understood him. "A car would be hard," I told him, "but you can wait here until the Russians come."

"We would rather reach the Americans," he said hesitantly. A buzz of agreement ran through the bunch of men.

"I know," I said. "But it's impossible. The trains aren't running now."

"A shame," said the sergeant.

"How far is it from here to Prague?" asked a guy with a

red mustache and wearing a bright Scottish cap. I noticed they were all cleanshaven.

"One hundred and forty-three kilometers," I said.

"Which is. . . ?"

"About a hundred miles," said the tall man with the gaunt face.

"We'll never make it," said the bowlegged sergeant.

"No. The Russians'll catch up with us," said the Scotsman.

"But you can stay here," I said. "We'll put you up and feed you." I said it without even thinking but I knew people'd be interested in Englishmen.

"Do you know where the Russians are now?" the sergeant said.

"No. But they ought to be here any day."

I was feeling pretty proud of my English. The Tommies started talking about what they should do. They stood around the sergeant, talking in low, calm voices. It seemed to me now that the whole street was full of people. I looked around and saw a weird-looking crew in moss-green uniforms streaming across the square. There were slews of them. Me and my Englishmen stood there like an island in the midst of that sea of people. Lots of them had Mongolian faces and droopy walrus whiskers and they milled around, most of them without any knapsacks, and more kept coming in all the time. They all had big su's painted on their backs with whitewash. "Soviet Union," I realized. Prisoners of war from the eastern front. The sun shone into their oriental faces and they had a queer smell which I rather liked. They streamed in and around like a great wave. Jesus, no wonder that the SS, even with death's heads on their caps, had gone under in a sea like this. Seeing so many I felt a strange awe, and maybe fear, too. The POWs must have mutinied somewhere in Germany. And now they were on their way west. I saw Berty Moutelik with a white armband and his camera dangling over his belly. He grinned at me from a distance.

"Hi, Danny. You an escort, too?"

"What do you mean?"

"What have you got there? Frenchmen?"

"What?"

"Well, you're taking them over to City Hall, aren't you?" Berty stopped and I noticed that a ragged little cluster of men with canes and knapsacks stopped behind him.

"Listen, Berty, what's going on anyway? I was sick in bed yesterday."

"You mean you don't know? They're POWs escaping from Germany ahead of the front. They're all supposed to report to City Hall."

"Why?"

"Well, for order's sake, I guess. And they all get a coupon for lunch at Lewith's."

"Oh, I see. Who are those guys with you?"

"Poles. And yours?"

"Englishmen."

"Englishmen?" Berty's eyes lit up. "They're the first, then. There haven't been any up till now."

"Maybe they are, then. You say they're supposed to report at City Hall?"

"Yes."

"Well, I'll show 'em the way then. So long and thanks."

"Oh, you're quite welcome," said Berty and went on. I turned to my Englishmen.

"Listen," I said. "You're all supposed to report at City Hall."

"Why?" the old sergeant asked suspiciously.

"I don't know. An order from the City Council."

"And we must?"

"Well, it's an order."

The sergeant studied me for quite a while. I could feel he was slowly beginning to trust me. Because I spoke English probably. It had probably been quite a while since he'd met anybody who did.

"You see," he said, "we don't like registering—any-where."

"I understand, but you don't need to be scared."

"We aren't scared, laddie. We just don't care to register anywhere," said the tall man with the hollow cheeks.

"Okay," I said. "Only you've got to. I'm very sorry about that."

"Don't you think, sir," said the sergeant, "we might simply pass through town—without going through all these formalities?"

"But what do you want to do?"

"As I say, we want to reach the Americans."

"But you can't get through to them. There's a revolution going on in Prague."

"What?" the sergeant asked, shocked.

"A revolution."

"The communists?" he asked in a tense whisper.

"I don't know. All I know is it's a revolution against the Germans."

"Oh, I see," he said. "But then the Americans must surely be there by now."

"No. They aren't there."

"But we heard that the Third Army was already in Czechoslovakia."

"They are. But they stopped at Pilsen."

"Where's that?"

"About two hundred miles from here."

"Great God!" said the sergeant. "Why aren't they advancing?"

I shrugged. He turned to his companions. The men—there must have been about twenty of them—huddled around me and the old bowlegged sergeant told them something which I couldn't make out because he spoke too fast and too English for me. All around us the stream of fleeing men flowed on. The Englishmen stood in a tight group by themselves, keeping their distance from the swarm of others. They were English. Then the sergeant turned to me.

"Listen, friend," he said. "I take it we can trust you?"

"Sure," I said with a real American accent, which made me feel good.

"Tell me then, is it true that war's broken out between the Russians and the Western allies?"

"What?" I yelled and this time I sounded even more American than before.

"A war," said the sergeant slowly and distinctly so I'd

understand. "Between Russia and Great Britain and America. Understand?"

"That's nonsense," I said, and suddenly remembered a nice expression I'd read once in some article about Ford. Ford, apparently, had used it about history. "That's bunk," I said.

"You're quite sure?"

"Absolutely."

"But that's what they told us."

"Where?"

"In camp."

"Oh, they've been pulling your leg," I said, this time in very British English. "That's the Germans for you. That would suit them fine—a war between Russia and the West." I was surprised myself how well my English came out.

"Perhaps you're right," said the sergeant.

"Of course I'm right. How long ago were you captured?"

"I was in the rear guard at Dunkirk. It's been five years now."

"Oh, I see," I said and felt respect for the old guy. "Listen, you can trust me completely. I think the best thing for you to do is wait here for the Russians. You are welcome here in Czechoslovakia."

"Thank you. Well then, I suppose we should stay," said the sergeant. "What do you say, men?"

The Englishmen started muttering among themselves.

"There wouldn't seem to be much choice," said the Scotsman.

"All right," I said. "Then come with me." I walked between the tall thin man and the sergeant as we headed toward the square. The stream of people swept us along. Flags were flying again from people's windows and the morning sun made their colors look brighter than ever. The white-lettered backs of the Russian POWs bobbed along in front of us and the sun brightened the letters. I noticed that the Englishmen stuck close together. You could tell they felt strange in that seething mass of people. I felt strange and different there, too. I felt there was danger in the air, as if all those heads were full of hidden violence, though I knew very well they weren't, and that all these poor Mongolians were thinking about was food. I was still subconsciously parroting the racial lines that Goebbels had drummed into us. As we passed the loan association building, a whole troop of police came out of a side street, led by Chief Rimbalnik. They marched quickly off in the direction of the ghetto. Mr. Rimbalnik was pale but otherwise as pompous as ever in his corset and white gloves. The blue-uniformed police plunged into the dirty gray sea of prison camp fugitives and made their way over to the other side of the square. A couple of bearded, ragged old gypsies respectfully stepped aside for Mr. Rimbalnik, probably out of respect for that corset of his. No wonder. That corset had made lots of people respect him. That and those gold epaulets on his uniform. An SS man made a pass at Mrs. Cuceova in her store once—she was the pastry shopkeeper's young widow—just as Mr. Rimbalnik walked in. He had a crush on the widow himself and when he saw how that SS man was trying to feel around with her, he turned red as a beet and bellowed at him in perfect German and the SS man just clicked his heels, saluted, and left. Probably never seen a blue uniform like that in his life, with all those gold epaulets, and thought Rimbalnik was some kind of admiral. Or else that corset subconsciously reminded him of Prussian drills and he forgot all about race. God knows. Anyhow, after that performance, Mr. Rimbalnik nearly fainted and the widow had to revive him with rum in her kitchen in the back of the shop. Though maybe Mr. Rimbalnik was just putting on an act. He had a crush on her and finally, they say, he got what he was after.

We made our way past the loan association office as far as the square. It was bright with the sun and swarming with people. A long line of people, some in uniform and some not, stretched all the way from the City Hall to the church. Most of them were men but there were some women, too. And mostly they were the bright green Soviets, lots of them, with bunches of civilians and people wearing other uniforms mixed in. At the corner just ahead of us stood a handful of soldiers wearing blue uniforms. One of them, a swarthy little guy, came up to us and asked something in French. My bowlegged sergeant started talking to him. I couldn't understand a word.

"Wait here," I said. "I'll see what's going on at City Hall." I took the army armband out of my pocket and put it on my sleeve. Then I started elbowing my way toward City Hall and the armband helped. People stepped back for me on both sides so I got through without too much trouble and also got a chance to take a look around. People were standing and sitting all around on the pavement, most of them silent. The Mongolians interested me. When I looked at them, they smiled broadly and their small eyes almost disappeared in the deep creases of their flat faces. Lots of them wore long, droopy Mongolian mustaches and all of them stank of straw or stables or something like that. It was as if they carried around the scent of vast virgin lands in them though, God knows, it was probably just a concentration camp smell, I said to myself, because the Germans hadn't pampered these inferior races like they had my Englishmen, yet even in spite of living in those camps they'd somehow never lost that country smell, that smell of horses and straw. I wanted to say something to them but I didn't know what, so I said in English, "Cheer up, boys," which made me feel pretty heroic, and then I passed by a bunch of curly-headed Italians and when I said "Cheer up, boys" to them they all clustered around and one of them, a handsome dark-skinned guy with a real beard already shaping up under the stubble, started jabbering away at me but I couldn't understand what he was saying until suddenly I realized he was mixing a few words of English in with a lot more Italian. "Americano?" he said. "Army Americano?" No, no, I said and kept right on going and finally there I was at City Hall. Two soldiers with fixed bayonets stood at either side of the door and between them was Mr. Kobrt, wearing a white armband with a red cross on it. They were only letting one small bunch in at a time. Mr. Kobrt was yelling at the weary, ragged fugitives in a mixture of Russian and German. They looked tiny in front of him because he had a hyperproduction of the hypophysis, or something like that anyway.

"Good morning," I said.

"Good morning," he said without even bothering to look at me. He'd collared a couple of gypsies and was bawling them out. I stood there watching him and gradually came to the conclusion that I wasn't going to get all caught up in this organization. I could just imagine that bunch of bureaucrats sitting around a table inside asking these bedraggled characters for their name and religion and all the rest of it so everything would be in order and so Mr. Machacek would have plenty of material for his history of the Kostelec uprising. Then I noticed they were roughing a Russian around and decided then and there that I'd look after my Englishmen myself. I'd been an Anglophile for as long as I could remember, especially since the time I fell in love with Judy Garland, and now here was my chance to do something about it. And I knew plenty of people around town. And suddenly I felt like taking care of these guys. And putting them up in the most comfortable houses in Kostelec. Sure. At Dr. Sabata's. At the Mouteliks's Wholesale Notions. At Dr. Vasak's. All sorts of places they could stay came to mind and I was convinced the ladies of the house would welcome them. Because they were Englishmen. Sure. The little Mongolians could sleep on the floor in Lewith's cafeteria but my Englishmen would snooze in Dr. Vasak's guest room. I glanced over at Mr. Kobrt and saw he was busy barking away at some muzhik in the doorway and I decided to skip the whole thing and turned and made my way back through the crowd. I was lucky.

Before I got back to my Englishmen, I bumped into Dr. Vasak's wife at the corner by the cigarstore. She was standing there in a white linen dress without any stockings on and the hair on her legs glistened like gold. She had a red string bag in her hand and around her neck a string of big blue beads.

"Good afternoon," I said, and smiled. She smiled back a very affectionate smile. Yes. Dr. Vasak's wife was fond of me. I used to sit with her and her husband and my parents at Sokol Hall Saturday nights during the war, and while other people discussed the war, we just looked at each other.

"Could I ask a favor of you?"

"Why, of course," she said with that same nice smile.

"Well, you see, the thing is I've got these Englishmen—boys who fought at Dunkirk—and I'd like to find a nice place they could stay for a few days, because . . . well, you can see for yourself," I said, gesturing toward the colorful, stinking crowds all around us. "And, after all . . . I mean, they're Englishmen." I paused and looked at Mrs. Vasakova as though she would naturally understand what that meant.

"I'd be glad to, Mr. Smiricky. Of course," she said. "How many do you have?"

"Well, how many do you think you could take?"

The doctor's wife thought a moment. She looked at me with her pretty blue eyes and tapped the sidewalk with the heel of her little white shoe. My God, I thought, those guys are in for some welcome all right.

"Would four be enough?" she said.

"Why, of course. Four would be fine," I said, and smiled at her.

She smiled, too, and then added quickly, "And how many do you have?"

"About twenty," I said. "But I hope I'll find other people as helpful as you've been."

"Wait a minute. Go to my sister-in-law's. Tell her I sent you, will you? Mrs. Heiserova, the managing director's wife." She looked happily excited, but when she saw I was still smiling, she blushed. "I'm sure she'll take in a few too," she said a bit more stiffly.

"Thank you very much."

"Be sure to call on her. And say I sent you."

"I certainly will. And thanks again."

"And now where are these Englishmen of yours?"

"Would you mind coming along with me?" I said, and took her over to meet her Englishmen. They were still standing there on the corner and they saw us coming but it wasn't me they were looking at.

"Do you speak English?" I asked her.

"Unfortunately, I don't. But perhaps some of them know French or German."

"I'm sure they do," I said. We stopped and Mrs. Vasakova smiled at the Englishmen. The Englishmen smiled back at Mrs. Vasakova and the biggest smile came from the bowlegged sergeant.

"Listen," I said. "I've fixed it so you won't have to register. Now I'll take you around to some of the best families where you'll be put up for a few days."

"Splendid," said the tall, hollow-cheeked redhead. "Thank you very much, friend."

"Okay," I said. "This is Mrs. Vasakova who's been kind enough to offer to take four of you in at her place."

They all beamed again and Mrs. Vasakova beamed back. I turned to the sergeant. "Sergeant, pick four men, and it would be good if they could speak French. Mrs. Vasakova speaks French."

"I speak French," said the redheaded Scot and turned to the doctor's wife. "*Je parle français, madame,*" he told her. The doctor's wife smiled again.

"Well, I know some French ways," said a broad-shouldered, smooth-shaven Don Juan with a bandaged head. He grinned. "*Merci, madame,*" he said to the doctor's wife. She smiled and I glanced at the sergeant and saw he was following the whole scene with great interest.

"Two more, sergeant," I said. "Two more to go." The sergeant snapped to attention and looked his men over.

"That's the lot. Nobody else speaks French," he said and then turned and, with a glint in his eye, added, "except for me."

"Yes, but I'm going to need you. You're the commander here," I said. Looking dejected, he about-faced, paused, and gave his order, "Kilpatrick and O'Donnell, fall out," and two well-built but wiry men emerged from the crowd. No doubt about it, he certainly knew how to pick a team for the doctor's wife.

"Aye, aye, sir," said one of the men and grinned.

"That's it, then," said the sergeant.

Looking very slim and pretty in her white dress, Mrs.

Vasakova stood there surrounded by the four Englishmen, and she laughed.

"Thank you very much," I said.

"Not at all. I thank you," she said with a wink. She'd stopped being so formal with me now.

"We'll all meet here tomorrow at nine," I told the four and they mumbled that that would be all right with them.

"Goodby," said the doctor's wife with a friendly smile, and started off down the street flanked by her imposing escorts.

"Well, let's go," I said and tried to think where to find places to put the rest of them up. We were walking along under the arcade when suddenly I had a bright idea.

"Would you like to go for a swim?" I asked.

"Sure," said the sergeant and then so did all the rest of them. Just the idea of a swim seemed to pick them up.

"Come on, then," I said, and headed toward the municipal pool in the loan association building. The door was open and there stood Mr. Vimler, the bank janitor and furnaceman, and the old lady who sold tickets.

"Good morning," I said to them. They looked at me and said good morning.

"These Englishmen here would like to go for a swim," I said.

The old lady looked at me uncertainly. "But they're filthy!" she said.

"That's just why they want to."

"Well, I don't know . . ."

"Don't worry, I'll tell them they'll have to take showers first."

"And you're going to pay for it?"

"Well, no. I thought you'd be kind enough to let them in free?"

"Free? Oh, we can't have that."

"Why not?"

"Well, because I would be held responsible."

"But look, these are Allied soldiers."

"Nobody's told me anything."

"Why should anybody tell you anything?"

"Well, because I'm in charge here."

"Now, look, I'll make out a receipt for you stating that you allowed twenty English soldiers in for a swim and then you make out a bill for it, all right?"

"I don't know . . ."

"Go ahead. Let 'em in, Mrs. Maslova," said Mr. Vimler.

"There. You see," I said.

"Oh, well, all right," said the old lady. "But you'll have to write out a receipt for me."

"Of course," I said. "Come on in, boys. You can undress in the locker room and you're supposed to shower before going into the pool."

The Englishmen filed in through the door. I led them into the big room where the old lady was already opening up the separate changing rooms one after another. You went in one side and the other door led out to the pool. I went out through to the pool. Shining through the tall frosted windows, the light made everything look clean and bright. The water in the pool looked green from the tiles at the bottom and the surface lay smooth as glass. It was quiet there and empty and the light was pleasant. I stood by the window and leaned back against the wall, alone, while the Englishmen got undressed. I looked around the pool with its greenish light and memories started filtering in and I could see the place lit by evening light, the way it'd been on winter evenings during the war and there was Irena in a yellow bathing suit, and I could see her thighs, a bit flattened from the way she'd been squatting down before slipping down next to me, and Christ, they were lovely, and her knees and her firm little belly in that yellow bathing suit and her girlish shoulders and that red mouth and I watched her swimming, slender and nearly naked in the translucent water of the pool and then standing under the shower with a rubber cap on her head, stretching her arms, her suit glued to her body, and then going into the changing room and I knew that there, behind that white door, she was undressing and drying herself off with a towel and I swam madly around the pool and suffered because I wanted her so. A long time ago, yet it had only been that winter. And now all that was over. Everything. And it would never be the same again because who could tell what would happen? We meet and we part and everything in life comes to an end, nothing lasts, and I felt like dying but then I thought supposing there's a heaven after all, and me with all my sins, and that got me off onto heaven and I wondered what it was really like and whether people there were the same as here when they died, which would be pretty stupid because, as a rule, pretty girls like Irena live until they're old and gray, but then I thought that in heaven everybody would have to look like they did when they were looking their best, which would make it quite a place to go, I thought. But then I wondered how things were arranged there when here on earth Irena went with Zdenek but in heaven, where people are supposed to be happy, would she go with me? But then Zdenek would be unhappy. But maybe Zdenek would go to hell or else maybe I would. Or maybe things are somehow secretly organized so everybody in heaven can go with whoever he wants to. For instance, Irena would somehow be split up into two Irenas. Only then it occurred to me that she'd have to be divided into at least five because I knew of at least five guys who are crazy about her. But I didn't much like that idea. I was dead set against her being all split into pieces. I wanted to have her all to myself and Zdenek and all the others could just go to hell instead. And suddenly a door opened and out came one of the Englishmen, naked and hairy, and he looked around the pool curiously.

"There. The showers!" I called to him and pointed them out to him.

"Thanks!" he said and by now others were already coming out and running toward the showers.

The place echoed with yells and laughter. I looked at all those naked, wet bodies and just then right in front of me a short, naked fellow clambered out of the pool. He had tremendously broad shoulders, narrow hips, and a farmer's beard and he grinned at me and said happily, "Wonderful feeling. Five years is a long time."

He stood there in front of me and started slapping himself all over his body, then laughed, turned, and his white backside flashed in front of me as he dove back into the water. All over the pool naked men were racing around, giggling and laughing and romping like kids. I saw one funny little bowlegged guy tramping around the edge of the pool toward me and thought it must be the sergeant. It was. He told me it was really wonderful and he'd missed being able to swim for five years, and then the tall one came over to tell me the same thing—the one with the gaunt face. But it was only his face that was so thin. Otherwise he had the build of a wrestler. A really fierce sight, with a big red scar on his chest. I watched them all and it was strange to see. It made you think about what they'd been through and where they'd go from here and what else they'd have to live through and it made me feel sad again. Then I heard someone calling me. It was the little old lady from the ticket office. She was leaning out the window of her booth, taking a sidelong glance at all those naked men. I went over to the window.

"Now then, write me out that receipt, young man," she said and handed me a piece of paper and a pencil. I thought a while, listened to the splashing and laughing behind me that filled the whole pool, and then wrote: *"This is to certify that on May 8, 1945, twenty soldiers of the British Army swam free of charge in the municipal pool."*

I signed it and handed the paper back to the old lady. She read it, glanced over at the pool again, then shut her window. I turned and watched them for a little while. Finally the little sergeant climbed up to the diving board and bellowed something in such an ear-shattering voice that, coming from a bandylegged and nearly-old-man's body like his, seemed incredible and suddenly all those who were still in the water scrambled out and rushed off to the changing rooms. I went out and sat down on a bench out in the lobby. It was empty and quiet. I used to wait there for Irena and she'd always come out, scrubbed and pink in her blue coat with the white fur collar. Well, that was all over now. And on the wide staircase with its rubber matting there was always a flock of Kostelec matrons coming from their steam baths and massages personally supervised by Mr. Repa, a professional masseur, who I was later assigned to assist at the Messerschmidt factory and whose hands looked like a butcher's and they always reminded me of the fat bodies of those women swaddled in white sheets and I could see Mr. Repa's hands, tattooed with a heart and an anchor, mercilessly and with sadistic delight kneading away at those doughy bellies and thighs and buttocks. A limp palm tree stood at the foot of the stairs and the light coming through the frosted glass had a warm glow. The tub baths were upstairs where Prema used to go with Benda to look at the girls because at the top of one of the compartments you could slip out a pane of that frosted glass so they took turns crawling along the concrete beam at the top and taking a peek.

The door of one of the changing rooms opened and a fellow came out in a beard and wearing an Australian sombrero. I saw it was the big-shouldered guy who'd gotten such a kick out of the pool. He grinned at me. Then the others started coming out. They looked refreshed and were in a fine mood. I got up and led them out. The street was in shadow but the rooftops stood out bright in the sun. It was a real spring day. I wondered where we should go now. Then I noticed Mr. Moutelik's shop on the other side of the street. His sign hadn't been touched since Haryk had painted it over on Saturday.

"Wait here for me," I told the sergeant, and walked into the shop. Nobody was there, not even a salesgirl today, just Mrs. Moutelikova at the cash register. She was wearing big pearl earrings and her hair looked fresh out of curlers.

"Good morning, ma'am," I said.

"Hello, Danny," she said. "What can we do for you?"

"Well, I've got a little problem, ma'am," I said, feeling my way.

"Oh? What is it?"

"Well, I've taken charge of a few Englishmen, you see, and I have to find a place for them to stay for a few days, and you know how Englishmen are," I said shyly, "always want to have a bath, can't stand to be dirty, and I wouldn't want to make them stay in an emergency barrack or anything like that."

"Of course not, Danny. How many do you have to take care of?"

"That depends, ma'am, on how many you think you could take."

"For how long?" she asked cautiously.

"Oh, just for a couple of days. Until we can put them on a train to Prague."

"Aha. Would four be all right?"

"It certainly would."

"Well . . . it's a pleasure to be of assistance."

"Thank you very much, ma'am."

"You're quite welcome. We've got to do our part. After all, they're our liberators."

"Absolutely, ma'am. Thank you." I would have loved to see what would have happened if I'd brought her four Mongolians with walrus mustaches, thanked her again and went on my way. I still had twelve left. We started down Jirasek Boulevard toward the station. The colorful crowds still kept coming toward us. They poured along the street in a cloud of dust and among them I saw various people I knew wearing white and red-and-white armbands. The crowd was still mainly green-uniformed Soviets, but I saw a couple of guys in khaki uniforms, too, with NEDER-LAND on their shoulder patches. Then a cluster of gypsy-looking Italians and some Frenchmen in blue uniforms. But I had my Englishmen—the pick of the whole crop, I thought. I was looking at all those different faces as we pushed against the tide and suddenly bumped into Benno and his sister Evka.

"Hi, Benno," I said.

"Greetings," said Benno.

"Hello there, Evka."

"Hello."

"Why didn't you show up yesterday?" said Benno.

"I was feeling lousy."

"You're always feeling lousy."

"Maybe so. Look, Benno, could you do me a favor?"

"What?"

"Could you take in a couple of Englishmen over at your house?"

"You mean they're English?" Evka asked, looking at my troop with obvious interest now.

"Yes. You can talk to them if you want to," I said, feeling like a barker at a sideshow. Evka smiled at the Englishmen and I looked at them and they were all scrubbed and refreshed now and they were all grinning at Evka.

"How do you do?" said Evka in English.

"How d'you do?" they said in chorus.

Evka smiled and didn't know how to say what she wanted to say next.

"Take them with you," I said.

"Yeah, all right. But not all of 'em," said Benno.

"How many?"

"Well . . . what do you say, Evka?"

"Well . . . about . . . about five, I'd say—all right?"

"Okay," I said. "Sergeant, five men with this beautiful girl."

"As you wish, sir!" said the sergeant and grinned. He turned to his bunch of men and barked out the names of five men. One by one they stepped forward and saluted Evka, and Evka shook hands with them. I felt proud of myself. They'd better be grateful, I thought—with me, like an angel of peace, providing them with deluxe accommodations, with beautiful young matrons and girls, after all those years of deprivation and hardship. I turned to Benno.

"You going to be home this afternoon, Benno?"

"Yeah. Come on over."

"I will. Any news from the brewery?"

"We've got to be there tomorrow."

"Why?"

"They put up an announcement that anybody who enlisted who doesn't turn up tomorrow will be treated as a deserter."

"Honest?"

"Honest."

"That's stupid."

"They're stupid."

"Are you going?"

"What can I do? We're in a big enough mess as it is."

"You mean on account of Sunday?"

"Well, Sunday's enough, isn't it?"

"Oh, that wasn't so bad."

"Don't kid yourself."

"Well, we'll see. So I'll come over this afternoon, right?"

"Right."

"So long then. Goodby, Evka," I said.

" 'By," Evka said to me. She was already chattering away with her Englishmen.

"Have fun," I said with a small smile that was half leer.

"I'll try," she said.

"So long," said Benno.

We left them and turned off to the left and took the path that leads around behind the spinning mill. I thought I'd take them to the expensive residential part of town where Mrs. Heiserova lived. To the left, the castle rose high above us, its red cupolas gleaming in the sun and a flag fluttering against the blue sky, while below off to the right the spinning mill sprawled, with its fire reservoir whose oily water made splotchy rainbows out of the sun, and then the endless rows of warehouses which made the place look even more desolate than usual—the barred windows crusted with dust, the pointless renaissance ornaments writhing on grimy towers, the big gravel yard, the abandoned freightcars standing on a siding. The whole plant was surrounded by an iron fence which curved off in the direction of the workers' district, and on the slope below the castle the villas and mansions of the mill's directors and assistant directors caught the full slant of the sun. Mr. Heiser was the general director and his house stood in the middle of a huge garden crisscrossed by sanded paths. It was a big two-story house with a big balcony and a glassed-in sunporch at one corner and the garage doors underneath it were green. We stopped at the gate. Vines arched overhead, and I pushed the doorbell under the brass nameplate with the inscription, ARNOLD HEISER, GENERAL DIRECTOR, UNITED TEXTILE WORKS INC., and we waited. The mansion shimmered against the green hillside and my Englishmen stared at it with open mouths. Then a voice came through the speaker by the gate.

"Yes. Who is it?" The voice sounded tinny, but I could tell it was a woman's, and I leaned up close to the mouthpiece and answered, "Smiricky. May I speak with the lady of the house, please?"

"Just a moment." I stepped back from the mouthpiece and we waited again. I looked at the yellow path that led to the sunporch. A couple of birds were hopping along it. I could hear them chirping and there was also a soft, rustling sound in the air, like wind blowing through a forest, but then I realized that it was a fountain. Everything was quiet here. I looked around at my Englishmen again. They were standing there with their knapsacks on their backs and when I turned they all stared at me. Then for the first time I noticed how wrinkled and torn and dusty their khaki uniforms were, how dirty their shoes were. The sergeant took off his cap. His head was shiny in the sun. He took out a red handkerchief, mopped his forehead, and smiled at me.

"Hot," he said.

"Yes," I said with a smile. "Awfully hot." Then I nodded toward Heiser's house and said, "Pretty, isn't it?"

"That it is," he said and put on his cap again.

The speaker crackled, "Come right in, Mr. Smiricky," and the door buzzer sounded. I opened the gate and stepped into the garden. The Englishmen remained standing where they were.

"Come on," I said. "You can wait for me in the garden."

One by one they came through the gate and we all started off toward the mansion. Their heavy shoes crunched in the sand. The door to the sun porch opened and there stood Mitzi, the maid, in a short black dress with a white apron and little white cap.

"Good morning," I said to her.

"Good morning," she said and her voice, which sounded like metal over the speaker, sounded very nice in the flesh. The white bib of her apron was loosely pinned over her well-rounded breasts. All I could do for a minute was stare.

"May I speak with Mrs. Heiserova?" I asked.

"Come in, please," she said with a smile, and stepped a bit to one side.

"Wait for me here," I said to the Englishmen, and started up the stairs to the veranda. I'd been in the big entrance hall before. It was full of potted palms and dark green rubber plants and paintings by Spala and Rabas hung from the walls. Mitzi went ahead and opened the door to the salon.

"Please go in," she said to me with that professional smile of hers, except I was sure it wasn't just professional. The skirt she had on was awfully short and she was wearing silk stockings and high heels.

"Thank you," I said and passed by so close I could nearly feel the warmth of her body coming out through her dress. I entered the salon. It was full of highly polished sideboards and china cupboards and alabaster figurines and Persian rugs and the sunshine poured through the big window and, filtered through an immense aquarium, fell on the wife of the general director, Mrs. Heiserova who, stuffed into a silk dress with a string of pearls stretched across her balloon-shaped bosom, was sitting in an armchair next to the silver smokingstand. Mrs. Kramperova, widow of a Lewith Mill attorney, sat across from her, a cigarette dangling between her fingers. Both ladies stared up at me, dumbly. I knew what they'd probably been talking about. And that they were both scared—Mrs. Heiserova, because she was always scared of something; Mrs. Kramperova, because of Krobe. Looking at her now, I couldn't figure out what Krobe had seen in her anyway. Krobe had been the chief German plant supervisor at the Messerschmidt plant, one of those blond, elegant, fanatical Nazis; during the war he had boarded and roomed with Mrs. Kramperova. And obviously bedded with her, too. They always used to go around together—Krobe in his leather coat with a swastika in his buttonhole, and that tubby little widow on his arm. I came across them in the woods a couple times and was always surprised at Krobe. So now the widow was probably scared on account of that and had come over to console herself with her best friend. Her bosom friend. The English expression occurred to me and, looking at their bosoms on display behind all that flowered silk, all sorts of wild and dirty thoughts ran through my head.

"I kiss your hand," I said.

Both ladies inclined their heads.

"Mrs. Heiserova, I have a request to make," I said smoothly.

"Go right ahead," said the general director's wife, and suddenly a mean bit of strategy crossed my mind.

"I'm in charge of a group of escaped prisoners of war," I said. "They've escaped from a camp in Upper Silesia and I'd like to place them somewhere for a few days until they can get a train to Prague."

"Yes," said the general director's wife in a neutral tone.

"Could you possibly put a few of them up for maybe two or three days?"

"You mean house them?" said the general director's wife cautiously, her face clouding over a bit. She was obviously already having visions of hordes of hairy Mongolians clomping around on her rugs in muddy boots and of her precious silverware vanishing piece by piece.

"I would be delighted to help you, but I don't quite see how I can at the moment," she said slowly. "You see, Mr. Smiricky, I have guests. My brother-in-law is here from Ostrava, and then, too, we already have some refugees staying with us—my brother from Brno and his family."

"Of course," I said. "I understand completely. I just thought that the primitive conditions in the emergency barracks might not be so pleasant for these Englishmen."

"Oh, they're English?" the general director's wife asked, clearly interested now.

"Yes. Prisoners of war from Dunkirk."

"Oh, I see. Soldiers!" she cried as though the idea had just then crossed her mind. "Well, that's different, isn't it? I could make room for one or two of them in the back room upstairs."

"Fine," I said in a respectful tone.

"As I say, I'd be delighted to help out."

"Certainly. Well, if you could I'd be very much obliged to you."

"Don't mention it. You're entirely welcome. How many would you want me to take?"

"That depends entirely on you, Mrs. Heiserova."

"Well, would two be enough? Two would be no trouble at all."

"Two would be fine. And, once again, many thanks."

"Not at all, not at all. It's our duty, after all. And how's your father, Mr. Smiricky?"

"Well, you know . . . with the way things are these days . . ."

"Yes, well," she broke in, "the main thing is we're rid of Hitler at last."

"Yes. Yes, of course."

"Please give my regards to your father and mother."

"I shall. Of course. And, once again, many . . ."

"You're very welcome," she said and lifted a hand.

She had pudgy little fingers and I kissed them between two large rings. One of them bumped into my lip. The hand smelled good. I turned and bowed to Mrs. Kramperova.

"Mr. Smiricky?" she said to me.

"Ma'am?"

"I might be in a position to take in one of your Englishmen, too, if you . . ."

"Oh, I'd be very grateful," I said quickly, and right away I knew which one I'd give her—that bearded giant, the farmer from Australia.

"But, Mr. Smiricky . . ."

"Yes?"

"If you please . . . I would prefer someone with manners."

"Of course."

"Not just any . . . well, but I'm sure you know what I mean."

"I assure you, ma'am—you can depend on me." The one I'd picked had manners all right. Among other things, anyway. Mrs. Kramperova would be satisfied. I could see his broad shoulders and narrow hips as he climbed out of the pool and I thought, you needn't worry, Mrs. Kramperova, you'll be satisfied. But then I looked at her and wondered how satisfied the Australian was going to be, but at least he'd be glad to have a place to stay for a while and maybe gratitude would make him overlook a few defects.

"Shall I bring him over to your house, ma'am?"

"Oh, you needn't bother. I was just about to leave," said Mrs. Kramperova, rising from her chair.

"Oh, won't you stay on a bit, Olga?" said the general director's wife.

"I really must be running along, Rosa. And then Mr. Smiricky would have to go to all the trouble of walking all the way over to . . ."

"No trouble at all, ma'am."

"No, no. I'm sure you have enough to do as it is, Mr. Smiricky. And I really must be going."

"When will I see you again, Olga?" said the general director's wife.

"As soon as I have a moment, Rosa. Don't worry, I won't forget you."

"That would be nice—forgetting your oldest friend. You see, Mr. Smiricky, we played together as children."

"Really?"

"Yes. And we've been friends ever since."

"That's wonderful."

"Yes, and now that everything's going to be so much more pleasant again, you have to come over more often, Olga."

"I will, Rosa, I will. Just as soon as things have settled down a bit."

"You must come too, Mr. Smiricky. And your parents. It's been ages since we've last seen you."

"Thank you. We'll look forward to coming over, as soon as things have straightened themselves out," I said

"Of course, of course," said the general director's wife.

"Well, goodby now, Rosa, and remember me to your husband," said Mrs. Kramperova. The two ladies embraced.

"I kiss your hand and thank you again, Mrs. Heiserova," I said and bowed. The general director's wife smiled graciously.

"You're very welcome, Mr. Smiricky. Do come again."

I bowed and turned and followed Mrs. Kramperova. We went out into the hall where Mitzi was waiting with her nice little smile. She opened the door that led out to the garden.

"I kiss your hand," she said, curtsying gracefully.

"Goodby, Mitzi," said Mrs. Kramperova in a completely different tone of voice than the one she'd used in the salon, and then stepped out into the sunlight. Now it was my turn to go by Mitzi's electrifying body again and suddenly I got this idea, though God knows where it came from—probably out of some movie or one of those novels—but there she stood with her breasts bulging out over that starched apron in the middle of all that luxury, so on my way out I slipped my right arm around her waist and tried to kiss her. She pulled away. I could feel her warm, supple back bending against my hand, and then I let go. I was awfully embarrassed, because actually I hadn't meant to try anything like that, it seemed the dumb kind of thing millionaires play around at, and I was scared stiff wondering how she would take it and awfully relieved when she pretended to frown but just laughed softly and whispered "Shh!" So I gave her a friendly wink and said, "Goodby."

"Goodby, Mr. Smiricky," she said and closed the door right in front of my nose. I felt tremendously grateful to her. Though why, I wasn't quite sure. I had the feeling Mitzi wouldn't spoil anybody's fun. And that she understood me. That she'd be able to understand what there was in me to understand. The fact that I didn't have any prejudices. That I longed to love somebody, somebody pretty like Mitzi or Irena, and that I simply went crazy when I wasn't given a chance to. Or when I bungled things badly. Right then, anyway, I was sure I could fall in love with Mitzi. That I was in love with her already. It seemed to me I loved her even more than Irena. And I realized how easy it was for me to fall in love with somebody else than Irena, that all it took was for me to be with a pretty girl, and I decided I'd give Mitzi a try as soon as possible. Mitzi was nice and she lived in nice surroundings, had a little room at the back of the Heisers's villa, curtains on the windows and a view of the castle and a moon between the turreted towers and the fragrant rustling of the woods at night outside the window—all this flashed through my mind as I plodded down the yellow path behind Mrs.

Kramperova and stopped beside my silent, dusty Englishmen.

"Well," I said, "you go with this lady," I told the guy in the Australian hat.

"Very well, sir," he said respectfully and took off his hat. His wavy chestnut hair shone in the sunshine. Mrs. Kramperova smiled at him.

"You can speak German with him, ma'am," I said and felt like a madam in a whore house.

"Yes? Wonderful! Thank you, Mr. Smiricky."

"You're welcome," I said.

"*Bitte, kommen Sie mit mir,*" she said to the Australian with an irritating smile.

"*Danke, gnädige Frau,*" said the Australian, then turned to me and said, "Thank you, sir." He loped off beside Mrs. Kramperova toward the garden gate. The sun shone down on them, he put on his hat again, and Mrs. Kramperova's pink slip glimmered through her thin dress. She'll have a good time, I thought to myself, and thought maybe the Australian would, too. If even a beast like Krobe had. I turned to the sergeant and asked him to select two men.

"Burke and Harris," said the sergeant, and the two men moved forward. That left me with only four now—the sergeant, the tall redhead with the gaunt face, then a pockmarked runt, and finally a big fat guy wearing a checkered shirt under his battledress and a funny peaked cap with a little pinned-on Union Jack. His cleanshaven face glistened with sweat. I turned to the two who'd been picked to stay at the Heisers's.

"Come on," I said and headed back toward the house. I went up the steps to the front door and rang the bell. After a minute the click of high heels came closer and Mitzi opened the door.

"Well! Have you forgotten something, Mr. Smiricky?" she said. I felt like letting everything else go to hell and just taking her off to her room. But those two Englishmen were standing right behind me.

"I think, miss, you've forgotten you've got visitors."

"What?"

"Here. I've brought you two guests for a couple of days."

"Who are they?" said Mitzi, peering suspiciously at the dusty Englishmen. Two little parallel wrinkles formed above her nose.

"Englishmen. It's all been arranged with Mrs. Heiserova. Could you show them in to her, please?"

"Goodness," said Mitzi. "We've got so many people staying here already, Mr. Smiricky."

"I know," I said quickly, and didn't move an inch. Neither did Mitzi. We stood there face to face and eye to eye, but all I could see were Mitzi's breasts under that white apron.

"Well . . . then . . ." she said slowly.

"Mitzi . . ." I said in a low voice.

"Yes?"

"Would you have any time this evening?"

She grinned. "Well, I don't know, Mr. Smiricky."

"Please, Mitzi. There's so much I've got to tell you."

"Yes? About what?"

"About how crazy I am about you."

"Oh, go on. Since when, Mr. Smiricky?" she said in a slightly sarcastic but still pleasant way.

"For a long time. Ever since we came here for a visit the first time."

"Mitzi!" a voice called out from the salon. Mitzi stiffened, glanced around, then turned to me and quickly slipped her hand into mine.

"At the edge of the woods at eight—all right?" I said.

"Behind the house?"

"Yes. Will you be there?"

"I don't know. Maybe," she said with a look that made my head spin.

"Well, goodby now," I said and Mitzi squeezed my hand and looked away. I was lucky. Like always. I was lucky with most women. Except with Irena. Jesus, it'd been going on like that for years already.

"*Kommen Sie herein,*" Mitzi said to the Englishmen. They went in. Mitzi winked at me and closed the door.

I stood there staring into the big mahogany door and then turned and looked out over springtime Kostelec. I could see the gray factory buildings down below and the backs of the apartment houses in town, the river, the railroad embankment and then the little houses strung out at the foot of Black Mountain and the woods and the hills and the blue sky above them and over to the left and the red roofs of the new residential section beyond the slums, and the air was clean and wonderfully fresh. Then suddenly, from a long way off, came a hard, low, steady coughing sound interrupted by louder repeated booms. The front —machine guns and artillery—and spring had come and the Protectorate was over. The remaining four Tommies stood there on the path, looking at me. The fat one was sitting on his knapsack, his shirt unbuttoned at the neck, his cap in his hand. He had a crew cut. I walked down the stairs and over to them.

"Shall we go?" I said, and we started off down the path toward the garden gate. I looked back at the mansion. Against all those green plants and shrubs it loomed up white and shining, with bits of mica glinting in the stucco and the windows bright with the sun, and in the garden the fountain spouted its plumes of spray into the air. I dragged myself away from the sight and strode along with the Englishmen, the white fence flickering by on the side. My destination was the Vevodas, where I planned to commit my last act of malice. The sidewalk dropped sharply down toward the creek, then went through Shanty Town and on up toward the new residential section beyond the factory-workers' district. Shanty Town was just a colony of old freightcars jacked up onto concrete blocks. Goats grazed and snotnosed kids were playing in the grass; blankets and bed linen lay draped over racks to air out. We crossed the creek above the weir and clambered up toward the newer houses. I told the Englishmen to wait at the corner for me and then headed for the building with the lion's head over the door. That was where District Attorney Vevoda lived with his sour, dumb shrew of a wife. I rang the doorbell. Nothing happened for a long time. Then I heard a faint noise as somebody first opened the peephole. They opened the door just a crack. I could only see a sliver of Mrs. Vevodova's face.

"Madame," I said, "I kiss your hand."

"Good morning. What do you want?"

"Madame, I'd like to lodge two English prisoners with you. The town is full of refugees and we're trying to put our Englishmen up with some of the better families."

"Prisoners?"

"Yes. English soldiers. Prisoners of war."

"Well, I really don't know . . . my husband's not at home."

"I'm sure your husband won't object. Dr. Vasak's taken some, and Director Heiser and the Mouteliks and . . ."

"And . . . uh . . . how many did you say there were?"

"Just two."

"Well, I'm not sure my husband will allow it. There's little enough room as it is."

"Oh, he will. And if he does object, you can always phone us," I said. I was eager to unload my two soldiers on her as fast as possible.

"For how long would it be?"

"Just two or three days."

"Well . . . what sort of people are they?"

"What do you mean, ma'am?" I said, playing dumb.

"Well, I mean . . . are they . . . they're not filthy, are they?"

"Ma'am, if they miss their daily bath, they get sick."

"Yes, well . . . I just don't know what my husband's going to say to this."

"No need to worry about that, ma'am. Thanks very much. I'll bring them right over."

"Well . . ." said Mrs. Vevodova, but I'd already gone.

"Go right in. She's waiting for you," I said, shoving the fat one and the runt toward the door. I caught one last glimpse of the runt's dirty boots and the fat guy's greasy rear and then turned and hurried off toward town with my last two Englishmen. Just the thought of the mess those soldiers would make of Mrs. Vevodova's place made me happy and I hoped they'd do a thorough job of it. I really longed to see them turn her house into one big pigsty. She was one woman I just couldn't stand. And so I prayed they'd really mess it up for her. We went down to the main street and headed off toward home.

I took the two Englishmen—their names were Martin

and Siddell—upstairs. Mother opened the door and I said they'd be staying with us for a couple days and then I took them to the bathroom so they could wash up. Here in the house, they both suddenly seemed very shy. I left them in the bathroom and went into the kitchen. It was two o'clock.

"What should I give them to eat, Danny?" Mother asked.

"Oh, anything. Boiled potatoes would be all right. Anything."

"But I don't have any meat."

"That's all right, Mother."

"How am I supposed to talk to them?"

"They know German. You have any lunch for me?"

"It's been ready for a long time, Danny."

"Could I have it then? I've got to go out again right away."

"My God. Where are you going this time, Danny?"

"I promised Benno I'd come over."

"Danny, be careful. I don't want you to get mixed up in anything dangerous."

"Don't worry, Mother."

The sergeant appeared in the doorway.

"Sit down," I said, and got up and brought them into the room. Embarrassed, they sat down at the table and rested their hands on their knees. Mother brought in plates and bowls and served us soup.

"*So, bitte,*" she said.

"*Danke, Frau,*" said the sergeant.

We finished the soup off and Mother brought some meat and potatoes.

"Danny, do you really think I can serve them this?"

"Why not?"

"It's horse meat. I don't have anything else."

"They won't mind."

"*Bitte,*" said Mother. "*Es ist nur Pferdefleisch.*"

"*Danke sehr, Frau,*" said the sergeant.

We ate.

"Where're you from?" I asked the sergeant.

"London," he said.

"And you?"

"Liverpool."

H*

"Married?"

"Yes," said the sergeant. "I've got three kids."

"Well, you must be glad you're on your way home."

"I am indeed," said the sergeant. After a while he said, "This is the second time."

"How do you mean?"

"This won't be my first homecoming."

"How do you mean?"

"I served in the first war, too."

"Oh, I see," I said.

"And I'd go again if there were ever another one."

"Really?"

"Yes. You see, I hate the Germans."

"I see," I said. I didn't know what to say to that. The sergeant, chewing away on his horse meat, looked at me soberly.

"Well, fine," I said and turned to the other one. "Are you married too?"

"No," he said, making a face as if he'd stepped on a nail.

"Well, then you've got something to look forward to too, don't you?"

"I should say so."

"We've got some pretty girls here, don't you think? You like them?"

"Oh, very much."

"They're pretty, aren't they?"

"Yes. But then, you see, I haven't had a girl for five years now."

That kind of shocked me. He said it the same way a man might say he hadn't had anything to eat for a week.

"Well, you can have one now."

"Really?" he said with interest. "But I don't have any money."

This time I made a face.

"You don't need money," I said. "Our girls are good patriots."

The Englishman chuckled. He was a big, redheaded, husky guy. I thought about Mitzi. Maybe I should do a good deed and let him go to meet Mitzi instead of me. No.

If he'd held out this long, he might as well hold out a little longer.

"Well, I've got to be going now," I said. "I'll see you this evening. In the meantime, get some rest."

"Thank you," said the sergeant.

"Well . . . goodby for now."

"Goodby."

I got up.

"Will you make up their beds for them, Mother?" I said.

"You're going already, Danny?"

"Yes."

"When will you be back?"

"Tonight."

"Be careful, Danny."

"Don't worry. Goodby, Mother."

"Goodby."

I went out the door and hurried downstairs. When I got to the landing I looked back and saw Mother standing in the doorway watching me. She looked worried. I blew her a kiss. She smiled and waved. Then she turned away. I hurried downstairs. Out on the street everything still looked the same. The same gray crowd as before except now, somehow, it seemed to me they were moving faster. I headed down toward the station but after putting away all that horse meat, walking wasn't easy.

"*Gnädiger Herr,*" I heard from behind me. Somebody touched my arm. I turned and saw an incredible filthy ugly woman in a striped dress.

"*Bitte, wo ist das?*" she said and held out a piece of paper. Behind her stood a whole flock of other women wearing striped clothing like hers. You couldn't even tell whether they were old or young. Hunger stared from their eyes. They looked like ghosts. I glanced at the piece of paper. On it was a typewritten message: "*For Lewith factory cafeteria: Serve lunch to fifteen Jewesses from Schörkenau concentration camp.*" At the bottom there was a round rubber municipal stamp and somebody's signature.

I handed the paper back to the woman and said, "Come with me. I'll show you the way."

The woman held up a bony hand and said a few words

in a shrill voice to the others. I turned and started off. The whole group followed along behind me. I turned to the woman with the piece of paper and slowed down.

"You just got out of a camp?" I asked. She looked up at me respectfully, then came to me as meekly as if I were her master. We walked on side by side.

"Yes. From Schörkenau," she said in an almost reverent tone of voice. I didn't know what to talk about. She trotted along beside me, alertly and expectantly, and I could tell she was ready to tell me anything I wanted to know, but for the life of me I couldn't think of anything at all. Just by looking at her you knew everything. I'd heard a bit about the camps. About Schörkenau especially. Some of the guys who'd worked for Luftmetal had told me about the Jewish women from the camp who were laying a spur line there. So I'd heard about the place already. The Jewish woman limped along at my side, her bare feet caked over with dust, her striped clothes hanging on her like on a skeleton.

"A good thing it's all over now, isn't it?" I said, and as soon as I'd said it I felt how dumb it was. I was sure it must sound insulting to her. I felt guilty. I wasn't sure why but I felt guilty anyway. For no good reason maybe, but there I was walking with a full stomach in front of all those women and then, in that same obsequious voice, the woman beside me said, "Yes. Yes, it's a very good thing," and then went back to being as alert and attentive and cautious as before. It was embarrassing how servile these women were. Hell, if I could only have told them they didn't need to act that way any more, that they weren't in a concentration camp any more and that they had just as much right to everything now as I did or something like that, but I didn't know how to tell them and I had the feeling it was impossible to, or that maybe I didn't have any right to tell them things like that, so I didn't say anything and just kept on going, wishing we were already at Lewith's. We'd been walking along the sidewalk on the right hand side of the street and, crossing over to the other side in front of the Grand Hotel, had to make our way through a swarm of people. The mixture was still the same

—Mongolians, French, Italians, Serbs, and clusters of people in rags—but it seemed to me there were more people than ever now and that they were moving faster. Every once in a while the sea of people parted and a wagon creaked by loaded with children or a skinny nag clomped past with two or three kids on its back. Sometimes somebody on a bike wove in and out along the fringe of the crowd—usually a man in uniform, a Frenchman, or a guy with a NEDERLAND patch on his shoulder—but the main current of that human flood flowed steadily by on foot, surging westward through the heat and swirling dust. I cut across that current, me and my Jewish women, and we walked on toward Lewith's cafeteria. The white concrete building of the new spinning mill—which the firm of Lewith had finished just in time for the Germans—gleamed in the sunshine like a palace and there was a line of refugees, standing or squatting, that stretched the full length of the iron fence. Small bunches of them, led by kids wearing white armbands, were being let into the cafeteria. I took my armband out of my pocket, put it on and turned to the Jewish woman.

"Could I have your paper now?" I asked. She handed it to me. We walked down the sidewalk, rows of squatting and exhausted people to each side, toward the factory gate. Two guys from the Red Cross stood at the gateway. Without a word I handed the paper to one of them. He read it and handed it back to me.

"Where's the cafeteria?" I asked.

"Around the corner to the left," he said, and the next minute he was already busy with another group.

"Follow me," I said to my Jewish women and led them around to the left between the fence and the white factory wall. Around the corner there was a little yard bright with sunshine and full of refugees sprawled out on the grass. We passed a long row of big windows until, almost at the end of that side, we came to an open door in which two women in white coats were standing. I handed the paper to one of the women.

"Fifteen lunches," she said to two other guys wearing armbands.

"Come on in," one of them said.

I told the Jewish women they could go in and one after another and each one looking as solemn and as close to dying right then and there as the other, they filed in past me.

"Jesus," the guy said to me as he counted them, "they must have just got out of a concentration camp."

"From Schörkenau," I said.

"Aha."

And just then, drifting in with the rattle and clink of spoons and the foul smell of cafeteria food, there was the sudden wail of a strange kind of music, a twanging, keening sound, something like mandolins, only much better I thought.

"What's that?" I asked.

"Russians," the guy at the door said. I listened. I couldn't see all the way inside, but I listened. It was one of those peculiar Russian melodies, sad but not maudlin, a melody that sounded detached and uplifted, above it all.

"Can I take a look?"

"Sure, go on in."

I slipped into the cafeteria and looked around. It was a big place with benches and tables, full of smoke and bad smells and food. Tattered POWs were sitting around the tables, stuffing themselves. Aproned women were clearing. A long queue stretched back along the wall from the serving window. I walked between tables toward the music. The room was L-shaped and around the corner another big hall opened up and there I saw a Russian orchestra seated on a platform, playing this song. Actually they weren't Russians. They were Mongolians or Georgians, men with wide flat faces and walrus mustaches. About eight of them sat there, smiling broadly and incessantly, twanging away on all kinds of odd mandolins and balalaikas. In front of the platform, where a couple of kids stood gaping at the orchestra, benches and tables had been cleared away and a handful of French soldiers were dancing with girls from Lewith's kitchen. The girls' cheeks were bright red and they looked like they were dancing in heaven. I squeezed my way up close to the orchestra and stood there. The Mongolians sat straight as statues, but every single one of them was grinning from ear to ear and their small hands flickered skillfully over the strings. You could hear the smooth, drawling, full-blown, mournful melody with a bass underneath and the little, high-pitched, tinkling tones of some sort of mandolin. The Mongolians played without stopping and without notes, grinning the whole time, blissful and mute and motionless in the midst of all that stink and clatter and talk. I watched them and listened to their song and wondered where on earth they'd come from and how they'd ever managed to wind up here and what a tremendous thing music was—how it was better than everything else put together and how, just because of their music, I felt some sort of fraternal feeling with these dirty muzhiks, and as I listened to them, I watched their hands, the way they played, wonderfully, their fingers moving over the strings with a marvelous calm and precision. For a few minutes some of them would stop, take a breather, then join in again, right on the beat, whether they were all playing in unison or harmony. Every once in a while a couple of them would play a lower-pitched plunking melody and the others would come up with something like trumpet riffs in jazz. I listened and forgot about everything. Then the orchestra stopped and a young kid played a solo on a huge bass balalaika or whatever it was. He played a low-pitched tune and the deep plunks of the balalaika sounded so weirdly and fantastically beautiful that it was almost like a miracle, almost as miraculous as when Armstrong sings "St. James Infirmary" and Kid Ory answers him on a muted trombone, and then suddenly that whole grinning and speechless bunch started singing and they sang a wild, wailing song in those Oriental voices of theirs and my hair stood on end and I felt they were lifting me straight up to heaven. The Frenchmen whirled the girls around the floor till their skirts flew up and you could see their silly pink panties and when the song was over one of the dancing Frenchmen yelled at me, "Vive la France! Vive les Soviets! Vive la paix!" and he smiled. I smiled back at him and wanted to yell something, too, but suddenly I was embarrassed. I would have liked to holler something back but I couldn't. The best I could come up with was a grin and I waved my hand and was furious that I didn't know how to shout like that and it ruined the music for me. I couldn't shout, "Long live Czechoslovakia!" or anything like that. I just couldn't. Maybe because Czechoslovakia is such an awfully long word. Still I might have yelled something shorter like "Long live Peace!" But I couldn't do that either. I couldn't bring myself to do it. I wasn't spontaneous enough. Sure, naturally it was good that the Germans were gone. But it didn't even start to make me feel ecstatic enough to holler. I'd never been able to holler or shout when parades went by or yell "Welcome!" and stuff like that. It was all very fine but, damn it, why couldn't they leave me out of all that? Why couldn't they just leave me alone? I wasn't dying to yell whatever it was I felt. I felt mad at that Frenchman. The damn fool. Why should I holler just because he had? I was glad the Protectorate was over but I didn't feel any urge to go crazy just on account of it. And I couldn't stand the feeling that somebody was standing there just waiting for me to go crazy.

I turned and elbowed my way out of there. The Mongolian melody pursued me, growing louder and stronger. They'd started singing again, a bouncy, yelping, beautiful steppe song, and a wave of sadness broke over me, a completely mindless and helpless kind of sadness, and I made my way blindly between the long tables. A sadness like when, out of the night air during the Protectorate, I picked up the Golden Gate Quartet or heard Wings Over Jordan singing "Swing Low, Sweet Chariot" or Leadbelly singing "Cedar House Blues" or the Mills Brothers or Bob Crosby's full four-part Dixieland with the tenor sax and knew it couldn't last much more than a minute and that maybe I'd never hear it again and that there wasn't much chance I'd ever have a record of it though I knew that any fool over in America could get one cheap and easy and there I was, stuck in the Protectorate and aching because that music was so beautiful and in a little while it would fade out and I'd never—damn it!—hear it again. And now here I was feeling that same longing and heartache I'd felt so often in the past and it made me sick to think how helpless people really were and how stupidly the world was organized after all, a world filled with marvelous things most of which you never get around to seeing or hearing or knowing and, even if you do, it gets lost in no time leaving you with a hole of despair in your heart so you feel like dying. I pushed my way out of the cafeteria, crossed the lawn between the sleeping people, and went through the gate and out into the street. New clumps of haunted, hungry people were headed toward me, escorted by boys wearing armbands and looking very eager and self-important. The sun was scorching and everything looked dusty. I started up the street toward the station and then to the Manes house.

But suddenly I didn't feel like going there any more. I just wanted to be alone and to wander around in that sea of people, to walk around Kostelec in the afternoon heat and look at them, at those unshaven old men in rags, at those Greeks or Bulgarians or God knows what, at those dark-eyed and elegantly ragged Italians, at seedy-looking Frenchmen and reserved Dutchmen, at the girls of every shade in kerchiefs and rags, wretched, smiling, and dirty, at the endless waves of little Mongolians with their mute grins and the white SU on their backs—that's what I really wanted to do. I wanted to stare at it all and be a part of it. But I also knew that I'd twice promised Benno that I'd be over and I couldn't just not turn up. Christ, everything in my life always gets fouled up. Always. Every goddamn time. I always have to go somewhere else when I feel like staying where I am and I've always got to stay when it would be wonderful to go somewhere else. Something always turned up to make things come out wrong. But that was me. Me all over. Maybe I just wasn't made for love or for happiness, for anything. I was just made to get through life somehow or other, to live it through and observe it and be a part of it, and to . . . But I didn't know why else I'd been made except I knew there must be some other reason, that I had to be made for something more than just that, like for playing the saxophone, maybe. That was the best thing I could come up with but maybe there was something else, too, something even better. There had to be.

I crossed the railroad tracks and went past Dagmar Dreslerova's house and saw her looking out the window, but I pretended I hadn't seen her and walked right on past that block of apartment houses with all those hopeless little mica stars in the stucco and turned off toward the Manes house. I rang the bell at the garden gate. "Who's there?" said the mouthpiece. "Smiricky," I said, and the door buzzed and I went in and up the path and up the columned stairs to the front door. The path and the ground floor lay in the shadows of the apartment house next door, but the second and third floors basked in sunshine. It was a great place. Benno's grandfather had built it, the millionaire Manes, about twenty years ago and it had lost none of the charm of the style of that time and it never left me with that feeling of showy luxury I got from the Heisers's place. Maybe that was because I was so used to it. We'd often played there, either downstairs in the drawing room or up in Benno's room which was plastered with pictures of Negro musicians and was next to Evka's room with its big portrait of her painted by Rosta Pitterman. It was a great place. I went up the curving steps and opened the glass door. It was nice and cool in the drawing room. A potted palm stood at the bottom of the steps like at Heiser's yet this one looked different and there were two wooden bears holding an umbrella rack. I was about to go upstairs to Benno's room when the doors into the salon slid open and there stood Mrs. Dvorackova, the old housekeeper.

"Benno's in the garden," she said.

"Aha. Thank you," I said, and went into the salon. There was a piano in the little bay by the window. I went through the French doors on the right, through the dining room and out onto the sunporch which was drenched with light but not stuffy or hot. There sat Mrs. Manesova and two of my Englishmen were sitting there in wicker chairs. The Englishmen—their jackets off, their green khaki shirts unbuttoned at the neck—looked very trim and clean as they sat there chatting in English with Mrs. Manesova. Two siphons stood on the table and two bottles of prewar whisky. I said hello and crossed the porch to the garden. There was Evka in a white silk bathing suit, playing ping-pong with one Englishman while another refereed. The ping-pong table was in the shade under a tree and Evka's white bathing suit flashed brightly against the shadows. Three deck chairs had been set up out in the sun and there lay Benno, Helena, and another Englishman. Benno was in his bathing suit, too, and with his bulging belly and female-looking breasts he looked like a Buddha. A couple of beer bottles stood sweating on a little table. Helena, wearing a two-piece blue linen sunsuit, was sitting in the second deck chair and you could tell she must be pretty chubby, too. There was a little sausage roll of fat between where her halter ended and her shorts began, so I looked around again at Evka's suntanned back and firm little fanny glistening in that silk bathing suit. The seam ran right down the middle so when Evka moved, each half glistened differently. The Englishman was sitting in his deck chair, smoking a pipe. He, too, had taken off his tie and unbuttoned his shirt. I walked over to the deck chairs.

"Hi."

"Hi," said Benno.

"Hello, Danny," said Helena.

The Englishman got up. "Good afternoon," he said.

"Well, how are you? Enjoying yourself here?"

"Very much."

"Good. I just came over to see how you were getting along. I've got to be going though."

"How come? Where to?" said Benno.

"Oh . . . I've got some things to do and . . . and I've got to pick up those snapshots Berty took on Sunday," I said with sudden inspiration.

"Hell, he could've taken our pictures, too," said Benno. "Sit down."

I stretched out on another deck chair opposite them. A long volley of clicks came from the ping-pong table. I stared at Evka. She turned around to pick up a ball and saw me.

"Hello, Danny," she said gaily.

"Hello. How do you like your Englishmen?" I asked.

"They're wonderful," she grinned and, as she bent for the ball, I gazed down the top of her suit. Then she straightened up and turned and I went on staring at that two-piece fanny of hers.

"Hey, you dummy!" I heard Benno say. I realized he was talking to me. I looked over at him.

"What?"

"Can't you take your eyes off her for a minute and listen to what I'm telling you?"

I laughed.

"You've got a great sister, Benno. I envy you."

Benno said nothing.

"I mean it. Evka's terrific."

"Yeah, but she's awful dumb."

"Benny!" said Helena.

"She's dumb and you know it."

"Well, but there's no need to talk about it like that."

"Anyway, she's terrific," I said. "She really is, Benno. I'm serious. Isn't she beautiful?" I said, turning to the Englishman. I must have broken some chain of thought because he sat up with a jerk and, quickly and without thinking, said, "I beg your pardon?"

"Isn't she beautiful?" I repeated, nodding at Evka. The Englishman beamed.

"I'll say she is!" he said in ardent agreement, then started watching Evka, too.

"See, you fool?" I said to Benno. "Even foreigners appreciate her."

"All right, all right," said Benno. "I guess you've heard that the SS are supposed to get here tomorrow?"

"What?"

"The SS."

"Who said?"

"They got word over at the brewery from Schörkenau. Somebody phoned. The old man told us."

"What's going on, anyway?"

"Well, the German Army's on the run but the rear guard units are SS divisions. And they're still fighting the Russians."

"Jesus."

"We're really going to be in for it then."

"You think they'll get all the way to Kostelec?"

"Why not?"

"Well, you don't think maybe the Russians'll finish them off first."

"I wouldn't count on it."

"Yeah . . . well, maybe we'll see some action around here after all."

"That we will."

Neither of us said anything for a while. Then I said, "What's your old man say about it?"

"He's scared shitless."

"Benny!" Helena piped up automatically.

"He's scared, like everybody else."

"You think the army's going to do anything?" I asked, saying the word "army" sarcastically.

"Why do you think they're calling up everybody tomorrow?"

"Yeah. Right," I said, and a chill ran down my spine. SS men! It was cool there in the garden with Evka bouncing around on the grass in her white bathing suit. So now things were really going to start happening. And suddenly I didn't want it to happen.

"What're you going to do?" I asked.

"I'll go over to the brewery tomorrow. Not much choice."

"I guess not," I said. We sat there, silent. "Jesus Christ," I said after a while.

Again we sat there in depressed silence. Then Benno reached over for a liter bottle of beer, snapped back the cap, and poured the beer into the three glasses on the table.

"Have some," he said to me and handed one of the glasses to the Englishman.

"Thank you," said the Englishman. We drank. The beer was warm but tasted good anyway. I drank off about half the glass in one gulp, then set it back on the table. Benno was still drinking. His Adam's apple bobbed rhythmically and he tipped the bottom of the glass up to the sky. We fell silent again, then finally I said, "Well, I guess I better be going," and got up.

"Don't go yet," said Benno.

"I've got to. I've got to do some things and I want to get a good night's sleep."

"Well, then off you go."

"You'll be there in the morning?"

"Yes."

"What time?"

"Stop at Haryk's. I'll meet you over there."

"What time should I be there?"

"Around eight."

"All right," I said. I said goodby to the Englishman and he sat up straight in his chair again and said goodby, and I shook hands with Helena and Benno. Then I called out, " 'By, Evka."

She turned and stepped into the sunshine.

" 'By, Danny. Come back again," she said. That warmed my heart. I thought yes, definitely, I will come back. In the sunshine, all her lovely curves radiated a dazzling whiteness. I made a V-for-Victory sign and the Englishmen grinned.

"See you later, boys," I said. I went through the house and down the sandy path out to the gate. This SS business really got on my nerves. But I shook my head to clear it and felt fine again. I knew Evka was in her white bathing suit in the garden behind me and that Irena wasn't far away either in the County Office Building. The whole town was full of girls. And I knew I'd be coming back to the Maneses tomorrow or the day after or in a couple of days anyway. And soon it would be summer and we'd all be going to the swimming pool. Then I remembered Mitzi. Life wasn't so bad after all. Even if there wasn't anything but that—and there wasn't—life would be worth it. To hell with the SS. And maybe up in the mountains this summer or walking together through Prague, maybe Irena would give in, maybe I'd win her over yet. Or maybe I'd meet that unknown girl after all. Maybe life really wasn't so bad. Then I remembered Berty and suddenly felt I had to have those snapshots. As if my life depended on them. So I could show off in front of Irena. So I could see how I looked with a gun. Snapshots were terrific. All they showed was what you could see in the picture—no words, no nothing, just the picture with nothing to get in the way. Pictures of girls always made a tremendous impression. If a guy shows some girl's picture around, it's kind of like a trophy, even if maybe he never got anywhere with the girl at all. It doesn't make any difference. All he needs to do is let his friends take a look at a couple of pictures and put on a mysterious look. His friends will take care of the rest. They probably know there isn't much to it and how it really is with girls' snapshots, how easy it is to get one, but they'll never let on because they like to show their pictures around, too, and it makes a guy feel good, a bit as if he'd really made out with all those girls whose pictures he has and that's a very nice feeling. And that's just how it was with that picture of me with the submachine gun. Nobody would know from my picture that they'd taken my gun away afterward. I went through the park to Zizka Square and hurried through the underpass and took a short cut along the railroad embankment to Berty's place. The side streets weren't so crowded, but when I turned off into the ghetto, I came up against a whole herd of ragged people milling around the synagogue. A truck loaded with blankets stood parked at the curb and four guys were busily unloading the blankets and carrying them into the synagogue. Moutelik's gleaming white apartment house stood at the corner, but their shop was closed. I went into their place and started up the stairs to the first floor. Through the stained-glass windows on the staircase which depicted various scenes of merchant life, the light streaming in from outside painted bright pictures on the yellow walls. I stopped to look at some of the figures—the half-naked Mercury and a muscular blacksmith—and suddenly thought of Mr. Moutelik himself who looked just like a billiard ball with a belly. I met Helena Reimanova on the stairs. She was wearing her tennis dress and the colors from the windows made pretty patterns as they poured over her. I rang the doorbell at the Mouteliks. Their aged maid opened the door and told me that Berty was in the darkroom. I went back downstairs and rang the bell at the back entrance to the shop. After a while Berty's brother Emil came to the door and let me in.

"Hi," I said. "Is Berty downstairs?"

"Yeah," he said and went back to his toys and puppet theaters. I saw he'd been taking apart some kind of a little machine; it was spread out all over the counter. I opened the door to the cellar and turned on the light. I went down the steps and came to a narrow little passageway between piles of crates and sacks and bundles. A lightbulb shed a little light from the ceiling. I headed through the yellow gloom to the back where Berty had fixed up his darkroom. It was kind of a booth made out of beaverboard and covered with black paper. A sign hung on the door: NO ADMITTANCE. I knocked.

"Just a second!" someone called from inside and you could hear a rustle of papers and the clap of boxes being shut. Then Berty opened the door. He was wearing a black smock.

"Oh, hello. You came for your pictures?" he said, and he bared his teeth at me like he did for customers in his father's store.

"Yeah. Are they ready?"

"Sure. Would you like to see them?"

"Well, if you'll show me—sure."

I went inside. It was a tiny little room with a work table on which the enlarger stood and three basins for developing fluid, the fixing bath, and water. Over the table there was a shelf for bottles and boxes and, over the shelf, three lightbulbs: one white, one red, and one green. A little cupboard stood against the wall on the left. Berty opened the cupboard and took out an envelope. The light of the low lamp on his work table, angling up from below, threw huge shadows on the opposite wall of the darkroom.

"Here you are," said Berty. "Come over here."

We went over to the table and Berty spread out the snapshots. There were six of them—exactly the number I'd ordered. I looked at them. They were excellent pictures. Gray and somber. You could tell the weather had been bad that day. There I stood with my submachine gun, my hair slanting down over my forehead a little. The submachine gun itself came out so clear you could almost count the screws and it had a real metallic sheen. I inspected the gun first and then myself—standing there in the foreground in just the right posture. Behind me and a little off to one side, you could see Benda with his submachine gun and fireman's helmet and Franta Kocandrle's back with a rifle slung across it. Over my left shoulder the long pale pins of a couple of bazookas jutted up. The background was a gray blur but I stood out sharp and clear against it, and I looked just like I really do and with the hair in my eyes and that submachine gun in my hands I looked pretty impressive. I don't think I'd ever seen a better snapshot of me—not even the one showing me with my saxophone because a professional photographer had taken that one and he'd practically flattened us out with all his spotlights so we all wound up looking as if we'd never seen our instruments before in our lives. This picture was worlds better. It made a strong impression. Berty was an artist. Or at least he had a marvelous camera. Actually, I guess it was the camera that counted. Anyway, the pictures were great.

"Very nice, Berty," I said.

"They came out pretty good, didn't they? Actually, I had to lighten it a bit at the edges but nobody's going to notice that."

"I can't even see it myself. No. They're great. How much do I owe you?"

"Well, the charge for postcard-size pictures is two crowns and I'll throw in the developing free so that would make it twelve crowns altogether."

I took out my wallet and handed him the money. When it came to money, Berty had no friends.

"Well, thanks very much," I said.

"You're quite welcome," Berty said, flashing his best salesman's smile. "If it's nice tomorrow, we might try a few more over at the brewery. Will you be there?"

"Sure. It looks like you may have an awfully busy day tomorrow."

"I took nearly one hundred and fifty pictures today," he said with a satisfied smile.

"Really?"

"Yes. Refugees. Some day those pictures may be very valuable."

"I'm sure they will be," I said, remembering Mr. Machacek's history. Those pictures would be a real goldmine for him! "You know they're expecting the SS to get here tomorrow?"

"I heard—yes."

"You going to try to take their pictures?"

"Well, I'll try anyway."

"You better be awfully careful."

"Don't worry. I've had experience," he said in a slightly superior tone.

"I guess that's true," I said. "Can I get out by myself or do you keep the upstairs door locked?"

"No. Just slam it after you."

"Well, so long," I said.

"Goodby," said Berty. I started back through the passageway between the crates. I heard Berty shut himself back up in his darkroom. I went up the stairs, turned off the cellar light, and went through the shop. Emil was in the back, still fiddling around with that machine. It was a mechanical bear brandishing a little bottle with the inscription: DER TEUFEL.

"So long," I said to him and went out into the hallway. I looked at my watch. It was after four. Four more hours till supper. I decided to loaf around on the street till six. I headed off toward the square. The crowds hadn't thinned out any. I stood at the corner by the loan association and watched them. By now the square looked like a gypsy camp. People, nothing but people—around the church and everywhere. They were all either squatting or standing around or munching on stuff they pulled out of their bundles and, though I saw them talking among themselves, a hot weary silence seemed to hang over the whole square. The crowd was thickest where the square sloped slightly up toward the castle. The sun beat down on them and the brilliant flags flying from the housetops flapped listlessly and drunkenly above that dusty mass of humanity. The crowd was waiting. Waiting for what would happen next. Waiting for peace and trucks with red crosses and liaison officers to send them back to all those different countries they'd come from. Or, rather, from where the Germans had taken them. I looked at them. Next to me sat an old fellow with a dirty beard, his head cocked back, his eyes like slits. But his mouth was wide open and inside there were stumps of teeth. A boy sat next to him and I couldn't tell whether he had jaundice or was just dirty. Though he looked sick, again I couldn't tell whether it was jaundice or just the fact that he was a gypsy, maybe, or an Italian. Then I looked out over the square and saw the Frenchmen in their shabby uniforms and they all looked weak and sickly though the Dutchmen standing next to them looked strong and healthy. I don't know why, or even if it was true, but anyway that's the way they looked to me. There was a filthy-looking family a few feet away whose kids kept chasing each other around a soup pot and, a bit farther off, a hunched-over, bedraggled-looking couple—the girl wearing a concentration camp dress and about eight months pregnant, the boy with his head bandaged up and his face covered with bruises and scars—and then Russians and Mongolians with that eternal grin on their faces and looking so carefree and relaxed and even happy it made me furious. And then suddenly I saw Irena. She was just coming out through the bronze doorway of the post office. Slowly she made her way through the crowd toward the loan association office. Ah, Irena! She was wearing a simple dress, white with a pattern of flowers. Ah, Irena. It almost hurt to look at her. I leaned back against the corner of the loan association building and stuck my hands in my pockets. It was a completely automatic reaction; I figured it would make an impression on her. Well, maybe not much of an impression but still it was better than nothing. It was the best I could come up with, and I was pretty sure Irena would like it. I waited until she was close up, then grinned my lopsided grin and said, "Hi, Irena," and, looking her straight in the eye, I couldn't help thinking how few brains she actually had, but it was all the same to me.

"You're beautiful, Irena," I said.

"Really? I'm glad you like me," she said.

"That's not the half of it, Irena."

"Hmm?"

"I mean, I don't just like you."

"Why? Did I do something wrong?"

"Oh, you know what I mean."

"No, I don't."

"You know all right, Irena," I said, drawling the words out.

"No. Really."

"You want me to tell you again?" I said.

She didn't say anything. All she did was look at me with those big eyes of hers. I could see she was enjoying it though.

"I'd be glad to tell you again," I said.

"Well, go ahead and say it then."

"I love you, Irena."

She smiled and slowly, very slowly closed her eyes. As if she was really taking it seriously, as if she was trying to show me that, even though the whole thing was only a joke, it was still a very serious matter, while as for me it didn't seem serious at all, just very pleasant, and if she'd had any idea of who she was really up against she would have said I was a mean fresh kid and walked off.

"I'm terribly in love with you, Irena," I said, as if I meant it from the bottom of my heart and I uncrossed my legs and straightened up.

The serious look suddenly slipped off her face. "Danny," she said, "you certainly do pick wonderful places to make your confessions."

"I don't pick them, Irena."

"Well, who does then?"

"You."

"Me?"

"Every time."

"What do you mean?"

"Well, sure. Because you never have time except when we meet like this. Not for me anyway."

"But . . ."

"I'd rather talk somewhere else, too. But you never want to."

She took my hand again the way she usually did at about that point and then looked thoughtful, wondering whether she ought to give me any time this time or not.

"Danny . . ."

"Yes, Irena?"

"Look, Danny. There just wouldn't be any point."

"That's what you say."

"I know it."

"Not for you, maybe. But it would for me."

"No it wouldn't."

"It would, too."

"No, Danny."

"It would, Irena. I know it would."

"You just think it would."

"Think? I know."

"You're kidding yourself, Danny."

"I am not."

"Yes, you are."

"Well, you can say whatever you want to, Irena. All I know is, it would mean something because I love you."

Just as I said that, Mr. Boucek from the post office passed by. I'd been talking pretty loud. Mr. Boucek looked at me and grinned. Irena saw him grinning and blushed.

"Danny, you shouldn't say things like that so loud."

"Why not?"

"Well, it's just not the kind of thing everybody should know about, that's all."

"You think I care?"

"Well, maybe you don't. But I do."

"You mean it bothers you that much?"

"Yes."

"Just knowing that I'm in love with you?"

"No, not that. Just that you say it so loud."

"So you don't want me to say it—is that right?"

"You can say it as often as you want just as long as there aren't a lot of people around."

Aha, I thought to myself, and let out a good long sigh.

"Oh, stop sighing, Danny, and come along if you want to."

I didn't say a word but just started off beside her. We went down Jirasek Boulevard toward the station.

"You're going home?"

"Yes."

"What're you going to do at home?"

"Oh, lots of things."

"Oh, come on. Like what, for instance?"

"Well, I've got to wash out some stockings, and then do some darning . . ."

"Oh, that."

"Why? What'd you think?"

"No, I just wondered," I said. "And when you're not busy with that kind of stuff, what do you do?"

"Think about you."

"Oh, I'll bet. That must really keep you busy."

"Honest. You can't imagine how often."

"You're right. I can't."

"When they led you away from the post office on Saturday, I was awfully scared for you and now I wonder if you even deserved it."

"Honest, Irena? You mean you were scared they were going to shoot me?"

"Well, naturally. So then I phoned Mr. Rimbalnik and he promised he'd see what he could do for you, and then I just waited and prayed for you."

"Really?"

"Really. Though I'll bet *you* wouldn't do that, would you, Danny?"

"Sure I would."

"You don't have to lie."

"But I would. Really, Irena."

"Sure, I know. And then Mr. Rimbalnik called me back and said they'd already let you go."

"And you were glad?"

"It made me mad that I'd gone to all that effort, because you're probably not even worth it."

"Yes I am, Irena."

"Well, that's what you say. Everybody thinks they're worth a lot. But whether it's true or not, that's something else again."

"I'm worth it, Irena. And I'm awfully grateful for what you did."

"Well, you should be," she said, and suddenly I had an unpleasant feeling that maybe I really was a heel for playing around with her and that maybe she really was a lot better person than I was, worrying about me like that. I just flashed her my Don Juan grin, though, and said, "And I am grateful—tremendously. For everything!"

Either I was a real devil or else just a bigmouthed fool. But so what, I thought. So I'm a fool. And if that's all you are you might as well make the most of it and be a really big fool. Maybe that's what I am then—the biggest fool in the whole wide world, and as soon as that crossed my mind I felt a big wave of relief, I felt a lot better, and the more I thought of it the more it struck me that it wasn't me who was such a big fool. No, I was as smooth as they come—a real operator—and if anyone was dumb it was Irena.

"Now, don't start exaggerating again," she said.

"I'm not exaggerating."

"But please tell me what else you're so tremendously grateful for."

"Just for the fact that you're who you are, Irena."

"I don't see why you should be so grateful for that."

"You're my reason for living," I said.

"Well, then, your life doesn't make much sense, does it?"

"I'll say it doesn't."

"Well, thanks very much, Danny."

"I didn't mean it *that* way."

"How did you mean it, then?"

"I just mean my life doesn't have any sense because you don't love me."

"And it would if I did?"

"Sure."

"You poor thing. So the only thing for you to do is to commit suicide—right?"

I changed my tack and went on in a different tone of voice. "Irena," I said, "you're just making a big joke out of the whole thing, aren't you?"

"No. I'm just telling you how things are, that's all."

I stopped and let my mouth sag down so I looked really pained. We'd just come to Zizka Park.

"Irena," I said. "I can't help it. I'm in love with you. Really."

Irena stopped, too. Her expression grew serious. She didn't say anything.

I waited a second and then added, "Tremendously!"

"I know," she said. There was another pause. Then she said, "What can we do about it?"

"I don't know."

She studied me. "It's an awful problem," she said and went on studying my face.

"Irena . . ." I sighed.

"Come. Let's sit down for a minute," she said and took me by the hand. We went over to a bench in the corner of the park. It was almost completely hidden under the bushes. We sat down and Irena was still holding my hand. I took her other hand in mine and then laid all those hands in her lap and gazed at her. I gazed and wondered if I looked enamored enough. Her eyes had their usual earnestness plus just a hint of affection. There we sat, holding hands like a couple of idiots, and just the thought of what she must be thinking made me want to burst out laughing. About how tragic our fate was, because how could she possibly make room in her heart for me when she was already in love with somebody else and in the meantime, as she sat there beside me with her breasts rising and falling under that white-flowered dress of hers, all I was really thinking about wasn't whether she loved me but whether she'd ever go to bed with me. She frowned. Little wrinkles formed on her forehead.

"What can we do, Danny?" she repeated helplessly. "Tell me, Danny, what can we possibly do?"

"I don't know," I said.

"But it simply can't go on like this."

"Why not?"

"Well, because it's senseless."

"What—my being in love with you?"

"No. Not that, but . . . Danny, I . . . If only there were something I could do to help you . . ."

"That wouldn't be difficult, Irena," I said lewdly.

"That's what all you boys think," she said.

"Well, would it be?"

Irena pulled a long, unhappy face. "Danny, please. Don't ask me to do that. I'd do almost anything to make you happy, but not that."

"Then how am I supposed to be happy?"

"There're lots of other girls around."

"But you're the one I'm in love with," I said, and suddenly felt a peculiar sense of responsibility. Christ, though, she was right! There really were lots of other girls and if I'd spent as much energy on them as I had on Irena there was no question about it—I would have made a lot more progress than I ever had with her. God only knew why I'd sunk so much time and effort into a girl that hard to get. It was God's business to know things like that. As for me, I wasn't about to give up.

"I don't even see those other girls," I said.

"They're pretty, too, Danny."

"Not nearly as pretty as you."

"It just seems that way to you," said Irena. You could tell she was flattered, though.

"No, it doesn't. Look at yourself. You'll see," I said and pulled out a pocket mirror. The mirror trick worked.

Irena laughed and said, "Oh, dear," and then turned an awfully unhappy face to me, though you could tell by the look in her eyes that she wasn't so sure of herself any more, yet she kept up this act like she was going through a rough inner struggle, as if she'd love to help me but since she was in love with somebody else how could she possibly —but why not? It would have been easy, the world was full of examples and not just the world—Kostelec, too.

"Irena," I murmured and took hold of her arm just under the elbow. Her arm felt soft and feminine. She drew back a bit and stiffened. I kissed her. Her lips gradually parted and I could feel the tip of her tongue. That really got me excited. Then she pulled back, stood up quickly and said, "Let's go!" turned and hurried off. Swearing to myself, I started off after her. Her dress sparkled in the sunshine and the façade of the County Office Building was practically glowing with the heat of spring. We made it to the entrance in no time at all. Irena stopped and turned to me. I could tell she was waiting for me to say something. Though I was still pretty mad, I smiled.

"Take care of yourself, Danny," she said. She held out her hand. I squeezed it.

"You too, Irena," I said. For a while we stood there looking at each other. Then I gave her one last passionate "I love you very much, Irena."

She reacted just like I knew she would—gave me a radiant smile, squeezed my hand, let go of my hand, turned and ran up the steps without looking back. I turned and moseyed back into town. I wasn't mad any more. I felt grateful to Irena. Tremendously grateful to her and to all the others, too. To the whole town, to all the pretty girls the town was full of, and to all the guys too—I loved them all. It didn't even matter that all the girls were so dumb. I loved them all anyway. The houses shone and shimmered in the spring sun, the sky was blue and high above the town, the castle rose with its lilac bushes and curving drive and there were girls everywhere and all these things made life worth living and beautiful. Irena must be home already, I thought to myself, talking to her mother probably but still, in the back of her mind, thinking about me, about how unhappy I must be, since after all she was only a girl and this was a man's world, a world in which women only served to provide pleasure and delight. I went through the underpass to Jirasek Boulevard and headed home. It still didn't look as if the crowds had thinned out any, but the sun hung lower in the sky and it was already late—five-thirty—and I didn't feel like hanging around outside any more because I didn't want to run into somebody I knew and spoil the great mood I was in, so I went upstairs and Mother opened the door for me.

"Shh! He's asleep," she said.

"Who?"

"The old sergeant."

"And the other one?"

"He went out for a walk."

"Aha," I said. "Can I have some supper?"

"Already?"

"Yeah. I'd like to go out afterward."

"*Now* where, Danny?"

"Oh, just for a walk."

"Don't you think you ought to stay home tonight?"

"Don't worry," I said and opened the door to the bathroom. "I'll be careful."

Mother went into the kitchen, looking worried. I turned on the faucet in the warm bathroom and washed my hands. Then, with the towel in my hand, I went into the kitchen. Mother was cooking something on the hot plate.

"What's for supper?"

"Potatoes. The Englishmen finished up all the meat at lunch, you know."

"That's all right. Potatoes are fine."

"That'll be enough for you?"

"Sure. Don't worry," I said, and went back to the bathroom. Suddenly I realized how short I'd been with her, that lately I'd just charged in, said what I needed to, got what I wanted, and taken off again. I realized I was behaving pretty mean toward her. It wouldn't cost me anything to talk to her a little bit, would it? But I didn't feel like it and so usually I only talked to her when I wanted something. Which made me feel ashamed of myself. Because I was fond of her. It was just that now there were so many other things and they were more interesting. Irena and Mitzi and the uprising. I wanted to say something nice to her though, just to make her happy and so she'd know how fond I was of her. I went back into the kitchen and sat down on a chair. It took me a while to figure out what to say.

"Those refugees are really weird," I said finally.

"I just hope they haven't brought all sorts of diseases," she said.

"Aw, no."

"Well, there were epidemics after the last war too, you know."

"I know, Spanish influenza. But there won't be anything like that this time."

"Goodness only knows. You never can tell."

"No. They've got all sorts of drugs and vaccines and stuff like that now."

"I don't know. All I can say is God spare us." She lifted the lid and took a look at the potatoes. "What did you do all afternoon?"

"I went over to Benno's for a while and then I just watched the crowds for a while and then I went over to Berty's and then I saw Irena and we . . . talked for a while. . ." I thought about showing Mom the snapshot but decided not to. That submachine gun might frighten her maybe and the war wasn't over yet and why get her all worked up over nothing? Then I remembered I hadn't showed my picture to Irena. How in hell could I have forgotten that! I felt so bad about that I almost felt sick to my stomach. But then I figured that I must have been saving it up for later, like an ace in the hole, and that made me feel better again.

"Oh, you saw Irena? What's she doing these days?"

"Working at the post office."

"Did she say what she was going to do when . . . whether she'll be going to Prague?"

"No. But I guess she will."

"And what does she want to study?"

"I'm not sure. Medicine, I guess."

"Medicine?"

"I think that's what she said once."

Mother was interested in Irena because she knew how I felt about her. Quite a lot of people knew because, for one thing, I hadn't made much of a secret of it and for another thing, Mrs. Moutelikova had told Mrs. Frintova and Mrs. Frintova had passed it on to Mrs. Baumanova and Mrs. Baumanova had told my mother that Danny had picked out a very nice girl and Mother acted like she didn't know anything but was glad about it and Mrs. Moutelikova told Irena's mother in the shop that I came from a good family and that Irena better hang on to me because I was such a serious and reliable boy and since nobody took this Zdenek seriously because God only knew who he was and where he'd come from. He was just in Kostelec on a labor brigade whereas I was young Smiricky and all the mothers took me seriously, even Irena's. Irena was the only one who didn't.

"What about you, Danny?" Mother asked me. "Have you settled on anything yet?"

"Not yet."

"You ought to be giving it some thought, Danny."

"Well, sure. But it's not all that big a problem, is it?"

"Remember, it's for your whole life."

"I know. Well, I guess I'll study English then," I said and smiled. For my whole life? I couldn't believe it. For a couple of years maybe, but it seemed impossible that I'd always go on doing the same thing my whole life—like a job, I mean. Playing the saxophone, yes. I thought I'd probably do that for as long as I lived, and falling in love with girls and telling them how crazy I was about them, but then I figured I probably wasn't going to live all that long anyway, and I couldn't imagine I'd ever fall into one of those ruts older folks slipped into and never climbed out of. Maybe I'd die any one of these days. The idea didn't worry me at all.

"Well, it's up to you," said Mother. "Your father and I won't stand in your way."

She set a plate of potatoes and a salt shaker down in front of me and sat down in a chair on the other side of the table. I started eating and the food tasted good.

"Then you'd be a teacher after you graduated?"

"Yes. Or I'd go on for my Master's."

"Master of Arts?"

"Yeah."

"Well—what can you do with a Master's degree?"

"It depends. I could get a job in a library somewhere or maybe as an editor—that kind of thing."

"You mean you'd like to be a journalist?"

"Sure, that too."

"I think you'd like that, don't you?"

"I guess so."

"You've always been good at talking, I mean, and always gotten the best grades on your essays."

"Well, we'll see," I said. "The main thing is, the university will be open again."

"That's true," she said. "God grant us good health—that's

all I ask. If only we can all stay well, we'll manage the rest somehow."

"Sure," I said and pushed back my plate. "Well, time for me to be going."

"Now, Danny, promise me you'll take good care of yourself," said Mother, and her eyes looked worried again.

"I will. Don't worry," I said and kissed her.

She stroked my hair and said, "And come home, as soon as you can."

"Sure," I said and went out into the hall. I looked at myself in the mirror and, in the shadow at least, I looked pretty sharp. I opened the door and stepped into the outside hallway. Mother stood in the doorway.

"Well, goodby," I said, and started down the stairs.

"Goodby," she said. At the landing, I saw her still standing there and blew her a kiss. Like I'd done at noon. Like I'd done every day for as long as I can remember. I decided to go over to Heiser's place through the castle grounds to make better time. I turned left and headed toward the square. By now the sun was shining only on the tops of the houses on the left side of the street; down below it was already twilight. Refugees were still camping in the square and flags dangled down at them from every side. The windows of the City Hall and the post office and the buildings on the left side of the square glinted in the setting sun, which bathed everything on the square in a lovely yellowish light—the refugee families crouching on the sacks and bundles together with all their children and sometimes dogs, all chewing away on something, and the French soldiers, too, in their dusty blue uniforms. An organ sounded from the church and behind one of the narrow windows in the Gothic bay you could see the glimmer of candles. I went around the church. In front of the door stood a cluster of stock-still people, bareheaded and respectfully silent. The church was packed. They couldn't get in. As I passed the door, I could feel a wave of heat coming out from inside and caught a few words of some song to the Virgin Mary and the weak bleat of the organ. I could just see the choirmaster sitting up there in the loft going off into a trance over that sloppy music which he'd had to put up with for years, and even worse since he gave violin lessons, and now there he sat probably glad to drown out his fear in that music, scared of what could happen before the Russians arrived and scared of what would happen once they did. I'd taken a few music lessons from him once and always had to wait outside until the kids ahead of me were done with theirs. I only played the piano then, so I didn't have it bad, but the kids ahead of me scratched away on their violins and the choirmaster would prance around clapping his hands to his head and sighing or shrieking while those kids calmly sawed away, flatting and sharping like so many tone-deaf mummies. That was our choirmaster. And up at the altar, the rector was working his way through his *trinitate personae et unitate substanciae* without believing a word of it, whispering it, mumbling it, whining it while the choirmaster went after those flat or deflated tones with his index finger on his organ, and everything about the priest was cheap and shabby—his cassock frayed, the monstrance battered— everything around him down at the heels, including himself in his medieval parish house with its weather-beaten image of St. Anthony out in front, and still there was really something beautiful about it all and somewhere in the world, in Rome or New York or maybe even in Prague, there were brand new churches whose priests believed in all this and sang about it every day as though each day they were singing it for the very first time, with reverent voices, wonderful, rich voices: *vere dignum et justum est aequum et salutare, nos tibi semper, et ubique gratias agere.* It sounded beautiful all that *Domine sancte, Pater omnipotens, Deus: Qui cum unigenito Filio tuo, et Spiritu sancto, unus es Deus, unus es Dominus.* I stopped to listen and I could actually hear the priest's rusty old voice croaking, *Oremus—praeceptis salutaribus moniti, et divina institutione formati, audemus dicere: Pater Noster, qui es in coelis*—and, oh, how I wished that our Father Who art in Heaven was really sitting up there, looking down at me and taking care of me as if I really mattered, but I knew the earth rotated around the sun and that the sun was only an immense disk belonging to the Milky Way and that it was spinning away in space in an orbit all its own and that, according to Eddington, there were about a hundred thousand million stars in any given galaxy and around a hundred thousand million galaxies in the universe and what good did it do me if the priest said *omnia per ipsum facta sunt, et sine ipso factum est nihil quod factum est* if I simply couldn't believe it? I looked away from the church and up at the castle, at its three rows of glittering windows, and I started past the parish house up the steep hill. Quickly and without looking back, I climbed the lilac-scented path up past the crumbling castle outer wall, and I didn't stop till I got all the way up to the circular drive in front of the castle. From there the square below looked flat and crawling with tiny figures headed every which way under the copper disk of the setting sun. There was something about that seductively blossoming May evening that made me feel so strange that I rushed over to the courtyard to leave that view behind. It was dark and damp in the first courtyard. As I passed the well, the door of the steward's apartment opened and out came Ema, the steward's daughter.

"Hello," I said and waited for her. Her big, potato-nosed face broke into a grin as she came toward me in her pink dress.

"Hello," she said.

"How're you doing?"

"Fine, thanks. And you?"

"Not bad. Listen, what're all your noble folks up to these days?"

"They're just getting ready to leave. You want to take a look?"

"Sure. You mean they haven't been jailed yet?"

"No. Why should they be put in jail?"

"Well, von Schaumburg-Lippe, for instance." Actually, I didn't really know either why they ought to be put in jail. "What's the Queen of Württemberg doing?"

"She's here, too. Come on, I'll show you."

"Oh, I know what she looks like. You showed her to me before—remember?"

"That's right."

"Still—so what? Another look can't do me any harm."

Ema grinned. "It'll be some day when Danny Smiricky doesn't have time for a look at things."

"Well, you know me," I said.

"Come on then," said Ema. You could see her corset or girdle or whatever it was under that pink dress of hers. She had mammoth hips topped by an unusually short torso—a real steward's daughter type. From the outside, anyway, she looked custom-made for living in a castle tower. We passed through the second courtyard and stopped in front of the stables. Three open carriages stood there, the horses harnessed and ready to go. A cluster of castle kids had gathered to stare. The count was already seated in the first carriage—an old guy, over ninety, with a neck like a giraffe and a head that wouldn't stop shaking. Next to him, her knees covered by a thick green blanket, sat the countess. They stared dully in front of them. Across from them sat two young girls as ugly as they come.

"Who's up in the first carriage with the count?" I asked.

"Countess Hilda and Countess Elis," Ema said.

I looked at them, both redheads, and then over at the second carriage where a butler in ordinary clothes was just helping a fat, gray-haired old lady wearing a black shawl up and in.

"The one that's getting in now is the Marquise von Stroheim, one of the count's cousins," Ema said.

The old lady sat down and as she did the carriage rocked slightly. Kozak, the castle gamekeeper, leaned out of a window over the stables and in his vest and with his sleeves rolled up settled down to watch the proceedings. His wife was at the next window and the two of them looked down without a trace of regret or respect. A young man with a little beard sprang up into the carriage, spread out and tucked in a blanket around the marquise.

"That's Count Hohenstein, her nephew. He's engaged to the queen."

"Oh?" I said. He looked pale and ordinary and completely insignificant.

"I wonder what she sees in him, anyway," I said.

"He's a nobleman. A blue blood."

I*

"Hmmm," I said. Well, that kind of thing probably meant a lot to those people. And maybe there really was something appealing about locking yourself up in your own private world like that and gradually becoming extinct. Which reminded me that I had blue blood in my veins, too, and why my ancestors couldn't have taken better care of it was beyond me. It made me mad. So here I was now, just another ordinary mortal on my way to meet Mitzi down below this castle.

"The one sitting across from her is the marquis, her husband, and next to him is the Princess von Blumenfeld. She's an old maid," Ema said.

The marquis was fat and redfaced and the princess looked pale and drawn. They were all bundled up under blankets and steamer rugs. Mr. Kozak spat from his window and lit his pipe. The marquis called out in German to somebody in the house. Princess Renata came out of the door followed by her two little kids in loden coats. She looked German and bony and wore a transparent raincoat over her dirndl. The old butler lifted the kids into the carriage and then helped the princess up.

"What's keeping the queen?" I wondered.

"She's probably still busy giving instructions to the housekeeper. She's got more energy than all the rest of them put together."

"Isn't the housekeeper going with them?"

"Yes. But the staff won't be leaving till tomorrow morning."

Everybody was already seated in the carriages. They were all just waiting for the queen. The coachman of the third carriage was letting a harness strap out a notch. The ramparts cast their jagged shadow across the courtyard and the last sliver of the crimson sun shone from the edge of the horizon straight up to the door. I kept my eye on the door and just as the shadow reached the threshold, the Queen of Württemberg appeared, all made up and wearing a light brown suit, as beautiful as Greta Garbo, her hair shining in the copper glow, and said something in German to the housekeeper bowing behind her and then, with a few elegant womanly strides, went over to the carriage, jumped in, and called out in a firm, deep voice, "*Los!*" The coachman cracked his whip, the first carriage rolled off, the second right behind it, and then the third. There was a creak of wheels and out they went through the gate and down the drive and in the last carriage I could see the copper-colored hair of the queen who didn't turn to look back, and then there was only her glow as she passed through the gate and she was gone. She impressed me, that Queen of Württemberg, and I felt sorry for her. But Ema was standing beside me.

"Well, there they go," she said, and giggled. Mr. Kozak left his window and the castle kids rushed out through the gate after the carriages.

"Yes. Well, I've got to be going, too. Thanks," I said, and shook Ema's hand.

"You're welcome."

"So long," I said, and walked quickly out through the gate and down the drive. I turned left, past the ball courts, jumped over a ditch, and plunged into the woods. It was almost dark under the trees, but as I went on light sifted through from the far side. I walked across the soft pine needles. At the rim of the woods there was a large grassy clearing. I sat down and looked at the Heisers's mansion and the factory buildings below. The sun still lit up parts of the town down in the valley; most of it was already in shadow though. In the shadow of Castle Hill the Heisers' place was turning blue. The long gray factory sheds behind it were fading out in the evening haze. From a long way off, coming in from the east, I could hear a faint rumbling and the muffled bark of gunfire. The stars in the eastern sky glistened as if they were wet. In the west, the horizon glowed pink. Again I heard faint but distinct bursts of machine-gun fire. You couldn't see anything, though, just a piece of the silent town below and the Heisers' handsome mansion.

I lay down on my back in the grass and looked up at the moist little stars that had started to twinkle shyly in the darkening sky. Right over me and a bit off to the east, the beautiful constellation of Orion's Belt stretched splendidly out across the heavens, all laid out in the same great pattern as always. To the left I saw a feeble reddish little star —the red giant Betelgeuse—and it seemed very odd that there was that ball bigger than our entire solar system and thinner than air, shining up there calmly and quietly in the remoteness of space, like a drop of raspberry juice on a patch of green moss, while down here below me was Kostelec and revolution and every once in a while the sound of gunfire rolling in from Germany. The sky and its little stars were calm and still, but down in the town there was a stifled rustle and a peculiar kind of springtime tension, like just before a thunderstorm. I could feel the cool blades of grass under my head and the hard ground under my back. I closed my eyes and started thinking about life and how I'd live it and thought of Mitzi, but only as an overture or transition into the new kind of life I was going to start in Prague, and I thought about how I'd tell her, Mitzi, I'm crazy about you, but then it struck me I'd used that line on every girl I'd ever met and I wondered whether I'd use it again on the girl I was going to meet in Prague and knew I would because it was the only one I knew and I'd used it on everybody and it had usually worked, though it hadn't helped much with Irena, because girls are basically all the same and I had the feeling I was far superior to them all, that I was just playing around with them, secretly laughing at them, and I wondered whether I'd feel the same with that girl I was going to meet in Prague and I was sure I would because she'd be just another girl no matter how pretty and smart and amoral she was because I just couldn't believe that besides me and boys and girls, there could be a fourth sort of people on earth or some kind of female counterpart of me, I mean, who'd come anywhere close to being a match for me. The whole idea struck me as being ridiculous, absurd. And then suddenly my thoughts got all tangled up and I was somewhere else and everything shifted and turned crazy and fast and I drifted off far, far away and suddenly I was cold and the sky above me was black and littered with cold white stars and I realized I'd fallen asleep so I sat up and I could see cracks of light shining out through the badly blacked-out windows of the houses on the hill and the dome of heaven was mirrored in the swimming pool down on Jerusalem Street and you could hear that springtime buzz coming up from the town and then I realized Mitzi had stood me up so I got up, even though I was half frozen, and said to myself, Mitzi, you bitch—so you didn't even bother to show up, did you? Well, that sure takes care of that, but it really didn't bother me now and I headed down through the grass toward the Heisers'. I looked in through the window of the salon which wasn't blacked out and saw Mrs. Heiserova. She walked toward the window, looked out into the dark, then turned and said something to somebody inside. You couldn't hear a word, you could just see her mouth moving. Mitzi wasn't in the room. The light from the window sort of melted away in the darkness. I turned and started back toward town. She'd given me the brush-off and now she was probably sitting up in her little room laughing at me. A machine gun was chattering away again in Germany. It was a warm night, more like summer than spring. Anyway, it served me right. Why couldn't I be faithful to Irena? Why did I have to turn to look at every skirt that went by, why didn't other girls leave me cold when I was so in love with Irena? Maybe that was asking too much of me. I wondered whether the sight of another girl would ever leave me cold and decided it wouldn't, ever. Or maybe when I finally met that girl in Prague. But I knew that even then they probably wouldn't. Anyway, that wasn't the point. The point wasn't to be blind to other girls. What point would there be to that? The trick was, not to be blind, but to stick to one girl. That was what counted in life and maybe that was what love was all about and maybe that was the way it should be. To stick to one girl, even though you liked them all, and be happy with her and have tender loving feelings for her and stay with her for as long as you lived. With Irena. Or that girl I was going to meet in Prague. I was in love with her already, just because she was alive, because she must be out there somewhere, just waiting for me, maybe. There must be girls somewhere who know how to love just one man, body and soul and always, and how to be faithful to him too.

I turned down the tree-lined street toward the workers' district and there, among the shadows, I saw the flash of a girl's light dress that was cut in half at the waist by a dark-sleeved arm, and as the couple strode quickly down the path toward the woods the starlight lit up a blonde head I recognized right away. It was Dagmar Dreslerova, but the guy with his arm around her waist wasn't Kocandrle. I stepped back into the shadows and watched. They cut across the meadow toward the clearing in the woods where I'd dozed off just a few minutes before. The guy boosted her along up the slope and then all of a sudden they stopped and threw their arms around each other. His cap fell off and his red crewcut flared up in the starlight. I stared. He was wearing what looked like a windbreaker. Then they pulled apart and Dagmar raced on up toward the clearing, the guy right behind her. He had narrow hips. Jesus! Of course. It was Siddell, my Englishman, the one who said he'd just gone out for a walk. Hell, he sure didn't lose any time. Less than half a day and more than halfway there already. The last thing I saw was the two of them tumbling down onto the grass and Dagmar's white knees gleaming in the starlight.

I turned and went on down the road through the workers' district. So that was girls for you. Well, so be it. Under the shadows of the blossoming trees small bunches of people, many of them in shirtsleeves, were standing listening in silence to the distant sound of the guns. From the other end of the workers' district you could hear a woman giggling and a man's laugh booming out through the dark. Some beginner was practicing on a bugle in one of the old apartment houses. I walked along next to the factory wall. Lewith's cafeteria on the other side was still lit up and through the barred windows I saw somebody's green-uniformed back. The doors downstairs were open and in the pale light of a single bulb stood a cluster of guys wearing caps, talking to some Russian refugees. I kept on going. The main smokestack of the power station loomed up in the sky. Betelgeuse stood balanced and glowing right on the tip of the lightning rod. Gunfire rang out again from the east. Mr. Pitterman was standing in a doorway with

Rosta. They were both gazing up at the sky and listening.

"Good evening," I said.

"Good evening," said Mr. Pitterman.

"Hi," said Rosta. "Where're you off to?"

I stepped up into the doorway. "Hear that?" I said.

"Yes. They're getting pretty close," said Mr. Pitterman.

"I'll say," I said.

"They'll be here tomorrow. Dad's already got his red flag all fixed up," Rosta said.

"Well. You know how it is," said Mr. Pitterman, embarrassed. We were standing in the doorway to Mr. Pitterman's house. Besides that place, he owned five others on Jirasek Boulevard, plus a store and an electric mangle.

"Yeah. They may come in pretty handy," I said.

"You have one, too?"

"What?"

"A red flag."

"No. But we don't own our own house either."

"Rosta thinks it's all just a joke, but it isn't," said Mr. Pitterman.

"They'll take everything away anyway, Dad. Because you're a bourgeois and a capitalist," said Rosta.

"You keep quiet! You'd do well to learn where to just keep your mouth shut, Rostislav!"

"You going over to the brewery tomorrow?" I asked.

"Sure. Listen. . ." Rosta grabbed my arm and pulled me back into the hallway. "I wrote one, too."

"Huh? One what?"

"Well, what . . . what we were talking about over at the brewery."

"Oh, your will," I said.

Rosta looked at me. "You think maybe I shouldn't have?"

"Well, sure. Why not? You can't lose anything by it," I said.

"Look, I know Dagmar's a tramp," said Rosta. "But still. . ."

"If you know that, Rosta," I said, "you know a lot."

"Well, sure I do," he said. "Still, she's a good kid and I'll bet if anything ever happened to me, she'd feel pretty bad about it, wouldn't she?"

"She sure would," I said.

"Aw, hell, I don't know. She goes around telling me I'm nuts and that there're more important things to worry about now, but that's where I think she's wrong. It's the only thing—I mean, what's between her and me—it's the only thing that does count. Not for her maybe but it sure is for me."

"Well then, it's a good thing you wrote it," I said. "Maybe you'll need it."

"You think so?"

"I was just up at the castle. From up there Germany's nothing but fireworks."

"Really?"

"That's right," I said and then added, "so maybe Dagmar'll be sorry after all."

"I'll say she will," said Rosta.

"Well, I've got to go. Good night."

"See you," said Rosta.

"So long," I said and walked back out to the boulevard which was empty now. I got home, unlocked the outside door, and went upstairs. Everybody was already sound asleep. The door to my room was closed. Mother's voice came from the bedroom.

"Danny?"

"Yes," I whispered.

"That Englishman hasn't come back yet."

"I know," I said. "He won't be back for a while."

"How do you know?"

"Well, I saw him," I said. "He . . . he's out having a good time, that's all."

"Gracious me," said Mother. "Already? And nothing happened to you? You're all right, Danny?"

"Sure," I said.

"I made up your bed on the kitchen couch."

"Fine. Good night."

"Good night."

I went into the kitchen and slowly undressed. Then I lay down on the couch and pulled up the blanket. The couch stood by the wall under the window and through it you got a wonderful view of the sky. I looked up and saw Betelgeuse glowing red above me again. It was following me. I started mulling things over again—Irena and then Dagmar and then tried to think about the revolution and shooting, but couldn't keep my mind on it and looked out the window at Betelgeuse which was almost directly above me and started thinking about that girl I was going to meet in Prague but somehow I couldn't quite picture her but that didn't stop me from thinking about her anyway and I was sure she existed, she had to, and I could feel she was there, coming toward me, like out of the sky and wearing that red Betelgeuse around her neck on a little silver chain, and exactly what color her eyes were I couldn't say but she was wonderful and I saw her but didn't know a thing about her except that she'd probably turn out to be a bitch, too, and then I fell asleep, sound asleep, a sleep without dreams.

Wednesday, May 9, 1945

The next morning, as soon as I walked out of the door of our building, I was caught up in a regular maelstrom of people. The German Army was pulling back from the frontier. The streets were packed. There were Germans in dusty uniforms, some armed and some not, and a few on bikes, all heading west as fast as they could go. And there were refugees—swarms of them. And townspeople. While I stared, Franta, the glassmaker, burst out of the house next door with his shirtsleeves rolled up and made straight for the Germans, grabbed for a rifle slung over one soldier's back and started yanking at it. The German tried to push him away—but not very hard—then unhitched the strap and let the rifle fall, and the next minute Franta had already picked it up and was heading back to his house, holding the rifle up high in both hands. This sparked the crowd. From both sides of the street, people moved in on the Germans, scrambling to lay hands on a rifle, but the Germans closed ranks and trained their guns on the mob. They stood in a huddle bristling with muzzles; the mob stopped, then just stood there swearing at the Germans. The Germans moved on again and the crowd let them pass and, when they'd gone on, followed along behind. I tagged along, too. Looking at the backs and rumps of those guys tramping in front of me in their tight jackets and bulging pants, I thought they looked awfully well fed. So this was our uprising. I trailed merrily along behind them and every once in a while caught a glimpse of the gray German helmets and guns near the street corner now. The crowd of guys just ahead of me were still yelling and shaking their fists. We'd already reached the antitank barricade at Novotny's and there the Germans had to slow down a little bit to get through the barrier. One soldier halted and waited for all the others to pass through. Then one guy jumped him and tried to wrest his rifle away from him. The crowd seethed. Two other Germans turned and lifted their submachine guns. I caught a glimpse of their faces for a second—expressionless and exhausted— and then both of those guns held ready to fire into the crowd. Then somebody yelled and the rear of the crowd started pushing up against the front. That blocked my view. All I could see now were those fat backsides working their way forward. Then two shots rang out, one right after the other. Immediately the crowd started to scatter. The guy in front of me turned and piled into me full force, sending me sprawling on the sidewalk. First all I saw were stars and then people racing off every which way and in no time at all the street in front of me was deserted except for those two Germans with their submachine guns. They were still standing by the antitank barrier. One of the muzzles was still smoking and the third German was still holding his rifle and they all just stared blankly in front of them. I sat there, dazed, staring right back at them. One of them glanced at me, but then quickly turned to the others and said, "*Los! Gehn wa!*"

"*Warte, Fritz,*" said the one with the rifle and, leaning it up against the barrier, he adjusted his helmet. It had been knocked crooked, probably when the guy from the crowd tried to grab his rifle away from him. The other two stood there, watching him. I looked around and saw Mr. Habr and some other guys flattened up against the walls at the entrance to the bank, eyeing the Germans. Suddenly, all around it was quiet as a tomb and it seemed to me I must look pretty ridiculous sitting there in the middle of that empty street, just staring at those Germans. So this was an uprising. The German straightened his helmet, then all three of them turned and, draped with hand grenades, moved on. As soon as they'd disappeared beyond the barrier, people swarmed out of the doorways and a big crowd gathered around me.

Mr. Habr hurried over. "Are you hurt, Mr. Smiricky?"

I scowled and got up. The crowd pressed in and stared at me.

"No," I said. "When you all took off, somebody ran into my stomach, that's all."

You could tell they were disappointed. Nobody had been hurt. The Germans had just fired into the air. The crowd broke up and drifted away. I went around the corner to Haryk's place. A family of gypsies was cooking something in a kettle over a little fire under a bunch of trees on Jirak Square. I rang the doorbell and Haryk leaned out the window.

"Hi," he said.

"Throw down a key," I said. Haryk disappeared and in a little while leaned out again.

"You going over to the brewery?" I asked.

"We've got to," said Haryk, and tossed down the key. "Come on up. I haven't finished breakfast yet."

Upstairs somebody was playing "Heartbreak Blues" on the piano. I opened the door and there was Lucie sitting at the piano, wearing a striped dress. Haryk was sitting at the table behind a big mug of coffee and Pedro was stretched out on the couch.

"Greetings," he said to me. Lucie stopped playing and spun around toward me on the piano stool. She spun too hard, though, so she had to spin it back down a little.

"Hi, Danny," she said.

"Hi. Are you going over to the brewery, too?" I asked

"No." She cocked her head to one side and, in an affected tone added, "Women have no business in a place like that." Her bare feet looked pretty in her white sandals.

"Well, I don't agree with that," I said. "So what are you going to do for your country?"

"I volunteered as a first-aid helper."

"Jesus," I said. "I hope I don't get wounded."

"Irena volunteered, too," said Lucie.

"She did?"

"Yes. We went over to sign up together." Lucie kept her face very blank and noncommittal.

"Well, then, guess I'd better let myself get wounded—but not too seriously."

"Oh? Why not?" said Lucie. She sounded disappointed.

"Why should I?"

"I thought you'd suffer anything for Irena."

"Well, sure. Within reason."

"Would you let them cut off a leg, for instance?"

"A leg? Sure," I said breezily.

"Or an arm?"

"Sure."

"Both arms?"

"Gladly," I said, but as soon as I'd said it I realized that'd be a dumb thing to do because then I couldn't even touch Irena.

"Wait a minute," I said. "One arm but not both."

"Why not?"

"One would be enough, wouldn't it?"

"But what if you had to lose both?"

"Why would I have to lose both arms?"

"Well, just supposing."

"Oh well, then, if I had to choose then I guess I'd rather lose an arm and a leg."

"But I want to know whether you'd give up both arms," said Lucie, swinging around on the piano stool and stretching out her legs.

"Well, okay. Sure," I said.

"But you had to think about it first, didn't you?"

"Well, it isn't so simple—losing both arms."

"You should have said yes without even giving it a second thought."

"Well, but I said I *would*, didn't I?"

"You're just like Haryk. You're all the same."

"I beg your pardon?" Haryk chimed in.

"Well, aren't you?"

"No."

"Oh, no?"

"Well, how do you mean—the same?"

"Well, for example I want you to shave off those awful-looking sideburns and you won't do it."

"And I don't want you to dye your hair and you don't pay any attention to me either."

"But *you*'re supposed to listen to *me*."

"Oh, well isn't that interesting? Why me and why not you?"

"Because you're a man," said Lucie and turned back to the piano. "Or at least you look like one," she added and she started playing "In the Mood" real fast, the way she'd heard it played over ABSE, the American Broadcasting Station in Europe. She played well. Her slender fingers with their red nails played a hard, sure bass boogie. She wore a wide blue bracelet on her bare wrist.

"What a woman!" Haryk said to the two of us. You could tell he was bragging. And she really was something to brag about, too. Lucie was as silly as every other girl but she really knew how to play the piano and dance boogie like nobody else and she took ballet lessons and she was awfully pretty. I liked her a lot. Irena didn't know how to play the piano. All she could do was plunk out some bad Beethoven or stuff like that, but she didn't know "Heartbreak Blues" or "Canal Street Blues" or "West End Blues" like Lucie did and which Irena never did and when Lucie played she looked like Mary Lou Williams, only prettier. And Irena didn't dye her hair either or paint her fingernails like Lucie and she didn't have a swell house with a swimming pool below the castle, but then again I remembered the cliffs and how I'd clung to the rope together with Irena that time at Spider Rock and all those evenings and nights I'd spent with her up there on the cliffs, but then Lucie started playing "Nobody's Sweetheart" and I was all wrapped up in her again and didn't know for the life of me who I really had a crush on. Oh to hell with it, I said to myself, and went over to the couch where Pedro was sprawled out and sat down next to him. Pedro pulled in and let go a big long yawn.

"Damn," he said.

"Shall we go?" I said.

"Just a second," said Haryk, and he got up from the table

and went over to the wardrobe. I looked over at his bed. It was still unmade and he had a big picture of Lucie on his bedside table. That reminded me to show him the picture of me with my submachine gun. I got out my wallet and took out one of the snapshots.

"Look," I said to Pedro, and handed it to him. Pedro took it, looked at it, and said, "Oho!" Then he turned and called over to Haryk!"

"Haryk!"

"What?"

"A portrait of Partisan Smiricky. Want to take a look?"

Haryk came over to the couch and Lucie noticed and stopped playing.

"Lord!" said Haryk. "I'd sure hate to meet you on a dark night."

"Let's see," said Lucie. She got up and sat down next to me.

"Lord!" she said, just like Haryk. "Very impressive, Danny!" She laid it on very thick.

"You think so?" I said, taking the picture and sticking it back in my wallet.

"Why didn't you have your picture taken too, Haryk?" Lucie said.

"We should have," Haryk said to Pedro. "We were stupid not to."

"We missed our big chance, all right," said Pedro.

"Okay, let's go," I said. "You can still get your pictures. People are taking the Germans' guns away from them all over the place."

"Really?" said Haryk.

"That's right. Let's go."

"Better take along something to eat, Haryk," said Pedro.

"Not a bad idea."

Haryk went into the kitchen and Pedro got up off the couch. He went out in the hall and I heard him go into the john. I stayed there alone with Lucie. She stretched out, one leg dangling over the side and the other on the couch. I felt like flirting with her like I always do when I'm alone with a pretty girl. Maybe it was a fresh thing to do but I've never known one of them to object. So I started right in.

"Lucie."

"Hmm?"

"You're beautiful."

"Oh, God."

"You're the most beautiful girl in all Kostelec."

"How about Irena?"

"Compared to you? Nothing."

"She ought to hear that!"

"Let her. It wouldn't make any difference to me."

"Oh, no?"

"I mean it, Lucie."

"Oh, I *believe* you, Danny."

"Honest. When I'm with you, I don't even think about her."

"Some love!"

I smiled cryptically.

"Well?" said Lucie.

"Lucie," I said quietly. "If there's anybody I'm in love with, it's you."

"Mmmm."

"Lucie," I said, "you're a wonderful girl."

"I'm surprised at you!" said Lucie. "Boy, I sure wouldn't like to be in Irena's shoes."

"Why not? You mean you wouldn't like me to be in love with you?"

"Well, not that so much, but I mean I'd rather have nobody than somebody like you," said Lucie "All right, you just said you love me, didn't you?"

"I do, Lucie."

"As faithfully as you love Irena?"

"Much more," I said, and slid closer over to her. She put her hand on my arm so she could push me away just in case.

"Well," she said. "And that's saying a lot, isn't it?"

Just then Haryk's voice boomed out from the hall. "Let's go!"

His voice startled me and I jumped, but when I saw nobody was looking in through the door I turned to Lucie again. She'd pulled back a bit but when she saw nobody was coming she laughed and her eyes sparkled and she got up off the couch, and as she did she ran her hand with those red fingernails of hers up along my arm and the side of my face and into my hair and then she tugged it.

"You stinker," she said and went to the door. I got up, too, stumbling after her as if I was drugged, and at the door ran my hand gently over her rump. She grabbed my hand and pushed me away. "Cut that out!" she whispered, and then ran up to Haryk, took the lunch bag out of his hand and, pretending to be awfully interested all of a sudden, said, "Let's see what you took!" She looked and then she said, "That's not going to be enough!"

"All right, all right," Haryk said impatiently, and took back his lunch bag. "Let's go."

"I won't be hungry," Lucie said.

"I'm sure you won't," said Haryk, and steered her out into the hall. Pedro was already standing on the stairs. Haryk locked the door. We walked along Jirasek Boulevard but had to wait a while before crossing over toward the side street where the movie theater was. The German Army, on bikes and on the double, was just making its way down the main street of Kostelec. Those on foot were mostly unarmed, had no helmets, and were being herded along by a handful of scowling Krauts, helmeted and armed with submachine guns, who were trying to carry out some sort of organized retreat. You could hear a steady crossfire of swearing and see the few diehard fanatical Nazis dragging their feet, marching slowly, still refusing to admit they were retreating. They stood out from the rest—their lips thin, their faces so full of fury their helmets looked like they were going to lift right off, like lids on top of steaming pots.

"I'll bet they've really gone through hell," said Pedro gravely.

"How do you mean?"

"Well, just think who's coming after them."

Pedro was a regular little Goebbels. But even I had a funny feeling in my stomach. I remembered the communist leaflet Prema had showed that winter—about how the uprising against the Germans would have to be transformed into a social revolution that would bring down the bourgeoisie and give the power to the workers, and so on. It had been printed in Rohnice and Prema showed it to me with that grim gangster face of his, looking like something out of a Blok poem somebody had loaned me in my sophomore year and that had stuck in my mind somehow —about men with cigarettes between tight lips, caps pulled down at an angle, jail staring out of their eyes—only now they were getting closer and God only knew what would happen next. Which was silly, too. If I was worried it was because all I knew about what could happen was what Goebbels had dinned into us and what Mr. Prudivy had told us ominously one night when he and his wife came over to our place and what Mr. Skocdopole had said. He'd been in Russia with the Czech Legion and he hadn't just filled us up with horror stories either. He'd simply said that "the poor people supported the Bolsheviks." The poor. That was the whole thing in a nutshell and that was just the trouble. We weren't poor. But then we weren't millionaires by a long shot either. My father hadn't even been able to save up enough to buy a car. Call that rich? Well, in any case, the best thing to do was to see the whole thing as a big adventure. Let the people who owned a lot of real estate worry. I didn't own anything. Just my saxophone, which I wouldn't want them to take but why should they? So what the hell. For now anyway, the best thing to do was just take in this big, mixed-up, shabby parade—all those men and cars and guns and pistols and the end of their splendor.

We crossed the street, passed the movie theater and went through the arcade to the patch of lawn in front of the Czech Brethren Church. Refugees in concentration camp rags or Allied uniforms were straggling across the lawn and here and there you could spot a gray German uniform. They were fleeing across the green grass under the hot sun. We crossed the lawn with Lucie in her flowered dress which stood out bright against the grass, but the fleeing people didn't even notice her. I was the only one who was looking at her. Her skin was a delicate, almost creamy white—the kind a few girls have and which you can hardly believe is real and that makes you want to touch it to find out—and her lips were rosy with lipstick and her blonde hair looked great and her skirt was long like in a fashion magazine she'd dug up somewhere that said women would be wearing clothes like that after the war. She dodged her way between the pack-bearing, heavy-booted men who trudged past in silence, their mouths hanging open from exhaustion. We crossed the little bridge over the creek and headed toward the Czech Brethren Church. It was surrounded by trees covered with white blossoms. We were just going by the front of the church when suddenly a coatless and unarmed German soldier came running toward us. Reverend Houba and Mr. Rebarbora, the Sunday school teacher, were right on his heels—Houba holding a rifle, Rebarbora a German Army coat. Then, without slowing up, Reverend Houba dropped the rifle and made a beautiful flying tackle, just like an American football player, and brought the German down. They both made perfect belly-landings, flat out.

"Wow!" said Haryk. The Sunday school teacher ran to the preacher's aid and they both started clobbering the German. Then Houba tried to pull off his jackboots and, though the German kicked like mad, finally got them off, too. It was a weird sight—Rebarbora straddling the guy's back and thumping away at his head, Houba pulling the guy's pants off including his belt with its revolver and hooked-on hand grenades.

"There! *Du Verdamntes deutsches Schwein!*" Reverend Houba said in good high-school German and then let go of the guy. Rebarbora stood up, too. The German got up and started running. His long white underpants flashed in the sunlight as he sprinted across the lawn, heading west.

"Good morning," I said to Reverend Houba.

"Good morning," he said, gazing after the fleeing German. "The scoundrel!"

"What happened?" I said.

"He wanted to hide in the church!" the preacher said indignantly.

"Really?"

"We caught him just in time."

"Well, you certainly got rid of him," I said.

"May it be a lesson to him—the barbarian," the preacher said. He looked around. "Where's his gun?"

"Here," said Mr. Rebarbora, picking the rifle up. It was a handsome though obviously battle-worn German rifle. The preacher took it, looked it over, and said, "God only knows how many lives this thing has on its conscience."

"Yes," I said. "Do you know how to use it?"

"Know how to use it?" said the preacher as if I'd insulted him. "I'll have you know I was a Czech Legionnaire. I've had plenty of experience with toys like these in my time."

"Maybe this one's different, though."

The preacher scowled and pulled back the bolt. The bullets flew out of the gun onto the grass.

"No different," he said.

"Well, then, that's fine," I said. "Are you going over to the brewery also?"

"No, I'm staying right here. I'd just like to see somebody else try to hide out in my church!"

"I'd hardly recommend it," said Haryk.

"I guess not," said the preacher with a grin.

"Not unless somebody's eager to walk around in his underwear."

"Well, goodby, Reverend," I said.

"Goodby," said the preacher, and everybody mumbled their goodbys and the preacher and his Sunday school teacher went back into the church and we went on our way. After awhile Lucie said, "Haryk, are you sure you're all going to be all right?" she said.

"What's there to worry about?" said Haryk. "You can see for yourself the Krauts are on the run, can't you?"

"Well, sure. I just hope the SS won't come through."

"Oh, no. Don't worry," said Haryk. We went along the path by the river till we got to the brewery. Others were headed there too—most of them wearing armbands. The brewery was completely hidden behind fragrant blossoming trees. Some women were standing around in front of the gate. Men and boys, their faces set in patriotic expressions, were saying goodby to them. A few of the women were bawling. We stopped and Lucie said, "Well, take care of yourselves."

"Goodby, Lucie," I said and held out my hand. She squeezed it and smiled at me. I gave her a meaningful smile. Then she shook hands with Pedro and said goodby to him, too.

"See you," said Pedro. I watched to see whether Lucie and Haryk would kiss. They held hands and looked at each other.

"Well, 'by, Lucie," Haryk said.

" 'By," said Lucie. Then she put on one of those vaguely distant expressions girls get when they're with their boy-friends, even when there are other people around. Haryk kind of grinned. I stared at them and knew I was staring and knew I shouldn't be staring but went right on staring anyway. Then Haryk leaned over and kissed her.

"Goodby," sighed Lucie and pulled away from him and then she said goodby to us all again and we all said so long and then she turned and hurried off. I went in through the gate. The first people I bumped into were Benda and Vahar. They were standing around at the edge of the crowd, looking disgusted. Benda was still doggedly wearing his black fireman's helmet. I said hello but they didn't bother to answer.

"What's new with Prema?"

"Still locked up," said Benda.

"You mean old Cemelik hasn't let him out yet?" asked Haryk.

"Hell, no."

"Are they going to let us in to see him, at least?"

"No."

"Boy, I sure don't envy him. Two days sitting around in that cellar," said Haryk. I looked around. The squad leaders were standing out in front of the main building, dressed in their hiking outfits, waiting. They were chatting together. They looked kind of pale. Major Weiss stood up by the door with Lieutenant Rubeš and Captain Kuratko. All three were in uniform.

"Well, what're we going to do?" I said.

"Some uprising," said Haryk.

"Three cheers for the Republic," I said.

"Bottoms up," said Pedro.

"Good morning, men," somebody said behind us. It was Benno with Fonda and Lexa.

"Hi," I said.

"Well, are you all steeled in your devotion to the holy cause of freedom?" asked Lexa. "You hear Sabata's speech?"

"No. When?" I said.

"Last night over the public address system."

"I didn't hear it," I said. "What crap did he come out with this time?" I asked, and thought back to what I'd been doing then.

"Oh, about devotion to the holy cause of freedom," Lexa said. "About how everybody should be prepared to sacrifice everything for their country if necessary."

"And especially about how everybody should obey orders so they won't have to sacrifice anything," said Haryk.

A bugle blew. The bugler disappeared from the window of the main building and Major Weiss took his place. Major Weiss was holding a sheet of paper. It was getting hot as hell. The Major's voice reached us clearly even though he was a long way off.

"Order number twelve," he read. "All those who have not yet undergone military training are to report immediately behind the icehouse where they will be given basic instruction in military technique. Signed, Colonel Cemelik." Then Major Weiss held up another paper. "I will now read the names of those to whom this order applies, compiled on the basis of the induction forms," he said and started reading off names.

Boy, they've certainly got things running efficiently now, I thought, and then I remembered Prema and his naïve Robin-Hood notions of how to stage an uprising. This was the real thing, all right. With lists of names and everything. And basic training in military technique. I watched the guys start off after their names had been called out, heading for the other side of the brewery yard. I saw Hrob's red head, then Benda, Prochazka, and Vahar, then that little squirt Dobrman, who was hardly five feet tall, trotting eagerly across the yard. Then Weiss read off Zdenek's name and I saw him in his mountain-climbing pants and his jacket with leather-patched elbows and left shoulder, wearing a Tyrolean hat with a knapsack on his back. He elbowed his way through the crowd toward the icehouse, his leg muscles bulging under his woolen knee socks. I still couldn't see what Irena saw in him. And at the same time I wished she could see the same thing in me and wondered what it was that makes girls like Irena fall in love with somebody. When I heard my name called, I straightened up and went over to the icehouse, too. The untrained forces were sitting on the grassy bank that sloped up to the fence at the edge of the woods. Most of them had taken their jackets off and were loafing around in the grass in the shade of the loading ramp trestle. The shadows of the trestle fell like a checkerboard across the men and the grass. Zdenek was sitting up next to the fence, already settling down to eat. He was just squatting there with his knees spread apart and his pants stretched tight across his thighs. He peered out at me from under his Tyrolean hat and I thought that with those big thighs crammed into those mountain-climber pants and with all those black hairs crawling out from under his sleeves and with that big suntanned mug of his he looked pretty repulsive. In fact, everything about him was repulsive. He was eating with his mouth open, gnawing away at some bread or whatever it was and I could hear him smacking his lips as I got closer. And this was the guy Irena had picked out. I couldn't understand it. I would have loved to sock him in that big munching jaw and I didn't have a doubt in the world but that I was better than he was and that Irena would be better off with me, but then it struck me maybe I really wasn't all that much better than he was and when it came to what really counted with girls maybe he was better than I was, and just better in general since, after all, Irena was so wild about him and so I went up and said hello and sat down beside him.

"How do you do," Zdenek said to me. "How's it going?"

"Same as with you, I guess."

"Look," said Zdenek. "I get the feeling all this doesn't make much sense."

"All what?"

"All this organization."

"Well, that's an original thought," I said.

"Boy, we had a troop that was really organized. All mountain climbers, see?"

"Must've been great," I said.

"I'll say," went on Zdenek. "Tonda was our leader and it was just guys from the club."

"What happened?"

"They disbanded us. I guess they've forbidden any kind of private organization. That's what this army's for and anybody who doesn't obey will be treated like an outlaw."

"A bunch of crooks themselves," I said. "What's Irena doing?"

"She signed up for the Red Cross. Hey, there's Tukes!" Zdenek said suddenly and whistled their signal. Tukes, another mountain climber, came across the grass toward us. He had buckteeth and was wearing a ski cap and two other guys were with him. They were both wearing mountain-climbing pants with leather knee patches and jackets with more patches and Tyrolean hats.

So I quickly said to Zdenek, "Gee, there's Benno. I've got to talk to him. See you later!" It was all the same to Zdenek. He didn't even hear me and he didn't even look at Benno.

"Well, greetings, gentlemen, greetings," he yodeled at them. "Come on, come on over!"

I went over to Benno and the other guys from the band who'd just shown up and just walking over there made me feel better. I'd always felt funny around Zdenek and all those sportsman types from the Alpine Club. I wasn't the athletic type. I belonged to the band. The Alpinists made me sick with their knapsacks stuffed with bread and butter and their patented butter holders and all their talk about the beauties of the sun going down on the cliffs and about traversing here and chimneying there and about pietons and etriers and belaying and roping down. The whole business gave me a big pain and I only went around with them on account of Irena, because she did, and that's why I floundered around, up and down the Ledecsky Rocks, dabbing my skinned knees and torn hands with iodine, and swinging all tangled up in loops of rope far out over the tops of the pine and spruce trees with the blue sky up above and gray cliffs in between whose sides had been gashed and etched by some primeval sea and flayed by the winds while down below, deep in the gulch over which I dangled, the moss grew soft and wet and dark in the shadows and there I was, clinging to those ropes like an untalented spider. Like the time I crossed from Five Fingers to Sleave Peak. It felt awfully weird up there on those ropes but it really gave you a good feeling, too, because there was Irena sitting over on Sleave Peak in her yellow sweater and those pants with the leather heart over her fanny, and she was watching me tensely and telling me what to do next so it wasn't half bad. It was kind of fun, in a way, to be a mountain climber and crawl everywhere with Irena and sleep beside her and the others at night in the cabin down under the cliffs. All that was great, except I was no mountain climber. They had to pull me along the rope with loops and I'd always fall at Chimney Rock and my knees would knock going up the side of the cliff. I just wasn't built for that sort of thing. I was just interested in Irena and I did all that just on account of her and, man, what all I hadn't done! But almost everything I ever did was on account of girls. Just like every other guy I ever knew. Only some were lucky enough to be able to do things they were cut out for, things they loved doing and were talented at and that the girl loved doing too. No such luck for me. I loved playing jazz and I was good at it and I didn't enjoy crawling over cliffs and I was clumsy as hell at doing it. Irena was all for cliffs and nature and for getting up at half past three to see the sunrise and she said herself she wasn't musical and she wasn't. She'd only taken piano lessons because her daddy wanted her to and she couldn't tell the difference between a trombone and a trumpet, but she didn't even care. I did. I was happiest when we were up in Benno's room, listening reverently to Armstrong's "Ain't Misbehaving" or else when I was sitting at the Port Arthur sucking on the tenor reed and fiddling with the valves on its nice, cool, metallic body. That was the life for me. That was life and none of these other things were.

I went over to Benno and the others and joined them without a word. There was a big crowd behind the icehouse now. It looked like things should start any minute. We waited a while longer and then Major Weiss appeared around the corner of the icehouse in his elegant uniform. There was some other guy with him, a short guy with sergeant's stripes on his arm. He was squat and stubby and looked like a stump.

"Jeezuz," said Benno. "Is *he* going to instruct us?"

"Looks that way," said Lexa.

Major Weiss blew his whistle and everybody stopped talking. He waited till everything got quiet and then said, "Men, I'm turning over command of this group to Sergeant Krpata who will give you the necessary basic training. His orders must be obeyed without question, as you yourselves pledged to do when you signed up. Good luck!"

"Thank you, sir!" a couple of idiots called out feebly. Major Weiss said a few words to Krpata who clicked his heels and saluted. Major Weiss touched his cap casually and left. Company Sergeant Krpata looked us all over.

"We're in for a great time now," said Benno.

"Don't forget, it's for the fatherland," Lexa said.

"Shit," said Benno.

"There are quite a lot of you here," yelled Krpata. "So Major Weiss and I decided that half of you will go out on patrol while the other half undergoes basic training here this morning and when the patrols return those who've remained will go out."

"Are we going to parade around town again?" somebody up front asked.

"Yes," Krpata told him. "Somebody's got to help handle the refugees and move mattresses into temporary dormitories."

"The same old grind all over again," grumbled Benno.

"And now I'll read off half the men on this list. That half will remain here. You others'll leave and report back in two hours," said Krpata. I looked at my watch. It was eleven. Krpata read off the names. All were present and accounted for. The sun was getting hotter and hotter and there wasn't a cloud in the sky. It was sweltering. Benno took off his jacket and unbuttoned his shirt all the way down to his belly. Drops of sweat glistened on his forehead and there were big wet stains under his armpits.

"Now what're they going to do with us?" he said in a low voice.

Krpata finished reading his list and said all those whose names had not been read should leave. Several guys hoisted themselves up off the grass and plodded off. I saw the mountain climbers leave with the leather patches on their behinds, looking like they were going to some kind of masquerade. The sun beat down on the green grass and on the guys clumping past the icehouse. The back wall of the icehouse was cracked and tiny useless bits of mica in the plaster glittered in the sun.

"Well, now," said Krpata and then out of the clear blue sky, he let out an unnatural bellow: "Ten-*shun!*" Though none of us moved, I noticed a number of boys jumping up off the grass. Hrob was standing in front of me, tense as a bowstring, his carrot top blazing in the sunshine.

"You! You back there! Didn't you hear me? I gave the order to stand at attention!" yelled Krpata, glaring at us. Wearily we got up and drew ourselves to attention while Krpata kept his threatening glare trained on us. I could hear Benno behind me whispering, "Jackass."

"You waiting for somebody to pick you up?" said Krpata with suppressed rage. I looked around. Pedro was lazily getting up off the grass, smiling wryly. But no sooner had he stood up than he leaned over again and brushed off his knees.

"Well? You about ready now?" roared Krpata.

"Take it easy," said Pedro. Krpata flushed and bristled. He strode sternly up to Pedro and stopped in front of him. Pedro straightened up. He was about a head taller than Krpata but the sergeant was very solidly built. Then he yelled right into Pedro's face.

"What's your name?"

Pedro twisted his mouth into a near grin. "Gershwin," he said.

"You know where you are?"

"Sure. At the brewery."

"Don't try getting wise with me, and don't think you're going to get anywhere with your Schweik tricks either, because you're not!" bellowed Krpata. You could see he was trying to make up his mind whether he ought to start off his glorious training program by marching Pedro off and locking him up in the cellar with Prema or not.

"Wouldn't think of it, sir," said Pedro. Krpata sliced him with another bitter look.

"And stand up straight!" he barked, but in a somewhat milder tone now. Pedro straightened up a bit.

"Stomach in!"

Pedro sucked his stomach in and tilted slightly forward.

"Toes out!"

Pedro stood there looking like a toe dancer.

"Not so *far* out!" bellowed Krpata.

Pedro stood practically pigeon-toed. Krpata studied him for a minute, then said, "All right. But I'm going to keep my eye on you." Then he turned and went back to stand in front of the crowd.

"Prick," said Haryk quietly.

"Form up behind me now, in a column of threes!" shouted Krpata, and he turned to face the icehouse wall. Everybody milled around for a while and three straggly lines formed up behind Krpata. Guys were pushing and shoving, trying to line up according to height, and meanwhile Krpata stood there with his back to them, one hand stretched out toward the sky.

"Let's get in the back," said Benno. We headed for the rear. We stood right at the end of the line. Pedro, Lexa, and Fonda stood in front of me; Benno and Haryk and I brought up the rear. Far away I could see Krpata's upraised hand. Then his hand came down and I heard him yell, "Line up!"

I took two steps to the right and stopped directly behind Lexa. I saw Krpata marching back along the column, checking every row. He was looking for us. I heard him stop behind us and then a roar: "About *face!*"

Feet flashed in front of me and I pivoted slowly. It reminded me of the time at the beginning of the war when I went to Sokol Hall on account of Irena and let myself be shoved and ordered around by Brother Vladyk. When I turned around, there was Krpata again. His eyes were sparkling with vicious glee. The dunce had tricked us. Now the three of us were at the head of the column. Krpata studied us a moment. Benno stood right in front of him.

"I can see," said Krpata, "that some of you don't even know how to execute a proper about face. Be so kind as to watch. I'll demonstrate."

He drew himself up stiff as a ramrod. "This exercise is executed in two stages. In stage one, you pivot on your left foot and move your right foot out to the side, like so. In stage two, you bring your right foot up next to the left. Like so." Like a billiard ball hit with just enough English, he spun around and clicked his heels.

"Once more," he said, and did it again. We stood there watching him.

"All right, now," he said. "Company! About *face!*"

You could hear feet scraping over the ground and clumping together. I did it in two stages as he said. We stood there with our backs to him.

"Wonderful!" he howled sarcastically behind us. "Company! About *face!*"

I spun again and saw Benno next to me, pivoting like an elephant. Krpata was watching him, too.

"You now. By yourself," he said to Benno. "About *face!*" Benno turned his back to him.

"My God," said Krpata. "Did you even listen to what I was saying?"

"Yeah," said Benno, with his back toward him. I could tell he was mad and embarrassed. He always used to get embarrassed in gym class and always did everything wrong. Like the time when that jujitsu instructor came to our school to demonstrate self-defense and, of course, picked Benno for his demonstrations and threw him around on the mat for a full hour, twisting his arms and legs until, finally, he sat down on top of him while he explained the theory of self-defense to the whole class.

"Then kindly repeat what I said," said Krpata.

"Well, first you pivot on one foot and put the other foot out and then bring it over," said Benno.

"Then why didn't you do it?"

"I did."

"Nonsense! Now try it again. Company! About *face!*" Benno turned back to face Krpata. A couple of clowns in back snickered.

"You're as graceful as a block of wood! See if you can't move that big right foot of yours this time! Company! About *face!*"

Benno turned again.

"Company! About *face!*"

Benno turned back.

"Shift some of that flab of yours around, for Chrissake!" howled Krpata. "Company! About *face!*"

Benno wanted to turn but just then Krpata bent down and grabbed his right foot and, as Benno turned, pulled. Only Benno, caught completely off guard, lost his balance and came down heavily on Krpata's foot. Krpata let out a hiss of pain.

In the middle of the silence, Pedro chuckled. It wasn't any joke, though, to have Benno sitting on your foot.

"Up! Get up, you!" roared Krpata and Benno scrambled up from the ground.

"I've never seen such a clumsy ox in my life," said Krpata furiously. Then he turned and slowly went back to his place. He limped a bit, but tried to hide it.

"Let's hope they have to amputate," whispered Lexa behind me.

Krpata started in on his instruction course again.

"The cornerstone of military training," he said, "is knowing what every order means. The order, 'Forward march,' for example, is done this way."

He made a half turn, stuck out his bemedalled chest and yelled at himself, "Forward, march!" Then he flung out his left foot and started marching past our line without making any mistakes that I could see.

"When the order 'Halt!' is given," I heard him say as he marched along, "you come to a halt on your right foot, take one more step with your left, then bring your right foot up beside it. Like so." He came along briskly till he got to us, yelled "Halt!" and clacked his boots together. Then he looked at us triumphantly as if waiting for us all to applaud.

"Now let's all try it," he said. "Just mark time, standing where you are. Atten-*tion!*" He looked imperiously around the yard. It was as quiet as a graveyard. Then he let out a yell like an Apache: "Forward, march!"

I looked back and saw everybody tramping their feet up and down, looking embarrassed. The sun slid behind a small cloud and three long lines of guys marched away without going anywhere. "Left!" howled Krpata. "Left! Shift that flab! Higher! Higher! Lift those feet!" I could see him glaring at Benno. "Get some life into it!" he bellowed. "You look like you're going to a funeral!" Benno was staggering from foot to foot like a camel, staring stupidly ahead at the sergeant, his eyes nearly bulging out of his head. He was red and shining with sweat. Then Krpata started off around the field. You could hear him howling remarks all over the place. The sun came out again and there we stood in the field behind the icehouse, marking time. Four guys went past the fence with a load of bazookas on their backs. I stood there treading up and down and watched them until they disappeared around the corner. Then there wasn't anything else to look at so I glanced at my watch. Quarter to twelve. We'd been tramping up and down there for a good five minutes. We kept it up a while longer and then Krpata bellowed "Halt" and started telling us all about half turns and oblique turns and marching doubletime and about field equipment and outfits and about how a platoon is made up of a couple riflemen and a reconnaissance man and a machine gunner and I don't know what all and the sun beat down and we were sweating like down at the beach on the hottest summer day and Krpata kept on instructing us tirelessly there behind the icehouse and its white wall kept on sparkling away in the sunshine. He showed us how to salute a lieutenant and a colonel and a general and how many steps ahead you start and how many steps after you can bring your hand down again and he picked out Pedro to demonstrate with and really kept him stepping, past him and back and over and over again, bawling him out the whole time, and making him do those turns and half turns and obliques all by himself out in front of everybody until even Pedro was red with anger, though he was usually the last person in the world to lose his temper. Finally we each got a wooden stick handed to us—dummy rifles from Sokol Hall—and Krpata taught us how to present arms, but he himself had a rifle and kept waving its polished muzzle under our noses. You couldn't wear that guy down. When we took off our shirts because of the heat, he buttoned up the collar of his old uniform which he'd unbuttoned earlier and when we croaked from parched throats during the break he went right on roaring till we thought we'd go nuts. When we could hardly lift our feet after finishing that crazy stand-still march, he showed us how to hurdle obstacles and slip under wires, wriggling past us on his belly like a slug in a hurry. At first I found the whole thing a big joke but then the humor wore thin and I started getting mad and finally wound up hating that idiot sergeant standing there, in the pink of condition though a bit overweight for his size, bellowing orders like one of the German guards out at Messerschmidt, like Mr. Uippelt, the supervising manager, a pompous fart, bursting with zeal and unable to get his voice down under a shout. Finally Krpata dismissed us and trotted briskly off toward the administration building.

As soon as he turned his back on us, Benno collapsed and rolled over on the grass. He was soaking wet with sweat.

"Jesus H. Christ," he said and stretched out his legs. We sat down around him.

"A turd. A genuine turd, that guy," said Haryk.

"What're you griping about?" said Lexa. "You've gotten a complete military education in one short morning."

"Up yours," said Benno.

"You're talking like a top sergeant already," said Haryk.

"What's wrong? Aren't you happy, Benno?" said Lexa. "Fonda, go tell your old man to give Benno some private lessons in how to be a soldier."

"Up that, too," said Benno.

"You know, your old man's really not very bright, Fonda," said Haryk.

"Maybe not. But this farce isn't his fault," said Fonda.

"Like hell it isn't. He thought this whole thing up."

"Sure," said Lexa. "And when we finally attack, old Cemelik's going to send us back and make us do it all over in step the next time." He turned to Benno. "Hey, Benno, got anything to eat?"

"Food!" cried Benno. "Food! The best idea I've heard all morning!" He reached over for his jacket and started taking little packages out of the pockets. We got out our supplies, too, and started in. Our mood picked up. Suddenly Fonda started tapping his feet and humming and after a while he gave out with some scat. Fonda was a great scat singer. He sat there, his skinny body jerking as he sang through his nose, just sounds, no words. Haryk and Benno joined in, Benno like a trumpet, Haryk like a clarinet in the high registers, and then Fonda came in like a trombone. They scatted on into "Drop Down Mama Blues" and as I sat there listening, I started feeling good. Guys around us turned to listen, too. The sun shone down as hot as ever, and we sat in that checkerboard slope of shadow and light and the blues echoed against the icehouse wall and when the boys had finished the final chorus, I started up in English, singing "Woman I'm Loving" and the boys picked it up but stayed down soft and easy. "One tooth solid gold," I sang, and when I got through with that verse, the boys broke out with a gorgeous dissonance that swelled to fortissimo and Fonda gave out with a great big glissando and then they faded off and I went on, "dat's de only woman," while they plucked staccato chords and I let my voice go down to a hoarse sob for "a mortgage on my soul," and then I joined in like I would on my tenor sax and we went on like that, drifting from one piece to another for at least a quarter of an hour. A circle formed around us, guys sitting there gaping at us and tapping their feet, their eyes full of wonder. Their eyes always looked that way when they heard jazz, like when they were sitting around a table at the Lion behind a glass of pink lemonade, listening reverently as we played "Chinatown" and Brynych took over on his drums for an ear-shattering beautiful solo or when we played in our overalls at the Messerschmidt cafeteria at noon and I could feel their eyes on me when I played Coleman Hawkins' solo from "Sweet Lorraine." They were staring at us now with the same sort of eyes you saw when you told them the incredible fact that "Big Noise from Winnetka" was nothing but drums and bass for one whole side, and this wonder in their eyes made me feel great and I loved them for it and figured they must be all right after all if they loved jazz so much, and that they'd run things differently than Mr. Krocan who owned the factory or Mr. Machan or Mr. Petrbok, the band leader with his simpleminded merry-go-round music, and maybe their world was going to be a great world, full of jazz, and just generally a great place to live in. We sat there on the grass and were just blasting our way into "Darktown Strutters' Ball" when men with armbands on their sleeves came around the side of the icehouse and started calling up the patrols. We stopped singing. Our good mood faded fast.

"Why the hell can't they just leave us alone?" said Benno, but just then we heard Dr. Bohadlo's piping voice, "Dr. Bohadlo's patrol, over here!" and you could see his chubby little hand signaling above his waterproof jacket.

"Screw him," said Benno, and didn't move.

"Come on, Benno. Don't try anything stupid now," I said. I figured it'd be good to get away from the brewery for a while.

"I'm not moving an inch. First they drill you to death and then you're still supposed to drag yourself all around town."

"Yeah, but once you're outside it's easier to take off," I said.

"A bright idea. And the next thing you know old Cemelik's stringing you up for desertion."

"Well, they'll do it right now if you don't get up pretty soon," I said. "For refusing to obey orders."

"Bullshit," said Benno.

The field in front of us was slowly emptying. I watched the centipedes marching off. Dr. Bohadlo stood there in his knickers peering around expectantly. He looked just as rosy and complacent as he had on Sunday.

"Ah, there you are," he called out when he saw us and his voice was full of patriotic enthusiasm. "All right, lads, come on, come on! We've got to be going!"

"I'll murder him," said Benno quietly, but he got up. We dusted ourselves off and went over to Dr. Bohadlo.

"All right, come on," he said. "I hope you won't run out on me again like last time," he said jokingly. I grinned.

"Are we going around the town again?" said Benno.

"That's right," nodded Dr. Bohadlo.

"Three hours again?"

"That's right, Mr. Manes. Three hours. This is the army. All right. Line up, boys, so we can be on our way. It's already quarter past."

I looked at my watch. It was quarter past two. We lined up.

"So long, guys," I said to Lexa and Pedro who were marching at the rear of the last centipede.

"So long," said Lexa.

"For the good of our country!" said Pedro.

"Forward, march," said Dr. Bohadlo, flinging out his chubby little legs, and once again we started off on that crazy circuit around the town. We turned the corner and plunged on toward the gate. A bunch of guys were leaning against the iron fence by the gate, looking out. When we got closer, I saw they were arguing excitedly with a crowd that had gathered on the other side. The guards at the gate had been reinforced and they were arguing in two directions at once—with guys inside who wanted out and with people on the outside who wanted in.

"What's going on?" I asked.

"I don't know," said Haryk. "What's going on?" he yelled

at a guy running from the gate toward the main building.

"The Russians are coming!" the guy yelled.

"Jesus!" said Haryk.

"Well, I guess that takes care of our revolution," said Benno. "Are we going on patrol, Doctor?"

Dr. Bohadlo looked bewildered. "Well, I don't know," he said. "The matter wasn't discussed at headquarters."

"Well, let's skip it then. The whole thing doesn't make any sense, anyway," said Benno.

"He's got something there," said Haryk. "Let's go out and welcome the Russians."

"I don't know, boys. Wait here, I'll . . . oh, Major!" shouted Dr. Bohadlo, and he ran up to Major Weiss who was striding from the gate looking grave and important. He wore a tricolor badge on his cap and the buttons on his uniform shone in the sunshine. He stopped when he heard Dr. Bohadlo calling, bent over to hear what he had to say, but meanwhile kept looking around. He looked preoccupied. Dr. Bohadlo was telling him something and Weiss was listening and then he turned toward him sharply and shook his head. You could see him saying, "No! Under no circumstances!" Dr. Bohadlo bowed courteously, then remembered himself, stuck out his chest, touched his fingers to his hiking cap, then turned and came back to us as red as a lobster.

"Well, boys, we've got to go out on patrol."

"Aw, but that's silly," said Benno.

"No. No, Mr. Manes. This is a matter of law and order."

"But what's the point of patrolling if the Russians are coming?"

"Orders are orders, Mr. Manes. We're in the army."

"Fine. But orders aren't supposed to be stupid," said Benno in disgust.

"It's a soldier's duty to obey orders," said Dr. Bohadlo, and then he addressed the rest of us, "Let's go, boys."

Benno grumbled. "Sure. *Maul halten und weiter dienen,*" he said in an undertone. Dr. Bohadlo flung out his leg again and we moved toward the gate.

"This is crazy," said Benno. "This is first-class lunacy."

"It sure is," I said, and looked around. Four soldiers on

guard duty at the gate were fighting off a bunch of women trying to push their way in. Most of them were old women in babushkas and they were waving red flags and screaming, "Let us in!" "Our husbands are in there!" "The Russians are coming!" "Long live the Red Army!" I saw the back of one of the soldiers in green khaki. Holding his rifle horizontally in front of him, he was shoving the women back. A lieutenant was standing behind the soldiers. When I looked closer, I saw it was Baron Rozkosny whose prep school diploma had cost his parents a house which they'd built for the chairman of the examinations board. There he stood, an elegant little revolver in his hand, behind his men. We stopped by the gate and Rozkosny noticed us. "Make way for the patrol!" he shouted, waving his revolver under the old women's noses. They went on cursing the guards but moved back. The soldiers made a corridor for us and our centipede jolted forward and passed through.

"Look at 'em, playing soldier!" screamed one old lady.

"Well, they won't be playing much longer!"

I looked at Dr. Bohadlo's back. No reaction. We turned down toward the bridge, trudging along in step. On the other side of the bridge we suddenly found ourselves caught up in a swarming throng of people. Flags were flying from the houses and buildings facing the station again, lots of flags. They looked fresh and bright in the sun. Our centipede was swallowed up in the crowd. The crowd was streaming past the station, heading for the German border to the east. A parade of old men and women was forming up at the corner of the Lewith Mills. They were holding a banner made out of red cloth with some kind of Russian inscription on it. I spelled it out: LONG LIVE THE RED ARMY. Some of them were carrying red flags, some Czech flags, and children kept tearing back and forth on the sidewalk. Dark masses of people poured in from the factory section, all headed east toward the border. And we were marching along the main street, due west. It was slow going because we were going against the confused current of women pushing baby carriages and trying to carry children, too, little boys, Italians who'd suddenly started singing for joy, Russian refugees in their torn green clothes, guys in shirtsleeves and kids in knickers or short pants. Well, well, I said to myself, so it's only the elite who signed up at the brewery. The elite of the town's prize fools. And these guys here, they'd probably been hiding out in their cellars just waiting for this, for the Russians to come, and now they'd come out to welcome them while we had to march around on patrol and as we marched on I had this feeling that I was striding through Bombay or Rangoon, a member of His Majesty's colonial troops, and the next minute I was living the part—tight-lipped, pith-helmeted, marching through a mob, our revolvers in their holsters, our carbines in our hands—called in to put down some native uprising and, goddamn it, maybe that was all our army was called up for, too. The crowds made way for us and on we went and the tropical sun hung high above us, baking our faces. Then I saw Berty on a bike, a Leica hanging around his neck, riding off toward the border, peddling like mad in his short pants, his face eager with greed. The feeling of being in Rangoon popped. Photographs by kind permission of Mr. B. Moutelik, Jr. "Our Liberators," the caption would be in the *Illustrated History of the Kostelec Revolution* under a picture of some triumphantly gesturing Russians. Flags flapped from the windows above us and people kept hanging out more and more and suddenly I noticed that there were an awful lot of Russian ones, particularly at the Kaldouns's where the long red and white noodle had hung on Saturday. Now there was an even longer red one. At Pitterman's, just like Rosta had said there would be, an immense violet flag flapped against the wall with a yellow star in the middle. It looked like something out of a circus. A Soviet flag also hung in front of the Krocans's house and in each window they'd stuck a pair of little paper Czech and Russian flags. The Russian flags looked new and homemade. I looked around—the town was ablaze with red flags. At the Jiraseks's, at the Mlejneks's, at the Burinohas's at the Novotnys's, at the Novaks's, at the Wenigs's, and as we went on, I saw more at the Mouteliks's, the Rydls's, the Sejnohas's—everywhere. Thousands of them. A car steered toward us across the square. Its windows were decorated as if for a wedding and the radiator covered with garlands. Mr. Vipler, a municipal employee, was hanging out a big WE WELCOME YOU! banner above the loan association floor. The whole gypsy encampment in the square was going crazy, dancing around between the piles of knapsacks and bundles. In front of the Lion Hotel you could see the gleaming instruments of the local brass band. That intrigued me. I looked closer and saw Mr. Petrbok, its leader, with his white admiral's cap and his baton topped with the golden ball, lining up his musicians while, behind, a parade was forming with flags and banners. The sun beat down on the chaos in the square. Somebody started to ring the church bells and through all the noise and singing and din of voices, the two big bells—Gabriel and Michael—tolled out as if sounding an alarm.

"Well, if this isn't the dumbest thing I ever heard of," said Benno, and he stopped. Swinging along at a good clip, I tramped on his heels.

"Go on, go on," I said.

"Boy, are we ever a bunch of idiots," said Benno, and he plodded on. We crossed the square over to Sokol Hall. Another parade was forming up there. Sokol members in folk costume. Men and women. There weren't very many of them, but the ones up front were carrying a heavy flag with lots of ribbons dangling from it. Mr. Sumec's brass band was behind them and flags everywhere. The band started to play. It sounded sour and tinny. The Sokol members set off, the men stepping along majestically behind their pot bellies, the Sokol women in berets, then a straggle of kids and people in ordinary clothes. We headed down past Pozner's factory. The crowd had begun to thin out. It looked as if these parades had been lining up and setting off for hours, so that by now the head of the procession must already be at the border. There were hardly any people left in this part of town, just a few old granddads sitting on doorsteps, watching us in amazement, and grannies on footstools. We'd marched through town in tight formation; now we spread out over the empty streets on the western side. We'd come to the edge of town, to the lawn in front of Serpon's factory. The sun was still blazing away at us.

"Dr. Bohadlo?" Benno said.

"Yes?" said Dr. Bohadlo without stopping.

"Couldn't we take a little break here? We're all pretty tired out after that drill this morning," said Benno.

"Yeah," I said.

"We sure are," said Haryk.

Dr. Bohadlo stopped and looked at his watch. "Well," he said. "I suppose we might be able to work in a fifteen minute break here."

Without another word Benno flopped down on the grass and we sat down beside him, facing out to the east. The sky was blue and a couple of thin white clouds stretched off from over the town toward Germany. The cherry trees glowed in the bright sun. There was no wind and from the center of town all you could hear was a vague buzz. We sat there, staring off at the distant wooded hills between which the German border ran. I stretched out on the grass and looked up at the sky. Behind me loomed the big white Serpon factory, built like a Scottish fortress. It was a silent factory now. But I couldn't look straight up. The sun was right overhead. The closer I tried to look at it, the more it looked like a huge, shapeless, molten blotch, incandescent and melting into the blue sky around it, turning the whole sky to white lava. And, looking up at the sun and with the big white building looming behind me and in that stillness which was like the quiet in a country where the people have all died, I felt very far away and an awful feeling of futility spread into every pore and cell of my body and everything, everything except me, myself, seemed worlds away. I myself was a snail inside the hard shell of that futility and very comfortable in there even though I couldn't feel anything and was all alone, and I'd just started to inch out of it when my soft vulnerable body came up against something that hurt. There I was, just coming out, and there was Irena and the hurt of not having her and the hurt of not knowing whether I really wanted her and the hurt of wanting her and of being jealous of her and the hurt of not really caring and the hurt of knowing I'd never have her and of knowing that everything was and always would be futile—those evenings and all those words and this revolution which wouldn't help me out with her at all, those pictures with me holding that submachine gun, and that clash by night with the gang of communists, and the triumphant celebration when the Red Army arrived and everything went back to normal again and we were all living together in a republic or a democracy or who knew what, since as far as I was concerned all revolutions were futile, not for people in general but for me, anyway, because I was lost and would never win Irena, from which it followed I really must love her after all, and so I did—that dumb, beautiful Irena who didn't give a damn about me, that dimwitted girl with that little thinking machine in her head equipped with everything except the short waves we needed if we were ever going to establish contact. Which meant it must be her body I loved, and her face, but it wasn't only that. It was also that magical aura that always surrounded her and that maybe I'd helped to create myself—that window open at night above the river with the stars, and the cliffs and the white rope and her hair and the sun that seemed to follow her wherever she went. Which meant I was in love with her after all and never wanted to get out of it either but then I thought about Lucie and how when I was with her I didn't love Irena at all, and then about Vera and Helena and Mitzi and I knew I didn't think about Irena when I was with them but now, now I was thinking about her and none of the others meant a thing to me now. And that this one thought only was important to me now, and only it was sure and everlasting and fixed. I lay on my back under the utterly pointless and monotonous blue sky and couldn't hear anything except Benno's snores and the hum of the town and up there in that pointless blue sky who do I see but Irena. There she is, and I'm with her, and at night I kiss her and caress her breasts and say, Irena, Irena, will you marry me? And she says yes and it's morning in the church now and no one knows and I'm kneeling with Irena before the altar and sunlight streams through the windows on us and soon we're mailing out little cards: *Daniel Smiricky and his wife Irena announce that their marriage was performed in St. Anthony's Church.* Then my thoughts grew vaguer and vaguer until I hardly knew myself what I was thinking about—about Irena or happiness, I guess—probably happiness since of the two it was vaguer and couldn't be found up there in that pointless blue sky but in me. And I'd completely forgotten whatever it was I'd been thinking about when suddenly a sound rang out, a dark and peculiar sound completely different from all the tones I was listening to inside. It came from somewhere else, from outside, and I couldn't figure out what was going on but then a whole series of fainter noises rang out, one after the other, fast and very regular, and then they stopped and then started up again and by then I knew something had happened and I sat up and Irena and everything else vanished and I was sitting on the grass again next to Benno and he was looking tensely off to the east and Haryk and the three other boys and Dr. Bohadlo were, too, and none of us said a word. For a moment, it was perfectly still and then came another series of muffled mechanical raps and then another and another and then I knew what it was but still couldn't figure out what was going on.

"What's that?" said Benno.

"Machine guns," said Haryk.

"Jesus, maybe . . . maybe they made a mistake . . ."

"What do you mean?"

"Well, what if it's not the Russians after all?"

"That's crazy," I said. "That's . . . well, who knows . . ."

"The Russians wouldn't be machine gunning anybody," said Benno.

"But, look . . . well, but everybody went out to welcome them, didn't they?"

"Sure. But who told them to?" Benno turned to Dr. Bohadlo. "Who told everybody the Russians were coming? Do you know, Doctor?"

"Well, I don't know," said Dr. Bohadlo. He'd suddenly turned pale and his usually optimistic face looked worried. "I have no idea, boys. Nobody told us at the brewery, that's all I can say."

"See?" said Benno, and turned to us. "Somebody got this crazy idea and the whole town fell for it."

"Oh, sure, sure," I said sarcastically.

"Well, what do *you* think it is then?"

"How should I know?"

Just then the machine gun started chattering again, louder and quite clear now. You could hear each shot, sharp, dry, and hard. It sounded as if they were getting pretty close now.

"There, you see?" said Benno. "That's not the Russians, that's the SS." He got up off the grass. So did the rest of us. The machine gun let go another burst.

"Let's take cover," said Benno.

"Wait a minute," I said.

"You wait if you want to, I'm going," said Benno, and started running toward the factory.

"Benno, don't be an idiot! Come back," said Haryk.

"Wait, Mr. Manes!" called Dr. Bohadlo.

Benno stopped and turned.

"Wait a minute. We've got to go back to the brewery."

"Not me. You're all crazy," said Benno.

I watched him and was surprised to find I wasn't scared at all. Benno stood there and I heard Dr. Bohadlo yelling, "Mr. Manes, you come right back! Leaving now would be desertion," and I watched Benno standing there getting all red in the face and confused and suddenly all I wanted was to be in the middle of the actual fighting, to take up my gun or my pistol and fight for Irena, to win her. The machine gun hammered away again and I longed to be out there firing back at it so I yelled, "Come on, Benno. Don't be silly. Let's go back to the brewery. Come on!"

"Sure, hurry up!" said one of the other boys and I knew that when he said that he wasn't just talking to hear himself talk like me but because he was really brave, but it didn't make much difference, the effect was all the same. Benno still just stood there. So I yelled again, "We're going, Benno! Don't be so stupid. Come on," and I started off and the other guys and Haryk followed and Dr. Bohadlo said, "Mr. Manes, I am ordering you to come!"

I was dragging my feet, looking at Benno.

"For Chrissake," I said, "come on." I said it as if I was trying to lure him off to go swimming with me and Benno shuffled up all red and sweating like a pig and then Dr. Bohadlo hurried up ahead to lead us back. "All right, boys," he said, "let's take it back at a good trot now," and off we went, with Benno jogging along behind us.

"Idiots," he said. "You're running straight into hell like a pack of fools. This isn't going to be any picnic." That was all he had breath for though. We had to catch up with Dr. Bohadlo and he was way out in front by now with his fat rump bouncing around in his knickers. When we got to the main street, Dr. Bohadlo suddenly slowed to a walk. The people who'd stayed home were all out on the sidewalks nervously looking off to the east. Dr. Bohadlo started trotting again. A good Scoutmaster's trot. We jogged down the middle of the street, our shoes clattering on the cobblestones. People turned to stare. The sound of gunfire rolled in from the east and here were people who would be hiding in their basements soon and there we were jogging along, in step, straight into the whole big mess. Calm and unmoved, the sun shone on as we clattered down the street. The street pointed straight as an arrow to the underpass and all along the sides I could see people standing on the sidewalk, looking smaller and smaller down the length of the street, and they were all waiting. A deep rumble came from the town. It grew louder. It was a familiar sound but I couldn't quite place it as we trotted toward it. I stared ahead and the noise grew louder and then suddenly the people down by the underpass started to scatter and then to run. The sound was practically a roar now, yet through it our footsteps kept on clattering as we ran straight for it. There was a scream and a woman picked up a little boy and ran into a house with him. Then those two long rows of people lining the street from the underpass to where we were started to break up. They started to push, they crowded into doorways, they ran for the side streets. The roar changed into an awful racket and was already coming from just on the other side of the underpass. We kept on trotting, then stopped as though someone had ordered us to. We huddled together and stared at the underpass. And there inside, under the iron girders and between the two stone pillars, a tank suddenly appeared, clattered up into full view and, making a terrific racket, made right for us going fast. I felt as if I was standing in a desert face to face with a rhinoceros. The tank's armored plates glittered in the sunshine and it was swarming with soldiers in camouflaged parachute-troop uniforms. That was all I stayed to see before taking off like a shot around the corner and into a side street. Benno was ahead of me and Dr. Bohadlo ahead of him. Haryk was running along beside me. The street led up a steep hill with a factory wall on one side and a warehouse fence on the other. We were trapped. It gave me a weird feeling as the roar of the tank grew louder and both that fence and that wall looked awfully long and the hill steep. I saw that Benno and Dr. Bohadlo had already made it up to where the fence stopped and I was absolutely certain the tank was right at my heels. The roar sounded so close I couldn't believe it could get any louder. Dr. Bohadlo and Benno disappeared around the corner. We weren't far from the end of the wall now. Haryk and I were both panting and the roar and clatter were unbelievably loud. There was only a little way to go. Suddenly I realized I was scared stiff. Then I made it around the corner, and Haryk tore in behind me, and we stopped because there were people behind the fence and others running along beside it out of town, away from that tank. We stood at the edge of the crowd and now all at once I wasn't scared any more. The tank rumbled along the street below us. I lay down on the ground and cautiously stuck my head out for a look. The side street we'd raced up dropped steeply and was empty and so was the patch I could see of the main street below. The sun shone on it and that was all. I lay there for a couple of seconds and could feel the people behind me watching, too, and then I flattened out against the ground because just then the muzzle of a cannon appeared at the corner of the factory wall below. The cannon kept on coming for what seemed like an awfully long time, and then the front of the tank painted in big irregular splotches of color, and then the squat turret, and then the whole tank hove into view with those soldiers all over it in those camouflaged uniforms with branches stuck into their netted helmets. Some were perched on ledges of armor above the clattering tank track, their legs dangling down in their heavy boots. They'd rolled up their sleeves, I noticed, and I could see the oily gleam of their long Lugers. A guy in black overalls and wearing earphones looked out over the open turret. Next to him, leaning against the side of the turret, stood a soldier holding on with his left hand with a submachine gun in his right, his uniform draped with grenades. For a moment everything was drowned out in the frantic roar of the machine and then the tank clanked out of sight—and the noise faded, grew fainter, and soon you could hardly hear it. All that was left were the bare cobblestones sparkling in the sun. I got up. Haryk came over and, in a hoarse voice, said, "Is it gone?"

"Yes," I said.

Then that whole crowd of people who'd been standing back of the wall came over and started asking me questions.

"Did you see it?"

"Yes."

"Were they SS men?"

"I guess so. I don't know."

"I thought you said you saw 'em," one huge guy said in a hoarse voice. He sounded drunk.

"Well, you tell me how I'm supposed to recognize them and I'll tell you who they were," I said irritably. "Why didn't you look for yourself?"

Then I turned to Haryk. "Let's clear out of here," I said.

"Hold on," he said. "There's Benno. Hey, Benno!" he yelled.

Benno waddled over, his eyes still popping halfway out of his head.

"Still think it's fun?" he said.

"Who said anything about fun?" I said.

"You know what I mean. You're both nuts and you know that, too."

"What are you complaining about? Nothing happened to you, did it?"

"No, but it could have."

Dr. Bohadlo came plodding toward us.

"I don't know about the rest of you," Benno said, "but I'm going to take off for the woods."

"On a mushroom hunt?" Haryk asked.

"I'm just going to wait up there till the Russians get here."

"You'll starve," I said.

"I'd rather starve than have some crazy SS man put a hole in my head," said Benno.

I laughed like a movie hero. It was fun acting tough, now that the tank was gone. "It's all a question of taste," I said.

Benno blew up. "Listen, Smiricky," he said, "if you think you're some kind of a hero . . ."

"It starts to look that way, doesn't it?" I said. "Compared to you, anyway."

"You're not, though."

"And you are?"

"No. But neither are you."

"So what am I, then?"

"Stupid. That's all."

I looked at Benno as if that had really hurt. I hoped my eyes looked sad and, just to make sure they did, I lowered my lids and looked down for a minute.

"Maybe," I said. "Maybe I am."

"You sure are," said Benno. "As stupid as they come."

"Maybe I am," I repeated, with my eyes still trained on the ground. Then I raised them abruptly, looked Benno right in the eye and said, "Things are different with me than they are with you."

I wondered how he would react to that. It would have worked on Irena. But this was Benno. I hadn't really stopped to think how he'd take it. I'd said it more to satisfy myself than anything else.

"Bullshit. Just what in the hell is so different, if I may be forgiven for asking?" said Benno sarcastically.

"Well, oh, let's not argue about it," I said. "I'm going back to town no matter how stupid you think that makes me. You coming?"

Benno wasn't the type to fall for my kind of act. He did, though, look a bit more thoughtful suddenly.

"Smiricky, don't be a fool," he said. "Don't tell me you want to get yourself killed just to impress . . ."

"Don't worry," I broke in. "I don't want to get killed."

"No? Then why are you knocking yourself out so hard to get into this?"

"I want to, that's all."

"You just want to show off for Irena, that's all," said Benno.

"Whatever you say, Benno."

"Don't be dumb, Danny."

"I can't help it. Maybe I just am."

"Maybe you are."

I smiled my pained little smile. "Well, Benno," I said, "you coming with us?"

Benno looked at me, his face very serious now, as if this was nothing to joke about, and said, "Boy, you've really lost your head on that girl, haven't you?"

"So you're coming?" I said with a smile.

"Don't say I didn't warn you. And I'll tell you one thing— I'd be sorry if you got knocked off."

"Well, so long then, Benno," I said and put out my hand. "Don't be mad at me."

"So long, Danny," said Benno. "Too bad about you. We'll miss you in the band and . . . well, just in general."

"Christ! All these goodbys. You make it sound like a funeral," said Haryk.

"Coming with me, Haryk?" said Benno.

"Hell, no. I'm going back to the brewery."

"Well, so long then," said Benno, and put out his hand.

"Oh, cut it out," said Haryk. "The look on your face is enough to make a guy vomit."

Suddenly there was a roar of a motor again. We froze. The next thing we knew a plane was swooping over us, flying low. All over, people were dropping to the ground as the plane's shadow flickered across the field and disappeared against the sun, but you could still hear the roar of its motor.

"Run for the woods!" shouted Benno, as he scrambled up and started running off toward the first big trees. The roar of the motor, faint a minute before, was growing louder again. The plane was coming back. You couldn't see it, though, because of the sun.

"Get down, Benno!" I yelled. But the motor made too much noise and he was already too far away. He was scrambling up the slope toward the woods. Lots of people were scrambling up all around him. The motor was roaring full blast and the noise was growing louder. I flopped to the ground next to Haryk and Dr. Bohadlo who were already flat out. The din reached a climax and through it came the long chattering bursts of a machine gun. I could hear the short dry strike of the bullets close by as they buried themselves in the earth. Then the sound of the motor faded again and the plane disappeared over the other side of the wall. I jumped up and looked over. I caught only a glimpse of a German fighter plane flying fast and low over the town. It turned east and vanished among the hills along the border.

"I'll bet that's the last we'll see of him," Haryk said.

"Let's hope so."

"We were lucky."

"We sure as hell were," I said, and all at once I felt how afraid I'd been. Christ, I might have been hit! I looked around. A few people were running across the field for the woods. Higher up, close to the rim of the woods, I made out Benno's well-rounded body swaying as he ran.

"Look," I said to Haryk.

"What?"

"Over there. See Benno?"

"Good Lord. It doesn't look like he's planning to stop till he gets to Ratejna."

"We can just let him go, can't we, Doctor?" I asked Dr. Bohadlo who was standing next to us. He looked completely washed out.

"Yes, yes, certainly," he said. "It's no wonder. He's never experienced anything like it in his whole life."

"Sure," I said. "Well, shall we go?"

"Yes," said Dr. Bohadlo, but he didn't sound so enthusiastic any more. I got the feeling he also knew, now, that you could get hit out of nowhere and it could all be over before you even had time to duck. We went down to the main street, turned, and headed for the underpass again. The three other guys in our patrol ran out of a house on the other side of the street and joined up with us.

"Where's the fat one?" one of them asked me.

"He got hurt," I said coolly.

The guy's eyes popped. "Yeah? How?"

I tripped on purpose so I could catch hold of him and push him off to the side a little. I didn't want Dr. Bohadlo to hear.

"He got it in the leg," I said.

"From that fighter plane?"

"Yeah."

"Well . . . you mean you just left him up there?"

"There was a doctor there. They're going to take him to the hospital." I filled in a few other fake details and then we were quickly making our way through the underpass. In the bright light beyond the underpass, the crowd of people looked nearly black. They were all huddled around something. Then somebody screamed, a terrible inhuman scream. My blood ran cold. Then the scream started up again. A long, endless woman's scream which, after a tense terrifying second, died out and then welled up again, then dwindled off and changed into an almost animal-like gurgle. I felt sick to my stomach. We pushed up to the edge of the crowd.

"What is it? Somebody hurt?"

A man standing in front of us turned around. He looked grim. "A woman," he said.

"Do you know who it is?" I asked.

"No."

A fat woman closer to the front turned and said, "It's Dr. Vasak's wife."

"What?" I yelled. I nearly blacked out. Then that half-animal gurgling sound started up again.

"Let me through," I said. "Let me through. Has anyone gone for a car?"

I shoved ahead and, since nobody knew who I was, people respectfully made way for me and stared. Mrs. Vasakova was lying on the sidewalk. Actually, only her feet in her little white shoes and her legs as far as her knees and then just a mass of ripped flowered material and scraps of blue cloth and blood and then all that was left of her in her flowered dress. Two Englishmen were kneeling beside her, the redheaded Scotsman holding her head up, the tall, handsome one with the bandaged head holding her hand. Neither knew what else to do. It took just one look to see there wasn't much that could be done. Silent and stunned, the people crowded around. I quickly knelt beside her. The Englishmen looked at me. Their eyes were calm and suddenly it struck me how hard their eyes were. They looked at this differently than the shocked crowd did. For them, this was nothing new. At the same time, however, they seemed to know, far better than anybody in that crowd, what it meant.

"Has anyone gone for a car?" I asked in English.

"Yes," said the Scot.

"Isn't there a doctor around?"

"No."

"Where's her husband?"

"At the hospital."

I looked quietly at Mrs. Vasakova. She wasn't screaming anymore, just whimpering and her face was drawn with pain. Her breast under the thin dress rose and fell unevenly but she still looked young and pretty. Poor Mrs. Vasakova. I looked at her suffering there and everything around faded out and I saw her again in a white pleated dress smiling at me over a coffee cup and her bright eyes sparkling at me those Saturday evenings at Sokol Hall, and our casual chats about the war and shortages of food and me whispering some political joke to her and everybody bending our way to hear and I could feel her warm face close to mine and the interest in her eyes looking into mine, not in the joke but in other things, and I could see how it pleased her to have me flirt with her. She was about five years older than I was and about twenty-five years younger than her husband and she never would have let me get anywhere with her, not really, but she was pretty and she liked me and when we'd say goodby and I'd kiss her hand, I could feel how she'd press her hand against my lips and once, when it was dark and her husband was saying goodby to my mother, she turned her hand palm up and, when I kissed it, caught hold of my face and squeezed it in her hand so hard I saw stars, but then I was overcome with a feeling of joy that she'd done it and afterward I watched her get into the car with her husband and saw her give a little wave and her smile glimmered in the dark and Father waved frantically because he thought it was meant for all of us but I knew it was just for me, and then I went out for a walk and felt wonderful and didn't think about Irena all that night because all I could think about was Mrs. Vasakova. I thought about her and now there she lay, as pretty as ever, and it was all over, her mouth pulled down in an arch of pain and blood spilling out of her stomach. A crimson puddle glistened on the sidewalk and the blood kept running out of her. I looked at her face and real tears came to my eyes.

"Poor lady," I said. "How did it happen?"

"The plane," said the Englishman with the bandaged head. I just knelt there speechless for a minute. Then I said, "Isn't there any way to stop the bleeding?"

"No," said the Englishman.

"You mean. . . ?"

"Yes," said the Englishman and fell silent, too. Then he said softly. "She'll die before we can get her to the hospital."

A car honked and brakes screeched. The crowd parted. It was Jozka the baker's car, a light delivery truck. Jozka jumped out from behind the wheel and ran over to us.

"Let's put her in the back," he said.

"You have anything we can lay her on?" I asked.

"There're some empty sacks in the back."

I turned to the Englishmen. "Can you lift her?"

"Yeah," said the Scotsman. "It would help, though, if there was something we could put under her. A sheet would do."

"Right," I said. I turned to the crowd. "Does anybody have a sheet we can lift her with?"

"Just a minute," called the fat woman and she ran into a house.

"She'll get one for us," I said to the Englishman. "She'll be right back." We waited. It was quiet. In what seemed like a second, the woman reappeared with a sheet. She gave it to me. Her face was wet with tears. She looked badly shaken.

"Thank you," I said.

"Put it down beside her," said the bandaged Englishman.

We spread the sheet out on the sidewalk. The Englishman took hold of Mrs. Vasakova under her arms, the Scotsman around her waist.

"Could you lift her feet?" the Scotsman asked me.

"Yes," I said, and did. I was scared to death her body wouldn't be able to take it. When we lifted her, she started screaming again, but feebly now. We laid her on the sheet. A guy stepped out from the front of the crowd to help us. We lifted the sheet by all four corners and slowly carried her over to the truck. Blood dripped through the sheet onto the cobblestones. Jozka ran around the side of the truck and opened up the back. There were empty sacks inside. He climbed in, quickly piled them up to make a bed for her, and then, very skillfully, the Englishmen crawled up and lifted Mrs. Vasakova inside. The guy from the crowd and I held her legs until they'd slid her all the way in.

"All right. Drive fast," I said to Jozka. "You go with her. I'll see you later," I said to the Englishmen.

They nodded and bent over Mrs. Vasakova. Jozka shut the door and jumped in behind the wheel. As the little truck moved off, the crowd stood wordlessly on the sidewalk, watching it go through the underpass and turn off toward the high school. There was a big pool of blood on the sidewalk. It reflected the sun. I stepped on something and, when I stooped over to look, saw it was a big bent antitank bullet from the plane's machine gun. The street seemed quiet. Then I realized the quiet had broken. I glanced around. People were running in from the square. They were all dusty and sweating, women and children and old man Baudys dressed up in his Sokol costume and carrying a furled flag.

"What's going on?" I yelled to a guy who'd run up to one of the houses and was opening the door.

"The SS! They're coming in from Prussia!"

"Were you out at the border?"

"Yeah. And it wasn't true. The Russians weren't there."

"What was all that shooting about?"

"SS tanks."

"Anyone killed?"

The man waved his hand. "You can't even count 'em. One tank drove right into the parade out by the customs house. Right into a whole line of kids."

"Oh, my God!" screamed a woman next to me. The man beside her exploded. "Who the hell was it then who said the Russians were coming anyway? Who started that rumor?"

"I don't know," said the man at the door, "but if I find him I'll flay him alive."

"And what makes you so sure the SS will be coming through here?" I asked calmly.

"Because you can hear the gunfire already, just over the border in Prussia. There's a full-scale battle going on over there."

Just then the big hollow voice of the public address system sounded. "Citizens," it said, "retreating German tanks are approaching the frontier. We call upon all men capable of bearing arms to report immediately to the local Czechoslovak Army Command Headquarters at the municipal brewery. We repeat," and the voice blared on into the noise spreading through the streets as frightened people ran and shoved and swarmed with confusion. "Women and children should take refuge in the air-raid shelters. It is possible that the town may be bombed," intoned the announcer, and all around there was the shriek of women's voices. I saw them snatching up their kids and running. All of a sudden, a bunch of men in green uniforms appeared in the milling mob, hurrying against the main current of the crowd. Russian prisoners of war. People tried to make room for them. The confusion was tremendous. I looked around. Haryk was standing next to me.

"Let's go!" I shouted, and we both started to run. A couple of men started running along with us. This is what I'd been waiting for, the thing, a voice inside me said. And it was a great feeling. The voice over the loudspeaker went on: "Citizens! Your city is in danger. Defend it against the Germans! Death to the German occupation forces!" We ran for the square. Russians with the white SU on their backs were charging along ahead of us. A few people had already panicked and hauled in their flags. Red and red-and-white flags flapped over the heads of the crowd and a cloud slid over the sun. I looked up. Clouds were gathering in the west. We got to the square. It was chaos. Women and children from the refugee camp had thronged into the church and, outside, men stood in little bunches. Others were racing toward the brewery and, meanwhile, people from the welcoming delegations poured back across the square from the border. A group of French and Dutch POWs joined us by the church. We ran across the square and hurried on down the narrow main street. The sun was completely hidden by clouds now and the street was as dark as at dusk. People with pale, frightened faces were rushing in every direction and bumping into each other. We ran along the right-hand side of the street. A brightly-polished tuba loomed out above the crowd we were struggling to make our way through; it bobbed past, heading in the other direction. Everybody was moving faster now. The public address system went on blaring above the murmur and cries and shouts of the crowd. Somebody was already taking down Novotny's banner—the one that had stretched all the way across the street with the inscription WE WELCOME YOU! We got caught up in the jam in front of the antitank barricade. Two streams of people, trying to get through the narrow passage, collided there. From both sides, people were crawling over the barricade. We were shuffling forward when I noticed a girl wearing a Red Cross armband coming out of a side street. Then I saw that it was Irena. In her white dress she stood out against the dark background of the street. She crawled up and over the barricade and jumped down. Her skirt flew up a bit so I could see her legs above her knees.

"Irena!" I shouted. She looked around, then saw me. I ran over to the other side of the street, elbowing my way through the people.

"Irena!" I said, and took hold of her hand. Her hand was

warm and soft and she looked at me wide-eyed. She was beautiful. The crowd moving in both directions along Jirasek Boulevard veered and eddied around us. She was wearing a red-and-white polka-dot kerchief. "Clear the streets!" the loudspeaker boomed. "German tanks are just passing through Chodov!" Irena smiled at me. I noticed how little and pink her ears were, and the tiny holes pierced in the lobes.

"Irena! Darling!" I said, though in all that noise she probably didn't even hear me. Still, her voice sounded awfully faint when she asked, "Are you going to the brewery?"

"Yes," I practically shouted. A big guy blundered into us like an ox. Irena held onto me. I held her close. It was growing darker and darker. Gray clouds were piling up above the houses and the wind was rising. Dust and papers swirled around people's feet.

"Goodby, Danny," Irena said. Her face looked white, her cheeks were flushed. The wind blew dust in our eyes. I closed mine. Somebody was yelling from over by the barricades; I couldn't understand a word. I opened my eyes and saw that Irena still had hers closed.

"Goodby, Irena!" I said quickly. She made a face from all that dust in her eyes. I kissed her quickly on her red lips and stood back. She opened her eyes and tried to look around. A couple of women rushed between us. I caught one more glimpse of her as she stood on her tiptoes and rubbed her eyes and looked after me. I blew her a kiss. Then the wind rose again and the dust and the trash swirled up again.

"Come on," I heard Haryk say, and felt him pulling me along by the hand. We threaded our way back over to the other side of the street to the antitank barricade. Men were scrambling over it. The place was swarming with people's rear ends, then I saw somebody's shoes, their soles right in front of my nose, and then I was climbing over the barricade myself. Mr. Panek, the schoolteacher, was next to me; we jumped at the same time. I turned. Haryk landed right behind me. We started to run. It was dark on the street and windy. We ran faster. I saw my parents looking out the window at our place but I pretended I hadn't seen them. I had to squint; the wind was blowing right in our faces. The crowds were all moving in one direction now, rushing along toward the station. Mr. Pitterman and Rosta were standing at the entrance to Pitterman's arcade; they looked undecided; they were staring at the crowd. We came closer. You could see how confused and unhappy they were. When we were practically on top of them, I called out to Rosta but he didn't hear me. Suddenly people rushed out of the arcade, bumping into both Pittermans from behind. Mr. Pitterman staggered, nearly fell, then was swallowed up in the crowd. All I could see was his bald head being borne along by the streaming throng. Then I looked around and saw Rosta's blond head bobbing behind us. We clattered past the Hotel Granada, under the railroad underpass and up to the bridge. The first drops of rain were starting to fall. I was feeling great. As we dashed across the bridge it started to pour. The crowd thinned out now that there was more room. A few men were turning in toward the Port Arthur. We ran up to the brewery gate just as a ten-ton truck, loaded with people, was pulling out. I stopped. The guys packed into the truck were all armed. Then I recognized them. It was the mountain climbers. I caught sight of Zdenek with his Tyrolean hat and a rifle. The rain started coming down in buckets and the men in the truck swayed back and forth and, as the truck drove by, I turned to look again and saw the backs of some of the guys standing on top. One was carrying a submachine gun and wearing an armband, but it wasn't red and white with gold lettering. It was plain red. I stood there watching but then somebody gave me a shove and we hurried into the yard. A line of vehicles stood in the driveway in front of the main building—trucks of all sizes and cars. Guys carrying rifles were piling in. In the field by the icehouse three trim columns of kids stood facing Sergeant Krpata who was waving a revolver over his head. Some of the kids were armed. Then Krpata roared some command, jerked down his arm, and the whole company put their left feet forward and started marching off toward the gate. At the gate, people stepped back to let them through and Krpata, looking awfully pleased with himself, led his company out into the street. I ran along the row of trucks. The first one was just driving off toward the gate. It was already loaded with people. I saw Mr. Krocan standing by the next truck, but he wasn't wearing his uniform any more. He stood there, in his shirtsleeves, no longer wearing his cap, beside a man who had on another of those plain red armbands. Guys were scrambling up into the trucks, holding their rifles out carefully in front of them. I pushed through to the next truck.

"Where're they passing out the guns?" I yelled at a man who held a German bazooka in his hands.

"At the armory," he yelled back. I ran over to the armory. A bunch of men was just coming out of the door, some of them in uniform, and I recognized Captain Kuratko, and they were carrying somebody. A line of guys shuffling in through the door of the armory turned to stare.

"Who was that?" I asked as I got in line.

"Colonel Cemelik," somebody said.

"Was he wounded?"

"No. A stroke, apparently."

I was shoved from behind into the armory. A couple of soldiers stood behind the long tables and also some more guys wearing red armbands and the janitor from the high school in his Czech Legion uniform and they were all passing out weapons. Nobody was writing anything down now. The line moved fast and once you got your gun you went right on out. Dear God, I said to myself, dear God, please let me get a submachine gun. There were only three guys in front of me now. They handed a rifle to the first one, a rifle to the second one, too, and then I saw a soldier give a string of grenades to the guy right in front of me and then it was my turn and the red-cheeked kid with sergeant's stripes was handing me a beautifully polished submachine gun with two clips and I grabbed it, said thank you, and ran out.

"Hey, wait!" I heard Haryk call out behind me. I slowed down and slung my submachine gun over my shoulder. The place was swarming with people; mud splashed as they slogged across the yard. Haryk ran up to me, holding a rifle with a bayonet fixed to it.

"Hey, did you see that?" he said to me.

"What?"

"Those guys . . . with those red armbands."

"What about them?"

"They're communists."

"Could be," I said.

"Well, we're really in for it now," said Haryk. "They've taken over."

"Jesus," I said. "You think maybe they shot old Cemelik?"

"No," said Haryk. "He went off all by himself. He didn't need any help from them."

"Let's hope so anyway," I said.

"Look," said Haryk, "what say we clear the hell out of here?"

"What do you mean?" I said. "We can't do that now."

"Benno was right after all," said Haryk.

"Like hell he was," I said. And even if he had been, it was too late to try to back out now. The best thing to do was get right into it. Even with the communists.

"Let's go," I said. We were running toward the trucks when I heard somebody whistle our signal. I looked around and saw Lexa and Venca Stern standing with their rifles next to one of the trucks. We went over.

"Hi," said Lexa. "Where's Benno?"

"He skipped out," said Haryk.

"You hear old Cemelik had a stroke?"

"Yeah, is it true?"

"It's true all right. It happened when that fighter came over."

"Up you go!" somebody yelled in my ear and I saw Venca scrambling up into the truck. Lexa followed him and then I shifted my submachine gun over to one side and swung up, too. Haryk climbed in behind me. We were standing way at the back and two guys behind the truck lifted the tailgate and slammed it shut. I heard somebody yell "Move!" Then with a lurch off we went. We drove slowly along the driveway toward the gate. Men who'd probably gotten there too late to get issued a weapon were sprinting across the courtyard in the drenching rain. We passed through the gate and when we got out on the road the driver stepped on the gas. The truck started swaying and we hung on to the tailgate to keep from falling. We went over the bridge and I looked up at Irena's window and then we turned right, onto the highway that leads to the border.

"Some fun," said Haryk, his voice shaking as the truck bounced.

"You said it," said Lexa.

"There will be more," I said, and it was all we could do to keep from falling when the driver cut the sharp corner by Jonas's factory. We passed Krpata's well-drilled company. They trudged slowly, but in perfect step, through the rain which was letting up now. You could see the sun dodging in and out behind the clouds. We drove through the outskirts of town where there wasn't a soul on the street. Everybody had gone in. Then we passed the bunch of Russian POWs again, still hurrying toward the border. They yelled something at us but we didn't stop. We drove through the spa section and turned left by the bunker that was still standing from 1938. Guys with rifles were lying along the railroad track by the highway. They waved. Then one of them in a leather coat with a red armband on his sleeve jumped out of the ditch next to the road and signaled for us to stop. The driver put on the brakes. The man in the leather coat stepped up on the running board and said something to the driver. Now that the motor was just idling, I could hear that familiar rumbling drone again. Tanks were somewhere not too far off. The man jumped down off the running board. We drove on.

"I don't like this," said Lexa softly.

The sun was breaking through the clouds in the west; it was still drizzling, though. To the east, right above the border, rose a rainbow. We were heading due east on the highway. Men stood waiting in the doorways of houses, with rifles in their hands. Empty trucks stood parked along the side streets. Then we could hear the roar of a tank even over the noise of our motor. By the old customs house we turned onto the asphalt road to the new customs house that stood between two rows of blossoming cherry trees. The rainbow arched over the valley and was reflected in the wet asphalt. And all of a sudden a German tank appeared just beyond the new customs house; it was coming straight at us. Frantically, the driver jammed on the brakes; the truck started skidding. All I had time to see was the cannon lifting slowly, then everything lurched and reeled as the truck swung around. My ears rang with the tremendous racket of motors roaring and men shouting. Jostled, and with guys slamming into me, I crouched and saw that some were going over the side of the truck. The sound of a machine gun cut through the noise of the motors; you could feel the bullets ripping right through the metal. I saw Lexa jumping over the side into nowhere. Then the rear of the truck was facing the tank and there I was, so close to it I could see the men in their camouflaged uniforms clustered around the turret. Another second and they were gone as the truck skidded further around. There were only a few guys left in it now. One of them rolled toward me, his face smashed, leaving a smear of blood. I gripped the side of the truck with both hands, then pulled myself up and over, came down on my hands, and rolled into a ditch full of water. The truck had slowed down by the time I jumped so I made a fairly soft landing. I lifted my head out of the water. A few yards ahead of me, the truck plunged into the ditch. Flames burst out of the radiator. Then the tank went by on the road above me. I could hear the loud chatter of the machine gun, the bullets whistling over my head into the field beyond. Men were running across the field toward the river. When I looked up again the tank was slowly moving off, its machine gun still blazing away. I was up to my neck in water. A man was lying in the field near me screaming. I glanced up to see where the tank was and heard it already clanking on the main highway that led into town. The machine gun was silent. I got up and looked around for the quickest way out of there. Lexa was just getting up on the other side of the road. He looked like he'd been rolling in mud and dirt. Blood was trickling down his forehead.

"Lexa!" I yelled. He saw me.

"Come on!" he shouted in a wild voice, and then turned and ran for a meadow that sloped up to the woods. There was a little stone dugout in the middle of the meadow; it was half fallen in, part of an old border defense system. I could still hear the roar of the tank motor but I couldn't see anything else coming so I crawled up on the highway, ran across, jumped the ditch, and started up through the meadow toward the woods. The sun was shining brightly now and, off to the east, dark clouds were piling up along the horizon. The rainbow still arched over the valley. Lexa ran ahead of me, limping as he ran. I couldn't feel anything wrong with me. Again I heard the roar of a motor from over by the customs house. Glancing back over my shoulder, I saw another tank moving rapidly along the highway. I ran as fast as I could up to the dugout and stopped for a second to look out over the whole highway and saw two more tanks headed our way. Then I didn't look back, but made for the woods, which were close by now, stumbled into their shade and dropped. For a while I just lay there, then I realized I wasn't alone. Dark figures with rifles were lying all around me, trying to dig in behind the trees. They'd scraped up little mounds of dirt and stones and were peering out over them toward the highway. I rolled over to an unoccupied tree and stretched out behind it. It was dark in the woods and you had a good clear view of the highway shining in the sun. Another tank pulled out from the customs house, turned and headed slowly along the asphalt road toward the main highway. A couple of men were crouched inside the dugout straight ahead of us, about halfway between the woods and highway. I recognized Hrob's red head. As the tank clattered along the road, Hrob knelt by the bunker and then I saw him aiming something at the tank. Flames and smoke flashed out of the end of the tube as a rocket flew out. It landed on the highway in front of the tank and started to burn. The tank stopped and men in camouflaged uniforms tumbled off onto the asphalt and scrambled into the ditches. The tank turret started to turn and the cannon was swiveling toward the stone dugout now. The crouching men stood up and ran for the woods. I watched Hrob, but he was still kneeling there, getting ready to fire off another rocket. The cannon was aimed straight at him now. I looked back at Hrob. Again something flashed next to his head and smoke rolled out of the tube. Quickly I glanced back at the tank. But the tank just stood there and then something exploded a few yards in front of it and Hrob jumped up and made a dash for the woods. There was a terrific noise, then the whole dugout flew apart in a flash of flames and smoke. I saw Hrob pitching forward just before I pressed my face down against the ground. When I looked up again, he was back on his feet and running again. I heard something click next to me but didn't look around. Down on the highway, a tall SS man got up from the asphalt, swung his rifle around and took careful aim at Hrob. A short dry shot rang out. Hrob threw out his arms and fell face down in the grass. The other SS men got up, scrambled back up on the tank, and off it went again. Again I heard a click next to me. I turned to see what it was. His Leica up to his eye, Berty Moutelik was crouching behind the next tree, taking pictures. The last tank passed along the highway. The rumble of the motors grew fainter. The sharp quick crack of rifles could be heard from town, then the longer rattle of machine-gun fire. I looked off toward the east. The highway was empty.

"Well, they're gone," I said and got up. Berty stood up, too, then he recognized me.

"Oh, hello, Danny," he said.

"Hi," I said.

We stepped out of the woods. Men started coming out from all over. Some had guns, some didn't, most were covered with mud, a few were limping. I and a few other guys ran over to Hrob. I knelt down. He was lying with his face in the grass and in the back of his neck there was a big bloody hole. I turned him over on his back and could see he was dead. I got up.

"Dead?" somebody asked.

"Yes," I said.

Some of the men were heading back down toward the road. I looked around and saw Lexa wiping his face with a handkerchief.

"You hurt?"

"No. Just tore up my face jumping out of that truck, that's all."

"Where's Haryk?"

"I don't know."

Then, from around the side of the woods, came the sound of a motor again. We were racing back up for the woods when I heard people yelling and I looked around and saw that they'd stopped farther down the slope and were looking off to the east, and then I saw a tank coming down the highway and this one didn't look like the others.

"Russians!" somebody shouted. The tank was still glistening from the rain and on the side of its turret there really was a red star. It was true. It was the Russians. The tank disappeared for a minute behind the customs house, then there it was again. People swarmed out over the highway, waving and cheering. The tank stopped. Lexa and I walked over slowly. Soldiers wearing wide Russian blouses were jumping down from the tank and our men rushed up and hugged them. We walked slowly over toward the highway. My submachine gun thumped against my back as I walked and I shifted it around under my arm. We came up to the tank. There was a crowd of people around the tank and, all across the field, people were running over to join the crowd.

"What say we see if we can find Haryk?" I said to Lexa.

"Sure," said Lexa and we headed toward the overturned truck in the ditch. The crowd around the Russian tank was screaming and laughing and shouting. We jumped down into the ditch and started looking for Haryk. Next to the truck lay a guy with his skull cracked open. Another lay on his belly a few feet away from him. He was still moving. I went up to the cab of the truck and looked in. There was the driver, upside down and all shot up and splotched with burns. In the meantime, Lexa had crawled into the ditch under the truck.

"Is he there?" I called.

"No," came Lexa's voice.

"Come on out," I said.

And then the shouting around the tank changed pitch. Out of the old customs house ran a bunch of men waving their rifles. Lexa scrambled out from under the truck and stood next to me. The men with the rifles were running toward us now, yelling something we couldn't understand, and then the roar of motors started up from somewhere and I stared at the men and I knew then what it was they were saying.

"The Germans are coming back!" they yelled. The crowd around the tank suddenly dispersed, leaving only the Russians who glanced around for a second, then understood, too, what was going on. I wanted to get back to the woods but it was already too late. A couple of Russians jumped into the ditch in front of us and flopped down on their bellies. We got down, too. I swung my submachine gun around and rested its barrel on top of a highway marker. The Russian tank gunned its motor beside me and clanked off. I looked up the stretch of road ahead. A German tank had just emerged from between the two last houses in town. The Russian tank stopped and I saw the German cannon swing around and then both tanks started firing at the same time. The noise was earsplitting as chunks of metal whistled and sang overhead and the highway flashed with bursts of light. Flames were coming out of the Russian tank. A shout rang out right in front of me. The Russians leaped out of the ditch and rushed forward. The German tank was burning, too. I scrambled up onto the highway and took off after the Russians. Somebody was getting set to jump off the German tank. I heard the crack of a rifle and the German fell. I ran along after the Russians. They stopped running some way off from the tank to see if anything else was going to come out, but nothing did. Suddenly it was very quiet. Then more men came up out of the ditches. Flames were licking out of the German tank and smoke billowed out of it. I stood there next to the Russians. A guy wearing a red armband rushed up and started talking to them. A couple of seconds later a whole crowd had gathered again.

"Any more Germans coming?" someone called out.

"It doesn't look like it."

"We ought to get the wounded out of here."

The guy with the red armband waved his hand. "You all ought to get back and take cover. There may be more Germans coming through."

L*

"And the wounded?"

"Take them over to the old customs house."

"You mean you think there're more Germans coming along behind that Russian tank?"

"Yes," said the guy with the red armband.

"How could *that* happen?"

"Well, that's what comrade captain here says anyway."

It was the first time I'd ever heard the word "comrade" used seriously.

"The Russians must have got ahead of them somewhere along the line."

"Looks that way."

"All right, come on, let's look after the wounded."

"Come on, Lexa," I said.

"Aren't we going to look for Haryk?"

"Oh, he's probably just lying low someplace. Let's go down to the customs house. If he's been hurt, they'll bring him there."

We went to the old customs house. The men had spread out in groups across the fields and some were already carrying back the wounded. A truck pulled up in front of the customs house. We stood there, watching them bring in the wounded and lift them up into the truck. The guy with the red armband was supervising the loading.

"Leave the dead here. We're just taking the wounded this time," he told the men who'd brought Hrob down. Soldiers carried in two Russians from the tank. I looked at my watch. It was five.

Somebody yelled, "Here's an Englishman or something."

"Where?" I said right away.

"You know English?" the guy with the red armband asked.

"Yes."

"Go over and talk to him."

A man in an English uniform was lying on the ground groaning softly. I bent over him.

"Are you hurt?" I asked. He opened his eyes and nodded.

"Where?"

"Don't know," he said between his teeth.

"He doesn't know where he's hurt," I told the guy with

the red armband. There were no obvious wounds that I could see.

"You better go along to the hospital with him," said the guy. "You may have to translate."

"All right," I said. They loaded the Englishman into the truck.

"We get everybody?" the guy asked.

"I guess so," somebody said.

"Then get going."

"So long, Lexa," I said and got in next to the driver.

"So long," said Lexa. I slammed the door shut and looked out. Some guys with rifles were standing with a bunch of Russians on the wet highway. A clouded sun shone on them and there was a singed smell in the fresh air. The truck started off. I leaned out the window for a look at the two still-smoking tanks facing each other on the road. A light breeze blew the smoke low along the ground and across the meadows to the river. Above the hills of the frontier, big clouds were stacking up in tremendous mountains of their own. The figures on the field receded. I looked around at the driver. Gripping the steering wheel, he stared ahead nervously. The wet pavement shone and, in front of the houses, men and kids stood, rifles in hand. Lots of them, I noticed, were wearing red armbands now. As we turned off the highway toward the bunker and the spa, I saw a gang of German soldiers. Wearing camouflaged ponchos and walking along with their hands up, they were being herded along by a few raincoated men with their rifles at the ready. We'd passed the bunker by then and were driving through the outskirts of town. I leaned back and lay my submachine gun across my knees. For the first time my muscles and brain relaxed. I felt a tremendous calm relief. This was a real uprising! With a feeling of deep satisfaction, I closed my eyes. Again I could see the wet asphalt road, the rainbow, the German tank glistening from the rain, the steam rising above its hot motor, and then that frantic moment when I was so close to it I could smell its mammoth steel body and the whole world started to spin and then falling into the cold water in the ditch and the treads of the tank clanking above me over the asphalt and the bullets whistling through the air into the field and everywhere and always that terrifying deafening din.

The truck drove through the outskirts of town--and the little red-roofed houses flashed past and, thinking back on all that had happened, I was glad. I could still see Hrob throwing out his arms before pitching over onto the grass and the turret of the tank rotating with deadly calm and the speckled figures of the SS men leaping down onto the asphalt and into the ditch. I felt the submachine gun lying across my knees and realized I hadn't even fired a shot. I was overcome with regret; I'd missed my big chance. And I could just see me lying there in the ditch, the muzzle sticking up over the side of the road and that gray iron German giant coming toward me. My God, why hadn't I fired? My fingers longed to pull the trigger now but now it wouldn't do much good. The gun lay in my lap, silent and cold, and it was too late now to feel sorry. My God, up there in the deep shade of the woods with the whole landscape in front of me like in the palm of my hand and that bunch of SS men clinging onto the tank—I could have fired then. But I hadn't. I hadn't fired a single shot. All I did was gawk at the tank and then run away. It made me furious. We drove past the station and across the bridge and up toward the hospital. I was furious. The wet branches of a weeping willow swished against the window. The hospital gates were wide open and a man in a white coat stood off to one side waving us in and, as we got up to him, he jumped on the running board, leaned in through the open window and hung on to the handle of my door.

"You got casualties?" he shouted.

"Yeah," I said. There was an odd look of respect in his eyes as he looked me over. Then I realized I must look pretty impressive with my mud-spattered submachine gun lying in my lap and my clothes caked with mud and dirt. I must look pretty terrific, in fact. I just wished Irena could see me like that, and the thought made me feel pretty satisfied with myself again.

"Many?" the man asked.

"Enough," I said.

"It must have been pretty bad up there."

"It was."

As we came up to the entrance of the surgery pavilion, a hospital attendant ran out. The white robes of the Franciscan nuns glimmered in the doorway. I got out and jumped heavily to the ground. I could practically feel everybody watching me. The tall figure of Dr. Preisner, his glasses shining, loomed up over the nuns. He came over.

"How many do you have?" he asked.

"I don't know, Doctor, but we have quite a few," I said. Stretcher bearers hurried out to the truck. Some of them were still wearing street clothes.

"Careful," shouted Dr. Preisner. "Take them to the hall in front of the operating room." Then he went back into the hospital and the men set down their stretchers and I stood in the doorway next to the nurses watching them unload the wounded. The nurses eyed me and my weapon with awe. The first two stretcher bearers trotted into the hospital. One of them was Mr. Starec who taught at the high school and whose son was a doctor at the hospital. Then the second stretcher went by. I noticed they were just unloading my Englishman.

"I'll go in with this one," I said. "He's English—doesn't speak any Czech."

The bearers glanced up at me, then carried the Englishman in on their stretcher and I followed them down a dim, rubber-carpeted corridor. It was quiet in there. People in pajamas and hospital bathrobes stood at all the doors, looking out. As I walked along, I realized everybody was looking at me and that I was tracking mud all over the clean floor. Nuns hurried on ahead of us. We turned a corner and stopped. Three stretchers had been set down on the floor next to the wall and through an open door at the end of the hall came a wedge of light. The stretcher bearers set the Englishman down. Dr. Capek appeared in the doorway, his rubber-gloved hands held out in front of him, his surgeon's gown spattered with blood.

"All right, next," he said, and Mr. Starec and another guy lifted their patient and carried him inside. The other guy was Jirka Hubalek whose father was chief of the internal medicine department. We shoved our stretcher up closer to the door. Jirka came out of the operating room, picked up the empty stretcher and some rags that had been left lying on it, and came toward me.

"Hi," I said to him in a low voice. He didn't seem to recognize me. He was just walking along staring ahead of him, as blank as a sleepwalker, but looking worried. Then he recognized me.

"Hello," he said.

"You helping out?" I said.

Jirka nodded. Then he suddenly just took hold of my arm and led me aside and said, "I've got something I want to show you."

"What?"

Jirka leaned the stretcher up against the wall and hunted through the rags he'd picked up. They were all that was left of a pair of Russian army pants. There were splotches of blood on the pants.

"Look," he said. "Look at what that Russian was carrying around in his pockets." He held out his hand, then opened it in mournful silence. There lay two wrist watches and a silver pencil.

"Hmm," I said. "Well, so what?"

"Well, so it's true," said Jirka somberly.

"So what's true?"

"Just that."

"Well, what?"

"About the watches."

"Well, sure. I can see they're watches, but what of it?"

"Well, so that proves that what they said in the newspapers is true after all, that's what."

"You mean about the Russians stealing?"

"Stealing—and for instance in Moravia they're already confiscating private property."

"Crap," I said.

"And this? These things?"

"Nothing to get all steamed up about, that's for sure."

"Well, and just think what's going to happen when they're here. You thought about that?"

"Oh, Jirka, don't be crazy."

"Crazy? I'm not crazy. I'd rather be out of here when they all march in, that's all."

"Well, but what'd you expect? They're soldiers, aren't they? After what they have to go through day after day, you think they're going to worry about some dumb bugeyed civilian losing a wrist watch? That's the spoils of war, right? You think English soldiers don't steal? Or the Americans maybe?"

"But . . ."

"Anyway, he probably took it from an SS man in the first place. They're coming straight in from Germany now. And who the hell knows? Maybe that SS man killed the Russian's wife somewhere in Russia a year or two ago."

"Not very likely. The Russian I found these things on can't be more than eighteen."

"Well, some other Russian's wife, then. It's all the same thing."

Jirka shook his head. "I still don't like it," he said.

"Oh, for Chrissake, don't make such a big tragedy out of a couple of stupid little watches!" I said. What made me even madder was that I realized I didn't know what was going to happen either. Still, this whole thing was ridiculous. Idiotic. Wrist watches! As though everything that had already happened and was still going to happen had anything to do with a stinking little wrist watch.

"So some Kraut's going to have to look up at a church clock instead of at his wrist, for Chrissake, so what?" I said. "Worse things can happen to a person."

Jirka stuck the watches back into the Russian's pants pocket. "I'm still not so sure. So long."

"So long," I said, and without another word Jirka started off down the dimly-lit corridor. They were carrying somebody out through the door on a stretcher and you could see Dr. Preisner in a white cap, the front of his gown dotted with blood stains. Two more casualties were taken into the operating room. The Englishman was shoved right up next to the door. A nurse hurried out and knelt beside the stretcher.

"Now, where does it hurt you?" she asked him.

The Englishman shook his head.

"He's English," I said. The nurse glanced up at me; she looked scared. I shifted my machine gun around to my back.

"I'll translate for you," I said. She nodded with a little smile and I asked him in English where it hurt.

"I don't know. I can't move my arms," he said hoarsely.

"He can't move his arms," I said.

"I see," said the nurse. "Can you help me undress him?"

"Certainly," I said. The nurse lifted the Englishman and, while I held him up, deftly stripped off his jacket, then unbuttoned and took off his shirt revealing his broad chest. A tin tag dangling from a chain around his neck lay half hidden in the hair on his chest. Under each shoulder was a small bloody hole.

"There. You see?" said the nurse.

"Yes," I said, and bent over the Englishman. "Probably from a submachine gun. One right after the other."

"Next," called Dr. Capek. The two bearers lifted the Englishman's stretcher and carried him into the operating room. I went in after them. Dr. Capek looked me up and down—an unfriendly look.

"You can't . . ." he said.

"I'm an interpreter," I broke in, "in case you need to ask him anything."

"I speak Russian," said Dr. Capek.

"He's English."

"English?" Dr. Capek raised his eyebrows. "All right, come on," he said, and turned, and when he turned I noticed that the buttons on the back of his operating gown were buttoned up wrong. There were two operating tables with bright lamps hanging down over them. Dr. Preisner was working at one; a nurse stood over at the patient's head, letting something drip onto the mask tied over the man's face. Dr. Preisner was amputating the man's hand at the wrist. The instrument nurse stood on the other side of the operating table silently handing him the instruments. I looked back at the empty table. The bearers set the stretcher down and two nuns lifted the Englishman up on the operating table. Dr. Capek leaned over him.

"Hmm," he said. "Just under the shoulder bone. Both shots. Sit him up."

The nurses propped him up. There were two identical holes on the Englishman's back, one on each side.

"Let's take a look at this," said Dr. Capek, and held out his hand. The nurse gave him some sort of instrument through which the doctor closely scanned the Englishman's chest. It must have been some sort of manual X-ray or something. First he looked at one side, then the other. Then he set the X-ray down and said, "He's lucky. They're both clean wounds."

"I'm glad," I said. Dr. Capek looked at me and waited. "Is there anything else I can do, Doctor?"

"I don't think so. Thank you," he said.

"Well, goodby," I said, and left the operating room and plodded down the hall where the patients, silent and stunned, stared at me from the doors of their rooms. I walked out onto the damp pavement of the driveway in front of the hospital and there the western horizon spread out before me its brilliant colors and small puffball clouds. The sun was already setting; the air was cool and fresh after the rain. I took a deep breath. From far off came the tough stutter of a machine gun. I pricked up my ears. From somewhere beyond town came the faint rumble of a tank. Then there was the clear blast of a cannon. Then another. A pair of machine guns started chattering simultaneously. Quite a racket for a spring evening like this, even though it came from pretty far off. Guns boomed again.

I looked out across the town, then turned into the street the Port Arthur's on. It was quiet and the street was dim and unlit, but the sound of gunfire around the frontier went on. Another machine gun started hammering away. There were pauses and then it would start up again and each time it sounded louder. I started to run. The wind felt cool against my face and I felt strong and dangerous. I sprinted past the Port Arthur and down toward the brewery with only the noise of gunfire and my own footsteps to keep me company. Above the woods, off to the east, the sky had already darkened; the tops of the tall oaks and lindens swayed in the glow of the setting sun. A couple of people were running down the path to the brewery. I looked across the bridge toward the station and could see dark figures running in opposite directions. Shots flashed and cracked around the station. I turned and set off again for the brewery. I held my submachine gun in both hands and, jogging along, heard the whiz of more bullets. When I got to the gate I slowed down. Inside, in the yard, it was a sea of confusion. Crowds of men and guys my age, some with guns, some without, were milling around and I saw a couple of guys making their way up and over the fence out back by the woods. On the driveway, a little man in uniform was trying to line up a bewildered corps of young riflemen. The chestnut trees blocked the sun; the brewery yard lay in shadow. Major Weiss, capless and wearing a civilian topcoat, raced by. Suddenly somebody shouted from the gate, "The SS! They're heading for the brewery!" Confusion turned to chaos. Rifles and grenades, tossed aside, lay all over the place. I went over to the main building without really knowing what to do next. Men burst out of the door and started piling into a car parked by the steps. I recognized Mr. Kaldoun, Mr. Krocan, and Mr. Jungwirth. The car started off with a jerk and honked its way through the milling crowd. I figured I'd go through the warehouse, hide in the bushes along the river bank, and wait until it all blew over. Tanks couldn't cross the bridge anyway. It wouldn't hold them. I hurried along, keeping close to the wall. The savage bursts of gunfire from town were getting closer and closer. I jumped and dodged between little piles of abandoned weapons. Amazing how many guns we'd already captured from the Germans. Then all of a sudden I saw somebody inching out through a small low window next to the sidewalk just ahead of me. Already more than halfway out, supporting the front of his body on the flat of his hands, he was handwalking forward trying to get his legs and feet out. I stopped. A smudged figure sprawled on the sidewalk, picked itself up, and turned to face me. It had on one of those little caps like Masaryk used to wear. It was Prema. Prema! His cap was cocked over a coal-dusted face and his white eyeballs shone through the black. Prema! I felt a wild rush of joy. Just the guy I'd been looking for. Things would really start happening now.

"Prema!" I shouted.

"Danny! What's going on? Where're the Germans?"

"They're supposed to be coming this way." I still couldn't get over how glad I was to see him again. "How'd you get out of there anyway?"

"I've been filing away like mad for three days. Come on, let's get moving."

"Wait! Where are we going?"

"My place. Let's move!"

"What're we gonna do there?"

"I've got a machine gun all ready to go."

"A machine gun?"

"Yeah. Come on, let's move!" Prema pulled my arm. Machine guns rattled from the bridge.

"Wait! The Germans are out on the streets!"

Prema stopped. "Christ! That submachine gun's the only thing you got?"

I looked around. "There're guns lying all over the place," I said. Prema ran out onto the driveway, grabbed up a rifle, hunted around for something else like his life depended on it, stooped, and stuck whatever it was in his pocket.

"Come on!" I yelled. "Let's go around the back way."

"And then?"

"Under the bridge."

We ran over to the warehouse. You could still hear shots coming from over in front of the brewery. The warehouse was dark; we ran straight through and out the back door to the slope down to the river bank. We forced our way through the wet shrubbery at the top of the slope. Shots rang out to our left. Prema ran ahead, plunged down the slope with big long strides and I slid down after him. By the river bank, we looked up from its reflection in the water to the bridge itself, arching against the pale sky. Along the railing you could see the running silhouettes of people wearing hats and caps. Only a few carried rifles. A tank roared along a street on the other side of the bridge. We crouched there under the bushes, water dripping on us from the branches, the dark river murmuring along a few feet below. A machine gun chattered in a series of short bursts above the roar of the tank. The figures on the bridge dropped out of sight. On the opposite bank, a couple of shadows headed down toward the river and off toward the edge of town.

"Let's go," I said to Prema.

"Wait," he said. The roaring of the motor stopped. In the silence you could hear the crunch of hobnailed boots up on the bridge. Prema rose and pulled something out of his pocket. It was a hand grenade. He pulled the pin. Up on the bridge the black silhouettes of German soldiers stood out very sharp and clear, the noise of their boots resounding above the river. Prema stretched his arm way back, then pitched the grenade. Then he threw himself down on the ground beside me. I pushed my face in the wet earth. There was a big blast and chunks of metal came down, tearing leaves off the trees. Prema jumped up.

"Run!" he yelled. Then I was up and running too, along the river bank under the bridge. I saw that a piece of the railing had been blown out of the middle of the bridge and was bobbing in the water now and the air was dusty and full of smoke. We ran along under the bridge. Prema stumbled. Suddenly an SS man loomed up from behind the bridge pillar. He was right in front of me, wearing a camouflaged poncho. For a fraction of a second I looked at his wet helmet, the ammunition belt slung across his chest, and then I pulled back on the trigger. Flames leapt from the muzzle and I felt something jerk up sharply in my hands. The SS man leaned slightly forward and then fell hard and we went by him without even stopping. He lay there, wet, big, strong, in full camouflage, his helmet shoved back, his eyes wide open, and his blond hair, wet from the rain and sweat, stuck to his forehead. We ran on and didn't look back. Along the bank of the river, which reflected the brilliant colors of the western sky, we hurried away from the bridge. A machine gun barked behind us but I didn't hear the bullets coming by. We scrambled up the slope to the path at the top and ran on to the first weir. There we stopped and looked back. A light cloud of smoke was still lifting from the middle of the bridge; at the town end of the bridge stood a tank. Its flaring machine gun was firing off into the woods somewhere. Nobody seemed to be running after us. Then a couple of helmeted figures jumped back onto the tank. It backed up and turned.

"Step on it! Let's move!" said Prema. We turned and loped on down along the river bank, the western sky looking more fantastic than ever. The tank growled somewhere behind us and we ran on a little farther, then left the path and got down by the river again. Behind the weir the river was hardly more than a creek. Prema jumped into the water, I went in after him, and we waded over to the other side. After we'd clambered up the slope on this side, we took off across a vacant lot toward the courthouse. There wasn't a soul in sight. Above the city, the castle glittered in the rays of the setting sun, its windows a smoldering gold. Below the castle, the lilacs glimmered like lanterns. We tramped along the foot bridge over the stream, past the place where women used to do their washing, then turned into Skocdopole's warehouse. The corrugated-metal overhead door was shut. Prema took a key out of his pocket and unlocked the door.

"What's the plan?" I asked.

"We're going to take the machine gun up to Sugarloaf Hill and wait for 'em there."

"You think they'll head over that way?"

"We'll see." Prema pushed up the rumbling overhead door.

We went in. It was dark inside. Prema switched on the dim bulb in the ceiling.

"Come on. Give me a hand with this thing," he said, slapping a crate that stood in a corner. "We'll just tip this thing off."

We tipped the crate forward and let it down. My eyes popped. On little steel wheels stood a heavy, well-polished machine gun. The fat cooling sleeve around the barrel glistened and its funnel-shaped muzzle looked deadly.

"Where'd you ever get hold of that?" I asked in amazement.

"I had it down in the cellar. Ever since the mobilization."

"But where'd you get it in the first place?"

"Robert got it when he was still around. Come on, let's push it out." Robert was Prema's cousin, the one who'd left the country. We leaned against the gun and pushed it out in front of the warehouse. It was awfully heavy. There was nobody around out there.

"How're you planning to get it up to Sugarloaf?" I asked.

"We'll drive it up," said Prema, and vanished around the corner. I stood beside the gun, looking it over. It had a steel shield with a sight slit and two hand grips for aiming. This was really something. You could stage a real uprising with a thing like this. Like in that picture I'd seen in *Signal* or somewhere of communist bandits disturbing the peace and tranquility of Warsaw by staging a bloody uprising and up on a rooftop, his cap shifted to the back of his head and a cigarette dangling out of his mouth, behind a machine gun just like this, one guy all by himself firing away down at the street. Prema reappeared pushing Skocdopole's red motorcycle. It had a sidecar.

"You going to put it in the sidecar?"

"Sure."

"You think it'll make it with all that weight?"

"I know it will." We lifted the machine gun up and into the sidecar. The gun almost pulled us in after it, it was so heavy. The sidecar sagged over to one side.

"Boy, I don't know whether we're going to make it up to Sugarloaf or not," I said.

"Don't worry. I've tried it," said Prema.

"Tried it? When?"

"Not with the gun, though. I weighed it and then drove up there with a load of rocks."

The machine gun stuck way out in front and over the top of the sidecar a bit.

"Okay. Hop on," said Prema. I got on behind him. We could hear a tank going down the main street.

"The bastard—he's going to jump to get away from us," said Prema. Then he jumped into the saddle, tramped hard as he gripped the handlebars, let the motor bang and pop for a minute, and then off we went. We turned the corner toward the high school and then boomed up the street. As we bumped over the cobblestones. I could feel my submachine gun thumping my back. Some guys were running from the underpass. Prema slowed down and yelled, "Some more Germans coming?"

"Yeah," one of them shouted back as he kept right on running. "They're out by the customs house—big fight out there with the Russians!"

"Good," said Prema, and stepped on the gas. We took the corner onto the main street at full speed, using the machine gun as a counterweight. The street led straight out past Serpon's factory to Sugarloaf, whose crown looked blood red in the sunset. I could feel the motor chugging away between my knees as houses whizzed by on both sides of the road. Up ahead and a long way off a German tank disappeared around a bend. The cool evening wind slammed into my face and the springs in the motorcycle seat bounced like mad. Holding onto Prema's waist, I could feel the tight-stretched muscles of his back. The gun he'd slung across his shoulder dug into my chest. And then, for the first time, it struck me that I'd really fired after all. That I'd killed somebody. We tore on down the street that was as red with the sun as if the whole block was on fire. I couldn't worry about it. That was life, that's all. We shot across the cobblestones, past Serpon's factory, past the last scattered houses, then up the highway toward the woods. Looking off to the side I could see the town below us in the valley looking very peaceful and the same as always, with lights in the windows, and, above the housetops, the honey-colored crowns of the hills. Prema slowed down and turned off onto a bumpy path. He stopped at the edge of the woods: we got off. There was a stretch of meadow between us and the highway now and at the bottom of the steeply-climbing highway lay the city glowing in the last minutes of the day's light.

"We'll set it up here," said Prema. There wasn't a soul in sight. We stood there alone at the edge of the woods beside the motorcycle and then we lifted the machine gun out and set it down on the ground. Prema went a little way into the woods.

"Good. The hollow's right over here," he called. Then he

reappeared and said, "Let's put it here at the edge of the woods. Over by the bushes."

We put our shoulders against the gun and shoved it toward the woods. There was a low clump of hazel bushes growing there. That's where we set it down. Behind the bushes there was a long shallow dip in the ground. Prema fixed the gun in position and ran back to the motorcycle. He took two boxes of ammunition belts out of the sidecar and dragged them back to where I was waiting in the hollow. We sat down by the gun and Prema locked in the ammunition belt. It was already almost dark just beyond the bushes; I felt like I was off camping somewhere. From way off in back of the town you could hear gunfire.

"Watch out, now," said Prema. "You'll hold the belt for me. I'll shoot."

I held the belt. Prema sat down behind the gun. Then there was a short loud burst and my ears popped.

"Good," said Prema. The air was thick with the acrid smell of burned powder. Prema stayed where he was, in position. We looked out over the highway. As the sun set, the highway darkened and the slope to the right of the road filled up with dusk. We sat above the road, silently waiting. From town you could hear the distant roar of tanks. Something inside me eased. Everything that had happened to me flooded through my brain and all at once I felt awfully tired. I began to feel as if I'd had just about enough of this. The roar of the tanks was coming closer.

"It won't be long now," said Prema.

"Mmmm," I said. I started to think about Irena, but she seemed awfully unimportant now. After all this, I figured, Irena wouldn't mean a thing. I'd been an idiot. After this was all over, everything would be different. If, that is, we didn't get ourselves killed right here. My brain was worn out; scraps of thoughts blew around in my head; not one of them made any sense. The roar of the tanks grew closer and suddenly far down the highway, a big black shadow appeared like some huge bug, crawling swiftly up the steep gray road.

"All right. Watch out now!" said Prema, and he leaned over the handles of the gun. I crouched over and lifted the ammunition belt and felt the long cool weight of the bullets in my fingers. The sun had just gone down; dusk took over the countryside. The tank advanced along the dark road rapidly, its motor roaring as it came. It was about halfway up the hill when a second appeared behind it. Christ! I suddenly realized, there we were, all by ourselves. Still, there wasn't much we could do about that. Beside me Prema sat like a statue, following the lead tank with his machine gun. It was pretty close now, and I could see SS men perched all over it. They were everywhere—up by the turret, along the sides, under the cannon—and they were loaded down with submachine guns and grenades. As they headed west through the darkening hills, the treads of the tank clattered over the road and its motor droned on monotonously.

"Here goes!" said Prema. I could sense him tightening up and then the machine gun barked. Flames lashed out of the barrel into the darkness and in a second we were wreathed in a light cloud of bitter-smelling smoke. The ammunition belt slipped through my fingers and I looked off at the highway and saw bodies falling head first from the tank and then all of a sudden the tank swerved and tilted. More shadowy figures jumped off the tank now, their arms flung out, from all over the body of the swerving tank that tilted even farther and tipped at last into a ditch at the side of the road. Then it went right on tumbling, over and over, down the hillside into the valley. Its motor whined and then stopped as the huge shadow tumbled and lurched down the dark slope. Below us, a few scattered figures crept along the highway. I glanced at the second tank. It had stopped and soldiers were jumping out of it on both sides of the road. It was only about halfway up the hill and was hard to see. About all I could see was its black, sharp-edged silhouette. Flashes burst from the turret and bullets whistled above our heads, cracking into the tree trunks behind us. We lay flat out on the ground. The tank fired a few more rounds, then held fire.

"Let's go," said Prema and he sat up and grabbed the handles of the machine gun again. I picked up the ammunition belt. On the highway you could hear a motor roaring at full speed. Prema pulled the trigger and flames started lashing out of our gun. They blinded me; the tank vanished for a second in the glare. But just then there was a deafening explosion and a brilliant light burst on the highway. Heavy chunks of metal tore through the air. The tank split apart before our eyes and started to burn. Prema stopped firing. In the silence we could hear the faint rumble of a truck coming down the road.

"What the hell's going on?" said Prema. "We couldn't have knocked out . . . ?"

"I don't know," I said. We peered into the thickening dark as the flames licked up from the tank. I could make out the black shadow of a rapidly approaching truck. Shots rang out; the truck stopped. Dark silhouettes of soldiers spilled out of it.

"Christ," said Prema. "Those are . . ."

"Russians," I said.

"Hurray!" yelled Prema.

The tank's motor roared, then died. Then it started up again, then again died out. A few scattered shots cracked. We crept out of the woods and looked down. The flames lapping out of the German tank lit up a bunch of soldiers— Russians with submachine guns and Germans in camouflaged ponchos, their hands raised over their heads. A bit behind them stood a truck with a white star on the door and, in the deeper dark behind the truck, the black bulk of Russian tanks.

"They got it with an antitank gun," said Prema gleefully. "Let's go down."

Leaving the machine gun where it was, we ran down to the burning tank. In the meadow we met our first Russian.

"*Halt!*" yelled a voice in German out of the darkness.

"*Partisani!*" Prema shouted.

"Ahhh, *partisani!*" drawled the Russian, and then suddenly we were in the middle of a whole crowd of men. The Russians in their belted blouses and funny looking submachine guns with round drums and perforated barrel sleeves were darting back and forth in the flickering light of the burning tank. They looked fearsome. The Germans stood huddled together on the highway, their hands up.

They kept glancing around as if looking for a chance to escape. There wasn't any. More and more Russians kept coming across the field, their broad faces laughing and grinning. Every once in a while a shot cracked out, but the soldiers around the tank paid no heed. We stood there staring into the midst of it all. Then all of a sudden a civilian walked up to us. He was carrying a rifle and wearing a red band around his sleeve and a greasy cap on his head.

"You're from the brewery?" he asked us sharply.

"No," said Prema. "We've got a machine gun up there on the hill."

"Whaaat?"

"A machine gun. We were the ones that got that first tank."

"Just who the hell do you think you're kidding?"

"The one that was ahead of this one," said Prema coolly, and he turned and pointed up the highway where a black space gaped between the regular white teeth of the road markers. "That's where it went over."

"Well, I'll be damned," said the guy, and he went over to one of the Russians with wide epaulets full of little stars and he said something to him in Russian. The Russian looked at us suspiciously, then yelled something back into the truck. A spotlight switched on and started probing the slope below us, moving down across the grass until it stopped on something big and dark. It was our tank. It lay overturned in the flat stretch at the bottom of the slope, its treads in the air. The Russian shouted and the spotlight went off. Then he said something to the guy with the red armband, who turned to us.

"Let's have a look at your machine gun, boys."

"Come on," said Prema. We set out across the field, the guy with the red armband and three Russians following us up. It was pitch dark now. When we got to the woods, one of the Russians turned on his flashlight. Its cone of light picked out the muzzle of our machine gun.

"*Oi!*" said the Russian.

The guy with the red armband just stood there. "How the hell did you ever get that thing up here?" he said.

"By motorcycle. In the sidecar."

"And where did you steal it?"

"We've had it since the mobilization. Since 1938."

The guy started talking to the Russian again. Then he turned back to us. "What's your name?" he said.

I was just about to tell him when suddenly it dawned on me he probably just wants to know so they can decorate us for it, and I could just see the whole thing: the town square and the brass band and all the ceremonies and Dr. Bohadlo and Berty with his Leica and, in the back, the guys from our band making wisecracks. No. I didn't want that. Especially not the brass band. And it struck me that right up until then everything had been great—the night and the shooting and the tanks and the Russians—but afterward, all that would be left would be the ceremonial speeches and articles in the local paper and Mr. Machacek and his *History of the Kostelec Uprising*. No, that wasn't for me. But then it flashed through my head that Irena wouldn't hear about it, either, so that wasn't any good. Irena had to find out about it. Maybe then I'd finally get somewhere with her. And I was just about to tell them my name when it occurred to me that Irena was bound to find out anyway because as soon as they started looking for us under false names everybody would know it was us because Prema would have to tell somebody sometime and, besides, nobody's ever, since the beginning of history, been able to keep a secret in Kostelec. It'd be just that much better because we'd be spared the brass band and being decorated by the mayor and, at the same time, word would get around fast and it would give me a kind of halo. I'd be a hero—in Irena's eyes anyway—and otherwise being a hero was something I could do without, since what did I want a medal for or an article about us in the Kostelec paper? The only reason I was eager to be a hero was so that Irena would finally go to bed with me. I knew that using a fake name now and letting the truth get known later was the cleverest way to go about it. For a minute there, though, I wondered—what if the word doesn't get around, after all? But, hell, I thought, that's just a risk you've got to take and so, after stuttering a little, I finally said, "Syrovatko."

"And your name?" the guy asked Prema. Prema gave me a puzzled looked and then said, "My name's . . . Svoboda."

"You're from Kostelec?"

"Yeah."

He jotted something down in a little notebook and then patted our backs.

"Good work, boys. Report to the National Committee tomorrow. Wait a minute, let's have your addresses."

"132 Palacky Street," I said.

"Me, too," said Prema.

The guy wrote it down and then the Russians crowded around us, slapping us on the back. They grinned and we grinned back.

"Well, that's that," the guy said. "Come on, we'll give you a lift into town."

"I've got my motorcycle," said Prema.

"Good," he said. "Well then, see you at City Hall tomorrow, right?" And he held out his hand to Prema.

"Right," Prema said, and shook on it. Then I shook hands with him and then with the three Russians, one after the other. We stayed up by the machine gun and watched them walk back to the highway. The German tank was still burning. The Russians were loading the German prisoners into the truck, then a few Russians climbed in after them, and the truck lights came on and it started slowly driving toward town. Part way down, it stopped again and I could see a couple of men hitching on a small long-barreled mobile gun. Tank motors growled and three tanks, one after the other, started off. They crawled past us along the highway, heading farther west. Behind them came a few more trucks with guns hitched on behind. The German tank was almost burned out now. The Russian tanks and trucks rolled past it like black shadows and vanished in the dark to the west under the starry sky. Gradually the drone of engines receded and everything grew quiet again. Not even a single shot broke the silence now.

"I don't get it," said Prema after a minute. "Why didn't you tell 'em your real name?"

"I just didn't feel like it, that's all," I said. "They'd cart us around from one dumb celebration to the next."

"Right," said Prema, and we stood there in silence again. From the west all you could hear by now was the occasional faint rumble of the departing tanks and from town nothing at all. Nothing but the usual rustle of night. It was the same kind of a night as yesterday. Betelgeuse glowed red in the sky, the air was nice and cool. We stood there at the edge of the woods, looking thoughtfully out into the dark. The revolution was over. And now, I thought to myself, life was just beginning, but suddenly realized, no, it wasn't just beginning, it had just come to an end. My young life in Kostelec. Nostalgia and regret welled up in me. I swallowed hard, tears came to my eyes. I felt like crying and then I felt ashamed of myself. Still, something made me feel terribly, terribly sorry. What it was I didn't know. It was the ninth of May nineteen hundred forty-five and this had probably been the very last battle of the whole war. A new life was starting. Whatever that meant. With blind eyes, I stared down toward the town lying in darkness, a town that had turned all its lights out because everybody was afraid, and inside me all sorts of memories tumbled around in my head, memories of all those years I'd lived here, of Irena, of high school, of Mr. Katz my German teacher, of all the good old familiar things, of evenings at the Port Arthur and the music we played, of student carnivals and girls in bathing suits at the pool, and then of Irena again, and I knew it was all over now, over and done with forever, as far away now as yesterday's wind, as those Russian tanks on the other side of the hill, as the gunfire and grenades at the customs house, as everything else in the world, and that I could never go back to it again, no matter how much I wanted to, and it seemed to me that nothing ahead could ever be as wonderful, that nothing could be that tremendous or glamorous again, and that all that was left were these memories framed in gold. Everything I'd lived through before had been lovely. But what I was feeling now—all this nostalgia and regret and despair—was silly and dumb. Still, let the mood pass and things would look up again. That's the way it always went. I knew that. I knew damn well that nobody's ever really happy, or happy on time, since happiness belongs to the past.

"Well, let's pack up," Prema's voice came out of the darkness; it sounded tired and sad. We walked silently into the bushes toward the machine gun. Prema unfastened the ammunition belt and we dragged the machine gun into the meadow. The spring sky glittered gloriously overhead and suddenly I felt I had to have some kind of hope, something to live for, and from somewhere out of the night and the stars that strange girl emerged, the one I hadn't met yet and who'd be more wonderful than all the Irenas and Veras and Lucies put together and she was kind and sweet to me and I strained all my muscles and Prema and I lifted the steel gun into the sidecar and the springs twanged under it. We went back for the boxes of ammunition, then got on the motorcycle, and Prema tramped on the starter and the cylinders of the 500 exploded into the nocturnal stillness. Prema turned on the blackout headlight and drove carefully down the path to the highway. The motorcycle bounced over the bumps and the cone of pale light danced over the rough ground. There ahead of us we saw a dead SS man lying on his stomach, a submachine gun slung across his back. Prema stopped and got off the motorcycle.

"Wait," he said, and went over to the SS man. He raised him up and slipped the gun off his shoulder. The man's arms swung limply in their color-splotched sleeves. Prema slung the submachine gun over his back, then took the SS man's pistol, too. He stuck the pistol into his own belt as he walked back toward the motorcycle's headlight. His face, with its high cheekbones, looked thin and gangsterish. He sat in the saddle in front of me and we started out onto the highway, our headlight cutting across the silenced cooling wreck of the German tank. Going by, you could still feel the heat and smell the smoke and oil and burned rubber. Then we left all that behind and we went on down the hill and into town between the rows of darkened houses, our motor blasting away and echoing back, past Pozner's factory and the high school and down Miller Street to Skocdopole's warehouse. Prema turned off the motor and we got off the motorcycle and he went over to the overhead door and it was still up just the way we'd left it. He turned on the light inside and came back.

"Well, let's put it back again," he said.

"Under the crate?"

"Yeah." We lifted the machine gun out and dragged it through the doorway and into the warehouse. We set it by the wall, then tipped the crate back over it. "There. Maybe it'll come in handy again."

I looked at him and Prema looked at me. Under his Masaryk cap with the tricolor badge, his face looked grave. I didn't say anything. So maybe this wasn't the end yet. Or peace either. I didn't say anything. Prema straightened up and swung his submachine gun around under his arm.

"Let's go," he said.

I didn't say anything. Silently we went outside. Prema turned off the light and pulled down the overhead door. I stood there waiting.

"Give me a hand with this motorcycle," he said. I leaned against the sidecar and we pushed the 500 around the corner into the shed. Prema locked the shed.

"Want to go over to the brewery?" I said.

"Sure," said Prema. We cut across the vacant lot to the foot bridge.

"Listen," I said. "Aren't you scared they'll lock you up again?"

Prema laughed.

"What was it like down in the cellar?" I said.

"I was bored stiff," said Prema. "What was going on in the meantime anyway?"

"You mean since Sunday?"

"Yeah."

"You didn't hear anything at all?"

"Not a thing. They didn't just lock me up—those clowns forgot all about me."

"Really?"

"I swear to God. It was a good thing I had enough food

with me to hold out for two days. And I shit their cellar full for 'em."

I laughed.

"So you don't know old Cemelik's dead?"

"He is? What happened? He get shot?"

"No. He had a stroke."

"Shit," said Prema. "Well, at least that takes care of him. How about the other guys?"

"I don't know what's happened to them. It was a real mess though. You never saw anything like it."

We crossed the foot bridge and went past the Czech Brethren Church. The path was absolutely deserted.

"What was all that shooting this afternoon?" said Prema.

"Out by the customs house. Hrob got killed out there."

"Which one?"

"The short redhead. From grade school—remember?"

"Oh, him. Hell, that's a shame."

"And Dr. Vasak's wife got killed."

"The blonde?"

"That's the one."

We turned toward the bridge and for a while neither of us said anything. Dark figures drifted out of the brewery and disappeared in the dark. Over the woods the stars glittered and in their pale light I saw corpses lying sprawled on the bridge. As we walked across it, we had to sidestep our way around dead German soldiers. The left railing of the bridge had been blown out near the middle by Prema's grenade and there was a big hole in the sidewalk. Down below, the river flowed on as calm as before; it was black and mirrored the stars. The lantern over the brewery gate was on. Underneath it stood a reinforced guard detail. They were in uniform and armed with submachine guns. One of the guards brought his gun up to stop us but let us in when he recognized us. There was another lantern on by the icehouse. We walked along the path to the main building. A silent bunch of figures was sitting on the ground in front of it, huddled close together; two armed men were strolling back and forth in front of them. A broadening band of light fell on the ground from the warehouse and you could hear voices. We headed over. Kramm the butcher and Mr. Panozka were standing under the light staring at a wildly gesticulating German. A small crowd had gathered around—men with rifles. We could hear them swearing. We moved up behind them.

"Ich bin kein SS-mann, ich schwöre Ihnen, ich bin kein SS-mann!" the German was saying in a terrified voice.

Kramm the butcher just glared at him.

"Take off his clothes!" he said. Two guys grabbed hold of the German and started pulling his jacket off. The German struggled as hard as he could. One of the guys gave him a hard slap across the face. Through the V of his open shirt you could see white skin and tufts of red hair. The two guys were trying to pull the German's shirt down off his shoulders but he fought back until suddenly there was a rip and his arm was bare. Kramm leaned over to look.

"So!" he said mockingly. *"Du nicht SS, nicht wahr? Und was ist das?"* He pointed at something on the German's arm. The German turned pale and he was trembling and when he tried to talk he could only stutter and all you could hear was *"Nein, nein."*

"Take a look for yourselves at the bastard," said Kramm. People crowded around the German. I looked, too. Two tattooed S's, like two lightning bolts, stood out against the white skin.

"Take him away," said Kramm and the two guys yanked the German toward the door. They dragged him out to the silent huddle in the yard. Then one of them gave him a shove and the other kicked him and the German sprawled on the ground and then quickly got up and crawled over to the others. The two guys started back to the warehouse.

"Prisoners?" I asked the guy standing next to me.

"SS men," he said. "They're just waiting around for morning." There was an odd undertone of irony in his voice.

"For morning?"

"Yeah. We're going to finish 'em off in the morning."

My stomach clenched.

"Look," the guy said and turned his flashlight into a corner of the room. There, on a bunch of rags, lay two bodies with their noses and ears cut off and their eyes gouged out. Their crotches were a mass of blood. I felt sick.

"Who is it?" said Prema hoarsely.

"They're brothers . . . or they were," the guy said. "It was bastards like those over there that did that to them," he said, jerking his head toward the SS men out in the yard. I thought I was going to vomit. "Come on," I said to Prema, and we left the warehouse. The Germans sat hunched over on the ground under the lantern, waiting. One of them raised his head, looked around, then let his head fall back on his drawn-up knees. Most of them were sitting like that —their knees drawn up, their arms around their legs, their heads on their knees—and they had neither helmets nor weapons.

"They're going to kill 'em tomorrow," I said.

Prema looked at me. "What say we get out of here?"

"Come on," I said. We went past the SS men toward the back of the brewery yard. As we passed them, one looked up at me. Our eyes met. His eyes were grave but alert in the dark of the night. He looked down almost immediately. He leaned his head against one shoulder and his blond hair shone in the lantern light and against the light the hunched-over backs of the men, their heads bent toward the ground, stood out very clearly. They sat in silence. The only noise was the sound of their guards' boots on the cobblestones. I looked away. People appeared on the path leading over to the main building.

"We could go through the warehouse," said Prema.

"We'll go over the fence," I said. "I know a good place."

We went along the side of the main building, then back behind the woodshed to the place where Benno and Haryk and I had crawled over Sunday. It wasn't so dark this time. I shinnied up and over the fence and jumped down onto the other side and suddenly, as I came down on all fours, I felt the full load of that whole day. Now that it was all over, I was exhausted. Prema jumped down after me. We came out onto the path.

"Let's go home," I said.

"Mmm," said Prema. "I'm starved."

We walked fast, leaving the path and going down

through the dark pine woods to the river. Dead branches cracked under our feet and the wet underbrush felt cold as I pushed through. We finally made it down to the river bank and then headed toward the bridge. We stopped underneath it. You could hear people's footsteps up above; a black band of shadow lay across the river under the bridge.

"Well, good night," said Prema. "I'll go on down this way."

"You going to go over to the brewery tomorrow?"

"Me?" said Prema. "They can stuff their brewery."

"Right. Well," I said, "so long then." I went up the bank to the bridge and looked down and saw Prema hurrying along the river toward the weir. I turned and stumbled over a helmet lying on the sidewalk. Irena's window was blacked out; only a crack of light showed through. I wished I knew whether Irena was there or just her parents waiting up for her. But I was tired and Irena probably had her hands full down at the Red Cross place. As I went along the path toward the station, I tried to imagine her giving injections to the wounded and smiling that sweet smile of hers at them, but even that didn't help much. I was tired, but it wasn't only that. Irena just wasn't the center of my world any more. I turned onto Jirasek Boulevard and hurried toward our house. The stars shone warmly above the canyon of the street. I unlocked the street door and started up the stairs. My footsteps echoed up the silent stairway; a door squeaked. Then I heard Mother's worried voice call, "Danny?"

"Yeah, I'm coming," I said. She stood in the open doorway and the light shone into the hall from behind her so all I could see was a dark shadow.

"Danny, Danny, my dear, thank heavens! You're all right, aren't you?" she cried. She threw her arms around me and kissed me. "Thank God, you're home. But you're all wet," she said. "Where were you during all that shooting? What have you been doing? And what's that on your back?" She touched the gun.

"It's nothing, Mother. Nothing to worry about," I said, and I kissed her and swung off my submachine gun. "I'm okay."

"Get out of those wet clothes right away, dear, and I'll make you some tea."

"Fine," I said. I looked around. Father was standing in the hall.

"I'm glad to see you home again," he said. "You were out there in all that shooting?"

"Yes," I said. "I'll tell you all about it tomorrow but right now I'm completely worn out."

"Well, then," he said, "you go right to bed."

I took off my jacket. "I'll just wash up first," I said.

"Wait, Danny, I'll make a fire so you can have hot water," said Mother quickly.

"No, please. Don't bother."

"It'll only take a minute," she said and ran off to the bathroom. You could hear her raking the ashes out of the waterheater. I stayed there with my father in the kitchen. He sat down on the bench next to the stove.

"A costly day," he said.

"Many people get killed?" I asked.

He smiled nervously. "Oh, yes," he said. "Very. And the saddest thing is that none of these deaths were really necessary."

"Maybe. It's hard to say," I said.

We sat there in silence.

"You heard that Mrs. Vasakova was killed?" he asked. His voice trembled.

"Yes," I said. I knew he'd always had a soft spot for her. Everybody liked her. Why did it have to happen to her? We fell silent for a while.

"Where are the Englishmen?" I asked.

"The younger one came back this morning but they both left when the shooting began."

"They'll be back tomorrow," I said.

"Probably."

Mother came into the kitchen. "Your water'll be ready in a minute." She went over to the table and took off the tea kettle and said, "Where've you been all this time? We were so worried, wondering if you'd been wounded."

"Me? No. I took good care of myself."

"Yes. You're a sensible boy, Danny," she said.

"Well, tell us all about it tomorrow," said Father, and he got up and went out of the kitchen and into the bathroom and you could hear him tapping the hot-water tank.

"Another minute or two and it should be all right. Good night."

"Good night, Father," I said. I heard him shuffling off to the bedroom. Then Mother went into the bathroom again and called out, "You can come in now, Danny, dear," and I got up and took my pajamas and when I got to the bathroom Mother was standing in the doorway.

"Good night, Mother," I said. "You ought to get some sleep now." I kissed her.

"Good night, dear. Is there anything else you need?"

"No. Good night."

"Get a good long rest," she said, and then she closed the door behind her and I was alone in the bathroom. The light shone down from the ceiling into the white tub. I pulled off my wet pants and stepped naked into the tub. I caught a glimpse of myself in the mirror on the wall. I was really filthy but the way the light fell on me from above I thought I looked pretty handsome with those sharp Grecian moldings and angles around my hips and pelvis. In fact, I liked my looks so much I went on staring at myself in the mirror and then I turned on the shower. A thin stream of warm water started pouring down on me and dripping off my body. My skin glistened in the mirror. I turned the shower off and soaped the wash cloth and started scrubbing myself all over, and as I moved the body in the mirror moved, too, and I watched its hips move when I raised my arms and its arm muscles bulged when I leaned over and I started thinking about Irena, about her body, and how we could be together. I was young. Or at least that body in the mirror was, and so was Irena, and it was a damn shame that here was my handsome body just going to waste, doing nobody else any good. I'd love her. Or at least my body would. Since, after all, that was what love was all about—my body with those great classical Greek angles around my pelvis and Irene's smooth, wet, white skin, and nothing more, nothing, nothing. . . But what if Lucie and Evka Manesova and Helena and Mitzi had bodies just as nice and if it was just the same with them as with her and if that was all there was to it? It was crazy. And as soon as I thought about Irena again, I suddenly saw her in the middle of that mob down by the barricade and then the way she walked across the square from the post office as the sun set and then I wanted her again and only her. It was crazy. I rubbed myself with the towel, put on my pajamas, turned off the bathroom light and went out. I picked up my tea, put in lots of sugar and crawled in under the quilt on the couch in the kitchen and turned off the light and, looking out the window, started to drink my tea in the dark. A few lights still shone on the hillside; everything was quiet. I looked over toward the brewery and thought of the SS men sitting there by the drive, waiting for morning. I drank my tea and it warmed me up. I thought back over the day, about the tank coming up through the underpass, about the truck and how it went over into the ditch, about Hrob with his rockets and Prema with his machine gun, and about the revolution and what would come of it, but after a while my thoughts turned back all by themselves to Irena and to Prague and then to that girl I was going to meet there. I finished my tea, set down the cup on the table beside me and lay down. The stars were still shining. I looked for Betelgeuse and, when I found it, thought about the girl. I thought about how I'd meet her and how elegant and beautiful she'd be and a café came into it and comfort and pleasure and pleasantness and dreams—and so I went on thinking about her and drowsily started saying my prayers but she kept interfering with my prayers and I spoke English to her because she was American, a girl out of some movie or other, somebody absolutely different from everybody else and then I started in again, "Hail Mary, full of grace," and thought about that girl and she turned into Irena and I said something to her and she said something to me and I felt very comfy and tired and drowsing off and then I fell asleep and didn't even know how I'd done it, how I'd fallen asleep, and I slept a deep dreamless sleep.

Thursday, May 10, 1945

Next morning Irena's window overlooking the river was open and a bouquet of red flowers stood behind the green window guard. I stopped on the bridge and looked up at the window. I could see the glass chandelier hanging from the painted ceiling in her room and imagined her sleeping under it in her crumpled pajamas. It was all over now but she was still there. I went on. When I'd gone through the brewery gate, I stopped short. Terrible screams were coming from somewhere, like Mrs. Vasakova's screams yesterday. A chill ran down my spine. I stopped thinking about Irena. People on the path turned to listen, too. Sounds came from the warehouse, then more screams. All at once I knew what was going on, and had an odd urge to look, to see it. I hurried over. The SS men weren't sitting in the yard any more. The place where they'd been sitting was empty except for their rucksacks and other stuff which they'd left behind. I was almost up to the door when I heard more screams. I opened the door and went in. The lights were on inside the warehouse and a bunch of men were standing around something lying in the middle of the floor. You could hear thuds and groans and sobs. I stepped forward and then saw what was happening. Several naked bodies lay on the ground. Mr. Mozol, the time-study man at the Messerschmidt plant, was swearing and beating one of the Germans with a cane decorated with hiking badges. The German lay on his stomach, his back covered with blood. He no longer moved. "You German swine," Mr. Mozol kept

360

yelling. "There's another for you," and so on, hitting him hard with his cane. I knew he had good reason. I shuddered. Some of the others in the crowd were yelling and swearing too; a few, though, just stood there. There was a funny smell in the air; the place was stuffy. Then I noticed a few more SS men still standing off in a corner. They were still wearing their uniforms and were tied up. I turned. I wanted to get out of there. And then I saw Rosta's pale face a little way off.

"Hi," I said in a low voice.

"Hi," said Rosta. He was leaning against a crate. "Boy," he said.

"Let's go," I said.

The moaning started again.

"Lie down, you son of a bitch!" said somebody in a deep voice. I went over next to Rosta. "Take him out and finish him off," the voice went on.

"Next customer!" another voice yelled. Two guys ran over to one of the remaining SS men and dragged him over under the light. His eyes were bulging and he struggled automatically and then they started ripping his clothes off. They went at him like madmen, tearing away from every side and in no time at all he was completely naked. He had a sweaty white muscular body.

"Come on, Rosta, let's go," I said and we went out. Out in the yard a dim sun was shining. People had stopped to stare at two battered SS men who were being dragged off somewhere behind the icehouse. We followed them. I looked around. Major Weiss, in full uniform, again was striding solemnly around the corner of the icehouse with Mr. Kaldoun. We went around the icehouse, too. There stood another bunch of people and under the cooling pipes lay a pile of corpses. The walls of the icehouse gleamed white in the sunshine and the bits of mica glittered in the stucco. The men leading the SS men stopped. Sergeant Krpata and some other guys stood by the wall. Krpata had his revolver out.

"Stand 'em up over there," Krpata commanded. The men lined the SS men up against the wall.

M*

"*Also!*" yelled Krpata. "You can thank your *Führer* for this!"

Then he pressed the muzzle of the pistol up against the forehead of the first SS man and pulled the trigger. Then he shot the second one. The men let go and both bodies crumpled to the ground.

"Take them away and bring in the next," said Krpata.

"Come on," I said.

We turned and left. Neither of us said anything. The sun was burning through the morning haze; it started getting warm. People were streaming back and forth along the path to the main building.

"Where were you yesterday?" said Rosta.

"At the customs house. You?" I said.

"Nowhere."

"You hid out?"

"I didn't have a weapon. They gave me a rifle and ammunition but the bullets didn't fit."

"You didn't miss much," I said.

Rosta was silent for a little while. Then he said, "What do you think about all that anyway?"

"You mean back there?"

"Yeah."

"I don't know," I said. "What can you say? It's just—just Goya."

"Goya? He's shit compared to that."

"You're right." I didn't feel like talking about it. We went over to the gate. I remembered those two brothers that guy had showed me last night at the brewery. With their eyes gouged out. The bastards, I said to myself. Except the ones that did it had probably cleared out and these others were paying for it. What the hell, maybe they have the same sort of thing on their consciences, too, but how could you know for sure? And how could you tell whether they had on their consciences what Mr. Mozol and the others here were loading up on their own right now? I knew a few people who had plenty on theirs. Regierungs-kommissar Kühl. How he bellowed at the Jews when they were standing in line in front of the station, waiting to be taken off. He'd never been sent off to the front. *Ein alter*

Mitkämpfer, he'd been a member of the Nazi Party since 1928. Then there was that bastard Staukelmann who'd turned in Lexa's father, who was later shot because that was the easiest way to get hold of Lexa's father's apartment. And then later, when we already had our band and we donated the proceeds of two concerts to Lexa's mother, Staukelmann informed about that, too, because informing had become a habit with him by then, and the only reason nothing came of that was because Dr. Sabata had bribed some big wheel from the Gestapo with a case or two of slivovitz. Or Zieglosser, head of the personnel department at Metal, who used to pad around the factory picking out girls and then he'd have them called in to his office and if they didn't come across, they'd be shipped off to the Reich. Like that seamstress Bozka I'd worked with. God knows whether she'd ever get back alive. The bastard. And all of them had cleared out in time. That kind always did. And then when you'd forgotten all about them, they'd turn up again and in the meantime somebody else had to pay for what they'd done. Maybe these SS guys they were killing now hadn't been half as bad as Kühl and Staukelmann and Zieglosser had been.

We stopped beside the pile of the SS men's things. Somebody was screaming again inside the warehouse. A German rucksack made out of calfskin lay at my feet; a pamphlet had fallen out of it. I bent over and picked it up. It showed tanks marked with Prussian crosses moving across a field; the Gothic-script title was *Woran Wir Glauben—* What We Believe In. I flipped through it, stopped at one passage, and read:

> For us, there are only two possibilities: either what we believe in is a mistaken belief and history has not called us to this task and we have only deluded ourselves as to our mission, in which case we will not complete it and, sooner or later, will vanish from the stage of this life and none of us will shed a tear for this great movement but say, instead, "We were weighed in the scales and found wanting." Or . . .

I shut the pamphlet and saw a hay wagon loaded with corpses creaking by. It moved slowly and I could see a hand dangling out of the pile and it seemed to be groping around as if it was looking for something.

"Where you taking them?" somebody asked the wagon driver.

"Into the woods," he said.

We went along the path to the main building.

"They've shown what sadists they are underneath," burst out Rosta. "The bastards."

"You seen Dagmar?" I said. "Is she all right?"

"Sure," said Rosta. "She stayed inside and kept out of trouble."

"She did?"

"How about Irena?"

"She volunteered as a nurse."

"Have you talked to her?"

"Not yet." The thought of seeing Irena suddenly hit me with an almost physical force. To be with her! If only I could go to her right now! I felt as if somebody had grabbed my hand and started pulling me.

"I'm going home," I told Rosta. "So long."

"Wait," said Rosta. "Maybe the other guys are around some place."

"Well, maybe they are, but I've got to take off. See you later."

"Well, okay. See you," said Rosta, as if he couldn't quite figure out what was going on. I turned and hurried off. I felt driven to move. There was nothing I could do against it—except go. I decided I'd set out to find her and suddenly it seemed the easiest and most natural thing in the world. Sure. If only I'd done it first thing in the morning, instead of going to the brewery. The wagon with the SS men had just creaked through the gate and women were standing around outside gazing in horror. I went out through the gate and there she was—Irena. My heart skipped a beat she was so beautiful and I loved her so much. She stood there in her dress with the thin green stripes and her hair was drawn back and tied with a white ribbon. Her red lips were slightly open and her eyes looked worried. Irena! It was as if God had sent her to me.

"Hello, Irena," I said to her before she'd even seen me.

She turned her great big eyes on me and hurried over.

"Danny!" she said with relief in her voice, as if I was going to protect her from something. "Where's Zdenek?"

"Zdenek?" I said. The question came like a slap in the face. "I don't know."

"Haven't you seen him?" she persisted. "Don't you know where he was? Or where he went?"

"I don't know, Irena. The last time I saw him was yesterday at the brewery."

"Don't you know where he was when the shooting started?"

"No."

"Oh, God. He hasn't come back yet, Danny."

"He hasn't? Well, all I know is, he wanted to go with the mountain climbers." I felt a sharp pain. Not because Zdenek hadn't come back, but because Irena was in love with him.

"I know," said Irena with an impatient frown. "But he didn't come back with them!"

"You talk with any of them?"

"Yes. They were out at the customs house. But they haven't seen him since then."

"And . . ." I said hesitantly as my hopes began to rise. Except that was nonsense. I'd never be that lucky. "And did you ask—did you look at the casualty list?"

"Yes, but he's not listed. Danny, will you please run in and ask at the brewery?" She looked at me imploringly. I certainly didn't feel like going anywhere—I just wanted to be with her.

"They won't know anything. I can tell you that right now."

"I know, but ask anyway, will you please? I've got to find out somehow," Irena said, and grasped my hand. My God, but I was crazy about that girl. How could she ever have seemed dumb to me? But she was and I loved her anyway. Obviously that didn't have anything to do with it.

"All right, Irena," I said, as if it wasn't an easy thing

for me to do. "They won't know anything, but if you want me to, I'll go."

"Please, Danny. Thanks ever so much."

I squeezed her hand and she squeezed mine a little and smiled at me. I walked over to the main building and went in. The place was like a beehive except here it was swarming with people. I went into one room and elbowed my way up to the desk. Behind the desk sat Captain Kuratko talking to someone on the telephone and jotting things down from time to time.

"Captain, have you got the casualty list?" I called out over some old man's head.

The captain glanced up at me and, when he saw who I was, answered, "It's not complete."

"Could I take a look anyway?"

"Here," he said, and handed me a sheet of paper. There were around forty names typed on the paper. I read down. Hrob was listed but none of our guys were. There was Mrs. Vasakova and Lidka Jarosova, but no Zdenek. I read through it again with fading hopes, but there was no Zdenek this time either. I just didn't have that kind of luck. He'd turn up. I knew it and I felt like laughing so now I'd go out and comfort Irena and in a while Zdenek would surface somewhere and come back and walk off with Irena. In the end it was always me that had to clear out.

"Thank you," I said, and put the list back down on the table.

"You're welcome," said Captain Kuratko with his ear to the telephone. I walked out. Hell, no, they wouldn't kill Zdenek. Mrs. Vasakova, sure, but not him. I could just see those buckteeth of his and his fat lips and big face, and it made me mad. I saw Irena standing on the other side of the fence, holding on to the bars with her little white fingers, watching me nervously. If only I could tell her he'd been killed. That he was dead and killed and all shot up and done for, but I couldn't. And I never would no matter how much I might long to. I walked toward Irena and on out through the gate and, as she turned to me with fear in her eyes, I shook my head.

"Nothing," I said.

"Nothing?"

"He isn't on it."

"What'd they say?"

"Nothing. But his name isn't on the casualty list. It's not complete yet, though."

"And they don't know where he could be?"

"No. But we can ask again when they get more names."

"When will that be?"

I shrugged. "We could come back sometime this afternoon."

Irena sighed and leaned against the fence. She looked crushed and she was beautiful in her green striped dress with the nice legs under it and her white sandals. Jesus, why was she so wild about that guy anyway? He wasn't worth it. And what did she need to bother about anyone else for anyway when she was so pretty and when everybody would do anything in the world for her?

"Oh, goodness," she sighed. "Oh, goodness, I just pray he wasn't shot."

"Don't worry," I said.

Irena didn't say anything. She just stared at the ground.

"Don't worry, Irena," I repeated. There wasn't much else I could do now, except to try to comfort her. "Don't worry. You already been over to his place?"

She nodded.

"And the landlady doesn't know anything?"

"No."

"And you've checked at the hospital?"

Irena jumped. "Oh, Lord, I'm stupid," she said, but it was all the same to me. I was crazy about her anyway.

"Well, let's go on over."

"Will you come with me, Danny?" she asked.

"Sure," I said.

"That's awfully nice of you, Danny," she said, and we started off. Idiot, I said to myself. Still, the way she'd said how "awfully nice" it was of me had been like a caress. We started off toward the hospital. Irena walked fast. Neither of us said anything. I noticed how tightly her dress fitted across her hips and stomach and how nice it looked where it came together over her breasts. Beautiful, except they stood out as if they were on display and I couldn't help thinking that big jackass Zdenek had already sampled them and that that was probably all he was after, and now there she was, beside herself with anxiety—as if, in case he'd kicked off, nobody else would be interested. It was crazy. There I was who would have given anything to be able to sleep with her and practically dying of longing and there she was calmly walking along beside me in that tight provocative dress scared stiff about her dear little Zdenek and absolutely blind to me. Was I any worse or dumber or uglier than he was? God, how I hoped he was dead! If only they'd shot and killed and hacked him up into little pieces, just so you, Irena, would come to understand. But exactly what was she supposed to understand? And I didn't really wish the guy all that bad. Let him live, and even love Irena—fine. As long as Irena left him for me. But, no, her little soul wouldn't let her. That silly, girlish soul of hers said no. I looked at her, at her sweet creamy cheeks and the white ribbon in her hair and she was beautiful. We turned into the hospital yard and went up to the main building.

"You want me to ask?" I said.

"I'll go myself, Danny."

"Yes?"

"I know Dr. Capek, remember?" said Irena. I should have remembered. But then I was a fool.

"Well, I'll wait for you here," I said. Irena's striped dress disappeared through the door and I sat down on a bench in front of the surgery pavilion. It faced northwest and the sun was already high enough to reach the pavilion. I looked up at the western hills, at the edge of the woods and Prague was there beyond it, somewhere in the distance, and that gave me new strength. What the hell, I said to myself, I can manage without Irena and I'll go off to Prague and play Dixieland and somewhere there'll be an entirely different sort of girl and I'll go up to her room with her and she'll take off her clothes for me and let me touch her and we'll have an affair and I'll be able to do whatever I want with her. Yet I sensed it wouldn't be the same as if

I could have Irena now, that nobody would ever really replace her, not even the most beautiful girl in the world, and that I didn't care about seeing just any naked girl, only Irena, and the only person I wanted to touch and make love to was Irena. I felt awfully depressed. I shut my eyes and my temples ached. I sat there in dull despair for an awfully long time. Then, at first as if from a long way off and then close by, I heard Irena's voice saying "thank you very much" to somebody and somebody saying he'd telephone her father immediately if anything came up and I opened my eyes and saw her standing with Dr. Capek on the steps by the entrance, saying goodby. I got up off the bench and joined her. She looked at me gravely.

"Well?" I asked.

"Nothing," she said in a tragic voice and looked at her watch. "Danny, will you come with me?" The way she looked at me, I would have gone with her forever and anywhere.

"Sure, Irena."

"I'd like to stop by at his place again and see if maybe he's come back in the meantime."

"All right," I said and was all ready to go, but Irena just stood there.

"Danny, you . . . you're not angry at me, are you?"

"Why should I be angry?"

"For dragging you around with me like this."

"Oh, you're not dragging me anywhere."

"Yes, I am, Danny. I . . ."

"Oh, go on, Irena, don't be silly."

"You're sure you don't mind?"

"Irena . . ."

"Are you?"

"Irena . . . maybe I shouldn't say this right now, but . . . well, you know I love you."

"I know. That's why."

"Well, so I don't mind and I'm not angry at all, Irena."
"Really?"

"You know I can't get angry at you."

"Well then, all right. But then don't be angry with me and let's go, shall we?"

"Sure," I said.

"Come on," said Irena softly and soothingly and she stroked my hand and I was happy she was letting me come along with her and I knew I was being an idiot but maybe it was better to be an idiot like this than to be smart. I was glad I was so dumb.

"Irena," I said softly.

"What?"

"You love him an awful lot, Irena?"

"Yes."

We walked along without saying anything for a while and then I said, "Maybe he's already back."

"Oh, God, I hope so."

Then nothing again, until Irena said, "Did anything happen to your friends in the band?"

"No," I said. "Irena. . ."

"What?"

I came out with it. I couldn't keep it back any longer. "Irena . . . if Zdenek's been killed. . ."

"Danny, don't say any more!"

"But you don't know what. . ."

"No, no. I know what you're going to say."

"You don't either."

"Yes, I do."

"But you don't, Irena."

"Danny, I know what you're going to say."

"And I can't say it?"

"No."

"Why not?"

"Because I don't want you to."

"But why?"

"Because Zdenek isn't dead and, even if he were, it wouldn't be fair to him for me to listen to you."

"But, Irena. . ."

"No, I told you already."

"My God," I said in despair and I knew I'd say it anyway. So I asked her straight out, "Irena, what would you do if Zdenek was dead?"

She shook her head.

"Irena!"

"No, don't ask, Danny, there's no sense in it. I can't tell you. And anyway, he's not dead. He's alive and healthy."

"I know."

"Well then."

We crossed the bridge in silence and walked past the slaughterhouse toward the old power station. Lots of people were out on the street, and here and there you could see guys with rifles. The flags on the houses looked gay and the crowd was in a holiday mood. Sunk in our own problems—and Irena's were nothing compared to mine— we made our way through the crowd and past the power station, past the spinning mill, up by the high school and then toward the underpass and I remembered that only three or four days before the Germans had brought me the same way and how scared Irena had been for me then and it seemed a long time ago. We went through the underpass. At Sokol Hall, the custodian and another old codger were hanging up a huge portrait of Benes and all sorts of garlands. I looked down at the sidewalk and saw that, in spite of yesterday's rain, you could still make out a small red stain. Or maybe it was only my imagination. Why in hell couldn't it have been Zdenek's blood instead of Mrs. Vasakova's? We kept on going and turned left on the street leading up the hill to the army cemetery. The street was shady because it was narrow and there were little houses on both sides. Not an awful lot of celebrating going on in this part of town. I looked at Irena and could tell she wasn't with me at all any more, but all wrapped up in her thoughts about Zdenek.

"You want me to go in with you?" I asked.

"Of course," she said and I could see she didn't really want me to but that she didn't want to say no to me now after coming this far with her. That'd be a swell revenge, I thought, if I'd stick with her now and pretend I was crazy with relief and joy to find Zdenek still alive and then hang around in his room with them all afternoon. Only it wouldn't really be any revenge; it'd be idiotic and I'd feel more embarrassed than they would. We stopped in front of a small, yellow, one-story house and Irena rang the bell. We stood waiting and then heard footsteps shuffling along the hall and the click of a bolt and a wrinkled old woman opened the door.

"Good morning," Irena said sweetly.

"Good morning," the old woman said.

"Could you tell me, please, has Zdenek come back yet?"

"No," said the old woman.

"He hasn't?"

"No."

Irena hesitated for a second. Then she said, "Could we wait for him?"

"If you want to, miss," said the old woman, and stepped out of the doorway.

"Come on, Danny," said Irena. I went in and said "how do you do" to the old woman, and then Irena opened a door on the left side of the hall and we went into Zdenek's room. I shut the door behind me and there we were, alone. It was dark in the room because the brown windowshade was drawn; a dim yellow light poured over the old-fashioned furniture; in the silence you could hear flies buzzing. Along the wall opposite the window stood a bed—brown-painted pipes with brass balls on top, a faded bedspread. A heavy, beat-up, carved, and painted cupboard stood next to the door. Along the wall across from the door was a little wooden marbletop table with a flowered porcelain wash basin on it. Beside the table was a faded plush couch and a wall rack with lots of little vases and figurines of shepherds and shepherdesses. There was a desk by the window with a big photograph of Irena on it and, in the corner, a rubber plant on a stand and, under the stand, grapples and a coil of climbing ropes. In the middle of the room three chairs stood around a table covered with a heavy green cloth. Irena walked across the room and sat down on the couch. I went over and sat down next to her. Neither of us said anything. I looked around the room.

"Have you been here before?" she asked.

"No," I said. "It's a nice place."

"Well, it's not too comfortable, but I think it's pretty," she said.

After another long pause, I asked, "You come here often?"

Irena laughed and you could tell that that little head of hers was practically bursting with memories.

"Often enough," she said, and blushed a little.

"Doesn't the landlady mind?"

"No," said Irena.

"You're lucky," I said.

Irena got up and started pacing around the room. I watched her, thinking how beautiful she looked in her green striped dress and in that dim light that made her face look even sweeter because all you could really make out were her lips and dark eyes. She stopped by the table, picked up a little Buddha and turned it in her hand.

"I gave this to him," she said softly.

"Hmm," I said, unable to think of anything else to say or do. Irena set the Buddha back down on the table. She opened the cupboard and stood there in front of it. I saw a few of Zdenek's jackets and a coiled climbing rope on a hook and a neat pile of shirts and underwear. Irena stared at the clothes, lost in thought. I couldn't stand it any more.

"Irena," I said.

"Hmm?" she said without even turning around.

"Irena, how'd you meet Zdenek anyway?"

Then she turned, looked at me and said, "Why do you ask, Danny?"

"No reason in particular," I said and looked down at the floor. "I just wondered."

"Really?"

"Really."

"Well, I don't know . . . Danny . . ."

"What don't you know?"

"You sure it won't just make you angry or sad again?"

"No."

"Truly?"

"No," I said. "I'd really like to know. Everything about you interests me. You know that."

"I know. But this . . ."

"Tell me, Irena. Please."

"Well, all right," she said, and closed the cupboard and came over and sat down on the couch not too close to me and leaned back. She crossed her legs and her skirt rode up over her pretty knees which I noticed were a little bruised. But she pulled down her skirt right away.

"It was at Wet Rock," she said. "Just a year ago. I'd gone over with some friends and we'd climbed Chapel Cliff. You know the one?"

"Yes," I said. But in my eyes Irena didn't fit at all with Zdenek and his crew with their nature cult and all that sitting around on rocks to watch the sun go down. She belonged indoors, in a kimono and little slippers with pompons made out of bird-of-paradise feathers, lounging around in the bedroom. That's where she belonged and not all wound up in ropes, dangling over the side of a cliff. I listened to her husky voice which gave away a lot more than just what she was saying.

"And Zdenek . . ." she said, "was there with a group from Stare Mesto and they were going up over the Pehr approach to Chapel Cliff. You traverse to the overhang and, from there on up, you have to use pietons."

"I know," I said, but what I was thinking of wasn't what Irena had in mind.

"And I was right under the overhang and Mirek was already up and secured me and, all of a sudden, there was Zdenek up on the traverse and he saw me and he looked at me and then just stared."

Irena paused for a moment. Then she went on and her eyes had a remote stare now. "It was evening but the cliff was still in the sun and the tops of the trees down below were shining and the sky was already completely pink and Zdenek was wearing that leather jacket of his and I looked across at him and I liked him. He had nice wavy hair and it shone in the sun and he was looking at me, too, so I thought—though why, I don't know—maybe we'll get to know each other, and then he climbed up and helped the person behind him up too and then looked around and came over to me and said, 'Mind if I join you?' Or something like that, I don't remember any more, it was something like that anyway, and I said, 'Well, it was about time you asked, isn't it?' and I really didn't mean to put it like that but it just came out like that, that's all, and then he told me he'd been assigned to work for Messerschmidt in

Stare Mesto and I told him I worked at the post office and then we roped down together and went for a walk in the woods together and it was nearly two hours before we came back to the . . ."

Listening to her, I could picture the whole scene—the woods and the tops of the cliffs dripping with sunshine as if it was honey and the deep evening forest and Zdenek leading Irena deeper and deeper into the woods, and then kissing her. The most incredible thing about the whole business was that I also existed then and that all this was going on completely independently of me. I was being bored stiff at a welding course at Messerschmidt's in the meantime.

"We made a date for the following Sunday," Irena was saying, "because he was in the factory then where they worked from something like six in the morning until late at night. I was off duty the next afternoon and I went over to Honza's to get some climbing irons and I was just crossing the tracks by the station when all of a sudden I saw him getting off the train, and when he saw me he came right over. I asked him what he was doing there and he said he'd taken sick leave and had a whole week off so I told him to come over to Honza's with me but he wanted to go for a walk in the woods so that's where we finally went."

Irena fell silent. "Well, so now you know how it happened," she said after a while.

"Yes," I said. "And then?"

"Then? What do you mean?"

"Well, afterward. How did he manage to come to live in Kostelec?"

Irena laughed. "He was in Stare Mesto for a while and then he arranged to be transferred."

"To be near you, right?"

"Naturally," said Irena, and suddenly she looked very serious and said, "Oh, God, you really don't think anything's happened to him, do you, Danny?"

"Of course not," I said.

"I couldn't bear it," she said. A clock was ticking somewhere in the room and the shade was a rectangle of brown light over the window.

"Irena," I said. I uttered her name like a magic charm. Like balm for my own hurt soul.

"Yes," she said.

"Irena, have you ever . . ."

"What?" she answered softly and automatically.

"Is there—has there been—anything between you?"

She didn't answer. Her face was motionless and I couldn't for the life of me tell what she was thinking just then. I felt I'd gone too far and quickly and guiltily said, "Irena . . ."

"Hmm?" she said very faintly.

"Are you angry at me?"

"No, Danny."

"I'm glad. Because . . . well, you know how much I love you."

"I know," she said, and laid her hand on mine. But she still hadn't admitted that there'd been anything between them. I knew there had been but I wanted to hear it from her. Since I'd never gotten anywhere with her, I at least wanted to hear how far he'd gotten with her.

"Irena," I repeated, "did you have an affair with him?"

She bent her head and said, "Well, after all, Danny, we've been going together for a year now."

"I know," I said, and felt miserable. I'd have given anything if she'd only let me have an affair with her, too. But I knew I didn't have much to offer. I quickly thought about what really great thing I had that I could sacrifice for her. The saxophone! I could play the saxophone better than anything—nobody in the district could even begin to touch me when I was playing my tenor sax. So I could give that up. Rather never pick up my sax again than never once have an affair with Irena, I said to myself. Then, even head over heels in love as I was with her right then, the more I thought about it the less sure I was that I'd really do it and I said to myself, Sure you would! Damn right you would! By God, and you will, too! And I even swore to God I'd never play my sax again if only He'd let me have Irena and then I modified it a bit and swore I'd stop playing when

I was thirty—or forty—and at the same time, in some dark corner of my soul, I was pretty sure that something would come up which would get me off the hook somehow so that, actually, I didn't swear to do anything and I hadn't given anything up but, in spite of that, I was still in love with Irena, awfully and unbearably and deeply. I longed for her. Then I noticed she was squeezing my hand and I heard her say, "Danny?"

"What?"

"Don't think about it."

I switched on a melancholy smile. "I just can't help it, Irena," I said.

"You mustn't."

"There's nothing I can do about it. I have to."

"But you're with me, too, and you mean an awful lot to me, you know?"

"Honestly, Irena?"

"Honestly."

"Irena," I said yearningly, putting my arm around her shoulder.

"No, Danny," she said, taking my hand and setting it back on my knee. "There," she said.

I looked dejected.

"And don't be sad," she said.

"But I love you so much."

"I know, Danny, but there's nothing we can do about it."

That made me mad. Nothing we can do about it! She's always said that. And there was something we could do, if she really wanted to. Plenty, if only she had a little room left for me in her heart. But she preferred to play virtuous, getting me all excited, and meanwhile the only reason she was so virtuous was because I didn't appeal to her or excite her as much as Zdenek did. I didn't believe in fidelity and all that other rot. All it was was just an excuse girls waved around so they could make life miserable for not just one guy but for as many as possible. I was mad, but there wasn't anything I could do about it. It was up to her to make the next move. Irena looked at her watch.

"It's already two," she said. I wasn't hungry; the time had flown by. "Shouldn't we ask again?" said Irena.

"Wait a minute," I said. "I'll run over to Sokol Hall and phone." I wanted to keep Irena in that room with me as long as I could.

"That'd be awfully nice of you, Danny."

"Aren't I always?"

"You are. You're wonderful."

Wonderful. Well, sure. A wonderful idiot who put up with everything. I got up. "Goodby," I said. "I'll be right back."

"Thanks," said Irena, and she gave me a smile for the road. I hurried out of the room and the house and ran down to Sokol Hall as fast as I could so I could get right back to Irena again. I went inside and over to the telephone and dialed the brewery and waited.

Then a voice came. "Army Headquarters."

"Hello," I said. "Do you have the full casualty list already, please?"

"Yes," the voice said.

"Would you kindly tell me if a Zdenek Pivonka is listed?"

"Just a minute," said the voice. I waited tensely. I knew my wish wouldn't come true, but I waited anyway. It took a long time. I prayed he'd be on the list this time.

"Hello?" the voice came back.

"Yes?"

"No, he's not listed."

"No?"

"No."

"And that's the final list?"

"Yes. All the dead have been identified."

"But he hasn't come back yet."

"I'm sorry, but he's not on the list."

"I wonder where he could be then?"

"Possibly out on patrol somewhere."

"On patrol?"

"Yes. Some of the patrols went out to clear the woods of SS men."

"I see. Well, thank you very much."

"You're welcome."

"Goodby," I said, and hung up. Sure. Zdenek was probably out hunting Germans someplace. Nobody could kill that guy. Well, that's okay too—let him hunt, I thought to myself. Meanwhile, I'd make as much use of my time with Irena as possible. I hurried out. Or maybe they'd got him off after all—somewhere way off back in the woods—and just hadn't found his body yet. As I headed back up the hill, the idea that he really was dead and no longer stood in my way swept over me—I could see Irena grieving, Irena wearing a black dress to his funeral and then observing a period of mourning for a while and then getting tired of it and then going around with me. And as I walked along, I thought over my strategy in the time I had ahead of me and drew up a general plan of action. I rang the doorbell and suddenly there was Irena. The old lady hadn't even shown up to open the door for me. She was probably one of those landladies who don't worry too much about their tenants' visitors. Then I thought about all that had probably gone on here before between Irena and Zdenek.

"He's not on the list," I said.

"And do they know where he is?" said Irena.

"No. But he's not listed among the dead."

"So they don't know anything?"

"No. But Kuratko said they could still find some more corpses up in the woods. They're out searching the woods right now in fact."

I looked at her with a really demonic stare. It seemed to me she'd turned pale. She went back into the room and I followed her. I sat down on the couch and Irena started pacing the floor.

"Don't be scared," I said.

"It's this waiting that's so awful, Danny."

"I know."

She stopped by the washtable and leaned against it. She had a beautiful figure in that dress.

"Danny, you're very sweet," she said.

"Oh, go on."

"You really are—waiting like this with me."

"With you, Irena, I'd be glad to wait forever."

She smiled.

"Irena," I said. "I'd like to say something comforting, but I don't know what to say."

"You don't have to say anything, Danny."

"But I'd like to."

"You don't have to, Danny. I know how thoughtful you are," said Irena, sitting down on the couch and stretching her legs out onto the chair in front of the table. Neither of us said anything for a while. The clock ticked loudly into the silence.

"Irena," I said, "remember when we saw each other for the first time? That time in winter, I don't remember exactly when. All I remember is that you were walking across the square in your ski outfit and carrying your skis over your shoulder, I think, and you looked at me and it was love at first sight—for me, anyway."

Irena laughed. "I remember," she said.

"And you remember that time in spring," I said, "when you were standing on the corner with some other girl but I only saw you and didn't even notice the other girl and the sun was shining on your hair and you were saying something and wearing a flowered dress and, when I saw you, my heart stopped and I didn't know where I was hardly and just wanted to go over to you only I didn't have the nerve so I just said hello?"

Irena nodded.

"And that time in the summer, at the pool, when I came in with Salat and you were stretched out on the side reading a book and you were wearing shorts and the top had an anchor on it—remember?"

"Mmmm."

"Yeah, and we sat down with you and played cards."

"Yes, and you told my fortune and said I was going to have five children."

"You remember that?"

"Sure, Danny. How long ago was that anyway?"

I thought back. It seemed like an awfully long time ago. We'd been freshmen then. So sophomore year made one year; junior, two; senior, three; and then two years compulsory labor. Five years.

"Five years, Irena," I said.

"Five years. Good God, how the years go by."

"Yes. I've been in love with you for five years, Irena."

"You really love me, Danny?" she said, and there was a wavering, indecisive look in her eyes now.

"Very much, Irena. For five years you're all I've lived for."

"Oh, God," she said and took my hand. "Danny, if there were only something I could . . ."

"And there isn't, Irena?"

"No, Danny, no. I couldn't."

"Irena, if you really wanted to . . . just a . . ."

"No, Danny," she said and then after a while went on, "Don't think I don't care for you. But you know I can't."

"Why not?"

"I can't, Danny."

"Irena, if you only knew how painful . . ."

"I know."

"And I'm jealous, Irena."

"You shouldn't be, Danny. I'm sorry you . . ."

"I don't want you to be sorry for me, Irena."

"Still, I'm not so sorry for you that I pity you."

"Well, what's that supposed to mean?"

"Oh, you know."

"No, I don't."

"Well, I just mean that I can't do what you want me to do."

"And you wouldn't like to?"

"Well . . ." She thought for a minute. "Well, yes, of course I would, Danny . . . but it just isn't that simple."

"Irena, would you really like to . . . well, you know . . . be together with me?"

"Yes, Danny."

"Then why don't you?"

"Because I can't."

"But why not?"

"Danny, don't ask such silly questions."

"It's not a silly question."

"Yes, it is."

I didn't say anything for a while, and then I said, "Irena, if I didn't love you like I do and if you didn't care about me . . . Except you say you do . . . or don't you?"

"I do, Danny," she said.

"So then why don't you want to? There's nothing wrong with it, Irena, if you . . . if you care about me."

"That's something different, Danny."

I moved closer and took her hand.

"Irena, I know how good and kind you are and . . . and pure"—the word stuck in my throat—"and I know you're in love with Zdenek, but there wouldn't be anything wrong about our being together. Really, there wouldn't."

"Yes, there would, Danny."

"No, Irena. Why I wouldn't even want you to break up with him since you're so much in love with him. It's just that I'd like to have a little proof that you really care for me, see?"

"Don't you believe me when I say . . . ?"

"Sure I believe you, but a person needs a little proof and a little tenderness . . . and when I think about you and him, I feel dumb and inferior compared with him, you know?"

She stroked my cheek. Things were looking up.

"Oh, go on," she said.

I wondered how to keep things rolling along now that I almost had her where I wanted her. I put my arm around her shoulder and looked into her eyes.

"You understand, Irena?" I said.

"I understand," she said.

Then I let my voice grow softer as I went on. "Believe me, Irena, I don't want you to do anything wrong but I'm so madly in love with you and I want you so badly and you don't know how happy I'd be if we could just be together for a while, anyway."

I saw her eyes brimming with something that looked like sadness and sympathy but I knew what it really was. It was pleasure. She was flattered and at that moment she was already being elegantly unfaithful to Zdenek. Which made me love her even more.

"Irena!" I implored.

She smiled hesitantly. "Yes?" she whispered.

My moment had come. I drew her gently closer. She

didn't resist. She just kept looking into my eyes. Then I leaned over and kissed her. I saw her close her eyes. She was gone. I embraced her and sipped away at her love-hungry lips for a long time, but after a while she started to push me away. She smiled guiltily. "So," she said. "Enough."

I looked at her, my eyes full of loving devotion. Only this time I really was in love and devoted. "Irena," I sighed.

"Enough," she said.

"But, Irena . . ."

"Enough," she said. "Come on—over here next to me."

I moved over as close as I could and stretched out beside her on the sofa.

"Give me your hand," she said. I gave her my hand and she took it and held it.

"Are you a bit happier now?" she asked.

"Yes."

"I want you to be," she said.

I loved her. I was absolutely wild about her.

"Irena," I said, "I . . ."

"Well, what?"

"I'd like to say something nice, but I can't think what to say."

"Then just be quiet, Danny, and lie here next to me. You don't have to say anything."

I didn't say a word. We lay there next to each other and the room was flooded with the brownish-yellow light and flies hummed and buzzed around the ceiling light. I could hear Irena breathing and see her bosom rising and falling and I loved her and wanted to touch her breast but couldn't. The flies buzzed and the clock ticked and gradually my thoughts started to settle down. I lay there next to Irena, thinking about her, her lips and warm shoulder, and about how good it felt to be there with her, and the flies went on buzzing and then suddenly I noticed that Irena was breathing very regularly and I looked at her and saw that her eyes were closed and her lips parted and something glinted inside her mouth, and I realized she'd fallen asleep, that she was probably all worn out from last night, and I lay there without stirring so I wouldn't wake her up and I looked at her face, sweetly sleeping, and at her breasts under the green-striped material and at her stomach and lap and suntanned legs and as I looked at her, I started thinking again, thinking about her, about Irena, and about how things would be in the future. And I thought that maybe Zdenek had gotten himself killed after all. Then, I thought, I'd have sweet Irena all to myself and she'd come up to my room, but I didn't have a room all by myself and so I thought how it would be when I was living in Prague and I hoped I'd find a goodhearted landlady, too, and that Irena would come to see me at my place which would be in some dark old apartment building, a room like this one, and Irena, wearing a transparent hooded raincoat over her corduroy suit, would jump off the streetcar in the rain and the streetlights would be reflected on the cobblestones and Irena would come along barelegged, past the lit-up shop-windows and between the evening pedestrians in their raincoats, looking like a bright cloud, beaming and beautiful, and her coat would glisten with raindrops and then she'd turn into one of those dark and shabby apartment houses with two plaster Herculeses over the doorway and walk through the dim hall with its plaster stucco trim and pictures of castles and up the stairs to the third floor where there'd be a view out through the big window with its etched-in landscape, a view of the backs of other houses, and then she'd stop in front of a door and ring the bell and I'd come to the door in my bathrobe and let her in and Irena would take off her raincoat and then we'd sit down on the couch and Irena would tell me what she'd done all day and then I'd kiss her and then she'd stop talking and I'd kiss her again and Irena would put her arms around me and we'd lie down next to each other and Irena would press up close to me and I'd undo the buttons at her neck and keep right on kissing her and then Irena would take off her skirt and everything and so would I and we'd kiss each other over and over and then we'd be together and I'd say "darling" to her, "darling, you're so sweet"—and afterward we'd lie side by side and then Irena would get dressed and comb her hair in front of the mirror and I'd watch her and then I'd get dressed, too, or maybe just see her to the door and then there I am, all by myself, thinking about her again. It was wonderful to think about, so I started—thinking it through all over again: she comes up to my place, takes off her raincoat, she's sweet and affectionate, and then we're doing this thing together, and it's still with us, even in cafés and at the movies and the theater lobby and during the lectures we sit through and out on the street, and we'd always be doing it and we'd talk about it, too. I thought about it some more and then about how I'd graduate and Irena and I would get married and what the wedding would be like and how all my friends would stare when they saw Irena and be secretly furious at me for having walked off with such a sweet and lovely girl because in the meantime they'd married real cows or hadn't gotten married at all and we'd be married in church and my uncle, the one who's a priest in Budejovice, would perform the ceremony and somebody would be playing the organ and I could see Irena standing there in front of the altar in a beige suit and me putting the ring on her finger and then off we'd go to live together and we'd have children and I imagined Irena in a hospital with a baby boy or maybe a girl all wrapped up in a blanket and we'd call it Daniel or Irena and then I left off thinking about the future and only thought of all those kids we'd have—three or four or five, for instance, or three sets of twins or maybe we'd have as many as twelve—and suddenly I wished I had them already and I could just see myself, old and jolly, with about seven sons and five daughters and the Smiricky line growing and spreading out from me, from me, the last of the line, and how these sons would have their own children and so on and then I realized this was getting pretty absurd so I went back to thinking about Irena coming over to visit me, and her hair and her breasts, and my eyes closed and my head grew heavy and, next to me, Irena was breathing regularly and I thought about her and then my thoughts got all mixed up and I was so tired I started drowsing off and then I fell asleep.

When I woke up, the room was almost dark. The evening sun was just going down outside the brown shades

and the room was quiet. Even the flies had stopped buzzing. Irena lay beside me, her left hand under her head and
her face turned toward me, her eyes closed and her eyelids
dark, her eyelashes making two soft darker arches. I could
see two little white teeth gleaming between her parted lips
and I was overcome with an awful, yearning love. She'd
unbuttoned the collar of her dress and I could see the
tender white flesh of her body. I put my arms around her
and kissed her on the forehead. She nestled closer to me
and put her right arm around me. But her eyes were still
closed. I kissed her cheek again and whispered, "Irena."
She opened her eyes a bit and then suddenly moved very
close to me. I held her tight and wanted to kiss her on her
mouth. But she turned her head so I couldn't and just
hugged me.

"Irena," I said.

She hugged me again and started to say in a low, rapid
voice, "Danny, I'm so scared something's happened to him.
I just know something's happened to him."

"Don't be scared, Irena," I murmured into her ear. "Don't
be scared," and at the same time I had an awful yearning
for her and I was mad at her and it would have been fine
with me if he'd been drawn and quartered.

"I'm so scared, Danny, I'm so scared," she kept saying,
and she trembled as if she was cold.

"Don't," I said, and I felt awful. She didn't say anything.
I could feel she was still trembling, though. So I started
caressing her hair and mumbling, "Irena, darling, easy,
easy," and she stopped trembling but then all of a sudden
she was sobbing softly. I kept on mumbling, "Don't cry,
Irena, darling, don't," but she sobbed all the harder with
her face dug into the arm of the sofa and I drew her very
close and suddenly she turned her face to me and it was
wet with tears and all red but incredibly sweet, and I kissed
her on her wet cheek and then on her nose and one eye
and then her cheek again and then on the other eye and
I kept on kissing her and knew that this was what life was
all about and I wanted it to last as long as it could. It was
getting dark and Irena sighed every once in a while as we
lay there side by side in the twilight and I thought franti-

cally about her body and I could feel how fantastically hot and alive it was and I loved it, but suddenly it wasn't only because of the pleasure it gave, because she'd denied that to me, but for the life in it, for the fact that it was Irena and because of that little soul of hers which was dumb, maybe, but was still the living and tortured soul of a woman.

Then finally she sat up suddenly and put her hand to her hair. I watched her comb the tangles out of her hair and then she got up and smoothed her dress. I stood up, too, and smoothed back my hair. We both stood there. Then Irena said, "Let's go, Danny."

"All right," I said. I felt like an idiot.

"Zdenek won't be coming any more now," she said.

"Oh, he'll come back all right," I said, just to make her feel good. She turned to me and put her hand over my lips.

"Shh! Don't say that," she said. I didn't understand. "If we say it too often it won't come true," said Irena. So that was it. I stumbled out into the street behind her. It was already night outside and chilly and full of stars. The old lady hadn't even appeared. I took Irena's arm and we started off toward town. We went down the hill and along the main street toward the square. The front of the church shone in the starlight and the windows of City Hall were all lit up. The blackout was over now. There was a meeting going on at City Hall. People were standing around talking in the square. Irena and I walked past in silence. There was a big poster next to the church. We stopped and read that tomorrow at ten o'clock there would be an official welcome for the Red Army on the square and that General Jablonkovsky would be there in person.

"Are you going to go, Irena?"

"Hm," she said. We walked on. I wondered how to ask her whether she'd go with me if Zdenek didn't come back, how things were going to be if he did, but I couldn't. All I could do was keep quiet. We walked along together toward the station and crossed the tracks and walked past houses under the stars and on toward the bridge. Then we turned off and stopped in front of Irena's house. The dark river and the leaves in the forest rustled behind me. I took Irena by the hand and looked into her face. Her face was white as milk and her eyes and lips were dark. That was practically all I could see of her and yet she was all there.

"Darling," I said.

"Good night, Danny," she said softly.

"Irena . . ."

She stood there for a little while, then kissed me quickly on my mouth, whispered good night, turned and hurried into the house. She disappeared like a phantom right in front of my eyes. I turned around and felt a sharp pain in my heart. Yes. It hurt. I hurried home. I was almost bawling. I climbed up to the third floor, unlocked the door, and tiptoed into the kitchen.

"Is that you, Danny?" Mother's voice came from the bedroom.

"Yes. Good night," I said.

"Good night," said Mother.

I tore off my clothes and curled up under the blanket and closed my eyes. I couldn't think of anything but Irena. I lay there, feeling like I was going to die. That it was impossible to go on living in such pain. I remembered Betelgeuse and opened my eyes and saw it, red and glowing in the sky, and then closed my eyes again with Betelgeuse inside them. And then that bleeding pain took hold of my heart again and all of a sudden I started bawling, because of Irena, because she didn't want me, because there wasn't anything else in the world, and as I bawled under my blanket, I felt relieved just like everybody else, smart or stupid, feels when they cry and then I fell asleep and slept under the window while outside Betelgeuse went right on shining, and I slept without knowing whether I dreamed that night or not.

Friday, May 11, 1945

On Friday, I wandered over in front of the loan association office. It was nine. It was going to be another warm spring day and there were flags in the windows and bedding had been hung out to air. There were banners hanging all over the place. The shops were closed like on Sunday and there were all kinds of displays in the windows—pictures of Masaryk and Benes and little flags and flowers and colored streamers. The revolution was definitely over now and I sauntered on toward the square. Mr. Dluhon was standing in front of the open showcase of his book shop and rummaging around inside with a chicken-feather duster. I stopped behind his hunched blackcoated back and his shiny bald spot surrounded by a wreath of hair. Poor guy, he'd been practically driven out of business by Kulas' Kostelec Books, Inc. Kulas was one of those voracious businessmen whose showcases took up the whole ground floor of an apartment house so Mr. Dluhon's little shop next door was completely lost. Mr. Dluhon lived with his family in an empty garage because, before the war, he couldn't afford to pay rent for an apartment and, during the war, there wasn't anything to be had. I looked at his carefully-arranged window display and couldn't believe my eyes. There, on a Czechoslovak flag, flanked by a couple of geraniums, stood a bust of Dr. Kramar.* I didn't know much about politics during the First Republic, but I did know that Kramar wouldn't be very popular right now.

Mr. Dluhon was just brushing off Dr. Kramar's face with his feather duster. I decided to do a good deed.

"Good morning," I said.

Mr. Dluhon turned and bowed respectfully. "Good morning to you, Mr. Smiricky."

"I don't know, Mr. Dluhon," I said, "but maybe it would be better if you left that Kramar bust out of your window."

He smiled nervously. "Oh? You think so, Mr. Smiricky?"

"Well, it's just an opinion," I said, "but I think you'd be better off."

Mr. Dluhon smiled nervously again. "But your father was always a National Democrat. Just ask him."

"I know, but the Bolsheviks are here now."

Mr. Dluhon leaned over to me and said confidentially, "Oh, just you wait until all this blows over," he muttered. "After things quiet down, Dr. Kramar'll be respected again."

"I'm not so sure," I said.

"Wait and see, Mr. Smiricky. You're still young. You don't remember. But just ask your father."

I didn't know quite what I was supposed to ask and why he was sticking Kramar in his window right now when the storm hadn't even begun to blow yet that was supposed to blow over, but I acted as though I knew. So I said, "Yes, well, but maybe you might put in Benes until things do quiet down."

"No, Mr. Smiricky, I think not," said Mr. Dluhon. "I've always been a Kramar man and I'll remain one till my dying day."

Well, then maybe you won't be around very long, I thought to myself, but all I said was, "Well, it's up to you. But I'd stick Benes in there, if I were you."

His eyes twitched a bit as if he was thinking I was showing too little respect for a statesman, even if it was Benes. Then, with that same servile smile, he said, "Thank you, Mr. Smiricky, for . . . well . . . for . . . but I'll just leave Dr. Kramar in there."

There was no helping the poor guy. I decided to forget about it and take a look around the square instead. Maybe the guys would be there by now. And the girls. And I'd wait around for Irena.

"Well, maybe you can get away with it," I said with a smile. "I've got to be going. Goodby."

"Goodby, Mr. Smiricky, and thank you," he said, and bowed again. I walked on. People dressed up in their Sunday best were already heading toward the square. A smaller bunch was crowding around Mouteliks' display window. All those pictures he was taking, I thought to myself, and headed over. And there they were. I shoved my way up close to the window and saw that Berty, that fool, had put me at the top of his display and underneath my picture was the caption: *"Defender of Our Fatherland."* Jesus Christ! I hadn't wanted anything like *that!* I'd wanted the picture to show off with but not have myself put on display in his show window like the village idiot. I could already hear the other guys razzing me about it. Hell. I looked at my picture. Well, it wasn't a bad snapshot. But that awful caption underneath—"Defender of Our Fatherland." I could have socked Berty; it would be a pleasure. And then I almost burst out laughing. What had I been defending anyway? If only these people, with all their noses pressed up to the window, knew what I'd been fighting for. And how much I cared about "the Fatherland." And what I really cared about. If they only knew what I'd done on the eve of these great events and what I'd been thinking about and how worried I was about that other great defender of his Fatherland—Zdenek Pivonka. And how well it suited me that he'd disappeared while defending his country. And how his war widow fitted into my plans. Oh, God! I remembered Irena and glanced at my watch. There was still plenty of time so I started looking at the other pictures. There were captions under all of them, just like I knew there would be. One group was composed of Mr. Frinta, Mr. Jungwirth, and Mr. Wolf, all sporting armbands and standing in the brewery yard, grinning into Berty's Leica. Underneath was the caption, *"Everybody Volunteered,"* and under a portrait of Dr. Bohadlo, striding across the bridge in his knickers and with his hunting rifles, Berty had written, *"Into the Fray!"*

Most of the other captions were like that. A fuzzy picture of German tanks creeping away from the customs house bore the inscription, "*Enemy on the Horizon*," and for a shot of poor Hrob kneeling beside the shattered dugout holding a bazooka, Berty's incomprehensible fantasy had come up with, "*Neither Gain nor Glory—the NATION is All!*" Berty was obviously a chip off the old block. But still, Hrob's picture was poignant. Thinking about what had happened the day before yesterday, tears came to my eyes. I could still see the highway glistening in the rain and Hrob's red head and now here on Berty's snapshot, which had turned out exceptionally well, he knelt forever, full of enthusiasm, hunched beside the gray stone dugout wall with the strip of glistening highway and the black tank below, its long snout aimed at him. And in the background, the pretty rolling countryside and scraps of clouds in the sky. It was a masterpiece. But that wasn't Berty's doing. If anybody deserved the credit it was his dad for being able to buy him the Leica. Again I thought about Hrob and how he'd stood in line to enlist in the army, obedient and eager, and then lying so still there in the grass. If anybody had done anything real worthwhile, it was Hrob. But it went against my grain to call him a patriot, even in the privacy of my own thoughts. He didn't deserve it. Mr. Jungwirth and Machacek and Kaldoun and those guys—those were the patriots, and if they liked the word they could have it. But not Hrob. Hrob was something better. I remembered him at school, munching bread behind me and the smell when he opened his mouth; I remembered him always having patches on his pants and how he'd stare hungrily while Berty finished off a couple of sausages at the ten o'clock recess. I was sorry he'd had to die the way he did and so young and I thought about his mother, probably shrieking and tear-streaked and hoarse right now, and suddenly Mr. Kaldoun and Moutelik and the others—and me, too, stuck up in a window like an idiot—struck me as dumb and ridiculous. It was awful. Still, the best thing to do was not worry too much about it. I made up my mind I wouldn't say anything to Berty about it. Let him leave the picture where it was and to hell with it. I turned away from the window and walked slowly toward the square. Flags and banners fluttered in the brisk wind and the sun was shining brightly. I stopped at the corner by the loan association office. Long banners hung from the church and from the theater and City Hall was decked out with a whole array of flags. A regular Sunday promenade streamed along the streets and around the square. The speaker's platform in front of City Hall was draped with red cloth and flanked by propped-up birches. The sloping square, which yesterday had still been cluttered with refugees' bundles, gleamed clean and empty now. The refugees had vanished. It was a spring day and it was peacetime, and it struck me that I'd soon be setting out for Prague. It had been a whole year since I'd last been there. We'd gone there to play at the last big wartime affair, an amateur jazz festival in Lucerna Hall. There'd been an air raid that night and the concert had broken off in the middle. We'd played "St. Louis Blues," I remember, and "Solitude," only we'd changed the names to *"Die schöne Stadt im Süden"* and *"Liebling, mein Liebling"* concealing all that beauty under those awful words, and the Lucerna sparkled and shone with light and the balconies were packed and people hollered and clapped and stamped their feet and Emil Ludvik* was on the jury and he talked to us after the concert and the kids in the audience raised a terrific rumpus after every number and it lasted until late at night. Then we went home on the morning express, sleepy and depressed, and we had to pay a fine at the factory for missing half a day's work and they wanted to report me to the personnel office because I'd missed a lot of half-days. But it'd been terrific. The most wonderful time of my life. And now it was peacetime and there'd be jazz and night clubs and everything again. I looked around me and wondered.

I was still standing there thinking when suddenly I heard an odd far-off noise. It sounded like the clatter of hundreds of wheels; it was coming closer. There was a sharp whip crack and then through the gap in the anti-tank barrier two Steppe ponies appeared pulling a wagon with a Russian up front. The Russian was cracking his whip over his head and singing as the ponies galloped along, the wagon wheels rattling over the cobblestones. When I was watching the first one, a second wagon appeared, then another and another and another, as one after the other they squeaked through the antitank barrier and hurtled along the street and through the square, heading west. The air was filled with creaks and rattles and the crack of the long whips. Like a wild stampede, they rumbled past in rapid procession—the red-cheeked Russians towering above the rumps of their flea-bitten ponies, bellowing out their Russian songs. The people on the sidewalks gawked. The wagons hurtled by at breakneck speed, the wiry little horses tossing their manes. There was an endless line of them. Their smell filled the air—the smell of the tundra or taiga—and, breathing it in and looking at those weatherbeaten men's faces, it seemed incredible that such people really existed, people who knew nothing about jazz or girls either, probably, and who just shot by —unshaven, revolvers strapped around their greasy pants, bottles of vodka stuck in their hip pockets, excited, drunk and triumphant, not thinking about the things I thought about, completely different from me, and awfully strange, yet with something awfully attractive about them, too. I admired them. So this was the Red Army, dashing by at full speed, dusty, sweaty, barbaric as the Scythians, and I thought about Blok again whose poems somebody had lent me during the war and wasn't sure whether something new wasn't about to start, something as big as a revolution and I wondered what effect it would have on me and my world. I didn't know. Everything was tearing by so fast I felt lost in it all. I knew they'd be given a big welcome and that there'd be speechmaking and that everybody would be enthusiastic about communism and that I'd be loyal. I didn't have anything against communism. I didn't know anything about it for one thing, and I wasn't one of those people who are against something just because their parents and relatives and friends are. I didn't have anything against anything, just as long as I could play jazz on my saxophone, because that was something I loved to do and I couldn't be for anything that was against that. And as long as I could watch the girls, because that meant being alive. For me, then, two things meant life. I knew there was a hunger in those people riding past on those wagons and in those who'd be setting up the party and discussion groups and Marxist study groups and all that now—a hunger for knowledge. I'd already got to know them at the factory, from discussions we'd had in the john, and when I'd talked about the solar system and about galaxies and Apollinaire and American history they'd listened, wide eyed. There was hunger in them for things I was glutted with. It was different with me. With my past and my ancestors and education taken for granted for generations and just comfort and luxury in general. It was interesting to read about people like them. About the Negroes in America, the muzhiks in Russia, the way people had shot the workers and so on. To read about this thirst for knowledge, this struggle for a better life. It was interesting and even moving at times, so that sometimes actually tears came to your eyes, but only because you were sentimental, because you were touched by the idea of poverty and suffering like my mother at Christmas when she wore a silk dress and wept when she heard the carols. Otherwise, it didn't really touch us. It was remote. It wasn't something really close to my heart, it was outside and far off, remote. I'd had an education and so had everybody else I knew and we had all the comforts of life and civilization. Actually, education didn't even seem important; it was something you just took for granted, like railroads and aspirin, for instance. What really mattered was girls and music. And thinking about them. But finally, ultimately, nothing mattered. Everything was nothing, for nothing, and led to nothing. There was only the animal fear of death, because that's the only thing nobody knows anything about, and that fear alone was enough to keep a person going in this nothingness. I wondered whether some day this fear, too, would lose its importance for me.

The wagons kept rattling past and suddenly I felt terribly depressed. I turned around and saw Haryk and Benno with Lucie and Helena coming from the church against the tide of the wagons. Lucie was wearing a dress that looked like a Carpathian-Ukrainian folk costume, with a fringe along the hem of the skirt like Sokol teenagers wear on their pants, and it was funny but on Lucie it looked good. She kept stopping to yell at the Russians as they drove by and to toss them a rose from a huge bouquet she held in her arms. Benno, Helena, and Haryk walked along in silence; they weren't yelling at anybody. I waited for them and knew what Benno would say when he saw me, and he did: "Greetings, defender of our fatherland."

"Did you volunteer?" added Haryk.

"Shut up," I said. "You better just keep an eye on Lucie so she won't start necking with one of our liberators."

"You hear?" Haryk called to Lucie. But she wasn't listening.

"*Zdrastvujte!*" she screamed like she'd gone out of her head.

Haryk watched her in disgust. "She's gone nuts," he said.

"Listen, before I forget it," said Benno, "there's a rehearsal this afternoon at two o'clock at the Port. We're playing at six tonight in the square."

"Really?" I said.

"Yeah. We're going to celebrate peace."

"And there's going to be dancing?"

"Sure," said Benno.

The last of the wagons had rattled by. People were starting to crowd up in front of City Hall. Mr. Petrbok's brass band was lining up right in front of the platform. The clock in the tower showed quarter to ten.

"Let's go up and get a place," said Haryk.

"Come on," said Benno.

"I've got to wait here," I said.

"Who for?" said Benno.

"Irena," I said coolly.

Benno looked at me like I'd gone mad too and shook his head. "You were, are, and always will be a fool," he said.

"That's right," I said.

"Well, so long," said Benno.

"So long," I said. They left. I stood there alone on the corner again. The local dignitaries were assembling in front of the platform. There was the former mayor, Mr.

Prudivy, who'd apparently taken over again now that Kühl was gone—the Regierungskommissar under whom he'd been compelled to serve throughout the war as Czech deputy. Then there was Mr. Kaldoun and Mr. Krocan and Mr. Machacek—the whole bunch, including General Director Heiser, Dr. Sabata, Dr. Hubalek, the head of the hospital. They were all standing in front of the red platform in their black suits, consulting among themselves. The crowd was growing and the police were keeping everything under control. I saw Police Chief Rimbalnik, in his white coat and corset, majestically giving orders. I looked away. No sign of Irena. It didn't surprise me and as the minutes passed I got more and more irritated and then really mad at her. Only whenever I got mad at her because she didn't show up, I realized how much I loved her and yearned for her more than before. I thought over what had happened the afternoon before and the memory of it went to my head. When I came back to earth again, the square was already full and the clock said half past ten. I stood on tiptoe and looked for Irena. Still no sign of her. I couldn't have seen her anyway because the sidewalks all around the square were packed. She'd stood me up. Her promises were always like that. She'd stood me up and God only knew where she was. Maybe Zdenek had come back in the meantime. That was probably it. I felt depressed. Then I pulled myself together and elbowed my way through the crowd up toward the platform. When people glared at me, I told them I was on the welcoming committee. I was rude and I didn't give a damn if I was. I elbowed my way right up to the front so I had a perfect view of the platform. Irena—what a bitch she was. A little girl holding a bouquet and wearing a folk costume stood in front of the platform; she was shaking with stagefright. It was Manicka Kaldounova; I knew her and I felt kind of sorry for her, but not very. The gentlemen from the welcoming committee kept glancing at their watches and shifting their feet nervously. The brass band had been all polished up; they stood there with their tubas and horns all ready to go, waiting. People around me were grumbling. It was hot and already half past ten. Every now and then some kind of rustle would start on the street and people would stop talking but then nothing happened. I was sweating like mad and then finally shouting and applause drifted in from somewhere and I knew General Jablonkovski had entered town. Everybody turned to look off toward the corner by the loan association office. The applause swelled and you could hear the shouting and applause sweeping in toward us and then all at once one open car came around the corner, then another, and they drove slowly through the two lines of people toward the platform. The welcoming committee lined up. Somebody shoved the little flower girl forward. The door of the first car opened and out stepped a fat ruddy-faced man wearing red riding breeches with double stripes down the sides and a chestful of medals. The little girl recited her little speech while the general listened courteously. Then he bent over, hoisted her up in the air and held her there for a second because there were lots of photographers bustling around. I caught sight of the ever-present Berty taking the general's picture from an impossible angle just as the brass band let out a big blare. The general quickly set the little girl down on the ground and saluted, the gentlemen from the welcoming committee stood at attention, people started taking their hats off. The band was playing the Russian national anthem. I saw everybody standing there, stiff as posts, and noticed the deacon among the welcoming dignitaries. He was cowering at the back with a purple bib under his Roman collar and he looked worried. The band thundered to the end of the Russian anthem and launched into "Where Is My Home?" Then it clanked into "The Lightning Flashes over Tatra" and people started putting their hats on again. But Mr. Petrbok was just getting warmed up. The square resounded with the deep tones of the bass trombone and I realized they were starting off on "God Save the King." At first, the crowd glanced around hesitantly, then took their hats off again. The concert continued with "The Star-Spangled Banner," and wound up with the "Marseillaise." The band didn't play the Chinese anthem. They probably didn't have the music. The whole thing lasted for a quarter of an hour. General Jablonkovski's hand had fallen asleep from saluting so long and the gentlemen in the black suits were sweating. So was Mr. Petrbok. Finally he concluded with a majestic flourish and beamed triumphantly at the general. The general removed his hand from his cap and turned a crushing gaze on Dr. Sabata who was approaching him with a piece of paper. Dr. Sabata put on his pince nez and started stammering something. Once more the general stood at courteous attention, the sun shining right into his ruddy face, and a big shiny drop of sweat trickled along his nose. Behind him stood his bemedalled staff, looking bored.

". . . And on your brave shoulders you bring us freedom," I heard, as a breeze wafted Sabata's voice my way. Nobody could understand what he was saying. But then, even if the doctor had been stammering into a microphone nobody would have understood him. I remembered I really ought to be grateful to him since he'd saved my life just a few days ago. Or maybe not, since Prema and his gang would have turned up sooner or later. Sabata droned his way through his exalted rhetoric and the courteous general shifted from one foot to the other. Then finally Sabata said a few words without looking at the paper and held out his hand. The general pressed it with enthusiasm and Sabata's knees almost gave way. People started clapping and then the gentlemen, all gesturing wildly and stepping aside for each other, propelled the general up the steps and onto the podium. The applause and cheering grew louder. The general lumbered heavily up the steps and clutched the railing. He looked really magnificent. His uniform was a bit dusty and his medals glinted in the sunshine. His sweltering face broke into a large white smile and his thick-fingered hands waved in greeting. The crowd's excitement built to a climax and then slowly ebbed. Everybody quieted down to listen. The general glanced over the assembly and paused dramatically. Then his rough, rasping, heroic voice thundered out over the hushed square: *"Tovarishchi!"* And a submachine gun started blasting away from a window somewhere. Everything happened with incredible speed. Somebody pushed me from behind and I fell flat on my face. I saw the general bounding off the platform in a single leap, then a whole lot of little white holes suddenly popping up across the front wall of City Hall just behind the platform. I lay there. I watched the gentlemen from the welcoming committee pushing and shoving each other to make their way back to the entrance. The brass band ducked around the corner leaving behind only a couple of white caps and the bass drum. There was bedlam behind me; the square was emptying out fast. The gun barked again. I saw people dropping to the ground; those who were a little farther off were crawling toward the houses. It was quiet. The sun shone down. I looked around to see where the shots were coming from. The Russian officers peeked out from behind their cars; the general was standing bareheaded behind a pillar in the doorway now. He had red hair. He was holding a revolver. The submachine gun started blasting away again and you could hear the cracking impact of the bullets as they tore into sheet metal. Whoever it was was obviously trying to hit the Russian officers. I looked around and saw a flash in the attic window of the house next to the City Hall. Then there was a fainter shot. I turned around again and saw the general, cool as a cucumber, firing his automatic up at the attic window. Another submachine gun started firing from the Russian car; glass tinkled. Slate shingles around the window split. Then a couple of Russians ran around from behind the car and dashed toward the house, their pistols drawn. The Russian submachine gun covered them with a short burst. They ran to the door and disappeared inside. It was silent. I glanced around the square. People in their Sunday best were lying on the cobblestones. The whole square was strewn with sprawling bodies; heads peered out from behind the church, behind the well, and behind the statue of St. Jan Nepomuk. Two fainter shots suddenly rang out into the silence. The general stepped from behind the pillar, strode slowly over to the plaza in front of City Hall, putting his automatic back into his holster. His red hair gleamed in the sunshine. One of the Russians poked his head out of the attic window and shouted something down to the general. I quickly got up and dusted my knees off. The general looked around.

People started getting up and drifting back toward the podium. The general smiled and waved them to come closer. Then he picked his cap up off the ground and mounted the platform again.

"*Eto germanski barbar*," he shouted at the people with a laugh and a wave of his hand. The crowd burst out laughing and began clapping. Another head appeared in the attic window and then the upper part of his body with one hand dangling limply. I recognized the man's face. It was Kurt Schnobel. His father had a shop in that building. He'd been fifteen at the time of the invasion and he'd become a first-class Nazi. So he was the one who'd done it. His body dangled half out of the window and then the Russians gave Kurt another shove and he tumbled out and down onto the sidewalk. He fell like a rag doll with outstretched legs and arms and hit the ground with a splat. I watched the people run over and start to kick him but he was dead anyway. Then the general started off on his speech again. "*Tovarishchi!*"

I didn't understand a single word. After a while I got pretty bored; I looked around at the people. Judging from their faces, most of the others didn't understand him either. And then I noticed that the welcoming committee was slowly creeping back to its place up by the platform. They looked around cautiously as if expecting more bullets any minute, but when they saw everything was under control they started applauding like mad. The general kept raising his voice portentously and every time his voice went up a note the crowd applauded.

"He sure can talk," somebody said behind me. It was Haryk.

"I'll say," I said, and went on listening. About a quarter of an hour later, the general finally concluded his speech. After the applause, Mayor Prudivy stepped up on the platform, took out a sheet of paper, and thanked General Jablonkovski for his address.

"After six years of unutterable hardship," he said, "the fraternal Red Army has finally brought us freedom again. Once again we can breathe freely, and now our mothers no longer need to tremble in fear for their children. The hated German intruder has been routed by the heroic armed forces of our Slavic brothers and their Allies." He went on like that for half an hour. I gradually stopped hearing what he was saying and, instead, suddenly saw him wearing that same morning coat or cutaway or whatever it was and standing there, in exactly the same spot he was standing now, on that very same platform which they probably stored away somewhere in City Hall, except that then there had been a big V *für Victoria* painted on it and Mr. Prudivy was translating Regierungskommissar Kühl's speech and calling on all citizens to contribute to *Winterhilfswerk* and saying something—not very enthusiastically, granted—about somebody else's "brave shoulders" which "bore the brunt of the fighting" or something like that, I couldn't remember too clearly. Then one time he'd been at our place on a visit and had made a big fuss about how Kühl had forced him to translate that speech and both my father and Dr. Sabata had hastened to assure him how important it was to have trustworthy patriots in important positions, et cetera. Well, I realized he hadn't meant it seriously about those brave German shoulders. He wasn't a collaborator. It was just that he was always a trustworthy man in an important position. And that's exactly what he was. And always would be. They could count on him. People like Dr. Sabata and Mr. Krocan who owned the factory and, well, almost anybody. He was demonstrating that right now, with real flair. He stuck out his chest, stood on his tiptoes, and bellowed, "Long live the free Czechoslovak Republic!"

There was wild applause. Prudivy waited and then he shouted, "Long live President Benes and Marshal Stalin!"

This time the applause lasted even longer. When it died away, Prudivy gave it everything he had and screamed, "Long live our great Slavic ally, the USSR!"

"Watch out you don't bust a gut, you Slav slob!" Haryk muttered behind me. Haryk in particular had a bone to pick with him because Mr. Prudivy had made him have his head shaved once. It was when Moravec* issued that proclamation about zootsuiters. Potzl, a collaborator, was opening an exposition of paintings by an anti-Semitic artist named Relink or something and Haryk made a special point of turning up in a water-waved pompadour with a sharp porkpie hat on his head and he didn't take it off the whole time Potzl was speaking. He even offered his own opinion of the artist in question and Potzl heard him and started screaming that it was a provocation and Mr. Prudivy, who was standing nearby as a National Confederation delegate, got scared and he and Potzl led Haryk off to the barber shop. Later he apologized to Haryk's parents, saying he had no choice, that otherwise Potzl would have denounced him and so on. And the only reason he himself had gone to the exposition in the first place was because he had to, being chairman of the National Confederation. I kind of felt sorry for the guy. He always had to do things he really didn't want to do. And so now there he was again, welcoming the Red Army. He had to do that, too, so nobody would bring up all those other things he'd had to do before. All right. He'd always been dependable, as my father used to say. And he'd go on being that way. You could count on him. When I looked up at him standing there on the podium I figured this revolution probably wouldn't change things too much after all.

The crowd roared with enthusiasm and Mr. Prudivy concluded his speech. The general turned and started shaking hands. The brass band struck up a march. The celebration was over. The dignitaries surrounded the general and towed him into City Hall. I turned to Haryk.

"So I'll see you at two at the Port?"

"Right," said Haryk.

"You going home?" I said.

"I'm going to see that Lucie gets back."

"Well, so long." I turned and pushed through the crowd. I started home. I walked along thinking about Irena, wondering why she hadn't come. A funny buzzing started up in my head and people's backs seesawed pointlessly in the sunshine ahead of me. Everything started to seem unreal. The celebration, the general, the German terrorist, and Irena who'd been so close to me just the day before that she'd been the whole purpose of my life. I knew she was dumb but I needed her and her silly chatter. Right now I needed her somehow. It was as if something was wrong with me and with the people around me and I needed Irena so I could think about her and wouldn't have to think about those other things which suddenly, out of nowhere, were getting all mixed up in my brain—the general and Mayor Prudivy, the sweet stink of those Russian wagons, that leaflet we found last winter, Prema and the machine gun which had been put away again in the warehouse—and it all made a chill run down my spine and I was depressed or dissatisfied or something, God only knew. I just wished Irena were there. She didn't know beans about life or, when you come right down to it, that everything is just a lot of nonsense and suffering, and so she had her own silly, vague idea of some sort of gorgeous, happy, cozy life, and all I felt was that funny chill. And, still, I needed her. I loved her. Or else it was just because I was alone and suffering from depressive melancholy, as they called it, and from that strange confusion of the world which, up until recently, had seemed somehow simpler, in spite of the fact that there'd been the war. Or maybe because of it. In any case, life made some sort of sense. Now I was nothing but a living corpse. We all were. Me, Mr. Kaldoun, Mr. Moutelik. Everybody. They'd made a living corpse out of me and I didn't know for the life of me whether there was somewhere some magic potion that would bring me back to life. I went past our house in the direction of the brewery. I went up the stairs to Irena's apartment and rang the doorbell. Her mother came to answer it.

"Good morning, ma'am. Is Irena home?" I asked.

"No, she isn't, Mr. Smiricky. She went out this morning and hasn't come back yet."

"Aha. Well, I'll drop by this afternoon," I said.

"May I give her a message?"

"No. I'll drop by again. Thank you, and goodby."

"Goodby, Mr. Smiricky."

She shut the door and I went down the stairs. Everything disgusted me. And I knew where Irena had gone. I remembered the sofa and the brown shades and I was sick with jealousy. I shook my head and hissed between my teeth. That helped a bit. I went home.

Mother opened the door. "It's a good thing you're here, Danny," she said. "The Englishmen are leaving."

"Oh?" I said. "How come?"

"They've made up a special train for them."

"I see," I said, and I went into the room. Father was sitting at the table with the younger Englishman, Siddell. In front of them stood an open bottle of wine left over from New Year's Eve and Siddell's eyes were sparkling. He looked rested and he was freshly shaved.

"Hello," I said.

"Hello, Danny," said Siddell.

"Where's the sergeant?" I asked.

"He's already gone to the station," said Siddell.

I sat down. "Well, so you're going home, right?" I said.

"Yes," said Siddell.

"You're glad, aren't you?"

"It's been five years," he said.

I started to eat. Father was making conversation with the Englishman in his broken German. There was a white tablecloth on the table and our best plates. I thought about Irena. After lunch Father poured everybody a glass of wine. We stood up.

"*So*," said Father. "*Auf glückliche Reise nach Hause!*"

"Your health," said Siddell.

We drank. It was half past one.

"I've got to be going," said Siddell.

We all got up from the table and started saying goodby. The Englishman said thank you, Father shook his hand and grinned at him. I took my saxophone out from under my bed and went to the door.

"I'll go with you," I said.

The street was shady. Most of the people were indoors eating lunch. You could hear people singing from over by the station and the singing came closer and just then a column of Russians marched past the Hotel Granada in their rumpled uniforms with an officer in front and they were singing. Their chests were full of medals and they had submachine guns on their backs and the song they were singing was strange. It gave me the same feeling as that wagon procession this morning. Their voices sounded full and wild and alive and just then I felt a deep and awful longing for something and I didn't know for what—for life, maybe, God only knew, or for Irena, for a different kind of life than this one—and I stopped, under the spell of those bellowing soldiers, and looked at those men marching by and at their mouths that opened and shut rhythmically and out of which all those sounds were coming, and Siddell stopped, too, and then all of a sudden, out of the clear blue sky, he yelled, "Long live the Red Army!"

A couple of dirty faces turned toward us and grinned and hands, calloused from their machine guns, waved at us. The officer saluted. But they didn't stop singing. The street resounded with that weird, wild song of theirs and it was beautiful and then it faded, faded until it was completely gone.

"They look wild," said Siddell and he looked at me. There was a question in the way he looked.

"They do," I said. "Tell me . . ." I hesitated for a moment. "Are you a communist, Siddell?"

Siddell glanced at me. "No," he said. "Not really, I guess. But I am a workingman. A worker—you know what I mean?"

"I see," I said.

"And those chaps," he said, looking off to where the dusty column had already disappeared beyond the anti-tank barrier, "they look like workingmen, too."

"They probably are," I said. The idea had never occurred to me. For me, for us, for us here at home, they were Russians and Bolsheviks. For this guy next to me, they were workers. My head started to ache.

"Tell me, Danny," said Siddell and there was a touch of —I'm not sure what—mockery, maybe, in his eyes. "Are you glad the Russians are here? Or would you rather have the British?"

I looked at him. There was no doubt about it. He was making fun of me all right. He'd seen our place and all the other homes I'd arranged for them to stay in—like an idiot. I got mad.

"You're all workers, too, aren't you? You and the sergeant and all the rest of you?"

"Yes," said Siddell. "But . . . there's a difference."

"I know," I said. I thought a while and then asked, "Why do you ask these questions? You've seen my family. You know we'd rather have the English."

"No need to get sore, Danny," said Siddell, and he smiled at me. "You're a good chap. And your mother is a very kind lady."

"Thanks," I said. "Maybe I'd rather have the English. But the Russians are here now. There's no changing that."

"You're right. That can't be changed," said Siddell, and again it seemed to me he said it pretty complacently.

We went into the station and out onto the platform. There were lots of Englishmen and Frenchmen standing around waiting for the train. We went over to the bunch of Englishmen. The sergeant was prowling around, keeping an eye on things. As soon as he saw me, he grinned and saluted.

"Well," I said. "So you're going home. After five years."

"Yes, sir," said the sergeant.

"That's nice," I said. "I hope you liked it here."

"Yes. And thank you very much for everything you've done for my boys."

"Oh, never mind," I said. I didn't feel like talking about it. I knew my world was leaving along with them but I wasn't sure whether it had ever really been my world at all, whether it hadn't been just a world I'd known from the movies and that the only thing I really had in common with them was the English language. The train slowly pulled into the station. Conductors were standing on the steps with whistles in their mouths and red flags in their hands. The soldiers started running toward the train. The sergeant yelled a command. His men lined up, then started off on the double. The Frenchmen swarmed around. There were many more of them than there were Englishmen. But even before the train had come to a stop, the Englishmen overtook them like a rugby team on the offensive. In a few seconds, they were grinning at me out of the windows. I stood next to their coach and looked up at them.

"When you come to England," called Siddell, "don't forget to come to Liverpool."

"And to the West End," yelled the sergeant.

"I won't," I said. It was all a big act. The train slowly swallowed up the tide of uniforms and the dispatcher in a red cap blew his whistle. The train started to move.

"Farewell!" I yelled up to the window and shook a couple of hands that reached down to me.

"Goodby, Danny," I heard voices call, but I couldn't see very well because my eyes were full of tears. I was bawling like an old whore. And I wasn't any better than one. I was a fool, an idiot, a Robinson Crusoe ruined, beaten, lost. I was overcome by grief. Not just because they were leaving. But because of everything. Everything in the world. The train was leaving and I could hear the Englishmen's voices singing "Tipperary" in my honor. They're going, I thought to myself, they're going home and they'll kiss their wives and tell about their adventures and they'll drink beer with their neighbors who stayed at home. Life is beginning again for them. It had begun for me, too. A new chapter in a life that was always the same. What the hell. I picked up my saxophone case and went out of the station. The saxophone weighed me down. I walked past the sun-warmed western side of Irena's house, across the bridge with the broken railing and under the weeping willows, up toward the Port Arthur. I could hear them playing. I was late. I opened the door and there they were. They were sitting in a line, without their coats and with their ties loosened and the sun fell on them through the window, Benno with his droolly trumpet up to his lips, Lexa's pale fingers on the keys of the clarinet, Venca's swollen cheeks and sliding valve, Haryk with his legs crossed and his Gibson guitar in his lap, Jindra with his hat on his head, embracing his bass, and Brynych's freckled, mousey face behind the drums. They were just giving out with "King Porter Stomp," Venca's tailgate trombone snapping rhythmically while Benno played his teasing melody over it, sweet and sad and simple. At the table by the window the sun fell on Lucie's golden hair and on the lipsticked lips of Benno's Helena. I took off my jacket and opened the case. The music poured over me like a healing shower. Quickly I took out my sax, fitted it together, hung the cord around my neck, and hooked my sax on. Then, just as I was, I came right in on tenor, slowly walking over to my chair, playing as I walked. My fingers moved all by themselves. I played without thinking. It all came out right and free. This was life. This, right here, was life. I sat down and in one breath finished that wonderful, sweeping foxtrot along with the rest of them.

When it was over, Benno said, "Where've you been?"

"Seeing off the Englishmen," I said. I looked around. "Where's Fonda?"

"In mourning," said Haryk. "So no piano."

"You guys ready?" said Benno. "Let's play."

"What'll it be?" said Haryk.

" 'Rent Party'?" Venca suggested.

"Okay," said Benno, and we started in.

"What time do we start tonight?" I asked afterward.

"Six," said Benno. "Where were you all day yesterday anyway?"

"Why?" I said.

"Well, you didn't show up for patrol."

"You mean you went out again yesterday?"

"Naturally, stupid," said Benno.

"We cleaned up the woods," said Haryk.

"Yeah?"

"Yeah. And we nearly knocked off old man Petrbok."

"Why didn't you?" I said.

"Because they are stupid, that's why," said Benno.

"Shit," said Venca. "That was a real shit party all right."

"What happened?" I asked.

"Well," said Venca, "there we were cruising through the woods with our machine guns, see, all strung out about five yards apart, and all of a sudden we see something move in the bushes, so Haryk yells out 'Halt! Wer da?' and it was Petrbok and he screamed like somebody was murdering him, 'Don't shoot! Don't shoot! I'm a Czech!' So Haryk . . .'

"So I yelled 'Aaaa—ein Tscheche! Raus!' " said Haryk, "and Petrbok was scared shitless and started screaming 'Nein, nein, ich bin Freund, ich bin Deutschfreundlich!' So we just dragged him out of the bushes and sent him home."

"What was he doing there anyway?" I said.

"He was on his way back from Black Mountain. He'd lit out for his father-in-law's place the night before last, when all the shooting started."

"Come on, let's get with it," said Benno impatiently. We started in with "St. Louis Blues." I played like a madman, trying to drown out my thoughts. Then it was half past five and Benno said we'd have to go. We put our instruments into our cases and went out. In the meantime the sun had dropped in the west and was lighting up the first windows. The lovely, pointless city lay spread out beneath us in all its springtime color—lilacs on Castle Hill, cherry blossoms in the gardens, the fresh flags in the windows.

"We'll eat there," said Benno. "Prudivy said there'd be grub for all hands."

We pulled our cartful of instruments. Everything was over now and we were setting out to play the farewell serenade. We'd set out with our cart like this thousands of times. I remembered that winter afternoon in 1943 when we gave concerts in the neighboring towns and held jam sessions for our fans on Black Mountain and in Provodova and Hermanovice and all over in those little out-of-the-way mountain villages, mushing through the ice and snow with the bass fiddle and drums and a procession of faithful zootsuiters tagging along behind us, and I thought about the snow-drifted little taverns with their rickety chairs and the bartenders who looked at us as if we were crazy and the old-timers who listened in disgust to our carryings-on and then filed out one by one. I could still see the low ceiling and kerosene lamps in Provodova and the local zootsuiters dancing in their thick rubber-soled shoes with their girls who'd come in high felt boots with their dancing shoes in their pockets. I could see their shadows writhing and twisting against the whitewashed walls, dancing their own bastard breed of swing, and Benno in his green sweater swilling rose hip tea, and Lexa in ski pants, and I could taste the reed in my mouth and smell the ersatz tea and I thought about the moonlight rides on the sled at night with the black saxophone case on my lap and the dark rotund figure of Benno ahead of me, whizzing down into the valley where the sleeping town lay without a light in sight and there was only the hum of the factories and for me the whole scene still echoed with those blues we'd played all over the district and I remembered the midnight blues on New Year's Eve in 1944 on the ski jump at Black Mountain, four months ago, in the bitter cold dark with a dark half circle of faithful fans standing down below and how the icy air poured into your lungs at each breath and how Lexa goofed on his clarinet because his fingers froze and I remembered my hands in the knitted gloves with the tips of the fingers cut off playing "Basin Street Blues" which floated out over the valley and trickled down the snow-covered mountainside with the wind and the snowflakes and it sounded strange and new and wonderfully absurd on Black Mountain during the German occupation on the thirty-first day of December, nineteen hundred and forty-four. And I remembered the battles we'd had with the polka partisans and the apple cores they'd thrown at us and the faithful zootsuiters who tangled with the gang from Malina while we skipped out the back way with our instruments, and the illegal jazz magazine *O.K.*, which guitarist Ludvik "Louis" Svab* brought us from Prague, from P. L. Doruzka,* and the dead Fritz Weiss* who, according to Benno, actually started a jazz band at Terezin before being taken off to the gas ovens.

I was thinking about all this as we crossed the bridge and rattled triumphantly along with our cart on our way toward the square. Boys we knew greeted us from the sidewalks. "Hi, men," they said. They were all dressed up in sharp jackets and wide-brimmed Tatra hats and pretty young girls looked at me and that made me feel good. Things weren't so bad after all. I felt best here in this crowd with our instruments. I almost felt good. There weren't any Petrboks or Prudivys around. I walked along with one hand in my pocket, shoving the cart nonchalantly with the other. Flags were flying in front of the houses like a salutation, red flags with hammers and sickles on them, and Benno's rump was bouncing along in front of me again and his fat back in a plaid jacket. Except for Haryk and Lucie, who were having a fight, none of us said anything and I marched along behind our cart, silently, all wrapped up in my thoughts. Helena Reimannova came out of the Mouteliks's and joined us and I thought about Irena and about how happy I'd been yesterday but that happiness had vanished and would never return, and then I put my hand on my saxophone case and thought to myself, I love it—that live, silver, comforting thing lying there in that case. But as we approached the square and as the vivid colors of the girls' dresses flashed by and I saw all those made-up red lips and all those beautiful hairdos and legs, I yearned for Irena again. In vain. We came to the square and headed over toward City Hall. Near the speaker's platform they'd set up a bandstand wreathed with green garlands. A few chairs stood on the stand. A bunch of guys our age and their girls had already gathered around us. There weren't any older people. I knew they'd all be over at the Sokol garden where Mr. Petrbok and his brass band were going to play polkas. We had this all to ourselves. Benno went inside and came back with Mr. Pazler. They brought out some more chairs and we unloaded our instruments from the cart and took them over to the stand. Then we each got a bowl of soup and potatoes. We sat down next to our instruments and, while we ate, looked around. People were strolling back and forth around the church and a crowd was gathering near the bandstand. There were still plenty of refugees and soldiers in uniform mingled in among the local people and, right up front, some Russians stopped to gawk at us. The windows of the loan association office shone with a golden light; happy crowds streamed across the square. Everybody was laughing and talking. The customs house, the tanks, the shooting—it was all over now and had happened a long time ago. I thought about Hrob and the dead driver in the cab of the truck and the SS men over at the brewery and the two corpses in the warehouse. All over now. I took my saxophone out and adjusted the mouthpiece. The young guys and their girls stared as I slid my fingers up and down over the keys a couple of times, blew a few glissandos and smears, and then I took my saxophone out of my mouth and smiled at a pretty young girl down under the bandstand. I didn't recognize her but she looked sort of familiar. She had on a slippery-looking tight-fitting red dress and had a beautiful girlish figure. She smiled back and kept looking straight at me. We stared at each other. Who was she, anyway? Then she dropped her eyes and started saying something very quickly to another girl whose arm she was holding. Then I remembered. It was one of old Dvorak's twins, the guy who owned the auto-repair shop. I'd known her for ages but this was the first time I'd noticed she was so pretty. I couldn't remember her name but I made up my mind to give her a try before leaving for Prague. Before meeting that other girl there. I felt old in comparison to the twin, like somebody from another generation, and she warmed my heart. She was going to carry on from where we were leaving off. With this zootsuit stuff and jazz, this way of life of ours. Squares like Petrbok and Machacek and the others, they didn't understand it. According to them, we were no-good loafers and jazz was just something crazy and eccentric. Not for us it wasn't. For us, it was life. And for me the only life. The only one possible and the best one.

We finished eating and started tuning up. The crowd around the bandstand became alert. Benno was in charge today, instead of the orphaned Fonda, and Venca had his usual troubles with his trombone. Suddenly the people in the square were still. We stood and, like a priest lifting the chalice during mass, we put our horns to our mouths. Into the warm sun rays and into the shadows of the festive square we blew a theme we stole from the Casa Loma Band. We played it staccato and arrogantly, we blared the melody so that the burghers walking near the church turned toward us. I saw them shaking their heads, thinking "How can anyone listen to this?" But those around the bandstand listened. No, not listened—they swallowed it, they absorbed it. Our band caught fire, we were roaring and swinging until we finished the number. When we sat down, we immediately burst into "Organ Grinder Swing." The crowd around the bandstand started to move and in the next moment the plaza was full of jiving couples. I sat there on my chair looking out at the girls' skirts twirling up and the silhouettes of the zootsuiters with their built-up shoulders swinging in the sunshine. Benno's horn was aimed out over the dancers' heads, the sun glinting on it, and Venca's trombone slid in and out over people's heads like the wand of the god of jazz and I just poked along modestly under the fast sharp ripples of Benno's horn and I felt great. The sun was touching the roofs of the houses in the west and we sat there glittering in its rays, flashing our glorious music right back in its face. The sun was with us. Up on the hills the castle loomed, slanting across the blue sky. And the lovely Queen of Württemberg had driven off somewhere in her carriage, sleepy and bundled up in blankets, off and away to somewhere in Germany. I saw Mitzi down in the crowd, dancing with Prdlas, king of the zootsuiters, and Eva Manesova with Vorel, who wrote poetry, and over on the sidewalk I saw Rosta's blond head and the rosy cheeks of Dagmar Dreslerova and Rosta had his arms around her. And I was all alone, sitting up there on the bandstand with my saxophone in my mouth. And then suddenly I saw Irena down below in a light blue dress and she smiled at me. Her smile pierced right through me and made my heart stop beating. She was dancing beautifully on her lovely legs and keeping Zdenek, who was grinning like an idiot and clumping around like an elephant, a good arm's length away. But he was still holding on. And I'd hoped they'd shot him. No such luck. He could go off and leave her a thousand times but he'd always turn up again. He'd always pop back up again like a demon or the devil, with his buckteeth and chapped lips and Irena would always drop everything and run right back to him. No. I was the one who, finally, had only dreamed and imagined how it would be, and he didn't dream or even need to dream since he had it all right there. Finally, he was the only one who got anywhere with Irena, and she undressed for him and slept with him and loved him, and she was fond of me. Fond of me. That was all and there was nothing to be done about it. All I could do was be grateful she was at least fond of me. I got up, gravely raised my sax to my lips and sobbed out a melody, an improvisation in honor of victory and the end of the war, in honor of this town and all its pretty girls, and in honor of a great, abysmal, eternal, foolish, lovely love. And I sobbed about everything, about my own life, about the SS men they'd executed and about poor Hrob, about Irena who didn't understand and who was slowly but surely approaching her own destruction in some sort of marriage, about youth which had ended and about the break-up that had already begun, about our band which wouldn't ever get together like this again, about evenings when we'd played under kerosene lamps and about the world that lay ahead of us, about all the beautiful girls I'd been in love with—and I'd loved a lot of them, probably all of them—and about the sun. And out of the orange and saffron sunset clouds in the west a new and equally pointless life bent toward me, but it was good and I raised my glittering saxophone to face it and sang and spoke to that life out of its gilded throat, telling it that I'd accept it, that I'd accept everything that came my way because that was all I could do, and out of that flood of gold and sunlight, the girl bent toward me again, the girl I had yet to meet, and she caressed my cheek. The zootsuiters were dancing in front of the bandstand, kids I liked and whom I'd be leaving within the next few days since I'd be going away, going somewhere or other again, so I played for them and I thought about the same things I'd always thought about, about girls and about jazz and about that girl I was going to meet in Prague.

Prague, October 1948—Karlovy Vary, September 1949

Notes

CZECH LEGION: Units of volunteers who fought against the Axis Powers on the Eastern and Western Fronts during World War I.

P. L. DORUZKA: One of the most important writers and historians of jazz in Czechoslovakia; a principal organizer of the annual International Prague Jazz Festival.

ALOIS JIRASEK (1851–1930): Author of romantic novels with strong Czech nationalistic tendencies.

DR. KRAMAR: One of the leading figures, together with Masaryk, in the Czech and Slovak independence movement during World War I. He subsequently became Czechoslovakia's first prime minister. Kramar represented the interests of the industrial capitalists and later joined the coalition formed by the Agrarian and Social Democratic parties.

EMIL LUDVIK: Founder and leader, in 1939, of the first really swinging band in Czechoslovakia; founder and secretary of the Czechoslovak Society for Human Rights (1968–69), dissolved by the Czech Government during the post-Dubcek "reforms."

MORAVEC: Minister of Education and Culture in the puppet government formed under the German Protectorate.

BOZENA NEMCOVA (1820–1862): Novelist and short story writer closely associated with the nineteenth century Czech national renaissance movement. Her most widely read work is *Granny*.

OCTOBER 28TH: Czechoslovak independence day, commemorating the establishment of the republic and celebrated as a national holiday prior to February 1948.

SOKOL: A nationalistic physical culture organization.

LUDVIK SVAB: Guitarist of the Prague Dixieland Band founded in 1948 and still performing.

FRITZ WEISS: Jewish trumpet player and arranger for Emil Ludvik's band incarcerated in Terezin where he formed a jazz band called "The Concentration Camp Swingers." He died there.

$8.95

NEGLECTED BOOKS OF THE 20TH CENTUR

Josef Skvorecky's first novel, The Cowards, *was banned shortly after publication in 1958 by Czech authorities, who were outraged by its slang, its impertinent, youthful hero, and its mocking portrayal of the May 1945 German surrender to the Allies and the Soviet occupation.*

"Josef Skvorecky is . . . a novelist of the first rank."

—George Steiner, *The New Yorker*

"An important piece of history is marvelously recorded here, and anyone who wants to know how it felt to be young, idealistic and innocent at the end of the war . . . should read *The Cowards.*"

—*The Times Literary Supplement*

"I have enjoyed *The Cowards* as much as any novel I have read during the last year. A very funny and very sad story."

—Graham Greene

THE ECCO PRESS

1 WEST 30TH STREET, NEW YORK 10001

Cover design by Cynthia Krupat

ISBN: 912-9